The Fall of Light

'For a century, the natural conditions of the Irish poor were flight and exile. It is the story of this silent mass that Niall Williams tells so brilliantly in his third novel; the great Irish 19th-century narrative. Ultimately a heart-warming yarn, in the fashion of Charles Frazier's *Cold Mountain*, it deserves to be every bit as popular'
Guardian

'Williams's prose is bathed in poetry and moonlight, and the novel eddies and flows with the circularity of myth and ritual'
The Times

'On the run with a stolen telescope, Francis Foley and his four sons escape across country to the west of Ireland. The telescope becomes a touchstone for the family, especially for the resurrected father, and a connection with their vanished mother. The patterns of stars and myth it reveals are also a way for Francis to free himself from the narrow confines of Irish history'
Time Out

'Incidents from the recent and distant past become intertwined and, as the story unfolds, flowing backwards and forwards through time, it is the spaces of sky, landscape, the colours of the earth and water which dominate'
Observer

NIALL WILLIAMS was born in 1958 and lives in Kiltumper, Ireland, with his wife Christine and their two children. He is the author of three other novels including, most recently, *Only Say the Word*.

Niall Williams

The Fall of Light

PICADOR

First published 2001 by Picador

First published in paperback 2002 by Picador
an imprint of Pan Macmillan Ltd
Pan Macmillan, 20 New Wharf Road, London N1 9RR
Basingstoke and Oxford
Associated companies throughout the world
www.panmacmillan.com

ISBN-13: 978-0-330-48700-9
ISBN-10: 0-330-48700-0

A CIP catalogue record for this book is available from
the British Library.

Typeset by SetSystems Ltd, Saffron Walden, Essex
Printed and bound in Great Britain by
Mackays of Chatham plc, Chatham, Kent

For my father,
who first brought me to the library
where the stories were

Acknowledgements

This book is not a history, but several excellent history books published by the Clasp Press of the Clare Local Studies Project were helpful to me in writing it. Among these was *Poverty Before the Famine, County Clare 1835*, and *Two Months at Kilkee, 1836* by Mary John Knott, *Sable Wings Over the Land: County Clare During the Famine* by Ciaran O Murchadha, and *The Stranger's Gaze: Travels in County Clare 1534–1950*, edited by Brian O Dalaigh.

George Harratt's 'Scattery Island: A Guide', gives a true and fascinating account of the history of the island and its buildings. There is a Scattery Island centre in Kilrush, Co. Clare.

My deepest gratitude as always goes to Chris Breen, my first reader, without whose support the story would have fallen into silence. My thanks too to Marianne Gunn O'Connor and Peter Straus who have once again provided guidance and encouragement when my faith in stories weakened – of such support all writers dream.

Antonio: What impossible matter will he make easy next?
Sebastian: I think he will carry this island home in his pocket, and give it to his son for an apple.

William Shakespeare, *The Tempest*

This is a story that has been passed on. It is a story that begins in the time when my great-great-grandfather was a small boy. It has been told and retold for over a hundred and fifty years. It is not a history. As with all such telling each has added his own colouring, imagined and created details that were otherwise perished. These same were then forgotten or elaborated upon and others still added until the story itself became a kind of airy bridgework linking the living and the dead, the teller and those of whom it told.

It is the story of a family that is mine. Although its figures have grown outlandish in the telling, and dates and times and places been lost to the inexactitude of memory and invention, I recognize them yet. They are the Foleys. They are the ones that lived in this country long ago.

One

I

In an autumn long ago, the Foleys crossed the country into the west like the wind that heralds winter. Where exactly they had come from is uncertain. The family's origins vanish in the lost pages of Ireland's history. There was Francis Foley and his four sons. They rode horses through the night, travelling with all their possessions in raggle-taggle fashion, leading a small cart on which lay a large wooden telescope. The midnight creaking of the cartwheels, and the clattering of the hoofs on the road stirred those who slept on the edges of their beds in thin dreams. The Foleys fled through the fields of Tipperary and across the wide green of all that country until they reached the river. Then they stopped and slept beside their horses beneath the hidden October moon, their breaths misting on the darkness like visions and their eyes in sleep seeing the home for ever lost to them now.

The father did not sleep. He lay back on the cart and unfurled the green blanket to look at the telescope they had stolen from the landlord's house. He ran his fingers down the polished mahogany and up to the brass rim that held the eyepiece. He did not know its history. He did not know it to be one of the treasures of science. For Francis Foley it was simply the means by which to see the parts of the universe he would otherwise not see. It was something which he had taken in an act of revenge. Within it lay the limitlessness of space, the way to feel freed from the narrow confines of the history of his country. For amidst the stars there were no landlords.

Francis looked over at his sleeping sons. None of them was yet out of their teens. Teige, the youngest, was twelve years old. He had a gift with horses. He knew them intuitively. He knew more than men five times his age, and yet in sleep he lay with the innocent posture of a child who curls beneath the canopy of the night certain the skies watch over him with goodness. Finan and Finbar, the twins, were sixteen years, simple and distant and still sharing the one soul. While their father watched them they moved in the blanket of a sour dream, first one and then the other kicking at the same frightening vision as if it were a ball and could fly off across the dark. Tomas, at nineteen the eldest, was not quite sleeping. He was already the barrel-chested, flaxen-curled replica of his father. He had the same turn of lip, the same even curve of eyebrow that gave him the handsome expression of one who knows he is invincible. There was nothing from which Tomas Foley would ever step back. He had his father's recklessness, that stubborn indefatigable belief inherited from grandfathers lost that a Foley was as good as anyone and better than most. He no longer slept, but lay and watched his horse sleeping, and when it stirred or a sudden quivering passed along the muscles of its neck, he spoke to it from where he lay on the wet grass until its ease returned and the strangeness of the place was forgotten.

Francis Foley turned from them. He angled himself up in the dark on the cart that held all their possessions in the world. He was a large man in a small time, or so he believed, and his frame made the wagon creak. A tin pot fell free to the ground and the red fox that was circling through the copse of sallies skirted away. The old man did not pay it any attention. His mind was away. He had lifted and propped the telescope at an angle to the heavens and now stretched and lay sideways so he could tilt his head under the eyepiece. Then he looked up into the vastness of space, watching for the clouds to move and reveal the stars where some imagined all lives were explained.

When the boys woke they watched the dawn like a caress travelling the heavily misted veil of the river valley, and they supposed that they were near the landscape of their new home. Their father gestured them to breakfast, and they stood around the grassy space where they had passed the night and ate hunks of bread. A mist rain was falling softly. Softly the air was moving in opaque windblown patterns that the previous night Francis Foley had convinced himself tasted of the sea. He had never seen the Atlantic. His understanding of the country's geography was that across the plains of Tipperary the land grew more rocky and wild and the population more sparse. He believed that in the west was a place beyond magistrates and bailiffs and agents, a landscape unruly, shaped by sea storms and where, like many a man whose soul was full, he would find a place to live in that was empty.

But he had not calculated correctly. When he squinted into the mist that obscured the width of the river that morning he feared that they were in fact not halfway across Ireland.

'The country is enormous,' he said. He spoke in Irish, his words dropped into the air around his silent sons. 'The map-makers have it wrong. It is a plot. They have drawn the country small to make us feel small.'

He looked at where he wanted the sky to brighten and urged it to do so with the set expression of his face. He wanted the mist to lift and tried to stare it away, then he asked his sons if they could smell the sea.

The twins sniffed the air and smelled the deer that were not far up the river. Teige looked at Tomas, who was angled forward on his horse and like him he pressed his face outward to kiss the invisible. He paused a moment then sat back.

'Is that the sea?' he said.

The old man did not know. The scent of the morning was not bitter as he had expected. Though the small wind came from the west it did not burn the wound in his arm. There was no salt in the air, and although he told his sons this was a

5

victory, that their discovery of the size of the country was heartening, his spirit fell with the awareness of his own ignorance. The River Shannon, that on the map in the landlord's house where he had seen it was a thin blue line snaking south-westwards to the sea, was that October morning a wide grey swirling torrent whose width was unknown.

'If we follow it we will be too far south. We will cross it,' said the father.

He said it and broke away from the breakfast, as if between words and action there was not the slightest room for hesitation or debate. Not the slightest room in which one of the sons might have said, Father shouldn't we wait and find a bridge? For they knew their father well, and lived in the shadow of him like smaller animals. They could not take the bridge for the same reason that they did not cross the country by its main roads, for the telescope would be seen.

None of them could swim. There were three horses, the great chestnut that Tomas rode, the grey gelding upon whose back the twins sat together, and the black pony of Teige. The cart was pulled by a long-haired mule. In the poor rain-light of the dawn the Foleys rode down to the water's edge. The river ran past them, laughing. The horses caught the flash of the salmon silvering beneath and flared their nostrils and stamped at the bank and were stilled but not calmed by Teige. He dismounted and talked to each of them.

'It is not deep, it is only fast,' said the father, though he could not know and could not see the far bank. He had drawn from the mound on the cart a collection of ropes.

'Tomas!' He called the boy without looking at him. His eldest son came quickly and took one end of the rope.

'There,' the father said and pointed to one of the twisted trees that grew nearby.

Tomas secured the rope. Teige and the twins watched him in admiration. He had a kind of cool expertise, as if nothing in the physical world daunted him. He pulled the rope taut and quickly mounted again and without pause plunged his horse into the river.

It took him in its swiftness and at once he was swept sidelong. But while his brothers watched with that mixture of horror and awe in which they always beheld him, Tomas yelled and yahooed, his eyes wide and white and his body on the horse twisting with the power of the river. His horse thrashed and flared and swam with its neck, pushing his nose upward into the air and tilting its eyes as if afraid to see below it. The river swept them away, but not far. And still Tomas worked the horse, riding it the way horses are ridden in dreams where the world is infirm and progress seems at the whim of God. He rode the river and let the rope run away behind him. He rode it while the twins cried urgent cheers and Teige looked away and felt only the terror of the crossing ahead of him. The old man stood mute and patient without the slightest evidence of fear or pride. Tomas rode himself invisible. He crossed into the mid-river waters where they could no longer see him and passed as if through portals into some incorporeal world that existed beyond the midpoint of the Shannon river.

They did not see where he had gone. The mist hung between them. They did not hear him. Francis stood like the ghost of a father and did not move and did not show his sons the slightest uncertainty. The rope that Tomas held did not move but lay in the water. The sky had not brightened. The day was improperly born. Blotches of wet fog obscured its shape, there were loose long sinews of mist that hung and made blind and confined the space. It was raining and not raining. The only sound was the sound of the old river running in that green place where the family would come asunder. No birds sang. The river chuckled past and they waited, watching the washed-out light that was wet and thin and like gauze between them and the eldest brother.

'Tomas!' Finbar shouted.

Finan roared, 'Tomas!'

'Stop it,' their father said. 'He cannot hear you.'

They stood there and waited. The world aged in them another bit, each of the younger brothers feeling the impotency of their roles in the drama, mute witnesses to stubbornness and folly. They waited for their father to ride into the river and save Tomas, but he did not move. The rope was loose in the Shannon. The twins sank down on the ground. The old man's eyes stared at the wall of the mist as though he could burn it away, as though he didn't need anyone or anything and that the rescue of Tomas was in his gift and would happen without his moving from that place by the shore. They waited an impossible time.

Then the rope stretched taut.

They saw it lift and watched the line of it rise and drop the dripping river water back into the river. The old man moved quickly. He laid a hand on it and shook it and tested it for firmness. Then he tied another to a different tree and brought it over to the twins. 'Here. Go on, you,' he said. 'By the rope. Bring this one.'

The twins looked at each other and half-grinned, both at the danger and at the opportunity to imitate their eldest brother. They pulled back their shoulders and put out their chins and were like minor versions of their father.

'Go on, Tomas has made it easy for you,' said the old man. 'By the rope, go.'

He stood and watched, and carrying the second rope they rode down into the water, trailing behind them a line loose and wavering. The gelding tried to swim with its head impossibly high. It angled its long nose upward and snorted and opened its eyes wide and baleful and at first jumped at the current washing against it. Teige called to the horse. He said sounds in no language until the twins and the horse were gone out of sight into the wet brume and the only sign of them was the second rope running backwards out of the unseen.

Then there was stillness on that bank once more. After a

time the second rope was pulled taut. Now two parallel lines stretched, bridge-like, over the river.

Quickly the old man tied Teige's black pony to the cart. Then, with loops of rope and a leather belt, he attached the pony and the mule, one to each to rope, so the cart was linked on either side to the airy bridge that led into the mist. He called his son to get up and ride the pony and calm the mule and coax them into the rushing river. But Teige did not want to move. He had sat down on the ground and was turned away from the river. He was running a finger in the brown mud.

'Teige, come. Now.' The father's voice was large and full and like a thing solid in the air. Teige sat.

'Teige?' the old man said again and saw his son turn his face further away as if to study some distant corner of the mist.

The father said nothing for a moment. He looked up in the air then he cursed loudly.

'Get up!'

But Teige did not move. The river ran.

'I tell you now for the last time. Get up, come on.' The old man sat on the cart with the reins in his hand. He turned from his youngest son and looked away at the grey river and the rope lines running across it.

Still Teige did not move.

'You are afraid. Have you not seen your brothers cross it?'

'I don't want to.'

'Because you are a coward.'

'I am not. It won't work. The pony knows it. Look.' He pointed to the black pony whose ears were back and whose sides heaved.

'She is afraid because you are. It's your fear not hers. Did you see your brothers? They were not afraid. Get over here. Now, I tell you.'

Teige sat on the mud and studied the patterns he drew with his finger. His brown hair fell forward over his brow. The drizzle of rain made his cheeks glisten. His eyes were still, the world reduced to the two feet of mud about him. As if such were a door in the world for his escape, he stared at it. Then a blow knocked him on his face.

'Get up.'

Teige did not cry out or weep. He lay with his eyes open and his mouth bleeding into the ground. His pony stamped and turned and looked about with bewilderment.

'Get up,' his father said. 'Get up now and get on that pony and lead it into the river.'

The old man turned away from him and studied the thin light in the air and cursed wordlessly. In the wet emptiness of that clearing the year took another soft step towards dying. Teige did not get up. His father went over and went to kick at him but stopped short.

'Get up,' he said again in Irish, a single word in a sharp whisper. He was looking away, looking at some place where he raged against the world for not fitting his map of it. His blue eyes burned and his brow furrowed and his lips pressed against each other in a thin line of resolve; he would make things fit.

'I want to stay here. Leave me here,' Teige said.

'Because you are a coward? I will not,' Francis Foley said. 'I will knock you into the river if you don't get up.'

'I will stay here and wait for my mother!' the boy shouted.

'Your mother is gone. She has left us.'

'She has not!'

'She doesn't want to be with us,' he lied. 'She has gone off and now there is only us. Now do what I tell you and get up!' said the father. He waited a moment, and though it was brief it was long enough for him to consider going back to try to find her and then for pride and the knowledge that the law was pursuing them to banish the thought. No, they would go on. They would find a new home. He would make happen what he'd always told her, and then go and gather her up and bring her there and she would see. None of this he said, for he could not reveal his own rashness. 'Get up, *eirigh*!' was all he said.

Teige said nothing and the air stilled and in the stillness there was only the beating of their hearts and the rain now falling. The pony's tail whisked the morning, her foot stamped the ground.

And at last, without another word, but with a grey look of shame, Teige stood up. He did not face his father, but in a flash the old man had spun him around by the shoulders and holding him there an instant shook him hard, trying to contain the desire to knock him down. In his great hands the thin boy was like a bag of broken things. He shook him and saw the boy's spittle fly out of the twisting blur of his mouth. He saw the eyes flash past and lose their focus and sicken with fear and powerlessness. Then the vomit flew pink and curdled on to his shoulder and he let the boy go and watched Teige fall like a rag at his feet. The old man swallowed hard on the emotion that rose in his gorge, and his fists trembled. He looked away at where the spirit of the boy's mother was watching him. And he did not strike him again. This was not how Francis Foley had wanted to treat his son, it was not what he meant or wanted to do. He told himself it was how a father had to behave and he ignored the idea that his treatment of Teige was coloured by how much the boy resembled his mother.

'How are you going to live in the world?' he asked his son. 'Tell me that? How are you going to be a man and live in the world? If your father asks you to jump with him into the fires of hell you jump. If he asks you to swim in the sea when he knows you cannot swim and he cannot and the waters are filled with devils, you swim. Do you understand me?'

Teige did not answer. He stood up slowly and his father pushed him ahead of him back to the pony. The telescope was wrapped in a blanket and tied on the top of all their things. There were pots and tools and pieces of wooden furniture and cloths and rugs already tattered and various sticks and irons of uncertain purpose.

'Now!' said Francis Foley and swiped the air above the animals with the reins. They rode into the water and the whole cart swayed down-river at once. It was as though the world had suddenly been turned on its side and everything fell. The father stood on the cart and shouted at the mule and slashed at him with the reins and cursed the universe and cried out to Teige to keep them all between the ropes. The ties he had secured snapped like the river's toys. The whole of their belongings and the stolen telescope swung away. The animals tried to keep their direction, but were pulled backwards and sideways. They jumped and thrashed at the water. Then the lines that held them to the cart gave, too.

In a moment it happened. The cart sailed free and swung about and pressed against the rope of the bridge and snapped it. Francis cried out. In the river Teige looked over his shoulder and saw the old man falling back and clutching his precious cargo, the great telescope. Water spilled through the cart grey and fast and the old man was kicking away at it, making a small white splashing. Teige was ahead of him in the river. He tried to ride the pony back and over to his father but could not for the cart was floating away and was on the back of the current. The mule was swept forty yards then more and then was gone like a ghost dissolving from this world. Teige saw his father look with fury at the animal a last time, and then the telescope seemed to roll from its moorings and the old man pushed aside some of their things to keep room for it. Pots, shovels, bowls sailed away downriver. He clung to the telescope. He saw that he was drifting from Teige and that he could not be reached and he did not jump from the raft of the cart. He defied the world to drown him. He cursed it and shook his head and shouted out something that Teige could not understand. Then Teige called to him, and his words too were lost in the rush of the river water. The father did not hear him ask where was his mother, or if he did he did not answer. He looked back at the boy and then the whole cart sailed down the river and into the mist and vanished out of sight.

When Teige reached the far side none of his brothers could speak. They seemed paralysed. They did not greet his safe arrival nor move from that spot on the bank. They looked into the foggy river at nothing. It was as if their father had been erased and, momentarily, they were unsure if this was good or bad.

Teige looked back. 'I knew someone would die,' he said.

There was a pause and the brothers watched the river. It seemed to run without sound now. The twins turned and looked at Tomas.

'No one has died,' he said. 'Come on.'

'Come on!' said Finbar, in echo and perfect imitation and in this was joined by Finan, each of them mirrors of the elder. They mounted and rode and Teige came with them. They galloped along the grassy western banks of the Shannon river. They rode along the edge of the first light of that morning and found that no matter how quickly they moved the river moved quicker. They could not catch sight of the old man. All day the Shannon was sleeved in a fine mist and they could see nothing. After a mile the river was no longer even a river but had become a great lake that at first they mistook for the sea.

They rode the three horses all that day in search of their father. They scanned the grey waters where sometimes they thought they caught sight of him. At last they came to where they could ride no more and where the last sighting of Francis Foley turned out to be a singular lonesome swan riding the low waves.

'He is gone,' Tomas said.

The breath of the horses misted and faded. They sat crouched forward as though beneath a burden. The landscape thereabouts was a green and rumpled stillness. The silence grew heavy. Then Finbar said, 'He is gone to America,' and laughed a small laugh that faded away.

Finan looked at Tomas to see what he would say, but he said nothing at all.

They watched the waters.

'He is not,' Teige said at last, 'he is become a swan.'

Thin pale daylight fell out of the sky. Curlews flew over the water. The wind waved the reeds in a slow rustling where Tomas feared to find the body of their drowned father. But he was not there. He looked up at the bank where Teige and the twins were then making camp. He looked out at where the swan moved in the brown waters and the evening was falling. What was he to do now? Defeat was not in his nature. Yet in a few days he had lost almost everything. The vision of their home burning flared in his mind and he knew they could not go back there. He did not understand what had happened between his parents but from it felt an obscure guilt, as if it were the boys' fault. He wanted to go back and could not. He had to be the man now. He stood there a time and watched the river and the darkness coming. He wanted to be able to repair their losses. He wanted to right the crooked world, to go and bring back the dead. He wanted to rescue someone. He stood and then grew restless and came up to the others.

'The place he wanted us to go was further on,' he said. 'It was at the sea that has waves. We'll go on there tomorrow.'

'We have to go back,' Teige said.

'We cannot. They will arrest us. We have to go on and find a place and then I will go back myself,' said Tomas, looking away at the air above him as if to see how his words sounded.

Finan groaned then and rubbed at his stomach. 'We have nothing left, we have nothing to eat.'

'We'll eat the swan,' his twin answered and grinned.

'We'll not!' Teige said, and raised his chin and seemed momentarily pugnacious.

Tomas calmed them with the command to stay camped there by their horses while he went down the river to the town to get food.

'Don't be acting fools while I'm gone. There's only us now,' he said.

He left them in the darkness and rode away. The clouds blew eastward and the stars revealed themselves. In those days the night skies of that country were vast canopies of deepest blue, all the created stars glimmered there like the diadem of a king. There were none lost to surrounding light for there was none, and the patterns of the constellations were each clear and perfect as though drawn by a great hand in the depths of the heavens. As the cold of the night-time came around them the younger Foley brothers huddled together. They put the pony and the horse in the gap of the wind and gained a small shelter from the air that was blowing from Norway. They watched the stars.

'Do you think our father is dead?' Finbar asked.

But none of them answered him. They sat there in the night. Teige thought of his mother Emer and looked in the darkness for the image of her face.

After a time Finan said: 'Tell us one of the stories, Teige.'

'Yes, tell us one,' said Finbar.

And so, not to make the time move faster or slower, but to make it vanish altogether, to create the illusion that it did not exist and that all moments were the same, Teige told a story he had heard his mother tell. It told of the Queen Cassiopeia and her beautiful daughter Andromeda. He spoke in Irish and in that language the story seemed more ancient even than the versions of it first told in Mesopotamia or Greece.

'Who could say which of them was the loveliest? Cassiopeia or Andromeda?' he began. 'Queen Cassiopeia was full of pride in her daughter and in herself and announced that they were lovelier even than the sea-nymphs, the Nereids.'

'The Nereids?' Finan had forgotten who they were.

'The fifty daughters of Nereus, the wise old man of the sea.'

'Fifty?' Finbar asked.

'Fifty.'

'Oh ho!'

They watched the stars and imagined.

'The sea-nymphs were offended, they complained to Poseidon, god of the sea, who struck the waves with his trident and flooded the lands and called up the monster Cetus.'

'I love Cetus,' Finbar said.

'The king, the husband of Andromeda, was told that the only way he could save his queen was if he sacrificed his daughter to Cetus the monster. So Andromeda was chained to the rocks at Joppa.'

'She was eaten.'

'She was not,' Teige said.

'She was!'

'Stop it, Finbar!' shouted Finan and punched the other and the two of them fell to wrestling there and rolling over each other while Teige sat and waited. When they had stopped he told of how Perseus came and rescued Andromeda and took her for his wife, and made Cassiopeia jealous, and how Cassiopeia, in her jealous fit, helped arrange an attack on the married couple. How Perseus defeated the attack.

'Then Poseidon the sea-god, hearing how the queen had plotted against her daughter, cast her into the heavens for all time.'

'Upside down,' Finbar said.

'Upside down,' said Teige.

The story ended, they huddled there beneath the stars that were the same stars since for ever. And the longer they watched the skies the clearer they could see the kings and queens and jealous lovers and sea-gods and drowned fathers and vanished mothers and they forgot that they were cold. And after a while they could not tell whether they were in sleeping or waking dreams in that empty and merciless world where they were now alone.

3

Moments before dawn, Tomas returned without his boots from Limerick town. He dismounted his horse with a light jump and when his brothers raised their heads and stared at him he swung his coat on to the ground and fell down upon it. His body was exhausted but his spirit was elated.

'God!' he said, and astonished the others by rolling there on the ground.

'Are you sick?' Finbar asked him.

But Tomas did not reply. He shouted out a cry of no language, raised his bare feet and banged them on the ground. He let out a groan and wriggled in the mud.

His brothers did not dare to speak to him. They had never seen him in such an agitated state, but erroneously supposed it was the loss of their father and the new responsibility of leading the family. They lay there beside the flowing river and watched hungrily while the dawn rose in pink and blue ribbons.

In the dark Tomas had ridden his horse into Limerick town with the intention of stealing something for his brothers to eat. But from the moment he arrived on the hardened mud of the side-streets his resolve weakened. At that stage in his life, it was the biggest town he had ever seen. Dimly in the distance he saw the bridge named Wellesley with its elegant arches. The high steeple of the ancient cathedral appeared above the rooftops, and across the river were the neat plantations and well-made fences of the land of the Marquis of Lansdowne. He tied his horse and brushed the dirt off his clothes and walked into the night town. The smells of the outer streets were the smells of stout and whiskey and urine and cowdung. Cats and ragged dogs ran and stopped and sniffed at dark muddied pieces of nothing. He passed on into the town. From rooms above him he heard men's laughter and music from a piano. He was not sure where he was going. He was walking in the world for the first time without the shadow of his father. He let his hand rub along the fine stone of the buildings. He stood against one of them to let his back feel its perpendicularity and then looked upwards to see the straight line it cut in the dark sky. He paused there and gathered himself and thought for the first time that they did not have to follow their father's plans now. They could go anywhere. It would be up to him. We could come here, he thought. We could go anywhere. The country was suddenly big with possibility. He moved out of the shadows and walked the full length of the street that ran parallel to the wide river. At the far end of the town, when he was about to cross and walk back along the far side of the street, he saw a woman in a yellow dress.

She had bare arms in the cold night and a bracelet that glittered.

She was lovely. Her hair was high and pinned.

'Here I am,' she said. Her mouth was small and red, her eyes shining.

Tomas Foley had not known the company of women. He looked behind him in the street when the woman spoke, and when he saw there was no other, he imagined that the woman had spoken to him out of some distress.

'What is it?' he said.

And she laughed and covered her laugh.

'You're a sweet one,' she said and she moved to him and smiled.

'Are you all right?' he asked her.

She touched his face with fingers cool and soft and his head spun.

'Kiss me,' she said. Then her arms were around him and she was kissing and biting at his lips. She ran her hands along his chest. His eyes rolled. His head swirled within the cloud of cheap honeysuckle water that was her scent. She ate at his neck and then said, 'Come on, love,' and led him up the worn boards of a stairs to a room that was not far away. In that same astonishment, the same dumb innocence with which he later interpreted that simple act of economics to be the rare and absolute majesty of Love itself, Tomas found his clothes taken off and his body admired in the yellow candlelight.

The woman reversed the world he had imagined and told him he was a beauty. He stood there and she looked at him and saw the innocence that had once been hers and she asked him had he ever been with a woman?

'I have not,' he said.

She caught her lower lip in her teeth. Though she was not much older than he was her eyes showed an ageing sorrow as if she knew that she was always doomed to the fakery of love, its manner and appearance, but not its heart.

'You have a truelove?' she asked him. Then quickly said, 'No, don't answer me, come here.'

And he did then. And she reached and touched him and in an instant he forgot everything but her. She drew him down on the narrow bed and caressed him with such a ferocity that her movements could not be called caresses and the air in the room grew damp and white sweat might have dripped from the walls and the cracked ceiling. She loved him for two hours, then collapsed back on the bed, where suddenly she turned her head to the side and wept. It was an ancient if underused stratagem, and came from her own need to see him again. She did not know such performance was unnecessary with him. Tomas said nothing. Then, at the time when she feared he would be rising and pulling on his trousers and leaving his money by the door, he turned and stroked her hair.

She was a woman who did not believe any more in the

existence of tenderness. She had been a girl on the streets since she was fourteen years old. And when Tomas did not leave, when he lay there in the room that became cold as the night sky cleared, she asked him what he was doing.

'I love you,' he said.

She leaned up on her elbow. She drew the cover up across her breasts and shook stray hair from across her face to look more clearly at him.

'There is no need to lie,' she said.

'No. I am not.'

'You are,' she said, her voice turning hard and cruel from hard and cruel experience. 'You think saying that to me you won't have to pay me. You think I am some stupid witch.'

'I would give you everything I have in the world,' Tomas said.

'Pay me then.'

'I have no money.'

The woman shrieked and kicked out at him and kicked again until he came out the other side of the bed.

'I knew it!' she screamed, 'I knew it! A liar!'

The fierceness of her was a measure not of the loss but of her own anger in having, however briefly, believed in his innocence. She hated him then for having reminded her of a world she knew long ago.

Tomas stood and told her that he had nothing and she reached up and swung her right arm and caught him full in the face. His nose pumped a thick crimson.

'I love you,' he said and stood there bleeding.

On his declaration she let out a high long wail and got up and at him as if beating at the old lie of Love itself. Tomas did not move. He took her blows like proofs of something else and stood.

When at last she had surrendered and stopped in a wheezing breathlessness on the side of the bed, she heard with astonishment the handsome Foley repeat his vow of love. He stood there naked by the window and told her.

'Stop it!' she said. 'Stop it!' and held her hands over her ears and looked for a time like a young girl again. 'Don't even say that. Not you.' She turned away and looked at where the wall was flaked and cracked. 'Do you know how many times I've heard men say that?' she said.

'This is me,' said Tomas. 'I love you.'

She sighed and rolled back over on the bed so that she was near him. She looked at the beauty of his body and weakened. She looked at his softened sex and wanted to take it in her hands.

'If you love me . . .'

'I do,' he blurted.

'If, I said.' She reached up a hand and touched his stomach and drew it away again. 'If you love me you will pay me,' she said, and watched him for the dodge she knew would be coming. A bell in the town rang two o'clock. She should have been out on the street again. She heard it and waited, and then on the end of its second pealing heard Tomas Foley offer her his boots as payment.

'Here, I have no money. I will get some and bring it to you tomorrow,' he said. 'These are good boots.'

She took them in her hands. 'They are.'

'They show you,' Tomas said.

'I'd almost believe you,' she told him then, and with that he turned and walked to the door of that small room and picked up his clothes and put them on. 'They show you I love you.' He stood in his ragged trousers and held his shirt in his hand. He looked at her a final time. 'What is your name?'

With his boots in her hands, the woman, who through his eyes had seen herself again a girl in a time before the tarnishing of all such notions as truth and love, said her name was Blath, meaning flower.

4

With their eldest brother lost in the seas of love, Finbar and
Finan woke in the dawn with hunger eating at their insides.
They opened their mouths on the damp air to see if the pangs
might escape. They did not. They sat up and wondered what
to do. With Tomas sleeping they seemed grown in stature and
got up and stood with legs apart and stern faces as if serious-
minded captains. They walked about to the horses and back. In
manner they were minor replicas of their father and in the green
tranquil morning they were restless and impatient. They looked
for something to command. Finbar went over and pushed Teige
roughly.

'What is it?'

'Wake up. We have to get food.'

Teige sat.

'Light a fire,' Finbar said.

'Yes, light a fire,' said his twin sharply. 'We'll catch some
fish.'

They stood and watched him a moment, as if to see their
command taking shape. Then they went and from the small
collection of their things that were salvaged from the river took
a ball of line and a pin bent hook-shaped and walked away to
the water's edge.

The morning opened with ponderous clouds of pewter
coming eastward across the sky. Teige went to the horses and
spoke to them and then gathered sticks of ash and twigs and
dried leaves. All of us are like in a dream, he thought. Like

nothing has happened and we are just here in this place by the woods. He went deeper within the trees and walked across the softened brown floor of fallen pine needles and leaves long decomposed. He stopped and listened for birdsong and heard such whistled in the roof of branches above him. He stayed there with sticks in his arms and all seemed gone for the place was so greenly empty. He thought of how easily he might be lost there, and then he thought of his mother. Quietly into the screen of trees he called to her. He said the name he had for her. He said it in such a manner as one might use to speak with ghosts or others invisible. Then he stopped and stood and listened as if listening deep in the air for the slightest footstep or noise in which might be traced her presence.

When he came out of the trees the twins were already waiting with two trout.

'Where were you? Come on, light the fire!'

They threw commands and showed off their catch and had an air of swagger.

When the fire was lit they cooked the fish. Tomas was sleeping. Teige went and threw the heads and tails to the swan that had not sailed away. The morning in that place beside the river moved slowly as the clouds came on and dulled the light. Thin smoke rose in furls. A veil of misted rain fell without seeming to be falling.

When at last Tomas woke he arched his back like a cat and caught the after-scent of trout.

'I could eat a horse,' he said.

'We need to go back,' Teige told him. 'We have to find our mother.'

Tomas flushed. He looked away in the woods.

'We need to stay here – move into the woods for a few days until I get us somewhere in the town,' he said.

'We're supposed to be finding a place by the sea and then going back,' said Teige.

'Well, we're not. We're staying here.'

'It was father's plan.'

'And he's dead. So.' Tomas paused and in the rippling of the river water heard the name Blath meaning flower. 'I have to go. Make something there,' he said, and waved his arm at the edge of the wood. 'I will be back later.' Then he went and took his horse and rode back toward Limerick town.

His brothers did not know what had got into him, but they were too afraid to ask. Secretly the twins were pleased at his absence and thought of things they could get Teige to do.

They sat there, abandoned again, then Finbar said, 'We need to make a better camp by the woods.'

'Yes,' Finan agreed. 'A good camp, a fort.'

'That's what I said, a fort.'

They looked back at the trees. They knew stories of many that had disappeared in such forests, ones that had wandered off trails and vanished into the kingdom of fairies.

'At any moment something could come out of there,' Finan said.

They watched where the trees and their shadows met and dissolved in dark.

'It could, and it will,' agreed Finbar at last, drawing his knees up to his chest and turning to wait for when his prediction would come true.

While his brothers waited there that empty day, Tomas arrived back in Limerick. Along the route he had stopped at a number of cottages and stolen from cabins and yards what he could. He had an axe and a shovel and a number of irons. He had a blanket of coarse hair, and wrapped in it a fire tongs and a number of empty blue glass bottles. For himself he had lifted the eggs from hens and sucked them dry. He had eaten wild blackberries that grew in tangles in the hedgerows three miles outside the town. By the time he had encountered the ragged traders who were camped on the edges of the market, he had the wild look of one unstable with emotion. The traders were travellers from all corners of the country and they recognized at once the desperation in his bootless figure, and the tainted air of stolen goods. Squint-eyed, fox-headed fellows, they poked with their fingers at the little assemblage of things wrapped in the blanket and, while considering their value, measured it against the value of betraying him to the law. Nevertheless it was with a handful of coins that Tomas rode on toward Limerick town. He tied his horse outside an empty cabin with fallen thatch and washed his face with fingertips wetted in a trough. In the daylight the town was less than beautiful. A dreary rain fell. In the side-streets open sewers ran by broken footpaths and fouled the air. Tomas decided at once that their father had been right, the town was not for them, they would go to the sea. He hurried on, his feet cold and muddied. Small boys stopped baiting a rat and watched him pass.

He walked up the town to the place where he had met Blath the night before. But there were only two men worse for porter sitting on the street. One of them looked up at him and then grinned with an empty mouth.

'You're lookin' for 'em?' he gummed. His companion shuddered alive and dropped a loop of bloodied drool in the street.

'A woman,' Tomas said.

The first man began a laugh that became a cough. He coughed until his eyes ran.

'D'ya hear tha?' he said to the other. 'A woma.'

'No no no, you want to see de man,' Gums said. 'He's over dare, forty tee, up tairs on the lep. He pays ya for yer teet, look.' The two men opened their mouths at the same moment and showed Tomas their raw inflamed gums empty of teeth. 'Five pence the la.' They smiled, as if they had passed on to him some extraordinary felicity.

'The women will be here tonigh, after dar,' said the drooling man.

Tomas did not want to wait until darkness. He went directly to the room where he had made love the previous night but the door was locked. He walked up the town and down again and it was still not past noon. He weighed the coins in his pocket and briefly considered whether to buy food or boots. But in the end he did neither. He decided that he would give all the money to the woman called Blath because he had told her he would give her everything he had in the world, and she would give him back his boots. Then he would rescue her and take her with him back to his brothers and onward to the place where they were going to live by the sea. He did not include in the calculations that the rescue of Blath would in some way be the redeeming of other losses, the empty space that was his mother. But such existed, too, in the depths of his mind.

He walked up and down Limerick town. He saw fine coaches arrive and depart. He heard men talking in English. He watched a river rat run the length of the main street chased by small boys. He walked until his bootless feet ached. He walked the way a man walks when he is walking to meet a woman who is already lodged in the space before his eyes. Then, when he had reached the top of the town for the umpteenth time, had patted his horse and spoken to it, he sat down and waited for darkness.

Years later, when life had hardened the last softness of him, when he was living in another country and those days would seem to take on a fabled unreality, he would think of that afternoon. It would come back to him like the younger ghost of himself, and he would be walking the streets of a town where none knew his history or name and suddenly that afternoon's wait for the darkness would arrive in his heart like a spear.

If he could he would have given a year of his life to move the clock forward four hours.

But as it was, the time was much longer. It was long enough for all of his childhood, boyhood and adolescence to revisit him. All the battles of the small two-room house on the lord's estate where his father had knocked him down to make him grow up. Tomas sat and was revisited by them all while his feet froze.

When darkness fell at last he moved quickly down the cold pathway of the street. When he arrived at the place he had met Blath the night before she was not there. There were other figures in the shadows. Tomas went up the steps of the house. In the doorway there stood a woman. He thought at first that she was wearing a mask, for her eyes and lips were painted and shone glossily beneath the lamplight.

'Love,' she greeted him.

But he was already past her. He was already bounding the stairs two at a time. He was already at the bedroom door itself and turning the knob that was locked, making him knock at the cheap door with such fierce insistence that it was instantly clear he was not going to turn away. He stood back and then thumped at it with his shoulder, and then again until

29

it splintered down the centre and two boards fell apart and he pushed his way on in to the room of love.

The smells were the first thing to strike him. They were the smells of the night before, the smells he had lost on the ride back to his brothers and tried in vain to recover. Now the perfume assailed him. That there was another man in the bed with Blath did not arrive in his consciousness for a moment. There was a brief pause, a frozen nothingness. Then all proceeded as in bizarre phantasm and took the form of quickened nightmare and Tomas saw the arms of Blath lying by her sides and saw the man on top of her in his shirt. And she was trying to get up and get him off her and he was making a low moaning and hurrying as if in some desperation to finish even as he knew the other had crashed in the door. Then there was noise and cries of alarm and more people coming from rooms down the hallway. There was sudden pandemonium, floorboards creaking and some hastening away and others arriving down to where pieces of the door hung. But none of these mattered to Tomas. 'Stop, stop,' he heard Blath say. He saw her fists come up and hit the man on his sides, but then Tomas swung and cracked open his head with a plank from the door. The crack was loud and sharp and the fellow fell sideways and blood shot on the wall and there were cries and shrieks and the very air of the room itself seemed to pulse and beat. Blath screamed and sat up and held to her the blanket and she saw it was Tomas and was shaping some words to him when the painted woman arrived in the doorway with a pistol. The woman aimed at the broad back of Tomas and Blath shouted to her to stop and in the same instant still Tomas was dropping the plank and drawing from his pocket the money and spilling it on the bed. His breath was heaving. The bloodstain dripped on the wall. He wore the look of a man mad without comprehension yet of the violence and passion that had risen inside him.

'All I have, I said I would give it you.'

He said the words and may have imagined from them would

30

follow the rescue, and may even have thought they could both walk from there. But then through the door came a man called Maunsell with bald head and wide reddish sideburns who saw the dead man and the coins and called stop and grabbed the pistol from the woman in the door and fired it just as Tomas dived sideways. There were screams, there were yells from down the hall and men and women running. The room surged with people and then Tomas leapt through the window and shattered the glass and arrived bleeding in the street.

6

In the emptiness of that same day, Teige conversed with the swan. He knew the various mythologies of the swan that had been passed to him in the form of stories told by his mother. He knew of the daughters of Lir who had been banished into swanhood on Lough Erne for nine hundred years. He knew the tale of Leda and the swan that was Zeus, and the sons of God, the twins who were stars, Castor and Polydeuces. So he realized that the transformation of his father into the white bird that sailed by the shore of the river was neither unique nor fearful. It was almost fitting, he thought. For his father would have taken a kind of natural pride in at last becoming part of legend. So, while the twins hunted for sloeberries in the woods, Teige came down to the riverside and told the swan in plain Irish that he was sorry for what had happened to him.

'I knew we should not have crossed the river,' he said. 'I was not afraid of it, but I knew. As you know now,' he added. 'Let that be the end of it between us.'

Wind made the river into waves that lapped softly. The swan did not sail away. It stayed while Teige fed it the heads and tails of trout.

'Where is my mother?' he asked, but heard only the slow soft lapping of the waters.

'I suppose there are advantages in being a swan,' Finan said when they had returned with berries.

'Indeed there are,' his twin agreed, but could not think of

any until Teige told them: 'For him there's no time now. He's in the everlasting.'

'Here?'

'Yes, here, and anywhere he chooses to go. He can swim into the past or the future and be a swan there.'

'But not a man again?'

'No,' Teige said, and the three sat and pondered this and watched the inscrutable eye of the swan and the way its feathers ruffled sometimes when there seemed to be no breeze.

The darkness that night was deep and damp and starless. It painted the woods at their back into the sky and made the river before them into a black slickness that licked the air. The brothers waited for Tomas in the half-sleep of those who know trouble is on its way. The world turned with them lying but not sleeping beside their horses in the wetness of the night. They listened to Teige tell them the story of Orpheus and the Underworld. Then afterward they listened to the wind in the woods and heard there the voices of ghosts and fairies and other spirits who had nowhere else to be. They heard them and shuddered in the fear that a hand might reach out and arrive on their shoulders at any moment, and that it would not be the hand of agent or landlord but the inviting gesture into the underworld of the dreamless dead.

So, when they heard the first hoofbeats they did not move. They were huddled together in a grey blanket. Their eyes were wide. Though their horses neighed and moved about and beat at the ground with the smell of terror that was coming, and though soon the rider shouted out to them, still they did not move from the paralysis of fear. It was not until Tomas had ridden to within twenty feet of the bank of the river that Teige knew they were in reality.

The eldest brother's arm was dangling limply from his shoulder socket. He was slumped forward and his face was bloodied.

'Quickly now,' he said, 'we have a few moments, no more. They are behind me.'

The Foleys were used to flight. It was a family habit from the time before their great-grandfather. The twins were on their horses the moment they stood up. Teige ran to the river's edge. He called some words to the swan then came back and he too was on his pony and they were racing into the darkness.

They stayed ahead of their pursuers, riding with the abandon of the lawless. The younger brothers did not even know why they were being chased, but supposed that whatever the reason it was unjust and deadly, and was another event in the long catalogue of inequitable grief that was the family's history. The twins, riding together bareback on the grey gelding, became wild in the chase. Rather than seek the silent protection of the darkness, they yahooed in the air and shrieked loudly enough to rouse the birds from the tops of the trees in the great wood. Soon there were blackbirds flying, scattering the last dead leaves from the oaks and filling the air with a fluttering falling that in the darkness traversed like flakes of feeling, wild and ungathered. The twins yelled out. Finbar rode on the rear of the horse and waved his arms wide like a demented bird. Tomas was tilted forward on the chestnut, his arm like a rag and eyes glittering with the broken pieces of Love as he led the way into the nowhere that the Foleys sought for a new beginning.

They rode for ever. The pursuit was dogged, fuelled with whiskey and the twisted righteousness of those who know themselves equally guilty. The bald figure of the Law squeezed the flanks of his horse until white foam fell from its mouth. His men chased on, riding on a hot bed of lust, seeing in the capturing and killing of Tomas Foley a way to release what was twisting and burning inside of them.

How many of them there were the brothers did not know. They surged on through the darkness, racing blindly through screes where the gorse and hawthorn prickled and clawed and made scarlet ribbons of blood across their cheeks and arms. They rode down to the river's edge and found at once their progress slowed by mud. Teige's pony began to tire. Then in the water he saw the white gleam of the swan.

'They'll catch us,' Finbar said.

'Feck, they won't,' Tomas told them. His face was twisted in a mask of fury and pain and remorse.

They stopped in indecision.

Then Teige said, 'I'm not afraid of the river.'

They tied the horses loosely to each other and Teige spoke to them and told them they must fly like their horse ancestors into the darkness and lose the ones who were chasing them. Then he blew his scent into their quivering nostrils and smacked them free.

The brothers stepped into the Shannon. Teige floated on one side of the swan and Tomas on the other. Then, with the twins flanking them and holding on tight, they moved out into the river, and at once were borne away on the current.

7

And we can leave them there a moment. The part of the story that is the courtship and marriage of Francis and Emer Foley is told on winter nights when stars flock into the sky. It is told by the old to the young in cautionary tones. Sometimes the courtship alone is told and seems a story out of Arcadia. As tales of great-grandfathers and mothers are, it seems a thing unreal in a time of innocence. She was the daughter of a hedge-school master. His name was Marcus O'Suilleabhain. He was from the County Galway and had come eastward with his family when Emer was still a child. They lived in a place not far from Carlow. Sometimes he taught her Latin and Greek and spoke in those languages with an ease and eloquence that made him seem a figure from ancient times. He was blue-eyed and wore a grey beard. His fingers were long and thin as his daughter would tell, and by yellow candlelight he would sit in the evenings and dip ink and write words and say these out loud as he did so. He had rolls of scripts and other amber-coloured scrolls tied with frayed ribbons. He had books leatherbound and a few edged with gilt. He told his daughter stories in Irish and Latin both and made in this way obscure connection between times long distant and those of their living.

He loved the fair-haired girl, his only daughter, for the semblance she was of her mother and for the high-spirited way she had and how she held her head back when she walked in the street as the daughter of the master. He schooled her in pride and told her stories of proud falls and tragedies. When she was not yet twelve years old he first told her the legends of the stars. He sat with her and told her these though her mother thought she should be at bread-baking or other such things. Marcus O'Suilleabhain did not care. He had no sons. He had this beauty of a daughter. He sat by her bed and talked her into sleep. And just so, between her waking and her dreams, there walked on the mud floors of their two-room cottage Apollo and Artemis, and Pallas Athene, Hermes, Dionysus, such figures. She had been born in Virgo, and when in the spring and summer her stars could be seen, Marcus recounted to her the legends of the winged virgin. She was the Queen of the Stars, he said, the Goddess of the Corn. She loved one who was cut down in his prime, and she had to travel through winter to the Underworld to bring him back. But she did. For, see, the winter ends and she returns with him every spring. The master told her there were many names for her, the lovers were Venus and Adonis, or Isis and Osiris, but whichever there were always the grief and the journey and the promised return.

Like Virgo then, the independent and free, Emer grew more beautiful and fiery still. She sat at the classes her father held in an open cabin whose thatch leaked drowsily and sometimes she taught the very youngest ones. Then her father died. The school like a figment or a thing of air vanished overnight, its students gone. Emer lived on with her mother and then took work washing in the house of landlord Taylor. Her childhood and girlhood were like linen, taken up and folded away.

She was a young woman beautiful and proud and silent unless provoked. Then her anger would flash out in fierce indignation. Her mother caught fever in the wet autumn of Emer's twentieth year and died before Christmas. She was alone. For the natural elegance of her bearing she was moved into the position of dining maid and given a small room in the attic. She lived there some years and attended the table of people who ate lavish feasts served from silver tureens and platters and drank from goblets of crystal. There was a sorrow in her manner that beguiled the gentlemen. They spoke of her when she left the room. Some tried to draw her with remarks and soft flatteries but always she turned them away.

In the April of a year, Francis Foley saw her in the market of Carlow town. She was standing at a stall. Her hair blew about her in the breeze. He did not speak to her. He studied her until she turned and took her purchases and went back through the town and out along the road to the big house. Briskly he was behind her. He left his horse and went on foot and was a short distance back, as if it was she leading him, like a tame pony, leading him out of one life into another.

As a young man Francis Foley had been outlaw and rebel for his country. His father had been hanged for participating in treasonous and bloody plots. He had grown up hiding in woods, taking instruction from white-faced thin fellows who arranged attacks on magistrates and agents and spies. He had lived seemingly without life of his own, yet he was strong and powerful. He assisted at the assassination of plump men scented with cologne. He stood with others and stoned the gaoler MacCurtin in his bed for crimes of betrayal, and ate oaten porridge in the kitchen of the spy Lynch moments after he had slit his throat. In his youth, he had walked in the footsteps of his father, grandfather, and more great-grandfathers than he knew. He rode with his brother, Aengus, taking vengeance to be justice and thinking they were righting what was wrong in the history of the country. Then, on a failed raid on a barracks in Tipperary, Aengus was shot and died afterward beneath a hedge in a field wet with rain. Francis Foley lost his spirit then. He grew silent and went off by himself and did not again meet with those who promised freedom was near. He took work for short term in the harvest or spring. Anger still rose and bloomed within him sometimes. Sometimes he saw inequity and injustice and had to keep his chin set and knuckles deep in his pockets. Such times when he thought he should return to the life of a rebel he thought of Aengus in the field, and the anger did not so much pass as turn into grief. So his life was, working itinerantly and travelling between farms and estates, until the noon he saw Emer O'Suilleabhain at the market.

He followed her.

'*Ailinn*,' – 'Beauty' – he called after her when she turned in at the gates of the house.

She stopped in the road. She had known he was following her. She had already weighed the possibilities of the moment like pebbles in her palm and, with the intuition gifted her by a grandmother who spoke with fairies, knew that her life would roll from her fingers into those of this stranger.

'Is it me?' she said in Irish, turning her face into the fall of her fair hair.

When he came to her, Francis Foley fell into the first reverence of his adult life. He lost at once the hoop of words he had expected to throw over her. He said nothing. Emer smiled. The soft April noontime touched them both, then she said: 'I suppose I shall see you tomorrow on this road.'

There was no reply, though the air between them was already eloquent. Emer walked on. Francis lay himself in against the weeds in the ditch. The following day he awaited her there. When she arrived a thin rain was drizzling and a scarlet headscarf covered her hair. Without slowing her walk she passed along by where he stood and then felt the presence of him in her stride. It was as if she had collected him, and he her, and they were in each other's air already. So, without words, they walked off the road to the town and into the damp new grass coming in the meadows.

From the first, Francis Foley gave Emer his dreams. The dreams he had once dreamed for his country now became the condensed but powerful dream of a perfect place for this woman to live and bear their children. He imagined it fiercely. He told Emer the home he would make for her. He described it like it was its own republic, as if he hoped now to step outside the reality of history and find a place only theirs. Emer raised her eyebrows at him yet loved the way he made her feel again a queen. When she went out with him in the night-times after the dining was done and the ware washed he made her forget the disappointments of her life.

She lay back on his coat in a field under the night sky.

'Do you know the stars?' she asked him.

'Some of them I know.'

'My father told me their names and stories,' she said, and then told him something of the old master and of the stars' names in Latin.

He listened and loved her more still and in the following days went and asked of a schoolmaster thereabouts names of further constellations and these he brought to Emer like the gifts of courtship.

'I want a place for us,' he said to her.

'There are many places. Where will we go?'

'We'll have a house of our own.'

'Yes,' she said. 'A fine house. A house with a yard and garden and hens.'

'I will make it for you. I will make the finest house any man ever made.'

'You won't be able to.'

'I will.'

She angled herself on her elbow and looked into his face pale in the night.

'You are a man who thinks he can change the world.'

'Of course I can,' he told her and took her in his arms.

They married in May. Emer ran to him at the end of the avenue when the sky was releasing its stars and the night sweetening with scent of almond from the furze. The May night was warm syrup. The tenderness of the air, the hushed green of the world that was luscious, sensual, primordial, the soft low light, the sighing breaths of beasts in the fields, all these entered their memories that night as if such things were themselves the guests at the wedding. They met the priest at the roofless ruined chapel of Saint Martin's and were married with a twist of Latin over their heads like a cheap, invisible corona. When the priest had slipped bat-like into the shadows, Francis Foley and Emer clung to each other. It was long moments before they moved. Then they ran down the road and across the night-time fields to a stone cabin for cattle, empty now, and which was the first house of all those that fell short of Francis Foley's vision of paradise.

They began a home there. She left her work. He would not have her going there, and she herself was glad to walk in with her head high and say she would not be back. Then there was a brief blue summer of three weeks before the weather turned around and came at them from the east. The wind burned the hay. Seeds did not come to proper fruition, trees lost their leaves in August and by September a fierce winter had already arrived. Emer carried their unborn son like a promise of new spring and watched the dark days for signs of light. Her husband, who had dreamed so extravagantly, had to hire himself at fairs. He disappeared before dawn and did not return until the physical exhaustion of his body was brought about by those who paid him less than the cost of feeding their horses. Slowly, so slowly, a sour disappointment seeped into the cottage. Tomas was born in January when the snow was lying thick on the fields and there was no work even at the fairs. They ate small birds and berries. In the deep silence of the one dim room their marriage staggered under the impossible weight of dreams. Words were a reminder of other words and so went unsaid, but the vision of the place that had first been conjured remained. It lingered like a shadow in the corner, and soon Francis Foley could not look at the leaking thatch, or a place where the mud floor puddled, without hearing the reproach and mockery of his own words. Years slipped past them. The twins were born. Francis lay in the low bed at night and listened to the scouring wind and then for the first time in his adult life said a prayer to God for guidance.

He was too rash and independent a man to wait long for reply and the following morning when none had come he loaded his wife and family on their small cart and moved them north-eastward into the wind. Emer did not want to go.

'This is madness,' she said.

'Nothing is gained by sitting still,' he told her as the gale bit off his ears. 'This is not our home.'

'It could be.'

'No it couldn't. Look at it. We are going. This is not what I promised you.'

'What if I said I didn't care?'

'You'd be lying.'

'I wouldn't.'

'This is not our home.'

They wandered like biblical travellers looking for a sign, and were met with blizzards. Gulls were blown out of the sky. To keep his family alive Francis stole sheep and killed them with his hands. They slept under hedges of whitethorn, the father lying himself down and letting the others rest wrapped upon him as the cold rose into his bones and by the dawn made of his face a white bloodless mask.

When at last they found a place to live it was no better than the one they had left behind. They stayed a year and two months, then moved again.

And so on it went, that life of struggle and hardship that followed the innocent days of love so swiftly that soon they themselves were almost forgotten, and survived only as the thinnest faded memories of a once-upon-a-time sweetness. They did not find a home. They lived on for times in various cabins and ruined cottages, deeply mired in the disappointment of their dreams. They stayed awhile and then moved, each time at the insistence of Francis over the increasing resistance of his wife. At last when Teige was born Francis found work as one of an army of gardeners on an estate. They had a small cottage. The country itself was lost too in disillusionment. Spies and betrayals were everyday, the air of towns was opaque with mistrust and the yellow scent of greed. Those who owned the land did not live on it, and those like Francis who worked it imagined they were little more than the beasts in the field. It was a long hard kind of living. And, though he heard the whispered news of rebels, the perennial plots and hot dreams of those who promised a new country of their own, Francis resisted joining them. He bowed his head and stayed working, clucking the horse and leading the mower down the long lawns of the estate, trimming the hedges and tending the perfect gardens of Lord Edward James Fitzroy of the County of Essex.

Emer was by then almost contented. She was the mother of four boys. She tried to teach them classes in the Latin and Greek her father had taught her, but Tomas was impatient to be with his father and the twins rolled and knocked each other about and showed little interest. Only Teige sat and listened. His hair was first blond and then fair brown and he had a way of sitting in close attention that was serene and knowing. His mother told him he would be a master. She ruffled his hair and touched his face with floury fingers.

But trouble was already gathering. Francis had no garden of his own and tended another man's instead, clipping the laurel bushes that the lord himself never saw, grooming them into globes of green in case the lord should visit this year, and bringing home the clippings to add to the stew of their dinner. He planted potatoes, dug carrots and turnips and parsnips that were marshalled in such straight lines that they mocked the crooked stonewalled boundaries of the fields outside the estate. His hands grew black with earth. When the old angers rose in his chest he reached down and tore at the weeds with fury. And shortly he was noticed by the head gardener, Harrington, for none rooted at the ground like him or pulled up the stumps of dead trees or turned over the soil with the same fury.

The garden was a kind of paradise. It was made to defy the typical view of that country in the drawing rooms of London.

From there, the neighbouring island was a place unruly and wild where everything rioted in nature and a straight line was not to be seen. But in that garden was a proof of empire, a living evidence that in the hands of the educated and well-bred even the most inauspicious place, the damp dreary ground of that estate, could become transformed into an elegant country residence that would not offend a visiting lord. It would both reflect and inspire. It would show the natives the advantages of dominion, of what could be done, mirroring in its majesty the glory of its owner while subduing them to it at the same time.

Within it, Francis worked silently from grey dawn until the gloaming. The years ran into his hands and lined his skin like the knots in trees. The lord never came. The house was prepared several times, fires lit, woodsmoke hanging in the trees and every plant and bush in the garden balanced on the instant of its best display. Rain was prayed away. Maids ran about in black dresses with white aprons and caps and polished the dishes that had never been used. The world waited, and was disappointed once more.

It was the evening after one of those false visits, when all day eyes had watched the avenue for his lordship's arrival, and the gardeners had looked at their garden as though it were the painting of a garden, a masterpiece in which every detail had been painted just so, that Francis came home angrily to Emer. He sat at the table and placed upon it his hands brown with mud.

'What are we doing?' he said to her.

'We are living our life. Get yourself cleaned,' she told him.

'We have nothing.'

'Stop. Don't. I know what you are going to say and I don't want to hear it, Francis,' she said, and went to get the food for the dinner. The boys stood about and watched silently to see calamity coming. But that evening it did not.

Later that night Francis left the cottage in the falling

darkness and broke into the big house. He felt he had been scorned by the lord, and that this was only the latest of all those assaults life had made on his dreams. He opened a window and stepped inside that mute and perfect world. He walked through its ordered elegance, down the polished oak floors that reflected the stars and into rooms that offered themselves like nervous debutantes hoping for approval. He stood in the bay window and saw in the stellar light the long view down the garden. He saw it the way it was meant to be seen, and in those moments, hearing his own breath sighing in the empty house, he was struck with a cruel knowing of how completely he had surrendered his soul. Bulbs of anger exploded inside him. He was in the middle of his life and realized how much of it was lost. He touched the smooth painted sill with his fingertips, then he crossed the dark room and looked out at the western view of the rosebed, the eastern view of the boxwood. He moved from room to room to see out through each of the windows, and as he did, his rude boots making creaking noises on the floors, he felt a tightening in his heart. The whole country is a jail, he thought. They have us prettying it up for their visits and they never even come. He was in the library looking outwards, and when he turned away from the garden view in anger he saw behind him the great brass and wooden contraption that was the telescope.

At first he did not even know how to look through it. He did not know about angles or focus, but he knew the stars he had learned for Emer. The moment he touched the telescope his life had already begun to change. For he was at once vividly reminded of his courtship, of the innocent nights beneath the sky when he and she had imagined the world spread before them. It was a memory made bitter now. He turned his eye to the glass and looked up into the clouds.

It was three nights later before the skies were clear and Francis saw Venus from the library. He saw it and stared. He watched it with the kind of wonder children know and was still watching the stars when the light of the dawn thinned them into nothing.

When he told Emer, he thought he might have conjured magic and it would return them to the early days of their life together.

'I have seen Andromeda,' he told her in the dark of their low bed. 'Will you come and see tomorrow night?'

'You shouldn't be in there' she said.

'There are more stars than you can see with your eyes. They are like stars kept from everyone, like ones not for our viewing but only his lordship.'

'Francis.'

'Don't tell me we were not meant to see them.'

'You will be caught and we will be thrown out on the road.'

'Will you come with me tomorrow night and see them?' He leaned over and touched her arm in the dark. He brought his hand up to her hair.

She let the silence answer for her. She lay motionless and felt her life was about to come asunder. She thought of her father and his discipline and pride and how he had instilled in her a sense of who she was; they were not people who broke into the houses of landlords. There was nothing moving. Francis and Emer heard each other breathe and heard the breathing of the children in the vast stillness that fell out of the stars. At last, when he could bear no more the emptiness between them, Francis urged her again.

'Come tomorrow night. You'll see then.'

She said nothing at first for she was afraid. But he stroked her cheek then and whether out of fear or frustration or the feeling of loss that was deep within her, she said angrily: 'I don't want to see them, my feet are cold. What do I want seeing stars for?'

She thought it would end there. He drew away his hand. She turned her back to him in the bed.

'You want to see them through the telescope.'

'I can see them from my own window,' she grumbled.

'It's not . . .'

She sat up suddenly and turned to him.

'You're a foolish man. Oh God you are. And what if you were found? What if you were seen there, then what? We'd be thrown back on the road, that's what, think of that, will you? Or you'd be taken off to gaol, for what? For stars!'

Her words crossed the darkness like spiders and stung his heart.

'Forget that. Forget it,' she said, her voice breaking now with tears and disappointments that went deep into her past. She turned her back to him.

'You should not be going in there,' she said after a time. 'It will bring trouble on us.'

He did not answer her. She could not understand. They lay sleepless and separate in the dark.

She wished he would sleep. But instead Francis sat upright.

'What gives him the right to have it? To have it locked in there night after night not even looking through it, the empty eye of it! Not even seeing!' He crashed the crude wooden headboard.

'Francis!'

'It is a marvellous thing, Emer. If you . . .'

'Stop!'

She would have none of it. It was not because the poetry of her soul was so earthbound, or that she could not imagine the beauty, it was because she feared the quality in Francis Foley that once she loved the most: his ability to be enraptured. She knew he would not stop, and knew that the fragile world they had built would fall apart.

The lord never came. The seasons rose and fell on the garden estate and the children grew. They were not allowed to walk in the gardens their father made. They went instead up the rough fields and ran their horses and watched Teige gallop and let their giddy calls and cries in Irish fly across the wind. They were a country within a country and did not know it. Their father tried to make the boys feel like champions in the grassy spaces. He coached them in running and jumping and wrestling. He rolled with them on Sunday afternoons in the summer meadows and made his wife laugh when he pushed out his chest to show that he had still the cut of a warrior. He taught them the ancient game of hurling, and they played it with flat hand-hewn wands of ash, pucking the leather sliothar ball high through the air like some antiquated weaponry for the downing of eagles. Still, he had a kind of fierceness with the children that came from love but could become terrible. When they could not jump the stream that he could, he insisted they try again. He showed his disappointment and the boys leapt again and again until he walked off and left them leaping without audience and the vague stain of inadequacy spreading in their hearts. Nonetheless they grew strong and free-willed. They did not show their father their fear of him. And when he burst in anger at their carelessness or slowness they hung their heads in a greater shame for knowing that they had failed some standard of excellence.

And so it was. Francis worked the gardens by day and sometimes slipped by night into the big house and watched the stars and looked at the maps that were there, until at last the day arrived when his spirit broke free.

It was an October morning. He brought Tomas with him, leaving Emer with the others and going out across the dampness that hung visible over the lawns and made the songs of the hardy birds plaintive. There were leaves to be gathered. The evidence of the dying year must not be allowed to linger even for a moment on his lordship's lawns. So, father and son silently set about with wooden rakes the fallen black and brown leaves that fell even as they gathered them.

They worked through the still morning. Mounds of leaves were gathered and lay upon the grass, then these were lifted and barrowed away. When the scene was clean of even a single leaf, Francis stopped and told Tomas to stand and look with him. The lawn was like a carpet.

'Look at that,' he said. 'We might as well get to look at our work as no one else does.' They watched all that was tranquil and immaculate there and leaned on their rakes while from the oaks to the east walk late leaves unhinged and twirled down.

They did not hear the footsteps of the head gardener Harrington approaching. He came up on them while they were standing there, giving him opportunity to vent his resentment of the man who sometimes stole his praise.

'You're not paid for looking,' he said.

Tomas jumped. His father did not move. When Harrington came from between the trees their life there was already over. Softly he cursed at them for idleness though he knew it was not true.

'Look,' Francis said, and pointed at the lawn.

Harrington was not interested. 'Get on,' he said. 'The kitchen garden.' He did not look at what they had done or give them that credit. He walked past them and said beneath his breath a muted comment in which Francis caught only the word laziness.

That evening he told Emer he had wanted to hit the man.

'To knock him down into a load of shite,' he said. 'Christ almighty.' He drummed with his hand on the table.

'You have to forget about it. Just carry on. You can't take up against the likes of him,' said Emer.

'Why not?'

'You know why not.'

'I'm bound every way I turn,' he said. 'I can't piss in a pot without someone's say-so.'

'Francis.'

'Christ I won't.' He stood up. Her hands were white with flour at the table. She watched him cross the room and take a bowl and smash it against the wall. Teige was sitting on the

49

floor with a slate. Francis took down another bowl and threw it likewise through the air at the wall. Tomas and the twins came to the doorway. Their mother cried out to her husband to stop but something had snapped within Francis Foley and he knocked over the chairs and took one and crashed it against the floor. He said this was no life for his sons. He said what was he raising them for, was he raising them to be the slaves of the likes of Harrington? He said though Jesus wept he wouldn't. And then Emer was shouting at him and he was shouting in turn and knocking things over and picking up pots and pans and earthenware crockery and flinging all helter-skelter about. The room was like one hit by a storm. It was as if all the disappointments of their married life took form there and ran about and crashed and the air itself grew bitter and sharp. Francis railed and cried out. He said he would not stay there. He said they were not beasts in a field, they were not slaves. And Emer shouted that if they left there they would die on the roads like beggars. And the boys moved from that room into the bedroom they shared, and were like shamed and guilty things sitting with their faces lowered in the dark. And still pots and plates crashed and banged as the marriage broke in the room next to them. They heard the screams and the arguments. They heard their father shout at Emer that she must obey him and that if he said to go she was to go and that was that. But she was too proud. I have a mind of my own, she told him, I won't take my family and make beggars of them.

And then she cried out for Francis struck her.

She must have fallen down. Silence ripped like a tear in a garment that had once been precious.

The boys heard no more. They stayed in their room and after a long time lay and slept.

They did not see their mother walk away. Nor know that Francis went out with a lamp in the obscured moonlight and yoked the cart and rode it up the avenue to the big house and did not look back at her as she walked out the gates. They did not see their sundering apart like twin stars falling away into darkness and confusion. They did not know Francis let himself in through the window of the lord's house and went to the library and in the lamplight looked at the map of the country there. And then, grappling his arms about the telescope he lifted and dragged it down the hall and out the door where he loaded it on to the cart. He went then to the house of Harrington who was gone to the town and into it he wheeled barrows of leaves and dung. Then he came back and took what things of theirs were not broken and he woke the boys and told them quickly to come. He lit the thatch even as they were coming out the door. Tomas jumped on his horse. The younger boys were too frightened to speak. Then they all rode from there wordless and aghast in the dark. The father stopped the cart as they passed the lawn that was surrounded by boxwood hedge. 'Wait!' he said. Then he got down from the cart and took the lamp and walked up to the house, and moments later his large figure was running back and he was calling to the boys to go, go quickly, even as the flames were already rising from his lordship's library.

8

Now, the four Foley brothers floated and swam down the river and held on to the swan and caught in their teeth the cries that the icy water shot through them. They did not speak. The deep darkness they travelled through was myriad with the secret sounds of night, the beasts and bushes, the noise of leaves in motion, the falling twisting sounds of the dying of the year as the wind rose and made the water slap in their faces with small chastisements. The brothers did not dream though the time was dream-like and long and marked only by the gradual emergence of bruises of light in the wounded sky. They knew that they had escaped their hunters, and though the water was cold and the current strong, it was almost soothing for Teige and Tomas and the twins to surrender to its ceaseless flowing. They laid down their heads on the cool breast of the world and let it carry them forward. They did not know what lay ahead of them. Swollen puffs of grey and purple hung like resentments above the river. The dawn did not so much rise as ache sourly into the air, its grim clouds growing imperceptibly by the moment. The light was thin and weak and without hope.

The animals that woke and moved in the green fields above the river smelled the rain coming in the wind and ate hurriedly while the brothers sailed past. Soon the river took the colours of the sky. The water and air were one tone, that implacable dull iron that screened the blue heavens from sight and made the world seem burdened by an impossible weight which now must fall. It fell before the brothers had floated past the rocks of Carraig na Ron in the middle of the Shannon river and where the low shore of Kerry on their left was now erased. It fell as arrows of rain, the hard cold rain that announced winter and told the animals in their hidden places that the season had turned. It was as though the sky was squeezed through an iron sieve. It did not pour down, but seemed a stuff of thin metal that fell piercingly and killed the light of morning. Thunder rolled. The swan flapped in alarm and was at once free of the Foleys. It caught the breeze, sailed head-low as if in grief and within moments was thirty yards down river. The twins cried out. They kicked and splashed the Shannon as the rain struck them. Lightning arrived in the falling sky. It rent the air like old cloths and let the pieces fly away. Teige made the strokes of swimming but made no progress. He saw the twins' white faces flash in the waters and then lost them. Tomas was already being pulled away. Though he fought the river and arced his arms into it, trying to swim with his head swinging side to side in a thrashing motion, he seemed to go backwards. The green horizon retreated. The river sucked the rain and grew wild and capricious, swirling its currents, spinning a glitter of sand beneath the surface and rioting the fish so they eddied in quick schools of no direction sliding past the bodies of the swimmers with gaping amazement. The lightning lit the air again. The sky fell and rolled in booms. It was impossible to say in which direction the brothers swam. For none of them were swimmers. The gaol of the rain held them from seeing where they were, but, despite the urgency of their kicks and cries, they each imagined they were going down to where their father was waiting.

The rain struck Teige like a hook.

Then it struck Tomas, and Finbar and Finan.

It hooked Teige in the cloth of his shirt and he felt himself caught by it and being pulled backwards. He went below the water. He cried out gurgles and dark bubbles flew past his face. Then he reached a hand up and knew that he was dead or dreaming, for he felt the rain like a wire running toward the shore of Clare. And he clutched on to the line and fainted beneath a white zag of lightning and did not see the excited faces of the gathered gypsies who fished the thunder in the antique belief of landing the electric spirit of the world.

9

The gypsies' part in the story is long and intricate and fantastical. I think of it sometimes as a part invented by grandfathers later to explain the eccentricities and wanderings of other Foleys in years afterward. Oh that was the gypsy side in him, they say, and sit back and look into the distance.

The gypsies had travelled south in the dying of the year. Once, they had come from abroad, from Europe, in the hidden compartments of ships and through the secret ports that were used by spies. They had travelled to this country not from need or flight but simply because it was there, because it was marked on the outer edge of maps and looked the splintered part of some greater whole, and because they could not be still. Motion was natural, they believed. Nothing living stood still, and in their travels they had seen the variety of the world and accumulated its slow wisdom. Some of them had journeyed around the perimeter of the shore and then left once more. Others, drawn by the green mesmerism of the land, voyaged around it in covered caravans. They took to its crooked roads and found the circuitous routes that defied the usual measurement of progress to be an apt landscape for gypsies. These were roads that went nowhere. They were begun without concept of destination, or at best, no hurried sense of arrival. They were the grassy thoroughfares shouldered by hedgerows and stone walls along which the gypsies that remained lost all sense of time. Their lives, which had once been measured by the new places they discovered, now took on the dimension of a long somnambulant dream. They were not sure if the fields they passed were the ones they had passed only days before. And soon they did not care. The oldest among them, who they called Elihah, told them that they could not even be certain that the rain that was falling had not fallen on them before for sometimes they travelled into the past. One day's weather became the next and their ancient language was discovered short of enough words to describe the thousand different rains. The seasons were not the seasons of other lands, for here the summer might have been the autumn and the winter was sometimes not over until the leaves appeared and fell again in one windy week. They were accustomed to such seamless time, and rode their ragged cara-vans on through it, content in the simplicity of such living, their origins almost vanished from memory. Elihah remembered he had once been a child in a ship on the sea, but whether that was the journey that brought him there, or was a voyage even more distant in time, or simply one that he had dreamed in the seas of his mother's womb, he could not tell. His grandchildren were already old men, many of them gone back across the water to the great shelf of the continent, wandering untraceable paths and lost to their greater families, until by chance or design their roads might meet again at a campfire or fair in this life or another.

The gypsies of Elihah had remained on that rainy island for so long that they grew to know the ways of the natives. They knew the sympathy for outlaws that endured there in the hearts of men, and the evergreen curiosity of people to know what the rest of the world was like. And so they traded not only in tin and copper, but in stories, too. They learned a version of the native language. In it they told stories to those who would come to their caravans and peer in at Mara, the bearded beauty, or at Petruk, a giant who ate branches of the elderberry, and in the conjuring of places far away they could retouch their lost origins. They told of countries they knew but in truth had never seen, though they could describe them in such vivid detail that the listeners walked away with the dazzling vision of places more strange than fairy-tale. In all of their tales the heroes suffered outrageously, there were wrongful rulers and fierce oppression, exiled wanderings in strange lands, floods and famine. These were the stories the natives enjoyed, and the gypsies could link one to the other like threads in a fabric, making the tapestry longer and longer until it threatened a kind of madness. For only they knew that the telling of stories could rob the world of life and make Time vanish. And so, though the story might be yet in its vast middle, an hour before sunrise the lamp was always turned down, the listeners sent away and the curtains of the caravan drawn.

Such was their way. Although they did not follow the calendar, the gypsies knew the customs of the year. And on the morning they fished the Foleys from the Shannon river they were on their way to the last races of October held on the sands of the Atlantic. They had already been to the horse fairs that marked the end of the green grass, and were leading a new pony. On that shoreline in the dawn there were thirty or so men, women and small children gathered as the brothers were pulled ashore. They spoke their own language in quick guttural phrases and cut the fishing lines with knives in their belts. The men had black curls and smoky eyes and wore tattered shirts of once bright colour now open to the rain. The fingers of their hands were aged by the endlessness of the earth they had travelled, the muddied rutted roads, trackless bog and rockstrewn fields. Their women stood behind them with arms crossed. They were strangely beautiful in everything but their teeth, and made of their gaping blackish smiles a sensual virtue, painting their lips in vivid reds and opening them wide in a way that suggested they could swallow the world. They wore jewels and chains and bangles and brooches that were not seen yet in that part of the country. They had combs of tortoiseshell in their hair and wore skirts over their skirts that filled out the lower half of their figures with bounty and made their movements slow and swaying as if walking in another time. The children were like the ghosts of children. They appeared in brown and grey rags, thin and wan and dirty, their grave doomed eyes like pools of ink in which no expression could be read save that of mistrust, for death had moved recently among them. Their long arms hung limply. The rain ran down their faces.

The brothers were unhooked. They lay on the mud banks and looked at the faces peering down at them. The rain fell into their mouths tasting of blood. In the breaking light the storm rumbled and retreated begrudgingly. Then a large woman with a green shawl stepped forward and told the men to take the boys to shelter.

In three caravans they were laid on cot beds and undressed. The twins were kept together. Though they were living they imagined they might be dreaming and did not protest when the gypsy women took off their clothes and lay them naked on coarse blankets that smelled of hazel and hawthorn. The Foleys' senses were sharpened by the nearness of death. They came back to air like fish flapping in the bottom of a boat. They caught the deep and heady perfumes of the women in their nostrils, felt their heads swirl and fell asleep once more.

While the four brothers slept the women watched them to see the shape of their dreams and the men gathered and spoke excitedly of the catch the river had yielded. The gypsies read the adventures of every day for the secret code of the world and knew that the fish-men had come to them not by chance, but by design. For here was the answer to the question they had asked the universe.

The gypsies had had sixteen horses. From one of the diminished northern tribes, who had travelled to the fairs from Donegal for the last time, they had bought a white pony that was wild and fast. This they had watched and roped and lunged and groomed and fed with the berries of the year and with stolen hay from the farms they passed. In the evenings by fires of fresh ash that cracked and spat they had told each other stories of its future. They told the legends of the races not yet run but which had flashed before them all with the startling clarity of episodes of clairvoyance. They had told of how Mario, their champion horse-boy, would ride the white pony bareback on the horseshoe bay of Kilkee in Corca Baiscinn, how he would cling to the mane and slice the air on his way to victory. The women had rocked in their places on the ground, swaying softly backwards and forwards to the words of their men as white ponies ran across their minds and won the fortunes that would make easy the winter. By the low burning of the end of the fire they had laid down to love in blankets that smelled of smoke and horses, caressing each other's thighs as though they were the glistening flanks of the steeds of victory.

Then, in the morning, the world spoke to them. Mario fell ill during the night. He ran a fever and could not get up from his bed. His breathing was thin with a disease they did not know. The diphtheria made his throat narrow as though a leather thong was wedged inside it. His eyes watered a yellowy mucus. The gypsy women had gone out and gathered the flowers of the hollyhock and leaves of coltsfoot and made him a tea. They had made a poultice and placed it on Mario's throat and sat in the dead air of the caravan. They sang softly as was their custom, a singing that was neither song nor hymn but a wordless prayer that belonged to their own great-great-grand-mothers. It was the low music of despair, and sounded out from that caravan to the rest of them with the dread knowledge that the boy was dying. The women sang on through the night and watched the dim light of the boy's life flicker around beneath the canvas. When, near daybreak, the light slipped away the boy was dead. The women stopped singing. The hush travelled out across the camp and the men spilled their drinks into the fire. They sat with stones of silence hanging from their necks. On the long rope that linked them, the horses neighed and beat the muddy ground and twisted their necks about as if to see one who had passed. When the light had come up enough to force the men to see each other's faces, they moved away. They suffered a double grief, for beyond the ordinary loss the boy had been their talisman. They felt the guilt of those who imagine they have tempted fate by dreaming too hopefully of the future; it was as though they had brought the illness upon him through the outrageous good fortune of their dreams. Four days later, three more of the gypsy boys had died. The low singing sounded each night then and the gypsies wondered if they had ridden into a valley of bad spirits. When the fourth boy died, Elihah announced they must leave there. They marked the place by scorching the ground so that others might know it was the site of death, then, fearing the disease would not leave them but would chase their vanity, they had released the white pony.

No more of them had died. They had journeyed onward toward the races with no rider and no pony and no intention of entering the sports. They had gone there rather as a form of purgation, as though they bore witness to something larger than themselves, and the final act required of them was to watch the races Mario should have won.

Ahead of them the winter grew teeth. They felt it bite already in the cold rains that fell out of October. By the time they had arrived on the borders of Clare they were bedraggled and weak.

Then, the previous evening, when they were camped near the Shannon river, the white pony had returned, and brought with it three riderless horses.

The old man, Elihah, was asked if they were to fear them. Was it a portent of further deaths, they asked him. The storm was already moving in the sky. The wind whistled. The birds flew back into the trees. The old man said only the universe could answer. He said they should ask it and wait. He said death was not easily outrun.

Then the rain began. The skies fell in sheets. When the

lightning crashed in the hour near dawn the gypsies came from their beds and watched it like the ending of the world. The horses' eyes rolled. Their wild whinnying was lost amidst the fall of thunder. Then, with an unspoken accord that sometimes moved through their tribe and connected them with traditions of ancestors lost, the gypsies went out into the crashing electricity of the dawn and cast their hooks into the river.

Moments later, they had fished the Foleys on to the bank, and believed they had received their answer from the universe.

10

The brothers did not discover this story for two days. Then they rose from their cots in the caravans and walked out around the camp in the still morning. Smoke was rising in thin curls and men were standing watching it. Some of them looked at the Foleys from beneath their eyebrows. They studied them for the immutable signs of some hidden destiny and then looked away into the ashes as though not daring to face it. When Tomas saw their horses he crossed to them and they smelled each other and the horses made a quick whinnying of greeting. Teige stroked his pony's neck and blew in its nostrils and let its long face rub against his own and his brothers did the same, making gestures old as time. The gypsies stood on the wet grass and watched. They threw phrases to each other in their language. One of them bent down and moved the pot of their breakfast on the side of the fire. He blew softly on the sticks and then poured from the beaten blackened pot into four earthen bowls. He handed them up to one of the others and the two of them carried the food to the brothers. They ate without talk in the green stillness of the camp that was dripping with yesterday's rain. None of them began yet the telling of their story. From the fire the other gypsies stood and watched the horses and the brothers eating. They looked for how the men ate their simple food and if it found favour. When they saw that it did they felt the burden of their future ease a little and unbowed their shoulders. The Foleys ate. Birds sang minor notes in the crooked trees. After the deluge, the sky that emerged was clear with slow-moving white clouds that held no rain. A light breeze carried the air. When the Foleys had eaten they handed back the bowls.

'*Go raibh maith agat*,' Tomas said in thanks.

One of the gypsies took the bowls and nodded. He handed them away and then pointed to Teige.

'Him? Teige,' Tomas said.

'Teige,' said the gypsy.

'That's right,' Tomas said and named each of them. But though he did, he saw how the gypsies did not look from Teige to the twins. They looked at the youngest Foley and let their looking be seen now as though to allow it be translated and the desperation of their need be naked.

'Mario,' the gypsy said toward Teige and watched to see if that name would mean anything to him.

'Teige,' Tomas said, as though there had been some confusion.

The gypsy who had pointed nodded and waved his arm for Teige to follow him and they all walked down to where the white pony was tied on the raised ground by a stand of ash trees. When it sensed them coming the pony turned its head and pulled on the rope. Its eyes opened and rolled as though at the approach of ghosts. Its left foreleg trod blindly at the broken ground. The gypsies murmured to it. They spoke more softly than they spoke to women. But they did not come any closer. They waited for the brothers.

'That's the girl,' Tomas said. The brothers waited for the horse to smell them and smell their own horses off them. 'It's you they want to handle her,' Tomas said with his back to the gypsies and without turning to his youngest brother.

'Why?' Teige said.

'If you can explain gypsies I'll tell you.'

'Ride her, Teigey,' said Finan.

'Go on Teigey.'

'*Sos. Sos.*' Teige sounded the ease he wanted the horse to feel and stepped toward it. 'Sos sos sos.' He soft-clicked his tongue against the roof of his mouth. The pony turned her head and looked away from him but still watched him sidelong on the boundaries of her domain. Her pretend disregard did not mask her fear and stray electric flickerings of it ran in the muscles of her shoulders and made them jump minutely.

'She's a lively one,' Finbar said.

Teige raised his hand to let her smell it but she mistook the gesture and swung around and the brothers had to pull back and Teige whispered *shshsh* sounds and put his hands out with palms raised as if he could touch and smooth down the irrational and make the animal feel the radiance of his respect for her. The gypsies watched him. The women had come from their chores and were standing not far distant in the small clearing. The pony was turned into the trees. The brothers sensed the expectation of the audience behind them, and when Tomas looked back the gypsy who had led them there pointed once again at Teige and made a small rising gesture with his hand.

'They want you to ride her,' Tomas said.

'She's wild,' Teige said lowly, not taking his eyes from the eye of the pony and moving another half-step closer.

'Of course she's wild.'

'I won't be able to.'

'If she's a horse you will.'

'Go on, Teigey boy. Get up. Go on.'

The three brothers watched then as Teige angled his head forward and raised and lowered it in an exaggerated slow nodding mime that the pony watched from the corner of her view. He made himself smaller and then raised his right hand slightly and proffered it to the air between them. The pony let out a low whinnying sound and opened its nostrils as if to breathe in the message of the boy and discover for herself the veracity of his heart. Teige stepped forward and the pony did not move. Her feet were planted. He reached and held out his fingers inches from her face. He held them there proffered a long time. The pony did not turn away. She took hard short breaths and was as one growing slowly accustomed to something in which she did not believe. The company assembled may have been spirits to her eye and the boy the dead Mario. Her shoulders flickered. Quick skittish movements of uncertain purpose passed through her. Then Teige moved the hand that hung in the air and placed it upon her and stroked the warm hard length of her face. He ran his fingers under her chin and scrabbled softly while whispering not words but sounds. He moved inside her tethering then until his chest was against her. He pressed himself against the quickened breathing of her flank and ran his hand up and along her back. He stroked the length of her and kept the pressure of his fingers even upon her flesh as he moved across her back and down her haunches and round the hocks of each of her legs. Then he reached behind him with his left hand and untied the rope that held her and let it fall loosely across his fingers, moving her backward from that place with one hand on her side and the rope slack in the other. He took her a few paces and she moved easily for him, her step not full or graceful or true but marked by relief and the notion that she was free. The boy and the pony moved away into the trees and the gypsies and the Foley brothers walked after them and the gypsy women did the same.

In a place where the ash trees thinned and the ground was softer and gave beneath each hoof Teige swung himself on to the pony's bare back and felt the hushed inhale of the gypsies watching. The pony did not flinch. She did not run or buck or stamp. She stood with feet planted like the statue of herself and waited and felt the presence of the boy. The rope was around her as a halter, but Teige held it loose and then squeezed her with his thighs as softly as he could and at once rode quickly away.

The morning rose grey and still and held the air of new creation. The fields looked unfolded fresh in the dawn. The grass was wet and caught whatever light fell and appeared more green and young than it was. Teige held the rough rope of the halter loosely and tried to allow the pony to race her frustration and confinement away. He sat on the broad working muscles of her back and felt her power and crouched low and put his head forward to hers and spoke to her as the wind rushed past them. They moved away from the river. They galloped out hard and fast away from the small trees and tangled bushes and into the broader light. They beat away down the road and Teige rode the pony with his head close to her so that he felt her speed. The green of the land opened out before them and boy and pony raced into it, travelling with apparent fierce intent, so that to stray onlookers in that uncertain morning Teige Foley might have seemed a forsworn message-bearer, a figure out of Old Testament times charging headlong upon a secret and imperative mission. They rode away down the roads of the County Clare. Thin cattle in the fields lifted their heads to watch. The racing figure was there and then it was gone and the cattle lowered their heads to the poor grass once more. The road ran westward. There was a stonewall ditch that rose and fell and was diminished entire in places and left gaps where the rough wild grass and thistle and gorse grew awry and without promise. Rock shelved up out of the ground. A hare that stood in its tracks and studied them coming took off at last in pretend panic, playing an ancient pattern of zigzag before the horseman as though its flight and escape were not pre-ordained and guaranteed by nature. The hare delighted in the imagined chase; it tore away, sprung hindlegged then feinted right and leapt left into grass that did not seem long enough to screen it. They galloped on. They reached a small rise where again the river could be seen on the left, and suddenly, without the slightest slowing, from full speed the pony stopped short.

Teige flew over her head. Briefly he saw the country from the vantage of a ghost riding a ghost horse. He felt the airiness of his mount and it was momentarily pleasant and easy. He rode the air an instant then began to turn head over heels and then the knowledge of oncoming pain arrived somewhere in the front of his head and he saw the hard brown road and crashed down on to it. He landed and cried out and was only saved from breaking his neck by his youth. He lay in the road and the pony stood and watched him. She studied him with implacable eyes of no regret, but she did not turn and run away.

When he could speak Teige asked her what she was doing stopping like that. He looked around them to see if there was something that had startled her. But there was only the rolling green of that lumpy land. He said a curse in Irish and the pony lifted her nose as if to smell the words.

The pain shot down through Teige's left arm. He lay as flat as he could on his back in the road. He cried out loud and the pony turned half away and Teige called out to her to come to him. He had to call only a second time and the pony walked slowly down the road and he was able to pull himself up first by holding her hock and then the loose reins-rope and then he was sitting on her back once more. His left arm ached and sent crimson blooms of pain travelling toward his neck and spine. He sat there atop the pony sharply aslant and tried to will the hurt into subsiding. They did not move. As though contrite the pony waited for him, perfectly still. She watched the road where nothing visible was coming or going. Then twelve-year-old Teige cried out for his mother.

He cried out to her in the vanished world where she was gone whether living or dead and whence he longed for her now to reappear and take him from the pony and hold him in her white arms on that empty roadside so that a kind of goodness might be restored. He cried for her a second time and she did not come. The landscape ached with his longing. Blackbirds like small priests walked in the silent fields.

When he regained himself he slouched forward and patted the pony with the palm of his right hand. He whispered to her.

'It's all right,' he said. 'You are fine,' he told her, 'fine girl. Yes, you are.'

He felt the pain localize and he grew more lopsided to accommodate it, then he raised the reins and tried to coax the pony forward in a walk. They moved a short distance then the pony snorted and twitched and he stopped her on the crest of the road and looked out at the country. To the south he could no longer see the river but could see the blue shadows of the mountains that he did not know were in Kerry. The clouds were heavy and slow and faintly purpled. He sat on the pony and looked out for what she had seen as the weak sun climbed the sky behind them in a screen of cloud. Then he saw it. It was a man's legs. They were trousered in brown cloth without shoes and lay angled out of the ditch not forty paces away.

'Come on,' Teige told the pony, 'if I get down I mightn't be able to get up again. Come on, good girl. It's all right.' He clicked his tongue very softly at the pony's ear and she walked forward with an uncertain gait, her step inclining to turn sideways all the time and all the time Teige keeping her straight on. When they were ten yards from the legs, Teige stopped the pony and called to the man. He called to him the greeting that was part blessing and did not know if he was speaking to the living or the dead. The legs did not move. Teige was aware of the currency of outlaws and other rebels in that country and that the ruses and ways of robbers were not beyond feigning death in the road. So he walked the pony forward another three steps but did not dismount. He had no weapon to defend himself nor with his arm injured had he hope of fighting. He kept the reins tight in his good hand and prepared to heel the pony quickly, then he called out again.

From his fallen place in the rushes of the ditch the man moved. His toes twitched. They were dark and the blood of sores was blackened on them, a food for flies. The ankles appeared rude knobs on the thinness of the legs and did not seem as if they could support a man. But a man it was. He raised himself with slow and inordinate difficulty on his right elbow and Teige saw the face of an old man. The centre of his crown was bare and wore a lump that rose purplish and yellow both and was both sorry and comical and seemed to stare at the boy. The man lifted himself to an angle to see them and then attempted no further levitation but raised out a thin and quivering hand in a gesture of begging. From his crooked mouth drooled thin yellow-green stuff into the grass. He did not look like he could speak. The hand floated there in the air and Teige dismounted and stood before it and the flies rose off the man and buzzed the air.

'I only have one good hand,' Teige said. Then he took the man's fingers that were cold and yet firmly gripping and steadying his balance he pulled the figure to his feet.

The man swayed in his return to the world of the upstanding. The eye-lump glared around at the sorry world. Then the man said: 'Give me drink.'

'I haven't got anything,' Teige said. 'There is the river, it's . . .'

'Agh!' The man spat something of his disgust and clutched on to the shirt of the boy so his face floated up close to him and Teige cried out with the sharpness of the pain in his shoulder.

'Food?' the man said.

'No.'

The man sank back down in the grass of the roadside. Teige mounted the pony and rode away from him. He rode on down the way until he came to a small stone cottage where a woman was milking an old black goat in the sour-smelling mud of its pen. There he asked her for water and bread and though she was poor she was used to the traffic of beggars which were many and various there and she brought him some from the inside of her kitchen. Teige took them with gratitude. When he had said his thanks to her he got on the pony and rode back to where the old man was still lying in the ditch.

When the man had eaten and drank what of the water that did not run and leak sideways from the poor closure of his mouth, Teige asked him where he had come from and where heading. He told Teige the country was full of bastards. He said to one of them he had lost his farm. He had been turned out on the road and was now a man of no abode but walked vagabond and desolate on the face of the land. He laughed sourly as he told it and the hairless pate of his head tilted back and he opened his mouth full and revealed a blackish hole toothless and caked about with the dried riverbed remains of old dribblings. The man laughed in a high mocking manner. He told Teige the world was more cruel than he could imagine, and that his act of bringing him food and water was the lone act of kindness in that country turned barbarous and vicious as any Sodom and Gomorrah. But more, he said, the time was turning. He had heard it told, he said, that in the autumn now beginning was coming a bitterness. The birds had sensed it. The cuckoo had flown early without regard for calendar or custom. She had left the ragged trees of the west after less than a month's song.

'And why?' the man asked.

Teige said he had not noticed. He said he had come from the east.

The man rolled some nothing in his mouth and spat sideways. 'Because something is at hand,' he said. 'There is rottenness here. You will see. This is a cursed place. For your kindness I will give you this advice: turn back. Leave the west before you can start to smell the rottenness of it. Go home. Home,' he said again, and then began to laugh in distraught and hideous manner once more.

And was still laughing on that word home when Teige reined the pony around and rode away back across that country to the camp of the gypsies where the legends of his riding and songs about him were already shaping in the firesmoke.

12

When Teige returned he discovered that Tomas was gone.
He rode down to where the caravans were encamped by the
river and was greeted by the men with a waving of their hands
and shapeless felt hats. They came to meet him and touched
the warm flanks of the pony and patted Teige's leg where it
hung stirrupless. The boy did not know yet the significance of
his return and the taming of the pony, but soon the twins told
him. They came to him at once as he dismounted from the
pony and as the men took her away to where the best of their
hay was kept. They told him of Mario and the races. They told
him the story the way it had been told to them, with that
strange fated quality that runs through tales old and unfor-
giving. They told it with quickened voices and flushed faces,
for in their simplicity both Finan and Finbar were delighted.
They had been given an air of importance that had not been
theirs since birth. They had come from the river, see, they were
the answer to the old man's question. It was a kind of birth all
over again. They told it all to Teige and watched his face and
hoped to see there the reflection of their own excitement. But
Teige did not share it. In a way that he could not explain he
felt afraid as one who has been told the story of his own death.
He asked them what Tomas said of it.

The twins stared at him. They wanted him to talk about the
pony. They wanted the fabulous story of how the Foleys would
champion the world. But Teige asked again.

'What does Tomas say? Where is he?'

'He is gone to Limerick town.'

'Will he go to get our mother?'

The twins stared at him. They wanted to say their mother was gone from them, and that they were men now, but they did not.

'We are to go with the gypsies. He will come back and meet us on the road to the sea,' said Finbar and turned away. 'He has taken your pony with him.'

That night when the lamps were lit and the gypsies sang as they had not since the death of the children, Teige walked out by the banks of the river and sought for the swan. The sky cleared on a breeze from the west and the stars hung above him in vast and numberless panoply. He squatted by the small stones that made a thin crunching where the low waves of the waters collapsed upon them. The singing sounded in the night behind him. He reached and let the river run over his hand and thought of his father gone below the water.

In the morning before the dawn the gypsies began packing. They woke and moved about the camp gathering their things. Thin shadowy figures without speech in the moonlessness, they moved about the glowing embers of the campfire with slow care. They collected pots and tin cans and made small doleful tympani as they threw these things together in cloth sacks strung with cord. Their horses knew this morning music and sensed the departure even before the gypsies went to them. The men went to the river and brought their fill of it back in timber buckets and small barrels. They worked around the women without word or gesture of recognition, as though each were entirely separate races, or one the unseen shadow of the other. Coming from sleep into this grey dream-like traffic, Finan and Finbar held the horses while the old leathern harnesses were thrown over the backs of the animals and the buckles that were not brass but hand-shaped copper briefly jangled. Then, leaving a scattering of small potatoes and onions for the spirits of those who might be following them, the gypsies made a last reconnaissance around that ground. The place of their fire was like a black wound. They watched the sky for the dawn that was just then commencing, for it was their custom since time unknown to leave with the first light. Then they sat up on horseback and seatboard and clucked their tongues and led the caravans out of that place and away toward the west.

Teige did not ride the white pony. She followed with others on a rope. He sat in a caravan and looked out on the dark road ahead. They left the riverbank and he felt the regret of losing the swan and felt the foolishness of that, too. The road was the road he had ridden the day before and he watched it for the sight of the man with the broken head and the woeful laughter. But as the light came up behind them and followed them down that way there was sign of no one. They rattled on. The great wooden wheels bumped and clattered on the unevenness of the ground. Each of the caravans sang its own song, a weird jumbling of sounds individual and inseparable as the contents toppled from shelves, clanked and dully clanged within. Finan and Finbar rode their horse. By the time the sky was bright enough to show them, Teige could make out the first signs of their becoming gypsies. They wore their shirts open to the October morning and kerchiefs of cotton that had once been bright red were knotted at their necks. The complexion of their skin, even the fall of their hair, seemed to Teige indefinably altered. The twins seemed to live beyond any notion of regret. They rode with an easy silent gaiety, a lightness of heart, as though they were at last among their own and had discovered a fortunate destiny.

The day rose over them. They passed some small cottages that hung beneath the earthen roads where women heard them coming and stood in the doorways watchful and cautious and eyeing their hens. All of that country wore the same unmistakable look of hardship. The smoke of the hovels hung about their leaky thatch in the still and damp air and smelled sourly. From some places they passed no man or woman came to the door though it lay ajar. In the shadows of one such entranceway Teige thought he saw the shape of a man stretched on the ground and the furtive flickering of rats. But he said nothing. For the picture was all the time moving, as was in the nature of a caravan of gypsies, and one place became the next easily and quickly and faded away like childish painting in the rain.

They travelled down the peninsula of Corca Baiscinn. When they stopped for food the women fed Teige and his brothers a cold broth and rough bread whose crust was tougher than their teeth. They passed a knife among them. One of the women told Teige they had clothes for him and brought them out from the back of the hooped canvas. But Teige would not take them.

'I don't want them,' he said.

The women stood about and said nothing.

'They are the clothes of their children,' Finbar said.

'I know.'

'They wouldn't fit Finan and me. Take them.'

'I don't want to.'

'Do.'

'No,' Teige said, 'I won't!' And he was suddenly a very young boy with tossed and dirty hair, freckles on his cheeks, furious, fearful of things he did not understand which threatened to rob him of even his name.

'They are yours, you can have,' one of the women said, and then they stepped away from him and got back into their caravans as the gypsies were readying to leave once more. The clothes lay there on the ground. Then the twins hurried to their horse, and the wagons moved, and there was an instant in which Teige might have relented and picked the bundle up, but he did not. He walked past it and climbed up the wheel into the caravan and sat in. Then the signal was made for the horse and they pulled away from there in mute and profound dismay, each sorrowing for separate reasons, while left in the mud of the road behind them, like a body shed by a departing soul, was the small, sad pile of children's clothes.

Throughout that afternoon Teige thought Tomas might return. As they sojourned forward toward the sea he listened into the noise of the wagons for the sound of two horses coming behind them. The strange otherworldly air of the gypsies nearly made him lose sense of the world. Once, he noticed the caravans moving more and more along the verge of the road and threatening to topple. He called out and the line of wagons came right and he had the sudden insight that the gypsies were in fact asleep after their dinner and progressing in somnolent oblivion toward wherever the world tilted. Had they a destination at all? he wondered. They seemed to let the roads take them, and the further west they went the more the roads were broken and uneven, the hedgerows of fuchsia and woodbine and black- and whitethorn bushes coming closer on either side and scratching against the coarse canvas of the wagons. Rocks sometimes jagged up in the middle of the way and the horses steered around them. Sometimes the road softened and crossed boggy ground and the place was bare and treeless and the stones of the walls seemed placed by people that had long fled eastward. It was so dream-like, and as he shook himself there on the seatboard Teige wondered how it was that he and his brothers were now part of it. He could not understand it except to recall the moment when he had felt that he was drowning, and that their rescue had been foreordained in some way, that the gypsies and the races in the west were already there awaiting them.

Still, he longed for his brother. Tomas would know what to do, he thought. He would not let them be lost.

They moved on. Sometimes a man watched them from his place in a field, a feature in the landscape no different from rock or bush, a still twist of brown shade in the flow of greens. The man would watch the caravans coming with grave circumspection. They were like some weirdly exotic elephantine creatures, their hooped shapes lumbering high above the hedgerows and carrying an indefinable threat to the world he knew. And he would curse them and wish for them to pass and wait and watch from under his cap until they did.

And pass on they did all that day. The weak and pale sun caught up to the gypsies and crossed over their heads and dropped into the sea the Foleys had not reached. When the light began to die the caravans stopped and turned into a field. Teige thought that he could sense the nearness of the edge of the island. He thought that he could catch the sea in the air and opened his mouth wide and strained his eyes. He blinked at where the night was hemming the land with grey, where the fields stopped and were stitched into the sky and where green and blue became deeper shades of each other and were then the cloths of darkness. He stared but could not see the sea.

That evening the gypsies lit their fires and the twins sat with them and listened to the stories they told. They heard the tales of long ago and distant places, of vanquished kings and blind beggars become rich on the foolishness of men. They heard of strange and terrible plagues, of curses and blessings, the places now forgotten in the far world where once bejewelled princesses made the ground sweet as they passed upon it. Tales climbed on the smoke of the fire. There was devilry and laughter and many stories of how fate righted the wrongs of the poor, and made fortunate the suffering in the end of time. The twins listened with rapt attention. The fire burnished them, and they sat cross-legged in that colourful company, like the newest princes of a tribe, narrowing their eyes with concentration and falling inside the spell of those old stories. They felt elated and proud with a sense of their own belonging.

Teige did not join them. He stood at first on the edge of the campfires, but suffered still a tight unease. He wanted Tomas to return, he wanted his mother, and with the fall of night felt as though something cold and viscous had filled inside him. For the first time in his life he saw himself, singular, in the darkness. His brothers were laughing with the others in the firelight, there was no sign of Tomas, and for a time Teige had a vision of a thin transparent membrane separating him from the rest. In a matter of days, it seemed, he had all but lost his family. Where were the Foleys now? Without their father the boys seemed strangely disconnected, as though the notion of family itself was prefabricated upon the thinnest premise and the slightest breeze of chance blew it away. It dawned on Teige that Tomas was gone and might never return, and in that same moment he glimpsed a scene of his elder brother fallen to the ground and being savagely beaten by figures that wore the uniforms of the Law. The instant his imagination saw it, he let a gasp out of him. It sounded like a strangled cry, but was not heard in the raucousness and crackling of the camp. Teige turned his head. He waited to spew sideways the sour grey-white stuff of horror but it would not rise off his stomach and he blinked and sucked the air and walked a little away. Again it was there before him like a picture: Tomas in the town of Limerick, tied and beaten to death. What was he to do? He walked down along the dark to where the horses were tethered. He raised his hand palm first as though to press softly against something firm and feel the solidity of the universe support him and banish the phantasm. Then he curved his hand over and let the horses smell his knuckles. Their whinnying passed like a greeting down the rope. Teige went to the white pony and she raised her long head and lowered it and found the scent of him and he stroked the sides of her and tried not to think.

'That's the girl,' he said. He raised his arm up and over her shoulder and he hung there against the hard skin of her, pressing his face against her flank while the spectre of his eldest brother in pain dwelled in his mind. What was he to do? He was twelve years old.

At last he undid the cord that held the pony there. He drew her back and away from the other horses and said words to quieten them and then he seemed to slide upwards on to her back like a shadow. He rode her away from the caravans and the campfire and out across the heavy grass of the rough fields.

He rode into the lightless night and trusted the surefootedness of the pony. He squeezed her into a lithe speed and she carried them out to the road that led eastward toward Limerick and westward toward the sea. There he reined her back and lowered his head until it was close to hers. He turned her about and she was like a dancing indecision footing the air in all directions as if awaiting some prompt to fall from above into the cocked shells of her ears. None came. Teige looked down the road where Tomas was not coming, where his rescue must begin and where the dark made a wall into the sky.

Then he wheeled the pony about and galloped her instead down the blind road toward the sea.

Teige rode with the sickness of loneliness like bitter soup turning in his stomach. He rode with reckless abandon into the dark and charged down the way he did not know and could not see. He was a boy escaping from the world of men and did not heed the dangers of the road as it passed down along cliffs and sharp bends. He felt the sea before he could see it. His face was wet with it. The lids of his eyes tingled with the salt and his hair matted. Then, over the noise of his and the horse's breathing, came the sighing collapse and crash of the waves. He rode down through dunes that gave beneath him and he had to lean backward for balance and his moon shadow was like that of some stiff and proper gentleman descending on to the floor of sand.

The Atlantic was full and heavy. It seemed swollen beyond itself, and appeared to the boy as though the shore could not contain it. The flatness of the beach was strangely perplexing to him, as though just against it the sea itself could not be so deep nor the country fall away like that into the surging waters. Teige trotted the pony on the edge of Ireland where the white surf was combed out of the darkness like the frills of an elaborate gown. He trotted her the length of the soft sand in the splashing waves. Then he drew her in from the shoreline and slid down and stood there on that empty beach. He was at the place his father dreamed, he thought. He was there on the western shore where they were to begin to realize Francis Foley's vision. But it was in ruins now. His family was lost, he thought. Now there was only Teige and the great emptiness of the watery horizon where flashes of white appeared and disappeared in the far darkness of the sea. Teige stood there. He thought of the river where his father had drowned and which was now in that sea. He thought of the old man's boast that their country was bigger than the map-makers had drawn it and he suddenly saw it so. He saw the vastness of the sea was itself part of that wild country as was its great and million-starred sky and he dropped to his knees there in the sand and felt the despair of loss. And he put his hands together to pray and turned to the constellations that were cold and impassive and falling through the darkness ages away, and, knowing no God who knew him, he looked to Pegasus in the south and to it prayed the wordless prayers that rose off his soul.

13

Francis Foley woke from the dream of being a swan. He opened his eyes and immediately reached his two hands to pat his chest and feel there for his feathers. Even when he could find none he was not reassured, for the reality of his dream was more potent than the darkness to which he awoke. It was some time before his mind refound itself and he had left his swanhood behind, wondering if it was possible to dream within dreams. He touched the hard pallet of his bed but did not know where he was. He was in a stone building that was like a boat upside down and in which he seemed to sail in the world of the drowned. The doorway was dark without a door. When his eyes were opened long enough he could distinguish it and imagine the space that lay beyond. He feared for devils. He feared for the twisted shapes of white wasted bodies cast around outside in a sorry vision of the damned, and was no longer sure whether he had been saved or lingered in some netherworld awaiting judgement. He was not sure his body existed. He had the sense of time not existing as he lay there in the dark. Sometimes he imagined he was inside the stomach of something enormous. He saw in bizarre phantasm the thing that had swallowed him whose scales were stone-like and shone blackly, and he wondered how he might get it to vomit him back into the river. Or else he was in a womb and would be newly born into a distant world with other stars where the earth itself would be the smallest point of least significance and where all his travails and tarnished hopes would be forgotten and part only of the history of dust. Francis Foley imagined all possibilities and burned with regret at each of them. Why had this happened to him? He stared into the darkness at the doorway that led into the outer darkness. He watched it for a sign of anything, but there was only the nothingness of that empty space beyond.

So he sat up.

He held his hand out in front of him and brought it closer until he could see it just before his face. Then he put his hand out and moved it from side to side as though expecting to brush against some resistance. There was none. He moved his legs and stood on the ground, feeling the firmness of it and testing it with small jockeying actions of his knees. The ground did not give beneath him, and, coming from the aeons of his airy dreaming, was strangely reassuring. He could stand and walk. But he could not see. Then, as though declaring himself undead, making the shape that had first announced his birth on paper, he moved from there like an ambulant letter f with both arms outward high and low going slowly forward against the wall of darkness. He made his way toward the door. He did not know if when he stepped through it the world would end, if he would fall headlong, if the place where he had been waiting were the last sanctuary before the wailing and fires of purgatory. Still he went on. He could not stay there while he could still breathe. The image of his sons passed before him and he imagined them waiting for him.

Then he walked through the doorway of the dark and he cried out.

For there was God.

God's bald crown flashed like a lesser moon. Then God multiplied Himself and was a trinity of figures on a grassy hillock at the back of which lay a stone chapel. Francis Foley walked with his hands out before him in the f, though now he could see. He looked like he was feeling the world for a secret opening, or expecting to reach some invisible wall that would be impenetrable and leave him trapped the other side of living.

Still he stepped forward barefoot across the wet grass. The stars shone more brightly with each step. His eyes grew accustomed to the light of the night and revealed more clearly the strange trinity of identical bald figures in brown robes that were gathered on the small hill with their backs to him. Francis thought to shout out to them. But he did not want to discover that he might be dead and that his cry might be the soundless empty horror of screams in dreams. So he came forward in that odd manner and was with each step brought a little further back into life until the truth dawned on him at last: he was not dead and God was not God but a sinner like us all and that He was in fact three monks on an island in the middle of the River Shannon.

He realized this when he saw the telescope. The monks were clustered about it and taking turns to watch the skies for the evidence of heaven.

'Leave that!' He was surprised by the power of his voice. And used it again when he saw how startled were the monks, turning quickly to face him in the night.

'Leave that alone, it's mine,' he shouted. He waved his arms wide as though measuring his anger and the monks stepped back. The telescope had been set on a wooden platform. It showed no signs of having drowned and its long mahogany frame looked like it had been newly polished. Its brass mouldings and fittings gleamed and gave back the scintilla of stars. Francis's mouth opened when he saw it. It was pointed at the southern sky. As he came forward the monks, like figures caught and contrite, stepped away. They said nothing. The old man went over to the instrument and ran his fingers along it as though it were the final proof that he had returned to the world. He touched the telescope and he laughed.

'Oh God,' he said in Irish. Then he laughed until there was no sound but hard aspirated sighs that rose off his stomach and made him shut his eyes with effort.

The trinity stood and watched.

'Well,' said Francis at last, 'you saved me and I thank you. It isn't easy to kill a Foley. Now this is mine and I don't mind you having a look but I'll be taking it with me when I leave in the morning. Do you understand? And I'll need some kind of boat or someone to bring me across to the shore.'

The monks said nothing. He was not sure they had understood and so he gestured the same message to them and said it in pieces of English. Still they did not respond. Then, in an action slight and simple and yet filled with untold ages of humility, one of the monks raised his finger and ran it smoothly across his own lips like a sealant. Francis stared at them.

'Ye're mute?' he said.

The monk blinked his eyes yes.

'But you understand?'

There was the smallest nod, as if even that communication was in some way a compromise of their vows and betrayed them into the domain of sin. The night air blew softly and carried the small noises that were the slaps of the river and the running of the river rats in the blind dark.

'Ye have a boat?' Francis asked them at last.

They did not. They had sunk their boat years earlier and lived on that island on whatever the earth provided. When nothing was provided they took it as a direct epistle from above and remedied their souls with all-night confetiors, credos, and a diet of insects.

The river ran through the dark. Snout-up a badger arrived upon the four of them and stood striped and astonished before scuttling away. The monks were like stone monks. They offered no gesture or expression when Francis told them they must make him a boat. He listened to the water passing. The river was still between him and the home he had built in his mind. He could cross it by himself right then, but he would have had to leave the telescope, which had become something fixed into the corner of his brain like an obsession. He put his hand upon it and bent and lowered his head and met the eyepiece.

Then he squeezed shut his left eye and looked at the fixed constellations of the autumn night where the monks had been searching for the face of God.

The monks stepped away from him and were gone then to mute prayers and adorations. Francis watched the night and then slept. When he awoke the light of day startled his eyes and he remembered that he was not dead and lay on the wet grass of the hillock and heard come back to him all the minute sounds of the earth alive. He heard the insects and the birds and the wind that carried them. His eyes watered and he thought of his life to that moment and was burned with a sharp regret. He regretted all that had happened, how he had lost his wife and sons to the rashness of his will. He thought of Emer vagrant and alone. He thought of the home he so desired and how the dream of it lay in ruins now. He cursed himself then and wished he could undo the knots in his heart. He wished he was not who he was and as he lay he suffered a kind of soul-scouring in which there were revealed to him sins of vanity and pride. He lay long and still and was, in his sackcloth garb and turned-white hair, like a saint descended and discovered in the grass. When he got up he saw the one he took for the eldest of the monks waiting at the small stone church. The holy man beckoned to him and Francis went down the hill and felt the pleasant coolness of the dew on his toes.

'Well?' he said to the monk. 'What have you to say?'

The monk said nothing.

'I thank you for saving me,' Francis said, then added, 'even if it was really the telescope you were saving. It doesn't matter to me.' He paused. 'I was on my way with my sons to try to find a place to live, a home.'

The monk's face was impassive. He had once been a boy monk. Once his hair had been shaven off an unwrinkled crown that matched the curve of his young cheeks. Once his brown eyes had looked fresh and nut-like and saw the beauty of his own devotion as a natural offering to his creator. Now, the face was old and the apple cheeks sinking, deflated with the hard weathers of that life and the discovery that all of us are human. The boy monk was vanished, the nuts of his eyes like still shells. He looked at the big man he had taken from the river. He looked at him and shuddered at the vanity of their thinking he had been sent to them, that he had been a sign, or that the magnificent telescope was intended as a reward and means of communicating with God. The old monk stood there and visited the sin and stood within its black centre and said nothing. He looked inwards at himself without flinching and for a moment Francis did not know if he was gone blind. His eyes did not move from the pale air. Some who might have watched him very closely might have seen him face his own desperation, the long years of his living there on the island with fading hope, his diminished faith, and the longing grown ulcerous and sore in his spirit that the divine be revealed.

Blackbirds like smudges of charcoal appeared on the morning above them. Then the monk's eyes returned and he gestured Francis into the small building beside the chapel. Without opening his mouth, and with slow wearisome movement, he found a scrolled map. In the low light he opened it and showed Francis the island where they stood, and the river about it, and, in disconnected flecks of brown ink like the tracks of a creature long gone, an underwater pathway to the shore.

Then the holy man looked up at the man who had been drowned and considered a moment and then he ran his finger down the River Shannon and followed its curve and stayed within the drawn banks like a salmon or trout until the finger arrived at another island. It lay in the mouth of the river where it gaped with the inrush of the sea. The finger tapped the island twice and the monk turned his face to Francis and let him read the message that he should go there. It was wordless yet clear. And Francis knew from the look in the holy man's veined and yellowed eyes that it was part of some contrition, that within the grave and absolute laws in which the monk had passed his life and by a pure cleansing mathematics this was the given solution for his soul. He tapped the other island again and nodded toward the man he had once wished dead so that the monks might have kept the telescope.

Francis leaned over the table. 'Go there?' he said. He looked at the map and saw the round tower drawn on it and the cross-shaped mark that was once another dwelling place of monks. He followed the mapped river with screwed up eyes in the dimness there, and he leaned a long time without sign of any acknowledgement. And there arrived a moment of clarity, a purity in the air between them.

Then Francis said, 'I will. I will go there.' The monk made a slight nodding. 'I will leave you the telescope for a time. First I have to find my wife. And my sons.' Francis stood and looked as if at the things he had said and felt arise in his chest a strange lightness. 'Yes,' he said. 'Then we will go there.' He touched the island and left his finger upon it. 'I will come back for the telescope, mind,' he told the old monk. 'I will bring it there and set it up and if you want you can come and watch the stars with me.'

When they came outside the other monks were waiting. And they walked together down to the shore and mutely so, like figures engaged in matters of absolute secrecy, they showed him the place where once a path of stones had been laid beneath the river. Then Francis said his thanks and, promising to return, walked out across the water and back into the County Clare.

14

In the uncertain dawn the gypsies moved and arrived at the western coast with their caravans and carts and horses, the jangling of pots and dangling things announcing them to the small town of Kilkee. They gathered in the open field near the cliffs at the near end of the bay. The horses that pulled the caravans knew where they were going, and the arc of their passage through the soft ground of the field was a clean curving radiant of mud-marks that were only barely recovered from the gypsies' visit the year before. The gypsies got down from their horses and walked in scattered patterns while their women began at once the business of making camp. Finan and Finbar saw the edge of the country for the first time and yelled in manic celebration. In the grey light they ran in wild zigzags across the tufted grass and let the big breeze blow in their hair and open up their chests.

Teige was in the caravan. He watched them from the seatboard, and climbed down slowly and went to the white pony. Tomas had not rejoined them and with the passing of every hour it seemed to his youngest brother that he would not now do so. He was vanished and his erasure was made all the more striking by the vastness of that tumbling ocean. For nothing in the world had seemed as big to Teige Foley, and to watch the sea for only a small time was to become aware of the enormity of creation and the lies of maps that made it seem within the compass of man's understanding. When Teige had returned to the gypsies the previous night he had gone to the caravan of Finan and Finbar and asked them if they should not ride back toward Limerick. But the twins had dismissed him. They had been drinking the raw smoky whiskey favoured by the gypsies which inspired in them lewd visions of round women, and they had looked up from their cots briefly with the shadowed downward eyes of boys discovered in misdemeanour. Then they had turned back to the canvas wall and the dreams therein.

As the morning rose the wind carried swift clouds of all shapes across the sky. They crossed quickly over the grass below in elaborate shadowplay like out-of-favour toys thrown from the heavens. Brilliant blue appeared and disappeared in the spaces between them. The light kept changing. A shower of rain fell down through piercing sunlight and then vanished. From the edge of the field where the gypsies made their camp was a long view of the full strand and the line of low white cottages that faced the water. On that morning, the pristine surf of the Atlantic gleamed as it broke in frayed white chains that ran all the way to the pollock holes on the far shore.

Because it was their custom, and not because the population did not already know it, some of the men walked down into the town to announce their arrival and advertise the various wonders and entertainments they could offer over the coming week. When they met a man or woman in the blustery street they stopped them with a cry and told that there was one among them who could foretell all health, wealth and happiness. The fortune-teller would be in her caravan that evening and would tell all, they said. And all this with a swaggering waving of arms and floating eyebrows and squinted eyes. When they had finished in the little streets, the gypsies gathered by the shoreline and watched some girls in the sea. These had waded out through the tide and with dresses tucked up above their waists and baskets on their backs were busy harvesting seaweed. They were a sight as old as man's existence in that place and to the twins and the gypsies there was something true and uplifting in it. The waves did not come evenly. At times they rose many feet above the girls' heads and came at them in a back-combed wall of water crashing and foaming. Sometimes the girls lost their footing and were swept shoreward, their baskets bobbing in the distance and the seaweed spilling loose and slithering like so many snakes. Still the undrowned girl would get up, regain herself, and make a slow return out through the freezing waves. Renewed greetings were cried out to her along the ribboned line of workers. There was the appearance of gaiety, like that among those who travailing in underground darkness sing to assuage the terror. But there was no mistaking that the sea was a monster. For though the bay was sheltered the water at the turning of the year came in capricious twists and currents. The girls struggled to keep their line, but still worked on, hooking and gathering the seaweed that was valued as fertilizer for the potato gardens and could be sold or bartered in the morning market. There were not only girls in the sea that morning, but some older women too. Their hair was bound in bright headscarves, their hands moving in the blind foam without any of the quickened excitement of the younger girls. They watched the waves coming at the girls with both the protective and the deeply furrowed suspicion of new mothers-in-law. They waved their arms at the gulls that hung above them like a necklace of the sky. They called warnings and worked steadily, aware that the sky was changing all the time above them.

The gypsies sat by the sea wall and studied the scene. As the morning came on the tide withdrew and the line of the workers moved further out with it into the waves. Seaweed was mounded on the shore. There two men with carts pulled by donkeys gathered it up and moved away leaving wheel ruts across the smoothly hardened sand. They came and went while the women worked on. The sun passed behind a screen of cloud and the sea changed colour and was blue no more. It became the colour of gunmetal. The gypsies felt the cold and turned up their collars and pulled their kerchiefs tighter and moved as one man back toward their camp. Finbar might have stayed. He wanted to see what would happen, wanted to go on feeling the marvel of these sea-girls. He could imagine the cold in the white submerged limbs, the girl-skin that was beneath the surface for so long that it must not feel like the skin of those who lived only in the air. The toes that were vanished under sand traversed by crabs, clams, sea urchins and all assorted marine life. They were mer-creatures these, he thought, and wanted to wait and see them re-emerge on the land and see how they walked back up the town with steps like slow-motioned swimmers arrived in an element not their own. But when the gypsies and his twin moved he did too, as if connected, though he walked up the roadway with his eyes turned sideways to the girls below.

15

That evening high fires were lit and wind dragged the flames in twisting tongues of wild unpredictability, while the lanterns on the caravans marked a semicircle out of the darkness above Kilkee. From the streets of the town the place above on the hillside where the gypsies had camped was like a lightship. To there the people of the town made their way, scuttling up through the darkness to hear their fortunes and what their futures held. They lined up outside the caravans, and made in their waiting a trail of mud. Some went to the bonfires where the gypsies drank and paid money and tilted back their heads to sample the fiery liquids that shone in bottles of green and blue glass. Matches of fistfighting and wrestling brewed up there. Sudden and short-lived tussels broke out and there were cries and shouts and cheers, and then the gypsies gathered around again and one sang a song or made a remark that drew laughter. The scene grew loud with the night. More and more men and youths arrived from the town below. Some who were quiet and civil in the streets were here discovered wild and manic and leapt about and jostled against others and cursed loudly. The more these fellows drank of the gypsies' whiskey the darker their eyes grew. Smoke thick and heavy curled into the night. A man with reddened face and wide eyeballs took a run and jumped across the fire and was suddenly flaming as his jacket caught. Momentarily unaware, he stood looking back at the others with a boastful gaze even as they waved and shouted at him. The flames seared him then and he fell to the ground, rolling in the mucky grass and screaming as the others howled and laughed. But soon another attempted the same leap. He ran with bottle in hand and launched himself and flew flameward. His legs were out before him. He made the image of sitting in the air and yelled as the fire scorched him and he crashed smouldering on the far side of it. He stood and drank in celebration and spat back into the fire a stream that caught alight. And so it went on, in strange and terrifying carnival. The sea wind blew and smoke travelled sideways and enshrouded them coughing and red-eyed. Down at the caravans Johnny McMahon came from visiting Diado the fortune-teller, his face made scarlet and his legs bandy. The crowd surged toward him and shouted to know what he had been told. But Johnny, who was for many years the comical innocent of the town, stared bewildered at them and when he tried to speak could say nothing at all. Men grabbed at his jacket sleeve. There was a flowing pushing mob in the mud and faces were caught and profiled in the lantern light. The gabble of voices swelled around the poor man, then some lewd joke was cracked and laughter flew and Johnny staggered away.

By the fire Finan sat. His twin was gone to see the mer-girls that had come up from the town and were queuing now to learn of their lovers. Finan drank the sharp and bitter whiskey that burned the back of his throat. His eyes were glass. In the smoke and wavering of the heat he saw images of faces distorted. He thought he saw demons and blinked and screwed up his eyes and drank some more. A small fellow dared by others then announced he would attempt to dive face-first through the fire. He was wiry and thin and held up his arms that were like sticks. He was with another, a broad figure with scars on his face. Some tried weakly to dissuade him but many others urged him on. His companion said he would take any bet that his friend could not do it. There ensued then a rapid and heated calling of wagers and in bizarre fashion gypsies and men argued as to what would constitute a failed attempt. If the man was burned in the face, one said. If he was scarred but not if he was singed. If his clothes were alight it was all right. They considered this and other elements of the dive there amidst the crackling and spitting of the burning logs while the sea roared nearby. The night sky turned its stars. Men swayed as if at sea and held aloft glimmering glass bottles. They cried out and drank toasts of little sense to the thin fellow who would face the fire.

In this wagering Finan took the side of the diver. He thought the attempt brave and foolish both and yet was touched with admiration for it. Then, when the gypsies and others there were ready, the thin man seemed to swallow a clarifying reality for he stood back and said he had changed his mind. Bedlam broke loose. One pushed another and accusations and sharp words flew out on the air. Then the companion of the thin fellow turned on his friend and cursed him for being a coward, and these two wrestled and fought by the fire. The thin man was small and young and his manner of fighting was full of quick kicks and smacks, darts and shimmies. But he was worse for drink, and his blows flew wildly in the smoky air. He spun his arms about and was like loosened machinery coming asunder. He spat and said he didn't have to jump if he didn't want to. And it was clear to all that these were fellows who conspired to win money at gatherings such as this, and that in his way the thin man had reneged and his companion was shamed. Still on their feet they grappled and wrestled. The young man swung at the older and missed. Then the scar-faced man reached back and shot the full of his fist on to the other's nose. There was a crunch and stuff flew and the fellow fell backwards. His hands came up to his face and caught the blood running there. The other stepped forward again and delivered into his stomach another blow. The fellow fell to his knees. Then the bigger man leaned down and with two hands picked up his victim and lifted him full into the air and said the wager was still on for he would pitch the chicken face-first across the fire. He walked with the fellow in his arms and the blood dripping. He came to the edge of the fire and was so deciding the manner best suited to fling his companion when Finan Foley leapt at him and knocked him to the ground.

It was a rapid and unconsidered action. The man crashed into the side of the fire and sent aloft a scattering of sparks while his friend squirmed free. Finan hit the big man with his right fist and the fellow's neck snapped back. Then he hit him again. He felt the pain rush down the length of his own arm and as he did he was shouting out words that none there understood, and seemed to be fighting a mortal enemy against whom he had many deep and long unspoken grievances. He struck another blow. He hit the man and did not know he was dead, and the fire made of his face a twisted mask of red and brassy orange. Then the thin fellow was wailing out something and knocking him over and pulling at his dead companion and the gypsies were coming forward to ensure that Finan was not harmed. He was dragged back through the crowd and brought quickly away and taken to a caravan where he went inside and lay down and the world thumped in his head and he realized with horror the monstrosity of what he had done.

16

In the days following more tribes of gypsies arrived in the town of Kilkee. They brought their horses and ponies and made camps in random fashion on the grass that oversaw the sea. Soon there were scattered clusters of caravans dotted about the fields that ringed the town. The day of the races was not announced and Teige could not discover when it would be. He did not see Finan nor know where he was hiding, and when he saw Finbar it was always in the company of a group of gypsies and his manner did not invite conversation. Teige had already decided that the moment the races were over he would ride back into Limerick alone if necessary to find his brother, then go east to search for his mother. He wanted the race to take place at once, but when he asked the gypsies about it he always received the same reply, that it would happen when it was ready. There was no date set and time itself seemed an antiquated and overly formal invention so that days and nights rose and fell and the gypsies might sometimes sleep until noon or after and sometimes be risen and walking about the town in the pre-dawn like spectres come to visit. They showed no anxiety but rather now that they had camped by the ocean they took the arrival and gathering of tribes like a medicine of the spirit. Their hearts were lifted to see so many like themselves, and the buoyancy of their mood grew daily. It was the year's end in the gypsy calendar and the festive nights of ribaldry, of renewed friendships and fierce rivalries, revealed it as such. The constabulary adopted a policy of indifference and left the gypsies to their own affairs. Of the three officers in the town two of them had previously booked annual leave.

So, the town became for a time a gypsy island. Men and women continued to visit the fortune-tellers and story-makers by night. They paid for the gypsy whiskey and grew wild-eyed, watching men who could eat fire or swallow gold coins and find them again in the shells of their ears. They heard the stories of the animal called elephant and imagined him there on their own beach loaded with a mountain of seaweed, or, miraculously unsinking, tramping slowly across their bogs with the fuel for the winter. The children of the town suffered enlarged imaginations. They watched the exotic visitors with awe and dreamed of running away with them to far places that were not rainy and cold and poor and where kings and queens were glorious and beautiful and not the ones of which they had heard. They spread stories among themselves of the gypsies' scars and magic and these stories in turn grew other stories and became wilder and more ferocious with each telling and the gypsies became pirates, vagabond thieves or daring circus figures tumbled down from a highwire in the sky.

While the days passed, Teige rode the white pony on the strand of Doonbeg out of sight of the other gypsies. The pony ran well there, and Teige spoke to her and stood her on the sands and let them both look a long time at the breaking of the waves. The sea was slow mesmerism. The further out he looked the further it stretched, until it did not seem to be moving at all but was a steady line of grey without wave or wimple. He rode there in the nights too and liked the empty tumbling of the world beneath the stars.

'It's like a rim of iron,' he told the silent pony, 'where the world ends.'

In the darkness he watched it. The wind blew the sand in ribbons.

After a long time Teige spoke. 'Once,' he said in a whisper, 'Jason met a clever shipwright called Argus.'

The pony stood on the shore. It was an empty arc of pale light.

'And this shipwright had from Mount Pelion got tall pines, and of these built a fifty-oared ship so strong that it could stand all winds and waves, and so light that it could be carried on the shoulders of its crew.'

He stopped and thought of that magical craft and tried to think of nothing else.

'This ship was named the Argo. In it were assembled the best and the bravest, the sons of Gods and men, who were known as the Argonauts.' He watched the sea and the night sky. The waves sighed.

'And all were bound on a far course,' he told the pony, 'to the distant eastern shores, where they must tear free the Golden Fleece.'

Clouds moved and the stars came and went again. 'On a far course,' he said again, then said no more, the story stopped, its words gone in the wind.

17

On that very night the horses sensed the turning of the year and whinnied along their ranks and dragged their hoofs against the packed mud like creatures pawing for freedom. It was the beginning of Samhain, the time of dying and resurrection in the ancient spirit world of that place, and the ghosts of dead horses passed in along the seashore and made those living flick their ears and roll their eyes in the dark. Teige rose from his bed and walked out among them and ran his hand on the fevered flesh of the frightened animals. The night was cool and the sky charged with stars. The traffic of spirits was such that the horses would not quieten though Teige spoke to them in a soft voice and tried to make the very night-time calm with his presence. He knew it was the time of ghosts. He knew the tradition and belief of their coming from all graves on those nights and revelling in wild abandon, before taking some back with them to the kingdom of the dead. He thought of his father's spirit and wondered where it was, and in the still air of that night when he could not hush the horses he stood back and let them stamp and noise and grow accustomed to the strangeness. From caravans came the shadowy figures of gypsies drawn from their beds by the same presences that had disturbed the horses. Tousled, soft-shouldered figures, they ducked about in the dark as though expecting to encounter some flying debris, the blown souls of the vanished. Soon there was a small gathering. One of them began to hum and another took it up and then it was general, low notes in the pipes of their throats. They shambled around criss-crossing in the darkness and humming like things without language. The sound was not unsettling though and Teige joined in. And the horses stilled and listened. The small breaths of the wind carried the humming off into the fields about. The gypsies looked into the sky and sometimes here and there one of them made gestures in the air, waving their arms in a way that Teige could not interpret either as welcome or defence. Elihah, the oldest of them, came out and was brought across the grass by two of the younger gypsies bearing lanterns. When they stepped from his side he stood a moment by himself as though balancing one final time on the threshold between life and death. He then spoke words aloud that Teige did not understand and the gypsies brought him the lanterns and he threw them down in a pile of gathered branches and a fire sprang up. The Samhain had begun.

Within minutes the old man was gone and the other gypsies were about. Fires were lit and horses were released and ran wild off down the field into the dark. Across the bay other fires now burned with small tongues of light. From each camp around the town the same custom-worn and time-honoured gestures were taking place. It was as if a bell had tolled or a preternatural announcement had taken place. For though it was without clocks or even the rising of the sun, the moment of the spirits' resurrection and return seemed unanimously agreed. The gypsies' mood rose with the heat of the fire and soon they were singing and there were some who leapt in ragged trousers and bare chests by the flames and yahooed with wild ferocity. Women came out dressed in bright skirts with hoops in their ears, and though they had slept only a few hours they danced flamboyantly with different partners. They held up their skirts to show their legs and stamped in the muddy grass, laughing full-mouthed in the dance of the dead. Teige was pulled in by one such woman and spun to music of drum and whistle. He flew about in her arms and watched his brother Finbar do the same. The place was swept into a festive mood. The stars turned in the sky and the sea fell in sighs, exhausted.

From the town came those who knew what to expect. They had watched for the fires on the hill and slipped from the beds of husbands and wives to steal into that place where the spirits of the dead guaranteed a time of licentiousness and free pleasure. For the townspeople were even wilder than the gypsies. Girls pulled their skirts high and dragged and pushed the men about, throwing off lovers and taking others in a giddy and mad rush as though each had to be touched and tasted before that time of freedom was past and manner and decorum returned for another year.

In this way Finbar was pulled aside by one of the mer-girls of the sea and kissed hungrily on his lips. He tasted the salty girl almost before he saw her. In the firelight she flew him around so that she and he were one side golden and one side dark. Then she spun him away and out into the greater darkness and the tufted grass that grew by the cliffs. She held his hand and he climbed up into the fall of her hair and kissed her neck as they ran along. Then she slipped away in the dark. Finbar hurried after her. There was nowhere to go in the rising and falling undulations of the field that were like a calm sea. They chased and tumbled and she called him gypsy in Irish and laughed and threw her bare feet in the air and kicked as though treading deep water in the sea of the sky. Finbar held the calf of her leg and touched the skin and marvelled, and the girl turned into a fish there before him. She glimmered in the starlight and was slippery in his hands. She twisted about and was free of clothes and Finbar imagined her a salmon in the grass and he grappled her in his arms and she wriggled silvery and marvellous and beautiful.

The Samhain burned on. Cattle stolen or bartered in exchange for whispered prophecies to farmers desperate for love or fortune were slaughtered there. Though its blood was not fully drained a beast was dragged heavily across the grass spilling gore and scenting the night with fresh death as its head tilted with uprolled eyes of blind horror. Then the gypsies endeavoured to mount the animal on a crude and massive spit and many attempts were in vain with the spiked end bursting and tearing through the flank of the beast with cries and jeers and curses and men falling about.

Teige left and went to the white pony. He told her the races would be tomorrow, for he knew that the gypsies would bring all the animals down to the sands to meet the ancestors who had raced there. Then the sports would begin.

'We won't win,' Teige said and stroked the pony.

The fires did not die out that night but were kept burning into the dawn. As the light rose the sea seemed quickened and a white floor of surf lay all across the bay. Remnants of the night were scattered in the grass, wood and bones and fragments of clothing, torn or discarded.

When the gypsies stood in the morning there was a strange communal shyness among them. They blinked at the light and studied the ground. When they heard that two of their horses had plunged over the cliff into the sea their natural superstition caused them to suppose the white pony must be gone. Then Teige found her waiting beneath the wiry and back-combed shelter of hawthorn bushes and the men knew the day was to be theirs.

There was suddenly a renewed urgency. The camp came alive with the business of preparing for the races. A group of the gypsies came to Teige and stood about him and nodded. They smiled brown gap-teethed smiles at him and said nothing. Then when he walked across the field leading the pony they followed like designated escorts of Fate. There were other races and other horses for the gypsies to run, but it was upon the white pony they would gamble the wealth they had gathered over the previous year. They moved down to the beach where the wind blew the sand against their ankles and made powdery falls of each hoofstep. The sky was full of quick-moving cloud, the sea brilliant. Soon there were more than two hundred gypsies and their number swelled with the population of Kilkee spilling down toward the beach to watch. Dogs galloped in crazy circles with lolling tongues and flapping ears. Boys ran along the sand and mimed horses in ghost races. Girls looked for the ones that they had danced with in secret the night before and blushed when they could not tell which one or ones they were. All knew it was the beginning of the end, that when the exotic visitors left winter would be upon them with the colour and excitement of those days and nights passing into memory.

A way was cleared across the white strand. The gypsies had sticks they stuck into the sand. These were topped with ties of red and yellow cloth and made a start and finish. In the clarity of the daylight then all the gypsies were revealed, some one-eyed, some crippled, misshapen, round-shouldered, black, toothless, grin-faced, narrow-eyed, lipless, and handsome. Teige looked about at them as though looking at company kept in dreams. He saw his brother Finbar draw aside the mer-girl called Cait and take her away from the races down to the shore. He did not see Finan, and did not know that this brother was already on his way out of the town, that he had suffered deeply from pangs of remorse and guilt, faced the violence that had arisen within him and experienced a grim revelation that he must give his soul for the one that was perished. Teige did not know Finan was already gone, fissured from the family and lost to the obscured and traceless domain of zealots, that he was heading for the port of Cork and thence to the continent of Africa to begin work in the service of God. Out of some desperation Teige imagined that perhaps at last Tomas might arrive, that the road that wound down to the shore would shortly be dusted with the charge of his horse. But it was not to be and soon Teige could look nowhere but at the pony. He stood beside her and kept her calm while the noise and excitement grew around them. The first races happened, accompanied by wild frenzy. The gypsies had the habit of spitting, jeering, throwing small handfuls of sand at the horses of other riders. They made sudden large gestures, flinging both hands upwards like pantomime salutes to a rash inexorable deity, startling the horses and making the whole scene skitter sideways.

The white pony threw her head up and down and Teige laid his arm over her and made a matching nodding motion and then blew his scent once more across her nostrils. He had a rope halter but did not pull on it. When the pony moved about to evade the scene he stepped to meet her chest and was there in her view. He did not look at the men or ponies he was to race against. Instead he made the world small until within it there was nothing but his eyes and those of the pony. And he was standing so, his head upon the long white nose, when those gypsies that were self-appointed his guardians came and told him it was his turn.

Teige walked the pony through the crowd. They were a blur of colour as though his eyes were teared or blinding and he saw no face he recognized. Then there was a gypsy standing by him with hands cupped for his foot but Teige did not need him and swung up and on to the pony's back. Still he did not look at the other horses. He leaned forward and patted the pony's neck and spoke gently. There was a rope held raggedly across the way. Then a roar. The rope fell. There seemed a long pause, like a rip occurring in the fabric of time, and though the gypsies screamed and the riders crouched in a forward lurch, the horses did not race away. It was like the whole crowd inhaled at once and the poor and tattered, the small farmers and fisherfolk gathered there, were stilled momentarily and framed so as in a picture.

Teige would recall the scene for his lifetime. He would recall the snapped moment, though he was not even aware of seeing it at the time. He was sensing the way across the broken sand. He was breathing over the pony's ears and then somehow he knew that the race was on and the rhythm of it flowed through him like second nature. He became that strange oneness with the animal that was at once apparent to all there. He was crouched and low and his face was pressed forward and white where he galloped in the flying sand and spray. They were in the lead before the halfway turn and already the gypsies of his caravans were screaming and jumping along the inner edge of the course. There was a brown gelding at his side, and a sleek black animal foaming just behind it. But in the flash that was the race Teige barely saw them. The pony plashed the shallow seawater into a fine whiteness that rose majestic and ephemeral. The splash and speed made the scene shimmer, and perhaps was part of the reason why suddenly the gypsies saw the ghosts. There were the figures of the other horses in the race, and then behind them, and coming in a horde from the deeper sea, the charging shapes of a thousand more. They galloped out of the ocean and thundered down the bay. The gypsies all saw them at once and thought to run for they would not survive the stampede. Then they saw their own grandfathers as young boys with shiny black hair and flashing teeth and how they clung to the manes of the ghost horses and rode wildly along next to the boy Teige at the front of the race. They all came forward in one great mass, splashing the water and getting closer and closer. Then, the moment the pony crossed the finish line, to the gypsies' eyes it became two. Without breaking stride, the ghost of itself parted to the left and was ridden out into the sea with the boy Mario on its back and all the other grandfathers and spirit horses following behind until they vanished into the waves. The gypsies shouted and surged. Teige felt their hands grasp his legs and then he was toppled over into their arms and borne shoulder-high over the throng. He saw the sky and the white clouds in swaying bumping motion like the world coming to an end. Hands flew up and touched him. They patted against him and fell away and more pushed forward and did the same. He thought to get down and set off at once but his will was not his own and he was carried along down the beach at Kilkee and the sky spun about and his heart raced with victory. He was caught up in it, and, as the gypsies raced him along on their shoulders and threw him skyward and caught him and threw him up again, he did not know whether to laugh or cry.

Two

I

And three years passed.

The stars rose and fell across the sky and told their timeless stories. But of Francis Foley and his sons in this time there is little recounted. They have slipped inside a pause in the story, as if nothing good can be told and it is better for the silence to enfold them.

The old man walked the country in vain search for his wife and sons. He wore a long ragged coat of rough wool dirtied brown. He carried a willow wand. He crouched in the grass and caught pheasants in the dawn. He walked back to the lord's estate and came into it by darkness and stood in the charred ruins. He saw the gardens left ragged and unkempt. He slipped away and asked of some that lived nearby if they had seen a woman looking for her family. He met with vacant stares. He moved off and searched all the roadways running west. Sometimes he was befriended by the poor and sat in small dark cottages listening to their grievances with the turfsmoke encircling the room. He dug the potato gardens of widows and carried small boys on his shoulders. Then he travelled on again, beating his way back and forth along the roads of that country, all the time looking for his family. He encountered any number of constables, landlords, agents, and witnessed every kind of crookedness, cruelty and oppression. He asked if any had seen boys that looked like him. He heard of four boys that had died in a fire in Gort in the County of Galway and he went there with the ashes of grief and regret dry in his mouth. He stood with the mother and father of the dead boys. He worked for them in the little lump of a field they rented, pulling the rocks from it and bearing them over to make the walls higher. He left when the dream of his wife woke him one night. He went out under the stars and thought they were different, that they were beckoning him as they did others in the fabled past. And so he journeyed again in darkness with his eyes heavenward like a figure blind or visionary, being led by a light aeons away.

He walked that way, eyes skyward, through the winters of three years. In time the stars themselves seemed to reassemble in the constellations above him and were then the unjoined puzzle of a woman's face.

2

It was winter. In the plains of Tipperary snow fell thickly. It gathered in broad fields and rose high against walls. Cattle stood in stunned bewilderment and lowered their heads as though to look where the grass was gone. They did not move. They waited, dumbly. The snow slowed the world. It fell so thickly that roads filled and coaches stopped or slid into ditches. Horses crashed and broke their hips and were shot on the roadside. The distance across a valley was blurred to nothing and vanished altogether. It appeared as though the landscape itself were being erased and with it time and space and the whole history of man on that island.

The snow fell. Cottages smoked thin windless plumes into the pale grey sky. Women looked out from doors and threw crumbs for hens while their children scurried about barefoot and in wet rags. Briefly there was the holiday of it, the country-side made beautiful and pristine in a God-willed immaculate creation. It was not itself. The country was like a country in dreams. Birds flew in short inquisitive flights. They flickered on to the powdered tops of walls and settled for berries of the holly that were plentiful that year. The scene held. When the snow stopped the air froze hard and sealed the white country in ice. Skies were blue and cloudless, by night they were million-starred. No breeze blew. In God's slumber the entire island might have slipped its moorings and floated northward into a colder climate, defying the fixed certainty of maps. Such was the difference between this and the green country of everyday.

A still and iced Christmas passed, and the serenity of the season slipped away and was replaced by hardship. Ridges of cabbages perished and were like long white-mounded graves in haggard little gardens. As fodder ran short the cattle in the fields began to starve. Their thin flanks showed the cages of their bones, their hides were matted with the mud they now wore like crude clothing. At waterholes and by the sides of drains and rivulets brown mucked patches of ground opened and spread as animals made slow crossings back and forth each day to dip their noses in the glacial waters.

And across this frozen January scene, Francis Foley came. He was thin and bearded. He coughed hollow raking coughs that echoed across the stillness of the fields. His eyes were worn from sleeplessness and sunken in rims of darker skin. His lips flaked and broken, the hairs of his moustache overhung them in clumped straggles. He had walked the country back and forth following rumour and the pattern of the stars, but in that time he had found neither his wife nor his sons. Sometimes, in the middle of an empty road in the County Galway or Roscommon, he had imagined he saw one of them coming toward him. He saw some figure down the road and stopped and waited. His chest opened with the inflation of hope. The figure on the road was walking slowly. Francis blinked his eyes to clarify it but still he could not make it out. Was that not the way Tomas had of walking? Was that not his proud angle of head? The old man stood and was like a rock in the road. But his heart raced, imagining he had come to the beginning of the end of contrition, that here would begin the reunion of his family and that this time he would bring them all together to the monk's island and start anew. He stood in the road and the cold held his feet. Then there appeared before him the figure of one homeless and forlorn and wandering like him in the winter of his life. They passed with minor greeting or silence and went on. Other times, the figure seen on the road vanished entirely and was a figment of desire or something incorporeal, and Francis Foley at last moved from his stance and hobbled on.

Yet, as he travelled, he did not lose hope entirely. His death and resurrection by the monk had given him a sense that his life was not to be without purpose, and he endured. His fear was not that he would not find his wife and sons, but that when he did they would have starved or fallen to disease without him. At first he had supposed his sons would still be by the riverbank in Limerick where he had last seen them, and he had gone there and looked at the Shannon waters that in that time were not rushing or wild and seemed a gentle mockery of his failures. He had walked to the County Clare and asked of them there, but learned nothing and turned east again into the stars.

Yet all that was already long ago by the frozen January when he trudged not for the first time into Tipperary. The road was packed ice. He walked into the blown cloud of his breath and kept his eyes ahead of him on the emptiness of the way. There was a small breeze scouring. It polished harshly the skin of his cheeks and left him with the sense that his face was being peeled. His eyes watered, and in that way made uncertain the figure that appeared on the road not a hundred yards ahead of him. Francis saw the figure that he could not yet call a man or woman and screwed his eyes tight to release the tears. The figure was coming toward him. The old man stopped. He stood in against the stone wall ditch and laid his hand on the frozen stones. With an intuition that he did not understand he knew that this was not just another of all those wretches who had crossed his road. His fingers wrapped on to the top stone on the wall. He held it there readied like a weapon, for at first he imagined this one coming to be none other than the fallen angel himself come to take Francis Foley to Hell. He held the stone also out of the need to feel contact with the tangible world and for the reassurance it gave that he was not already dead. The figure moved slowly in the white scene. It was a man, he saw at last, a small man on a small horse. Still he did not lose any of his mistrust, and prepared to throw the top of the wall. His heart was hammering now. Blood was awakening in his feet and they were throbbing. The figure was thirty yards away now and he was suddenly afraid of it there on the road in Tipperary. It wore a hat. Its face was unseen. Francis lifted the stone off the wall and another rolled and clattered out on to the road. He shook and looked about in fright but the landscape was placid and empty and blanched in the grip of that season.

'*Dia duit*,' he called out, for he knew the name of God was abhorrent to the Devil and reasoned that he needed to know at once if such was his adversary.

The figure on the road stopped, and slowly raised its head in such a manner as to suggest that the man had been riding the horse in sleep and now lifted his face into the breeze to see if he was waking or in dreams.

And it was Teige. Father and son saw each other and did not move. There was a stalled moment of disbelief, puzzlement at the work of fairies or madness that threw such a likeness on the snow-road. For Teige had long supposed that his father was dead and similarly imagined this to be only the most recent of a long catalogue of his family's ghosts although the one with the most verisimilitude. Francis Foley was no more certain that this was Teige, and the beating of his heart raced up the side of his neck and into his right temple where he could hear it like a drum. He touched his tongue to the crisped edge of his lips and tasted the sting. He looked at the boy now grown almost into an old-looking young man and there flashed before him the last moments they had seen each other in the flooded river. Then he said the boy's name.

'Teige.'

He heard how old and thin his own voice had become since he had last said the name and could not imagine what he looked like as it was so long since he had seen himself. The stone fell from his hand.

'Teige, it's me.'

And his son stopped and looked and blinked his eyes and then climbed down off the white pony and walked directly across the slippery road to the old man. And in the moment when his father thought that he was about to embrace him Teige struck him with both hands in the hollow of his chest and sent Francis flying backward on to the snow.

He lay there for some time. He lay there and Teige stood over him and kicked at the snow about him and cursed and then shouted. The loneliness and anger of those three years came from him now sharp and heavy as stones. He yelled out curses and was weeping as he did so. Birds crossing the noontime in the daily hope of a thaw and the emergence of worms wheeled about and flew elsewhere. Cattle in the rumpled fields turned their heads to listen. Teige spat and coughed and spewed the words out. He told his father that once he had had brothers. He told him once he had had a mother and a family. He told the old man that he had ruined everything, that he had torn up the world and thrown it away. He told him everything was gone now, that Finan was gone, that Tomas had vanished, that Finbar had stolen a girl from the sea and ridden off with her and the gypsies and had not returned the following year. He told the old man there was no point in their even looking for them, that the Foleys were gone into the wind and it was all the father's fault, all his own stupidity and recklessness and stubbornness. The stones of his anger kept coming, and soon they were piled there all about Francis where he lay on the ground being buried alive in the evidence of his vanity and error.

Time passed and still Teige stood there on the road over his father. The glitter of the ice began to melt around the fallen figure of the old man while his beard strangely thawed and his eyes watered. He offered no resistance. His mouth was agape.

His hands were thrown to the side palms upward as though attempting to hold the unbearable weight off his chest. And they were still so a long time, the father on his back and the son standing over him. The winter night drew on. At last, Teige stopped. He stood over his father with his mouth open and no further accusation came out. His jaw ached. In the bluish light of the crescent moon he could not tell for sure if the old man was still living and he got to his knees beside him in the snow. Then he lowered his head until it lay on the other's chest.

'Teige son,' said Francis with his hollowed eyes staring at nothing. 'Teige son, 'tisn't all over. We'll find them, we will. I found you, didn't I? And I have been drowned and in a place from where none or few have come back and yet here I am. Teige son,' he said and raised one hand out of the wet and melted ground and lifted it to touch the boy's head.

They lay so a while. Then they rose and moved into the shelter of a roofless cabin, and Teige tethered the pony and they slept.

It was the pony and not the thieves that woke them. Dawn was rising with silvered streaks when they opened their eyes. There were figures there. At first they could not separate them from the gloom and they seemed like insubstantial fragments or velvet shapes come alive as the light thinly cracked the morning open. There were three or four of them. Francis sat upright and called out. The pony was being led away on its rope and was resisting and turning about in the road and making a long whinnying of dismay. One of the thieves smacked it hard across the face and shouted and pulled down on its rein as the pony's fright worsened and it tried in vain to rear on its hind legs. Teige was up and running then. He was a flicker of light and then shadow and his father was behind him. They hurried on the slippery road crying out and making such sounds as they hoped might ward off the thieves. These last, vagabond and itinerant, had come on the two figures lying on the road and had at first supposed them dropped dead from exhaustion and hunger and the ways of the road. They had approached them the way men approach blessings that have fallen from the sky. They had quickened their step and moved around the fallen examining their clothes and small belongings and beginning a whispered argument about possessing the pony. There were three and a boy, they were blackened, their heads hatless. One with the toothless and sunken expression not uncommon then shook his head and held a stub of finger to his lips when he had discovered the father and son were alive. In the obscurity they had moved with the infinite care of those engaged in detailed work of jewellery or silversmithing. They had fingered the rags of the sleeping in absolute silence like some flimsy wraiths or strange angels elected to divest and prepare the mortal for the hereafter. The dirty garments of the Foleys could not be removed without waking them and the fellows had taken only the boots and the pony.

Now, in the sliver of light, the Foleys charged at them. The thieves, whether grown accustomed to near-capture or out of natural fecklessness, seemed unafraid of punishment and ran about and yelped in high voices and called names. They were giddy and wild. Teige arrived first at the pony. He placed his head next to her shoulder and said some words and then ran his hand along her back, before leaving her to stand snuffling anxiously as he chased one of the thieves that had his boots. Francis was by him. He was concerned not for the robbery but only for the safety of Teige, and that nothing separate them again. He cried out to frighten the robbers off. But these would not let go of the boots they had and jumped about in weird dance. At last Francis caught hold of the scruff of one of them and yanked the man toward him and a piercing cry rang out. The others froze. They stood watching, poised between fight and flight. Francis held the man's head locked within his forearm. The boots fell to the ground. He looked for Teige and saw him turned to where the boy-robber was holding the pony.

'We have no fight with ye,' said Francis. 'Leave us something, and be gone along the road, and we'll not think on it again.'

The man within his hold grimaced. He felt the nearness of his neck to snapping and called out to the others. One of them took a coat then from three he wore and lay it on the ground. Francis released the thief and the fellow stepped away and twisted his head about. There was a strange sense of clemency there and a moment without words as the thieves stood in shambling pose with eyes downcast. Then the scene disbanded. The men scrambled away in the gloom, muttering and groaning, and the Foleys did not chase them.

'God in heaven,' Francis said, 'the people there are in the world, Teige, eh?'

The father looked at his son from the corner of his eye. He was not sure if he was to be struck down again, and balanced there on that moment, testing gently the relationship between them. 'Are you hurt?' he asked.

Teige was thin as a young ash. The curved branches of his ribs were plain even in that half-light.

'I am not,' he said. And then, without looking up and in a slender voice: 'Are you?'

'God no. No,' said Francis, and then added quietly, 'thank you.'

Francis bent down and picked up the coat and held it in the air. 'Well, isn't that fine style?' He smiled then and Teige saw it and it was like an image abandoned in the furthest corner of the boy's mind, for there was a sweetness in that expression that belonged in the days when he was much younger and the old man had carried him on his shoulders.

Teige did not say anything.

'Made of good stuff, too,' his father said. 'Here, take it, Teige, it'll be warm.' He offered it and his son took it and put it on.

Teige lifted a handful of the hardened sleet-snow to the

pony's mouth and she lipped at it and drew back her top lip and showed her teeth and moved her head right and left as if soundlessly laughing. Teige bent down and began to push the snow on the ditch away with his hands. When it was apparent what he was doing his father knelt and together they cleared the snow from the rough tufted grass that lay below. When it was so exposed the pony moved closer and, after nosing cautiously, chomped the frozen grass with a tearing sound. Father and son watched. Francis tried to figure out what they would do and how he would say it. They waited in the dawning light and each felt its revelation with shyness. There they were, the mismatched pair of Foleys, in the middle of the country of the lost. Their breath hawed. Blackbirds came and landed in the field over the wall, attending the pony's finishing the patch of grass.

In that tentative renewal between them, Francis did not know how to broach the subject of the boy's mother. Then Teige said:

'I have looked for my mother.'

'I went back there, too,' said his father. 'I searched every road. I asked any I met.' He had more to say but did not say it. He looked at his son, then when he could not bear it he looked away. He did not say that he feared Emer was dead, and Teige did not turn on him with recriminations or vent further his anger and loss. Instead each stood and the air between them was filled with tangled memory and grief. Teige's mother appeared there in form invisible and was a figure with fair hair falling instructing him in the stories of the stars. She lingered a time in the silence of the undisturbed landscape of field and hedgerow spread out before them. The two men tried in vain to hold her there but she was like a star retreating as the morning came on.

Francis felt the weight of his years and the immense loneliness of the road passed over his face like a cloud. Later, he thought, later he could go and look for her again, but he did not have the strength for it now. For now he had to be with this boy. He had to take him somewhere. He had to make a home.

'Well, son,' he said at last. 'Will we go toward the sea?'

4

As they crossed the country the snow melted. It was like a blanket of green being unfurled. The skies moved again and rain fell. Cattle stood in the timeless of drizzle, then crossed the fields in slow phalanxes, finding shelter in the hedgerows as squalls blew the hard rain sideways. When the squalls passed, storms crashed. Thunder broke over February. The stars in the night sky vanished. In the dawn, the light was pale and seemed a poor cheapened imitation, a grey murk that drizzled. The countryside itself looked strangely sorry, like a place in tales where the king has been banished and every plant, hill and valley suffers in punishment awaiting renewal. So it was. And across this through the falling weathers of the beginning of the year Francis walked westward, with Teige on the white pony at his side. They were not companionable, they did not speak in the day as they moved along other than to announce rests or the place where the pony needed water. Still, the presence of the boy consoled his father. He saw how Teige had aged, how loss had marked the expression of his eyes and stolen their brightness, and yet despite the chastening of such knowledge he was still grateful.

They moved west over the curves of the road. Sometimes Teige dismounted and walked the pony. He never offered his father to ride and Francis did not ask. They passed all and sundry on their way, a long and varied parade of vagabond unfortunates whose ills and complaints formed the whole catalogue of life's undoing. There were infirm old widows shawled and wrapped so as to lose all shape of womanhood and seem instead accumulated bundles of cloth, browned by the road. The feet in their broken shoes ached and they shuffled flatly with flawed ankles or torn tendons. There were all manner of mendicant and pauper, thin skeletal figures who drifted along with doomed eyes. Few stopped on their way when they met the Foleys. They eyed the pony and then turned their faces downward and shoulders sideways as if shamed by their home-lessness. With such figures in their squalor Francis and Teige were already familiar. They had each seen many on their separate wanderings, yet nonetheless in the passing of each of them father and son felt shivers of foreboding. Where had these come from? They were going nowhere. The road for them was the last hope, and upon it they carried the impossible burden of their untold stories. Day and night they appeared and disappeared. They were like fairy folk or the infinite population of the dead. None seemed to know each other, none said their name. Whatever their quest it remained in its secret history and travelled away with them.

On one evening when an army of such passed them going eastward on the road, Teige broke the day's silence and asked his father why they were all going in the opposite direction.

Francis stroked his beard. They were stopped beneath three leafless trees and gnawing at raw potatoes.

'We are going to the sea, Teige,' he said. 'They are going to Dublin.'

'But why? Why do they not stay?'

'Each one has their reasons. Our reason is to leave our name in that town of Kilkee for Tomas and the twins, and then we will go to the monk's island and make a place there. Then when the boys come back they will be able to find us. That is our reason. You have seen the sea, is it so terrible?'

'No.'

'Tell me what it is like.'

Teige was squatting on the ground, the pony grazing near

him. The cold was coming in his shoulders as the heat of walking faded. 'It's like the end,' he said. 'It's wild though.'

'Wild?'

'Oh yes.'

'Good. That's what we want, eh? Wild, wild sea. Did you go into it?'

'I did.'

'And were you afraid?' The old man had said it before he thought better of it. He remembered the disastrous scene in the Shannon river and looked down and tightened his mouth.

'I was,' Tiege said and lifted his face. There was a moment then in which their still fresh reconciliation might have come asunder, in which the father might have made a grunt of disapproval and shook his head leaving his son to feel the isolation of cowardice. But Francis said:

'Good. That's good. You were right to.' He glanced at Teige from under his eyebrows. 'There's many drown in it, I suppose?'

'There is,' said Teige.

'And it's fierce?'

'Yes.'

'You were right so,' said his father. 'You were right to try it and then keep well out of it.'

Another pause, then Teige added: 'I didn't though.'

'You didn't?'

The pony flicked her head. Her tail swished. The boy looked at her a moment and felt his father's eyes upon him.

'No,' he said, 'I still went in, three times.'

The father said nothing then. He sat there and the emotions he held made his lips quiver. He blinked. Dark clouds moved across the sky. The night fell and the stars came and went and wheeled above them and each lay down to the slender hope of their dreams.

The following day when they were passing a cottage a cry stopped them. The cottage was not unlike others, a small building of dark stone with crooked windows and a door open to the road even in that February. The cry was that of a woman, it came from the garden beyond. The Foleys stopped, the pony flicked her ears. Then Francis called out. There was no response and Francis looked to Teige who slid down the pony. Together they walked in around the cottage and found in a small garden a woman of fifty years trying to pull up from the earthen ridges the fallen body of her husband.

When she saw them she let go the man's shoulders and while he lay motionless with open eyes and mouth she slipped down on to her knees. Her black and silver hair was astray across her face. Her mouth twisted from effort. Her husband, a figure older than she with a face locked in an expression of astonishment, did not move. She propped him against her breast and though the Foleys were there kept saying over and over strange sounds of endearment and something that might have been a form of the man's name, Cathal. Francis bent down to them and Teige stood behind him. He told the woman they would carry the man into the house but she seemed unable to grasp this, as though she were from another country or already taken from sanity by grief. Francis gestured Teige to him and together they picked the man up and bore him out of the dirt and in through the open door. The woman followed them, her hands holding each other tightly in a knot. In the gloom of the kitchen something stirred and then two small girls pressed against the corner of the dresser. The man was laid out on a settle bed. He was breathing, but still frozen in that look of amazement, his left side locked in an attitude of bracing. The woman stood looking at him and brought her hands to her mouth making moaning sounds. The girls came to her then and she enfolded each of them in one arm and the three stood there at the feet of the stricken man. Francis got a bucket and traced the muddied track in the grass until he came to the spring well. He was back with the water before Teige was sure where he had gone.

'He has been out there a while,' the father said. 'Get the clothes off him. Make up the bed. Has he the fever?'

The woman did not turn to respond.

'Woman of the house,' he said again, and then one of the small girls stepped out from her mother's side and told them not to shout, that their mother could neither hear nor speak.

Francis lifted the man up against his chest. The woman was made to understand and, helped by her small daughters, she readied the bed. Teige took the man's feet and hoisted him upon it. The stiff figure was undressed and his clothes taken out the door by Teige who was instructed by his father to burn them. In the freshness of the day Teige felt relief outdoors and stayed awhile in the low corner of the garden. A black and white sheepdog met him there; it looked up at him with blank sad eyes. When the sod of turf Teige had carried from the hearth at last retook flame he dropped the clothes upon it and watched the thick smoke take the contagion and carry it into the sky. Back inside the cottage he watched his father trying to get the man to drink. His hand was cupped beneath the man's chin and the water spilled. The woman was sitting, watching. There was understanding now in her face, a stilled knowing and she did not weep. She looked at her husband in the bed, seeing in his eyes the entire story of their relation, the history of their time together now come to this.

'Did you burn them?'

'Yes.'

'The poor man is nearly gone,' Francis said behind the woman. 'I don't know how long he was out there, fallen. The girls told her they heard him cry. She mistook their meaning.'

'If it's the fever . . .' Teige said.

'I don't think it is.'

'But . . .'

'No. He's like a clock stopped. That's not the fever.'

That night the Foleys stayed in the house of the stopped man. Teige slept on the floor on blankets he was given and

Francis sat in a chair of ash and sugan rope that the man himself had probably made. The mute woman dropped her head, and the two girls slept in the one narrow bed and did not move in their dreams. In the stillness of the cottage mice scurried, their sudden dartings in the shadowed corners like tiny erratic pulses of life. The night was long and cold. Wind gathered in the west and blew against the door. The dog whimpered where it lay. The sash of the window whistled like a punctured sigh. In his sitting Francis watched the stopped man and thought of his own time between worlds when he thought he had drowned. He thought of the long darkness, the terrible sense that light and touch and taste had been taken from him. He thought of it all and then reached over and rubbed the man's feet between the palms of his hands.

5

The Foleys stayed on. The family's name was O'Connor. The mute woman made them meals from the end of their winter storage of vegetables. Flour was beyond her means and they had no bread, but some days they ate a kind of potato cake that was coarse and lumpish yet sustaining. The two girls who were aged about eight and nine were called Maeve and Deirdre and seemed to know their mother's will instantly. They spoke for her and told the father and son that they were welcome. Francis told them they would stay for a little time and help them until the man recovered. For already there were signs that he was not to die. The stopped quality of him had already begun to change although ever so slightly. The fixed lob-sided twist of his mouth had softened and he spoke a kind of flattened speech whose words were not yet comprehensible. Still, his eyes were alive. He watched the father repair the half-door where the boards had rotted. He watched Teige stand by him and hold the hammer and pieces of timber that had been salvaged from a broken cart. As the days passed on the Foleys fixed all about the house that they could find. There were windows that did not open, a thatch ladder with broken rungs, a broom without a handle, stone walls that had been knocked. Francis Foley went at each of them with quiet zeal. Though he was not gifted as a carpenter or mason, he set himself at these tasks like a man engaged on some complex and involved proving. It was as though he were to demonstrate in the house of the O'Connors that the world itself could be repaired, that no breakage was beyond remedy, and that soon all would be restored in the vision of the innocent. He hammered and banged. He whistled softly. The small girls skipped and danced steps to this rhythmic reparation, this making good of all that was damaged. For it was not unlike those cottages in fables that become for a time an island of their own and in which the laws of the world do not govern and the hardship of life is suspended.

Finally when all was done about the cottage and the weather lifted and the ground was crisp, Francis took Teige to the garden and showed him how to dig straight furrows. The two of them worked side by side, turning over the new ground as the birds flew about them and chirped and squawked in the hope of worms. At times the father stopped and leaned on the fork and sighed. He looked with satisfaction at the work they had done, yet recalled the old pain that reminded him that this place was not their own. His great chest rattled, he had a wheeze that came like an after-breath once he had exhaled. But he turned to the work again, moving over the brown earth and making it ready for seed potatoes. When they had finished, the patch of opened soil was a neat rectangle of promise. They stood at the head of it and leaned there and watched the birds alighting.

'You can feel the spring today,' Francis said.

'You can.'

And they stood so, and said no more and were like the guardians of something greater than themselves whose majesty could be felt in simplicity. They went and drank water from the spring and then the two girls came running and told them their father was able to stand. They hurried back and went in the door and saw Cathal O'Connor propped up on his feet with his arm over the shoulder of his wife.

'I am grateful to ye,' he said in thin words that could now be understood. His eyes were gentle and his face soft as linen.

''Tis a thing of nothing,' Francis said. 'Your potatoes'll be in the ground tomorrow. Come.' And he looped the man's arm over his and hoisted him in light and heavy steps out the doorway and was soon joined by the man's wife and daughters. Then in a pose redolent with hope and faith in the constancy of the world they stood and looked upon the garden with the dog scampering back and forth over the furrows chasing the birds.

That evening, Cathal O'Connor died in his sleep. None saw or heard his passing in the night and it was not until the light was already breaking that Francis woke and noticed the absence of his breathing. At first he did not believe it. Then he reached and lifted the man at an angle from where he lay next to his wife. Francis held his face close to the man's mouth to sense the slightest air, and when he found none he pressed his ear against the chest and then lay the man down and pounded at his heart with his fist. He was doing this when the wife woke. Her eyes stared wide and frozen in their expression. The daughters woke and stood. Still Francis hammered at the man's heart. He was shouting to him now. He was crouched upon the bed with one knee on either side of the thin man, one instant beating away at him and the next bent low to listen. Then he was thumping at the heart again. Teige came beside him.

'Come on,' the father hissed. 'Come on, come on come on.' He whispered low curses and paused and looked above him into the mud beneath the thatched roof. He whispered further prayers or damnations then to spirits in worlds above or below. His voice grew urgent and his words came through his teeth. He shook the dead man for the last flicker of life until Teige said to him:

'Father stop. He is gone.'

And so he stopped. There was silence. From outside the door the dog moaned.

Later then, in the garden that was to be for that spring, Francis and Teige Foley buried Cathal O'Connor.

Two mornings after, they found the body of the man's wife drowned in the stream that was called Abhainn Mine.

A voiceless scream was still in her eyes. Francis shut them with small pebbles and laid her in the ground alongside her husband. The following day they left there with the pony pulling the old cart and the two girls sitting mutely upon it.

6

And by that time, in the caravan of gypsies, far away, Finbar Foley was travelling south with a mer-girl called Cait. The gypsies, sensing some change in the stars, had not returned to the races on the sands. When the old man Elihah died, a younger voice had spoken and told that it was time to cross the water again. So they had left that country and journeyed by stages first into Wales, then through the Cambrian Mountains and across the Severn river and down on to Salisbury Plain. There they had camped some time until one night the stars or the unknown forces of the universe moved them and they woke and broke camp and crossed into the wider spaces of northern France. And others of their kind told them there was a new cruelty abroad among mankind, that gypsies had been killed for the look in their eyes, but that many now had foretold the end of the reign of those wealthy and privileged and the coming of the time of the poor.

These gypsies were not unlike those with whom Finbar travelled, though they spoke in a language he could not fully grasp. It was not French but contained it, as it contained in piecemeal the languages of all the other countries they had seen. But in a short time Finbar grew accustomed to it and, discovering a new gift, was soon so conversant in that strange hybrid of words that none could say he was not born to it. His manner and look now, three years after the races, were almost indistinguishable from those of the gypsies. He had let his hair and beard grow long and wore a ponytail of his golden curls. In the caravan at night he bedded his mer-girl with a passion that made the old axles of the wagon creak and caused the gypsies outside to cheer. He seemed gifted in sex. The truth was that from the moment he had first been kissed by Cait, his soul had been sucked out and he was left with an insatiable thirst for it. It was a craving that lived in him day and night and could only be satisfied in the moments when he was in her arms. Her kisses still tasted of oysters. Her tongue was a fish in his mouth. Though she was long gone from the days when she had strode the waves for seaweed her flesh was imbrined and in the dark hoop of the canvas Finbar swam in it and practised each stroke to perfection. She was a woman of ample hips and round breasts who laughed when the golden curls tossed about her. She liked to reach down and grab on to them as Finbar's lips travelled up and down her legs and back and forth across her belly in the search to find his soul. Mornings after such loving Finbar appeared with chafed mouth and the red-rimmed puffy eyes of the long-distance swimmer. He was become a man. Since last seeing his twin he had doubled the size of his chest. He did not show any regret for leaving his brothers, nor did he even tell Cait that he was a twin. All of that was like wreckage to him now and he dived into her every night to forget it and leave it deep fathoms in the past. Many of the gypsies thought that he would quickly tire of her. They had seen incandescent passions before, and watched them flare and burn in their own destruction like the extravagant tumult of Venetian fireworks. They expected it to be done by the end of the first winter and the woman to leave the caravan, curse the gypsies for the spell that had befallen her, and make her way back into the ordinary world. They thought, too, that Finbar must at last reach the end of passion, for he travelled through it so quickly that surely by the spring he would have arrived at its last unexplored corner, and then thrown aside the map with the sexual disillusion visited on many. But it had not happened in that way. With indefatigable fervour Finbar continued to love her and rock the caravan through the night. In the warm days of the first French spring the gypsy women had looked at Cait for signs of her carrying a child. They sought this as proof of some kind of fairness in the world, an inescapable truth of how the universe was balanced and beauty and pleasure to be paid for in the fullness of time. They had looked for it, too, as a means of dispelling their own secret mistrust of her, the stranger amongst them whose blue eyes and pale skin might steal their men. But as the seasons passed there was no sign of any child. By the second year rumours divided at the campfires. It was something she was doing to avoid conception and the risk of losing him. The women said that she was brewing odd potions and they narrowed their eyes and shook their heads at this defiance of nature. The gypsy men whispered among themselves that it was no such evil, that she was adept at strange positions of lovemaking that increased the man's pleasure almost to madness and made child-bearing impossible. They said she did so with Finbar's full consent, and was right too, for the fortune-teller had told her that from his loins only twins could spring.

So, as the caravan journeyed down through the fields of France, the frantic loving continued and for both of them the old country faded and was put away like the things of childhood. They did not speak to each other of the past. Cait was a capable woman with a lively manner, and she bore no sentimental attachments. She sat on the timber seatboard and sometimes held the reins and clucked the horse forward while Finbar sought sleep in the back. She learned the spices of the gypsies and soon cooked braised suckling pig and other assorted meats in such a savoury manner that the smoke itself was sustaining. Her only weakness was an occasional longing for fish. When it arose she could not abide meat of any kind and demanded that Finbar find her a river. He would set off then on the small grey horse that was theirs and be gone until the evening or the following day when he would return with a bucket of live trout.

The excitement would be immediately visible on Cait's face and she would reach in and take some of the fish in her bare arms and hold them slithering against her bosom. Although he knew what to do she would still command Finbar to fill their zinc bathtub, and he would do so, and later her cries would be heard like seagulls about the camp. For some nights after the caravan would groan and rock all the more and the gypsies at the fires would seem to see it as a ship sailing away across a dark sea.

As ever the gypsies had no destination or fixed itinerary. They wandered down through Normandy and found themselves crossing the Maine into Anjou and then further south still into the country called Limousin. They travelled down the map of France like ink dribbling down a page. Had they considered it, had they seen a map, they might have chosen a more south-easterly route, but they had not, and the leader now among them was too young and raw in the manner of command to show his inexperience and ask for opinion. His name was Masso. While the roads were easy and the weather clement he waved them daily forward. He did not show his own fright or uncertainty, or the reality that he had no idea where he was leading them. There were green fields. There were animals they stole and killed and others they hunted. There were tranquil farmhouses where the gypsies could barter tin spoons and ladles and other assorted oddments of their own manufacture. There were broad valleys where in the summertime they came to a somnolent stop and where in the buzzing of bees and flies they told stories and drank sweet wine. Sometimes armies passed them on the road. Men in blue and scarlet and black boots to the knee marched past heading off to some field of blood, doomed figures already called by Death. They looked at the gypsies with leering expressions, then looked at their women with a kind of hopeless lust, passing on all the time. Thirty, forty cannon rattled past and cavalrymen, too, with bridles of supple and polished leather and spurs that jangled in the after-dust. So the world passed by those gypsies, and it was as if they were living in a parallel domain where none saw or cared for them and where the history of the world was not known.

Then, at the end of summer, when lassitude had almost overcome them all and their faces were dark with sun, Masso announced that they must leave the soft valleys and go east once more. He made the announcement with no fixed idea of the geography of that country, but was secretly thinking that his position as their leader would be made secure if he brought them into Bohemia. So, they had set out just as the mistral was blowing. Under their breaths many of the gypsies cursed. Their eyelids were heavy and their eyes narrow and small. They had grown soft in the summer and now the journey into winter made each of them age rapidly. Within two weeks they were in the mountains and the wind blew knives past their ears. Then there fell upon them the infamous snow that was widespread throughout Europe that year. It fell in those mountains in large thick flakes. Each was like a piece of paper, torn fragments of some broken treaty between heaven and earth. It fell from the sky so quickly the caravans had to stop in the narrow passes. The drop to the valley below vanished, the peaks above likewise, and the gypsies were held there with frozen faces, amazed. They looked to Masso for enlightenment and were told to go back and sit in their caravans. The following day the snow was rising above the wheel axles. Men dug as the snow drifted upon them and made of their shoulders white epaulettes or poor wings. Food was thinned. Battered buckets of snow were melted and the water added to thimble measures of soup stock. As the hunger became first a sound and then a loud noise like a beast among them, Cait opened the barrel of salted fish that she had stored and Finbar carried some along the stalled line of the caravans. Still the snow fell. The mountains, that they did not know were the Alps, mocked them with their white peaks. In his caravan Masso stared at the canvas wall and slowly rocked. It came so that he could not bear to look outside and instead in the unearthly silence of that place he listened to the soft pounding and slide of the snow as it began to bury his caravan. Then, when Finbar came with other of the gypsies to ask him how they were not to starve, Masso stopped his rocking and looked them straight in the face.

'You must eat me,' he said, and stabbed a thin iron spike clean through his heart.

They did not eat him but took all of his clothes, his blankets and scarves. Under Finbar's direction they distributed these to the very young and old gypsies until they were like deeply padded polar creatures and not even their faces could be seen. The starving horses they released, and watched as they made slow terrified progress away down the road. Then they pushed Masso's caravan over the edge of the road and it crashed and splintered and echoed as the only sound of man in those mountains.

They endured another seven days and nights. Finbar Foley became their leader without election or discussion. He told them to gather six in a caravan and embrace each other's bodies as if in the strongest grip of passion. He told them to lock their lips and breathe into each other and seal there the energy of life in one long and continuous circuitry of warm air.

The caravans lay in the snowy pass and within each of them the gypsies embraced. Young and old clung to each other and worked an elaborate puzzle of connection so that no part of man or woman was left untouched. Giggles, groans, moans and other sounds travelled the length of the caravans and into the white air like the ghosts of pleasure. And then there was silence.

Years later, when the grandchildren of those gypsies told it, the snow would fall faster and faster. Each flake would become larger, they would spread their arms to show, and the snowflakes would transform until they were wide as sheets unpacked and tossed from some chest in the heavens. The gypsies would hear them fall upon them. In the darkness of their caravans they would sense the weight of whiteness thump as though it were landing on their spirits. Then by the magic of such memories, and the inheritance of the inexplicable that was theirs, the gypsy grandchildren would tell how the snow sheets defied science and were not cold but warm. The heat inside the hoops of canvas grew. Those who had prepared themselves for death and were starved and frozen into stilled pose like in some collapsed mosaic of Byzantine intricacy now moved their limbs. They stretched as the blood warmed and ran into their toes. Their faces felt the breath of those next to them. Their eyes dribbled a rheumy warm fluid and then their noses too. Sweat flowed off them and the heat was such that in their delirium or fever they rose and threw off the layers of clothes they were wearing and fell to the most passionate and sexual loving that surpassed even their own dreams. The caravans steamed. The young writhed upon each other. The leathery skin of those gypsies old and long-travelled softened like apples in October and filled the air with the fruitful scent of remembered Indian summer. Whether the gypsies were dead or dying they could not be sure. Whether this was the hereafter, or they were being granted a final night of loving on the futhermost edge of life seemed equally likely and they did not question it.

Their grandchildren would pause there to allow the story its own room in the minds of those who listened. And then, at last, they would tell its outcome, how the sheets of snow over the gypsies' heads had been melted by body heat. The sweat that dripped through the floorboards of the caravans made a river in that mountain pass and carried the snow away upon it. Then when the temperature inside the caravans grew too great the canvas had been thrown back and the green world revealed. They had survived, and when their bodies cooled and they put on their clothes and looked away from each other with low abashment, there remained the feeling that Finbar Foley had saved them. He walked along the line of them and shook each by hand and kissed them. Then he told them that without horses they could take only the best caravan and that each should put within it what was most precious and the men would take turns pulling it back down the mountain into France.

So they left there, walking out of the blizzard in the cold of dawn, a ramshackle collection of gypsies pulling a single caravan toward the dream of spring. At their head was Finbar Foley, and on the seatboard of the caravan sat the mer-girl Cait, pregnant at last with Foley twins.

7

Francis Foley and Teige and the young girls Deirdre and Maeve were similarly journeying. They crossed the open green land of Tipperary in the mild weather that followed the snow. The girls sat mute and impassive on the cart and behind them at a small remove followed the O'Connor dog. When the cart slowed so did the dog. When it stopped, the dog stood in arrested pose and watched from a short distance and then sat upon the grass verge of the ditch to wait. The young girls did not pay it any heed and seemed themselves, whether by sympathy, grief, or chance, to have acquired their mother's dumbness. They stared at the road. They ate their food in a trance and were like creatures fallen from another world. Their eyes could not be met. When Teige brought them the bowl of their dinner and was careful to kneel to their level to speak in his softest voice, the girls' eyes looked elsewhere. In the night Francis told Teige in whispers that they must expect it would take time. They were lying in a field on the blankets they had brought from the O'Connor house. The night sky was starless and the darkness falling in a fine mist. For an hour each had lain there awaiting sleep, listening to the small noises of the night and hearing the dog sneaking closer in the dark.

'It will be a while,' Francis said.

Teige lay and did not move. He was trying to understand how his father knew in the dark that he was not sleeping.

'Yes,' he said at last.

It was a conversation like that, fragments of speech and

response separated in the dark sometimes by pauses so long as to make each statement seem the end or beginning, or the inconsequential ramblings of the last awake.

'Those girls will come through it, though.'

The old man paused. His voice was low and edged with desperation. Teige heard him swallow nothing. The soft rain fell on them. In the dark the dog arrived at the cart where the girls were sleeping.

'They seem like birds,' Teige said, 'stunned and fallen down in the grass. Why will they not say anything?'

The sky was moonless and the world seemed lost and without light.

'They will,' Francis said after a time. 'They will come through.'

'They will,' he said after another moment.

Teige said nothing. He knew his father was not speaking only of the girls but of the terrible plight of orphans that weighed on him, filling the space about him with memories. Where were his other sons? Where was Finan gone? Had he really killed that man? Where were Finbar and the gypsies? What corner was Tomas vanished into and why had he not returned? Where oh where was Emer?

'We will give care to them,' the old man said when he had recovered. 'We will bring those girls with us to the island, Teige. Yes. We will.'

If he said more Teige did not hear him, for he fell asleep even as the dog claimed its place on the cart between the two girls and lay with low moans, hunting in its dreams the ghosted scent of its vanished master.

In the morning they moved on again and the dog resumed its place a little way behind. Teige drove the pony and cart and the two O'Connor girls sat upon it still like the daughters of Lot. The Foleys crossed the Shannon at a bridge and made their way across the County Limerick and into Clare. Sometimes the road they travelled gave way to such mud that the pony could not pull through it and Teige and Francis both had to pull and push, making slow progress with the girls useless to help and the dog watching from the ditch. The further west they travelled the higher the mud on the axle of the wheels.

In the late afternoon they came upon a farmer with a black cow in the road. In that season before the beginning of new grass, he was allowing her the poor grazing of the ditch outside his fields. Francis called to him a greeting and the man acknowledged him with the kind of low-voiced circumspection that seemed habitual there. When he could no longer avoid conversation the farmer asked them where they were going. The old man told him they were heading to the town of Kilkee in the west to see if there was news of his eldest son. The farmer nodded. He placed his hand on the backside of his cow. The cow did not move. She was thin and pregnant and exhausted. The farmer moved his mouth about as if trying to find some difficult word there. He looked over the ditch at the wet fields. He said a sound that was not a word, and then at last brought himself to ask them if they wanted food that night.

They ate in a small cottage that was unlit by any lamp even after darkness fell. There was a shadowy gloom there to which their eyes became accustomed. The woman of the house was robust-looking with greying curls that fell down her cheeks. There were the shapes of a half-dozen children standing. The O'Connor girls sat amongst them on a bench and ate the potatoes and potato-bread and winter cabbage and drank the buttermilk but did not speak. The farmer did not speak either and only made low guttural noises of response when Francis addressed him. His wife answered instead. She seemed lightened by their company, and it was apparent that the dour farmer had invited the Foleys there as a peace offering against some earlier argument with his wife. He had brought them to disprove his meanness, though he would not burn a lamp.

'You're like people who've seen a lot,' the woman said. 'I've seen no place but this parish and not even the furthest ends of that.' She glared down the table at her husband who did not raise his eyes to her.

'We've seen enough,' Francis said. 'But few places with the charity and welcome of your house.' He looked over at where she was standing by the deal dresser in the darkness. He nodded to her his thanks and was not sure if she saw him or not. The children who were standing along the length of the table had finished eating and were waiting to see what their father might leave on his tin plate. The youngest of them was aged about four. Teige watched as the man sopped milk in a semicircle with the butt of his potato-bread. There was a half of it left. He sopped the milk thrice and ate it. Then he took the second half of the butt and circled the hollow of the plate again although it seemed already dried. This too he mouthed. Then he stood up, stepped back and went from the cottage. The children scrambled forward amidst the shouts of their mother and found of the nothing he had left crumbs and flakes of food not enough to nourish mice but small trophies to them as they fell at each other and toppled noisily on to the ground. The O'Connor girls watched this in some alarm at first and Teige saw their faces and motioned them not to be worried. Then the mother of all those children assured the girls too and watched not without glee or pride as that mob of hers, boys and girls alike, tussled and squirmed and cursed and were general entertainment. A short time after the farmer came to the door. His face was twisted like a rag.

'Come,' he said, 'now.'

The Foleys and the eldest boy followed the farmer to the cabin. There a lamp had been lit. On a damp bed of mucked rushes the exhausted black cow was labouring. The farmer held the light high and they each saw the shine of her, the gloss of effort leaking out through her hide. Her eyes were wild and the pull and blow of her breath uneven and rasping like some faulty mechanics. The farmer hung the lamp on the wall, and then brought up from the ground a length of thick rope.

'She won't do,' he said to none of them in particular. 'You've pulled a calf?' he asked Francis.

'I have, and many, but she's not ready.'

'She'll die.'

'She won't,' Francis said.

'She's older than that boy,' the farmer said, nodding toward Teige. 'We'll pull her now.'

He ran his hand along the back of the old cow, but in her terror and hunger and weakness she frighted and turned sharply in the byre and knocked the farmer sideways against the wall. He cursed her with a kind of exaggerated violence, then stepped forward again and this time thrashed at her with the rope like a whip. He made connection to her backside only twice and she bucked and moved in a quicktrot directly at them. The boy jumped in against the stone wall of the cabin. Teige was pushed by his father sideways and felt the side of the cow against him as she passed. She reached the far wall and moaned. Then she bellowed loudly and arched her great head and roared once more. Pig squeals came from the next cabin over. The farmer strode up and whipped at her again. He shouted at her to stop that and be quiet, but she was still not finished bellowing and had her face now against the old door.

'Don't, she'll push the door out. Wait!' Francis called but the farmer was not to be deprived of his chance to whip her again. The rope flew back and was in mid curve high in the air when Francis stepped up and grasped the farmer and held him hooped in his arms. The man wriggled and cursed and tried to stamp on the other's foot but he could not break free and the son, watching, allowed a crooked smile to slide over his mouth as though at a circus.

'Let me off!' the farmer shouted, but Francis held him and kept him there imprisoned and told Teige to see to the cow.

Teige moved forward with his hands out wide and whispered sounds.

He said over and over words that sounded like a sea.

The cow had her back to him. The place where she had been whipped had welted in two clean lines. Still Teige whispered the sea until it was all about them and the farmer in Francis's arms quietened. Teige was next to her now, and the noise he made became instead a low moan that was almost unvoiced and sourced in some deeper part of his insides below his larynx. He came about until he was before her then licked his fingers and held them out and touched them against her foamed mouth. And she did not back away. The old cow stood in the low light with Teige putting his fingers inside her mouth and moving them within her mucus. The boy gasped at it. The farmer remained quiet. He watched as though at a dream. Then Teige licked his other fingers and withdrawing one hand slid the other there and the cow puzzled on them and turned her tongue upon them. Then Teige withdrew his moist hand and brought it down her back and softly inside her. He was knelt on the rushes, his head against her steaming flank and a hand inside her. She stood still some moments, her mouth working as though at the memory of her mother's udder. Then, very slowly, Teige moved his weight down along her and pressed his right hand deeper inside to feel for the calf. Sharp smacking sounds of suction and fluid escaped. She stood for him. His arm was lost inside her now and was vanished up to his elbow. The others watched his face in the lamplight for signs of what he found. But for a time they could not tell and Teige said again the sound of the sea and the low moans which spoke only to the cow. Blood and a heavy blackish stuff leaked there. The cow groaned. The boy's face was a white moon against the wall. Teige turned his hand inside her and twisted his elbow around until it was facing the thatch. Then back again. A spasm travelled through her. She lifted her left hind-leg and made a tiny kicking flick at nothing. A foamy sweat rose in separate places on her black hide. Then Teige began to withdraw his arm from inside her. He did so in slow stages, waiting and then pulling, easing his way from the depth of her as his arm came back out into the lamplight with skeins of blood flecked upon it and a transparent film of membrane. His arm withdrew as far as his wrist and then stopped.

'How is she, Teige?' Francis asked him.

'Backwards. But she's here now.' And again he made the sound of the sea. And while he was making it he withdrew his hand another piece and the bone-white tips of the calf's hind-hoofs appeared where they had pierced through. The farmer went to step forward.

'No, wait.' Francis's hand was on his shoulder. 'You'll start her. Teige knows. Wait.'

Teige's bloodied hand was free in the air and the calf's legs were out as far as the shins.

'Now, quickly,' Teige said, 'or the hip will lock and the calf will die.' And before another minute had passed his father and the farmer and the farmer's son had come and the rope had been secured over the hoofs and the calf pulled free on to the rushy floor. Teige bent to blow in its nostrils. The black cow turned her head and made a moaning. Francis moved his hand on her swollen udder until the beestings came and Teige and the farmer lifted the calf upright in the world for the first time. It stood and toppled like a thing of sticks. Now its forelegs were fixed solid and its hind buckled, and now the opposite. It tottered and was for a time like an imperfect creation. The men came and steadied it and held its mouth in place where at first it would not suck. Milk squirted and oozed out over it. Driblets ran across the calf's mouth but not into it. Teige had to slip his thumb in the side of the mouth and accustom the tongue and wait until the calf discovered sucking and could then have the hand-warmed teat wedged in its mouth.

The men stood back. In the yellowy light of the lamp they watched with the same mute reverence as was since time began. The calf milked at the mother and twice pushed its head quickly against the bulge of her udder for more.

'Tell your mother we have a heifer calf,' the farmer said. His son nodded and ran out. Still the two men and Teige stood. Teige's clothes were wet and stained. His father looked at him and had to blink his eyes then for the power of pride that coursed through him. Then he looked up at the old timbers of the roof and the thatch as though seeing through them and beyond into the heavens and the stars.

When the cabin door opened the woman of the house appeared and she looked at the calf and the black cow and said, 'Well, ye did well and thanks due to these strangers.' She smiled briefly at her husband and he made a timid return of the same. Then she looked at Francis and Teige and in the stillness of the cabin the intake of her breath was audible. She saw them for the first time in the light.

'It's yourself again,' she said.

Francis turned to her. Her face showed she was astonished.

'You,' she repeated.

'You have seen me before?'

'Yes. Only you were younger. Four days ago or so, wasn't it? On the road.' She stopped suddenly and became thoughtful; her hands came to her mouth and pulled at her lower lip.

'Perhaps it was a man like me?' said Francis and he came forward excitedly and took the lamp from the wall and held it next to his face.

'I'd swear it was you. You came along the road and you stopped at the door begging. You had that woman. She was out by the wall beyond.'

'It was my son,' Francis said in a low whisper. 'We are searching the country for him. Tell me.'

'I gave him bread and some grease of the goose and some small potatoes and a jar of buttermilk. He was thin. The woman beyond was coughing. I could hear her all the time he stood there. He took the things. He had a way of looking that said how sad he was to be begging there. I would have offered him a place for the night but I knew himself didn't like me to. He hates me thinking good of them as passes on the road and I know it is only misfortune that separates them from us. So I didn't offer and he went off and the woman coughing with him and I heard them like that some way down the road and I inside at the hearth. And when himself came in,' she nodded toward the farmer who studied the ground, 'we took to shouting at each other. I told him I would be gone the road and leave the children to him if he didn't invite the next beggars he met to come and eat with us. And them was you and your other son today.' She stopped and drew breath and looked at the calf. 'And see what good you've done us.'

'He was thin?' Francis asked her at last.

'He was.'

'But he was well?'

'I couldn't say that. I thought after he might have signs on him of whatever the woman had in her chest. His eyes, they . . .' she paused and watched the effect of the news on the two strangers, and then added, 'I am sorry for ye.'

The farmer joined her.

'Yes, we are sorry for ye.'

Francis stood absorbed in his grief. He aged as the knowledge twisted into him like thorns.

'How many days?' Teige said. 'How many days ago that you saw him?'

'Three, maybe four.'

'Think,' Francis boomed and the black cow shuddered a step away.

The woman pulled at her lip.

'What day have we? Yes, it was the day after Sunday last I'd say.'

'Three days so?'

'Yes.'

'Which way did they go on the road?'

'West,' she said. 'Making slow progress now, I'd say.'

'Teige, get the girls ready,' Francis said. 'We'll go now.' He turned to the woman. 'Thank you,' he said and swiftly went out into the dark and began preparing the cart and the pony.

A half an hour later, with Deirdre and Maeve O'Connor sitting on the front of the cart and a portion of a killed goose and a bundle of potatoes and hens' eggs and two winter cabbages on the back, the Foleys left. The farmer and his wife and children watched them under the held-high lamp. They knew there was nothing to say and witnessed their departure as though such haste and desperation were familiar and had often been re-enacted in the history of that country. Francis nodded to them a final time and told Teige to cluck the pony and they hurried westward, down the road under a thin light of few stars.

8

They went westward in the dark with the old man hastening ahead in a kind of soft-footed jogging that slowed and sped up continuously like a faltering engine of hope. The slap of his old boots on the road was a doleful music. Teige drove the cart and the dog followed some paces behind. The dawn opened before them and in the pale glow of its first light the father peered at all shapes and shadows that lay down the road as if each one might be the figure of his eldest son. They crossed the soft ground of the County Clare. They passed through the town of Ennis when it was still sleeping and its ghosted narrow streets echoed with the hoof clops of the white pony. The Foleys looked up at the curtained windows of the hotel, the shuttered boarding houses and the open doorless entranceway of the poorhouse, but they did not stop or make enquiry. They heard low groans and whimperings that escaped in slumber through the crevices of old buildings.

The dampness of the streets and the stone houses were like a cold purgatory and Francis quickened his pace and passed quickly on. He knew his son was not there. The rags of his coat fluttered. His long hair was plastered awry with sweat and rain and showed the bald places of his scalp like islands. Teige offered him his place on the cart but the old man declined. It was as if he imagined he was being guided now on the trail of Tomas, as if he alone knew which turns on the road to take and knew not by logical reason but by an inner prompting that would reunite him with his own flesh. Teige did not argue. He saw the look in his father's face, the sunken hollows beneath his eyes and the fixed locked mouth, and knew the old man's resolve was not to be questioned, that for him it was a kind of repentance and a journeying toward forgiveness.

Rain fell and stopped and fell again, as if such weathers were features of the geography. They went northward from the town and turned west at a crossroads and trekked through the wild open bogs and bleak land of Cill Maille. There by a place that might have been called Misery or Desolation were the grey waters of Loch na Mine, the lake with no bottom where watersprites lived. Francis stopped and held his right hand against his chest and was sucking at the air when the cart arrived up behind him.

'We can stop here a while,' he said, his breast rising and falling as if about to release something.

'Are you all right?' Teige asked him.

'Feed the girls, water the pony,' the old man said and slumped to the ground.

They ate some of the goose then and the girls went to the waterside for their privacy and returned and sat again mute upon the cart. Teige brought the pony to drink. The dog moved in a low crouching manner closer to the smells of meat. Before they were ready to leave she was eating from Teige's hand.

'They cannot be far now,' the old man said. He looked through the rain at the emptiness of the road.

'You think they . . .'

'I do.' The old man raised his head so his thin neck was extended, then he scratched at it as if deliberating a distance. 'We will find them today Teige,' he said, and did not say aloud 'or never'.

There was a still pause then in that eerie brown place of bogland and drizzle. The emptiness of the road shrunk their hearts. They said nothing. Waterfowl plashed in the lake and moved the time forward until the father finally stood and they left once more.

They drove on down through the townlands of Barsaile and Glean Mor and Cluain i Gulane. When they arrived in the village of Cill Mhicil it was late afternoon of the Fair Day there. Polyps of dung lay cooling in the street. Bootless boys in brown rags stood herding groups of two or three cattle while their fathers had adjourned elsewhere. The cattle were watchful and skittish and young and when the Foleys passed them they made small panicked movements and had their sides tapped by the boys' sally rods. There were curt cries and sharp commands. In the yards, tethered horses raised their heads dripping drinking water when the Foleys passed. Further down the village men eyed the strangers furtively from beneath their caps. They studied the white pony and chewed in the hollow of their cheeks, and awaited what trouble might brew. They did not let their eyes meet those of the Foleys. They did not show any sign of welcome or wonder or even of noticing that they were there. Instead, as if out of some inherited sense of distrust of anything they did not know, they leaned against one of the eating houses there and looked at each other's shoulders and waited.

Francis walked up to them.

One of them thought he was going to be struck and took two quick steps back. Francis was ragged and worn thin and wild looking. The dirt of the road was creased in his face. When he went to speak he felt his lips blistered along the insides.

'I am looking for a man,' he said.

The group of four men heard him but said nothing. One of them offered a hint of a noise and a small nod.

'I am looking for my son,' Francis said to them, this time in a louder voice and taking a step closer. Behind him Teige stopped the cart in the street. The men looked past the old man as though suddenly he was invisible. None of them wanted to speak, preferring the comfort of feigned ignorance until one with a screwed-up eye called out:

'Will you sell the pony?'

'What's the matter with ye? Are ye deaf or stupid?' Francis said.

One of them looked down at his boots, another made a quick grin and grinned it away down the road the strangers had come.

'We're neither,' the screwed-up eye said. 'I'll give you a price for the pony.'

'Have you seen a man and a woman walking down this road today?'

'We've seen many.'

The men murmured a sound that was not quite laughter. Their shoulders swayed with the signs of the day's drinking upon them.

'My son and a woman. That's who I'm seeking.'

'For some trouble is it?' said the screwed-up eye.

'For no trouble. For his good. The last he saw me I was drowned.'

'And a sight cleaner then,' the eye said to his companions who laughed.

'If you give me the price of the pony there I'll tell you,' he said.

'The pony is not for sale,' Francis said.

'I have a fine few laying pullets there and a banbh,' said the eye and touched the peak of his cap sideways to obscure his other.

'God bless you but you're thicker than the floor of the cart,' Francis said then stepped up and elbowed past them entering the eating house at their back while they followed him grinning and nudging as if about to witness a performance.

In the obscure light he could make out shapes of men there and sticks and the outward thrust of their legs on the mud floor. A noise of spoons rattling in earthenware bowls and the smell of potatoes with butter and milk met him.

'I am looking for a man and a woman,' he announced. 'It is

my son and I am certain he came through here. Has anyone seen him? He is with a woman and she is ailing, I'm told.'

The spoons paused. Amid the smells of cooked food rose the heated stench of farmers and their drovers. Some scratched themselves and unleashed the scent of old urine from their trousers. Francis heard their breathing labouring in the dark, but none answered.

Finally a woman at the counter said: 'There was a man with a woman passed through here no more than a few hours ago.'

'West?'

'Toward the ocean,' she said.

He could not even see her face. 'Thank you,' he said. Then he was gone from there and called to Teige that Tomas was indeed ahead of them not far and that they would catch him before dark if they hurried. Teige clucked and snapped the reins and Francis jogged ahead of them out of that village and into the light that was falling into the sea. They took the road west toward Crioch, meaning end, along the open country of no tree or bush where the fields themselves were winter-combed by the Atlantic breeze. It was a road Teige had travelled with the gypsies once before. It was the road that ran through the village of Doonbeg and on to the curved strand of Kilkee. The white pony seemed to recognize it and opened her stride on the road as if just ahead of her was the figure of her first love, the vanished gypsy boy Mario. She now trotted next to the old man so that he reached out and held on to the leathers and was sped on like that. The pony's eyes were wide and showed their whites, her mane fluttered in the breeze. Upon the cart the two small girls Deirdre and Maeve clung to each other. The road flashed past. Hares in the fields stopped dead and listened. The seabirds circled. Then, there it was.

A figure on the road.

But it was not Tomas. It was too tall.

Even knowing this the father shouted out. He let go of the pony, and Teige reined her to a walk as the old man ran on calling out and waving his arms. The figure that was like the figure of a giant stopped. It turned slowly, then, the way one might in a dream and Francis and Teige saw at once that there on the road to Kilkee was the aged and burdened figure of Tomas, carrying on his back the fevered body of the woman, Blath.

9

Tomas Foley had aged and was thin and weakened. The woman he carried on his back had shortened and curved him and though he put her down carefully on the side of the road he could not stand up straight to meet his family. He had been carrying her for so long that the skin across his shoulders was calloused. When he turned to look at Teige and his father he was not sure if they were phantoms or tricks of the fairies. He blinked beneath his fair curls and passed a hand across his brow.

'Tomas,' his father said, and then said no more for he had stepped forward and embraced his son and his heart broke to feel the thinness of him in his arms. They held each other and were still and wordless there in the road. Teige watched them and the girls in the cart watched too and the dog turned its head. Then Tomas stepped back and let out a groan and he held out his hand to Teige and then clung on to him.

'Teigy,' he said into the side of his brother's neck, 'I'm sorry.' They held each other tightly and shook with emotion. 'I meant to come back to you,' Tomas said, but did not release his hold. The sea sang down the cliffs to the west. Gulls buckled in flight in the sky. The three Foleys did not move as if afraid that any step would separate them again and this time for ever. They stood in the road. In a fable they might have remained so, transformed through the release of all their regret and suffering into stones or petrified trees. They might even have chosen such a fate, for in a family that had journeyed so much already none could now think of moving. They were still as the fields.

At last, Francis broke the spell. He went over and introduced himself to the woman Blath lying on the ground.

'You are the famous father,' she said to him and she smiled weakly and he could see that she was beautiful. 'He has spoken of you often.'

'You are welcome among us,' Francis said. 'I hope he has not told you what a fool he had for a father.'

'Indeed he did,' said Blath. 'But that father was drowned, you must be a new one.' She smiled again and there was in her expression such a tenderness that Francis saw at once how she loved his son.

'That's just what I am,' he said, 'a new one.' And he was stopped from further speech for she started coughing then, and in a swift movement he bent and picked her up and carried her to the cart.

They did not tell their stories then. They embraced again and looked at each other and stood back and then Teige shouted out cries of victory and threw his hands in the air.

'Tomas is back! Tomas is back!' he cried and made the others laugh at his manner as he jumped up and punched at the air. Tomas went over and climbed upon the cart, he told the O'Connor girls his name and they nodded slightly and Teige told him they were Deirdre and Maeve.

'And this is still your gypsy pony?' Tomas said.

'It is,' his brother told him. 'It surely is.'

'Finan and Finbar?' Tomas asked, but knew the moment their names reached the air that there was an answer already in their absence.

'Later,' the father said. His eyes were wet. He made motions with his mouth before speaking as if afraid to dare the words. 'We are going to see our new home now.'

And Teige handed Tomas the reins and went ahead and walked with his father, leading the pony forward.

10

This is the story that Teige and his father heard of what happened to Tomas. They did not hear all of it at once. But some of it they heard that first night when the Foley cart had arrived at the seashore and Francis had walked down to the edge of the country and stood alone a long time with his face to the sea. They heard it when he returned to the small fire Teige had built of sticks of ash and thin faggots scavenged from the fields nearby. They heard it while the wind played and they sat close to each other and even the two girls stayed awake with the dog taking turns in their laps. Tomas sat with the woman Blath lying curled and small beside him. As he told it his hand sometimes travelled down the twist of her hair. She lay, her eyes open all the time, and her face like worn vellum shadow-creased and burnished in the movement of the flames. Tomas told them some of it that night, and stopped when it seemed the woman grew distressed or the fever in her made her moan and her teeth jabber though they piled their coats on her. He told some of his story that night and more the night after and again over each of the four nights they stayed there on the edge of the town of Kilkee.

He had gone back to Limerick that day long ago. He had ridden in along the banks of the Shannon river with his head low on the horse and his eyes watchful for bailiff and agent and constable. He had considered the situation. He knew that she was waiting for him. He knew too the life that she was living and that her waiting was secret and silent and existed only in the thin insubstantial way of hope or prayer. Still he remembered a look in her eyes. He told Teige this. He said it looking into the starless sky when she was sleeping. There was a look in her eyes when he had told her that he loved her, he said, and that was all he saw that day riding back into the town of Limerick. He had no plan.

'No,' his father said, as though this was an inevitability of his birth.

Tomas had arrived back in the town in the evening. Rain was pouring down and the streets were mucked and the sewers ran like dark streams. Rats traversed the streets and carried leftovers from the stalls of the market. Apple cores, plumstones, flecks of potato skin passed into the shadows. Tomas tethered his horse in the narrow alley behind the building where he knew Blath was. The rain fell. In his wet shirt his chest hammered. He said he tried to swallow hard for it seemed he had bitten a huge apple and the piece of it was wedged in his throat. But there was no apple, he said. He went around the alley. When he approached the front door he saw it was locked. He wanted to bang on it. But for once he knew he shouldn't and crossed the street and waited. The curtains of the rooms upstairs were drawn poorly and frayed amber light showed. The rain threaded across it. There was the traffic of late gentlemen in their coaches passing up the street, there were dragoons in uniform cursing and laughing and kicking a bottle they had emptied. There were dogs that meandered night-eyed and low-snouted. So many dogs, he told them, dogs and rats and figures scurrying in the dark. He waited a long time and none came out or in. He waited longer still. He struggled with doubt and dark imaginings and when he could wait there no more he stepped into the rain and walked across the street up to the front door and banged on it like a hopeless emissary of Love. He banged again. Then he heard the noise of calling from within and footsteps coming on the stairs. He was asked his name through the door and he said, 'I am Tomas Foley, I am here for Blath.' And the door opened and there was a man there of small stature with bald pate and whiskers and the smell of tobacco. 'She's not here,' he said. His eyes were screwed near shut. He rocked on the balls of his feet as though a long time used to the sea.

'Where is she?'

'There's another Blath,' he told Tomas, 'there's as many Blaths as you want, eh?'

Tomas hit him then and the man fell back against the banister and his eyes opened wide for the first time and he rolled himself quickly to one side and stood with the swaying motion of a boxer though Tomas was nearly twice his size. He fisted at the air and made short jabs of no import as Tomas advanced upon him.

'Where is she?' he asked again.

The man did not say and Tomas reached across his fists and lifted him and flung him against the wall. He followed him across the hallway and pulled him upwards like a sack until the man's eyes were somewhere below his chin. He held him there and asked him again where she was. The man shook his head in quick motion as though his head was preparing to spin off. Then Tomas broke his arm. The man's screams brought an old woman to the top of the stairs. She held a candle and peered down at them. Her eyes were painted. Her hair was loose and those strands she possessed at the sides of her head were brushed outward by intent or accident and lent to her the weird air of one grotesquely masked. She shouted for them to get out in the street. Tomas asked the man again as he held him against the wall and this time he heard that she was gone, that all the girls were gone to the house of Lucius Stafford, cousin of the baronet. He heard the news but did not comprehend it. He stood a moment staring into the face of the man. The man fearing for his other arm said the name again and told him where the place was.

When Tomas left there it was the middle of the night. The

rain was still falling. He found his horse and rode out into the darkness to the south. His progress was slow. The rain blew in his face and the moonlight was lost to him. He had been told where the house was and so went there with the single purpose of getting Blath back. He was not thinking of the other girls or who they might be or what they might be doing. He was gifted the naive vision of the lovelorn and experienced a simplified view whereby the only significant measure in the world was the straight line between lover and loved. He rode on, an absurd servant of forgotten chivalry or like one bearing lit candelabra through the falling rain. He arrived at the house before dawn and saw its candlelit windows as he came upon the curve of the avenue. It was a tall house. Its chimneys smoked the scent of oakwood. Next to it, a smaller lodge nestled in the trees. Tomas tied off the horse and crept up across the lawns in the rain. When he reached the house, he knelt and looked in the window and thought he had arrived by some magic inside a painting.

'I could not believe it at first,' he told them. 'I could not understand it.' For there inside the long room were naked statues of women. There were a dozen or so of them. They were as like real as could be imagined. Yet they did not move. They were set about on alabaster podia through the room in a series of poses, some bearing fruits, some holding a hand out in frozen invitation, some covering modestly with draped arm or fingers their bosom or sex. It was not until he saw Blath there with flowers in her arms in the pose of Persephone that Tomas knew for sure that they were not statues. Then he saw Lucius Stafford in the gown of a Roman Emperor with a garland of leaves about his head and three others similarly attired. They moved among the goddesses. Lucius led a pair of fawn bullish dogs like mastiffs on a rope of red velvet. They passed down along the figures there. They laughed and made comments on each and restrained themselves to resume their performance and seem imperial. The goddess Diana holding a wooden bow wavered in her place and one of the men whipped at her with a tasselled cord.

'I saw no more,' Tomas said. 'I went down and broke the lock of the small lodge there. And I made a brand of a handle and cloth wrapped about it and I lay it in the ashes until it was alight. Then I came up the lawn to the big house and crashed in the glass and stepped in with the fire.'

Screams and glass shattering and the barking of the dogs and the astonished cry of Lucius Stafford announced him. The emperor raised his hand as though to call forth bolts of lightning. His companions held up theirs as if to hold firm the beautiful reality of the women in their power, but the goddesses had leapt down and were running naked in all directions. Tomas waved the firebrand in zigzag and briefly marked the air as he walked forward. The Romans backed away. They called out for him to stop. He struck the face of one of them with the burning wand and he fell writhing to the ground. Then he saw across the room that Blath had seen and recognized him and was standing there with her arms across herself unsure of whether to stay or run. And the room was suddenly full of people and the firebrand was wrestled from him and fell on the carpet and spread flame. There were two men on his chest. Another struck him in the ribs with a wooden baton. Smoke was thick. Flames ate up the curtains. Tomas could no longer see Blath or any of the women. He cried out her name. He kicked aside one who came at him low and saw the man's head twist sharply back as though the neck was broken. Then from behind he was hit with a poker and the room spun sideways and he fell senseless to the floor.

'When I awoke I was in Limerick gaol,' he said.

He said it in a whisper to his father in the small hours when the others were sleeping and the sea sighed in rhythm as though rocking the world.

'They had me there as a robber.' He felt his wrists when he

told it and Francis saw the marks of irons on them. 'I was, I don't know how long, in a place dark and wet no bigger than half the cart. It was a place of nothing. No bench, no bed, nothing. I stood in my own shit. I could not see my hand. I was in a place like under the world. Once in the day they slid back the hatch and threw in what I was to eat and it landed in the dirt many times until I learned to listen for it coming. There was a silvery kind of light for a moment then. Then it was gone. That was how I knew another day had passed. I counted them then. When I had counted a hundred I thought it was for ever. I thought they would release me. They would come any minute. But they did not. I began to count again. I tried to count each minute of each day and fell asleep standing and fell down along the wall and woke with my face in muck and counted again.'

Tomas stopped. They gazed dimly at the night sky a while.

'There were four hundred and thirty-seven days like that in that darkness and dirt,' he said, when he started again.

'Oh God,' the old man said, 'Oh God.' Teige awoke then and listened without stirring.

'I thought', Tomas said, 'they had forgotten me and I hammered on the door until my fists were numb. I beat my head against it. Still none came. I think they took days away and did not come at all for sometimes I counted the day longer than it could have been. Or it was that my mind was wandering. I thought of Teige and the twins then with the gypsies. I thought of the white pony racing on the sands and how Teige would surely win. I thought of Blath and where she could be and did she know if I was living or dead. I tried sometimes to see the patterns of the stars in the blackness, but my mind failed me. I could tell rough seasons by the cold in the floor or how the smells thickened and rose. But the darkness, the darkness,' he said, 'that is . . .'

His head bowed then and his shoulders curved. His father

placed a hand upon his back. The sea sighed. They said no more that night. Teige closed his eyes tight and drifted uneasily to sleep.

What he told them the next evening was how one day without warning the footsteps approached and the hatch was not opened, the door was. Two men reached in and lifted him out of the cell.

'I did not seem myself to myself,' he said, 'so weak was I. I could not walk. I was a flake of Tomas. I was bone with flesh fallen off it. They dragged me from under my armpits. My feet scraped and bled on the stones. They bore a lantern that burned my eyes and I hung my head and saw the nakedness and dirt of myself passing down that place that was like a sewer beneath the gaol. I tried but could not talk. My mouth was sores, my tongue like that in a leather boot. When I reached the stairs I felt the light on the crown of my head hurting. When I got to the top I discovered I was near blind in this eye,' he said pointing his finger to it.

'As they took me down along the corridor another in chains passed me going toward my cell below. He flinched when he saw me. I heard his irons shake and the sounds of struggle as they beat him forward. I was thrust on, dragged by my gaolers and brought at last to a large hall with barred gates and iron bars from floor to roof. Inside were maybe three hundred men and women. They clamoured toward the gate when the gaolers approached and were threatened back with lashings and the beating of batons on the bars. I was thrown in there then. The gates were locked and the gaolers went away.

'I lay on the ground. There were high barred windows. The daylight hurt me. I curled there and did not know if I was to live or die. Then the people came about me. They were beggars and thieves and rebel men and ones caught without means. The women were to be in separate quarters but all these were filled and so they were brought there to that large gaol instead and were to wait until such space became open to them. Some were there without trial or judgement other than the wishes and say-so of their landlords or some other one. They saw how I was and clothed me with abandoned rags. They carried me back toward the wall where the ground was driest for the light passed there each day. The women sat me then on cloths they had made themselves of their own rags. One touched water on my lips. I thought I fell in dreams then. I thought I lost the world and slipped into imagining for before me then I saw Blath.

'I thought one eye was blind and the other saw dreams. But she was small and bent and near to me and I smelled her, and her fingers touched on the place on my forehead that was bruised and bloodied from beating on the door. And it was her.'

They were seated again by the low fire beside the cart on the west coast of Clare. When he said her name Tomas looked to where Blath was now sleeping. He had thought that if they did not move for some days her health might recover, but as she lay her breaths came in broken parcels and her body still shivered beneath their blankets and coats.

'It was her,' Tomas said.

'She had been brought there after the fire in Stafford's house. Some had told against her and said that I had come to kill him because of her, and so she was brought without trial in the night and thrown in the gaol and forgotten. For one year she did not know if I was living. She hungered, she grew ill and her feet swelled. They had called for the surgeon of that place for her. Farley his name was, a man big in the stomach. He came there sometimes and ate with the captain. I saw him. He passed the gates of our gaol with a cloth over his mouth. The guards took Blath to him. They laid her on a table there and he looked at her feet and he cut them then.'

The wind came up from the sea and was bitter at their eyes and lips.

'He bled her to release the swelling. They told me he swayed with the wine of his dinner. He cut too forcefully and severed the backs of her heels.'

Tomas cupped his hands before his face and bit on his two thumbs. He stayed like that until his voice was steadied.

'When I saw her, she could no longer walk. She had to drag herself on the ground.

'"The fool," she called me. "There's my fool for love." Those were her words. And she lay in against me and the others stepped away and left us so in that corner of the gaol where the light sometimes fell.

'She made me well. I wish with all my might I could have made her so, too. But Farley had destroyed her. She was in and out of fevers then, agues, her blood froze. Sometimes her teeth chattered so that I wedged my fingers in her mouth to hold her jaw. She recovered a day, then fell hysterical the next and kicked at night-robbers she saw coming in dreams to cut off her feet. I thought to myself she would die there. I thought, she will die if she does not get outside this place again. And I thought of escape. As she could not walk, I carried her around the great room of our gaol on my back. I made myself strong. In the dark I dreamed of every way to get out of there. The walls were thick stone. The barred window was high and even if the bars were gone she could not climb to it. My mind knotted like a cord with it. I thought all the day and every day and still could not think of a way to get her out of there. I spoke with others who were there. Many were not guilty or their crimes were small. Some had come from the petty sessions in Ennis where they said the gaol was three times filled and the stench of shit and fever hung like a brown cloud. There was a father and son who had been convicted of killing a bullock out of hunger. They were being taken to Dublin and sent from there by ship to Australia.

'We lived four months on rye bread and water. Then the bread itself was rationed. We were given half of what we had been getting. We were told no reason. Some of the men grew wild and angry. Hunger made them fierce. Then, when the guards came to take a Mrs Doherty who had died, the prisoners rushed at them. In that,' Tomas said, and clicked his fingers, 'the guards' necks were broken. Then we were all pushing forward like a wave and I lifted Blath and put her on my back and we raced forward down the stone hall and one of the men had the guards' keys and opened the great gates and pistols were fired behind us. Some fell. I did not look back. We made the wall. The daylight was soft to us and the air fresh and we were dizzy with it. We had forgotten what air smelled like. But we pushed on. Then the outer gates were opened and we were pouring out of there with the guards following. There were more shots and calls and screams. But I ran on and Blath crouched low on my back, like a jockey, and many were recaptured. There were. But we were a great crowd and they could not take all of us and we scattered like insects do from beneath a lifted stone. I made it to the river and we stayed there among the bushes until dark.

'In the night I carried her away. I thought of you, Teige. I thought Teigey thinks I am dead now. I must find him. But Blath could not travel far and we were slow and had no food. The days passed us by. I could not go even to see if you were there. I sent prayers for you. I came on the workings then where the men were put to making the roads and I took work there so as to have food. We slept in a cabin where the thatch was partial. I made the road above Newmarket, lifting stones and breaking more of them. Then I thought, Teige is not there any more. He is gone from there. You will never find him. Stay here now and do this work and she might recover. I thought God might smile on me. And when that road was built there was another. And another. And we lived that way and had enough to keep death away. Until a week or so ago. Then the work was stopped and we were sent away. The hungry winter was over, the poor harvest of last year would not happen again, they said to us. Go back to your farms. And in the cabin where we were I looked at Blath and she was coughing a thick clotted stuff and I said to her, "Now maybe we should go to the sea."

' "The sea?" she said, "my sweet fool."

' "My father had wanted it long ago," I said to her, "and many say the air there cures the lungs." I did not tell her I wanted to be sure that you were gone from there, Teige. I did not tell her I was afraid that she would die.

' "The sea," she said. "I have never seen the sea. Let's go there."

'And so we left and were on this road where you found us.'

He finished his tale and his father and his youngest brother sat hunched beside him. It was dark. The sky was immense with constellations and they glittered above them like things new. None of them spoke further. They looked away at the stars and past the stars. Down at the end of the fields the sea turned softly, like a restless spirit come home at last.

11

The morning of the next day the Foleys left and crossed the narrow peninsula of the County Clare from the coast of the Atlantic to the estuary of the Shannon river. Blath travelled on the cart between the two girls and lay wrapped in blankets. The road was not smooth and they journeyed slowly now, conscious of each jarring motion from pothole and stone. With the presence of the ailing woman the young girls seemed to find new connection to the world. She was not their mother, but she re-sparked within them some filial response that had seemed perished. To soften the road they took her head upon their laps in turns. Then, on the road beyond Moyasta where the estuary appeared in mud and sand, they began without announcement to sing her a song. It was a slow air and might have seemed more mournful if not for the sweetness of the girls' voices which Teige and his father heard with some astonishment. They slowed the pony even more then and travelled rapt and lost in that music and their own meditations and dreams. When the air ended the girls sang another. Rooks in the flat fields seemed to quieten. Beyond the hedgerows a few thin cattle waited for drovers and fodder and hung their heads once more when the Foleys were nothing but that passing song on the breeze. And so they went on, like a caravan of exhausted minstrels in motley browns and greys; Francis, Teige and Tomas all walking ahead and trying each in their own way to imagine a future that might repair the past.

They arrived in the market town of Kilrush in the failing

light. There had been a horse fair and the streets were filled with its aftermath. Boys moved about with sticks and wore the air of men. Women disassembled wooden stalls on wheels and cried out at cats, dogs and children. A pony and trap came with speed and the flickering of a long whip as a youth of fifteen made a show of recklessness and skill and galloped wildly past. Boys yahooed and ran after him. Some shabby genteel men in ornate waistcoats and ragged jackets posed like men deserving of their idleness and studied the crowd. Others, beggars of all description, moved in broken file with hands out offering prayers for pennies or food. Those who had abandoned even this slumped by the roadside as the sun went down.

Francis Foley walked the pony and cart through them all. He walked with his head erect and his nostrils drawing hard on the air as if to bolster a thin faith. It was over three years since he had left the monk. It was three years since he had seen the map with the island sketched upon it, and in that time he had often wondered if he had imagined it, or if it had been a ruse of the holy man's to get him to leave the telescope. He wondered if the monk was dead. There were a dozen elements of chance spinning like glass balls in his mind. He shook his head at them. He realized suddenly the full weight of the hope that pressed upon this moment. Here was to be their destination at last. Here was to be that home for which he had set out so long ago and in so doing all but destroyed the family for whom he wished it. He walked down the streets of Kilrush to see if the future existed. He screwed his eyes tight and opened them again and as he turned down Francis Street he kept his eyes low on his opened and broken boots. He watched them take each step of the road. He watched how they swung up into the air and fell again in that mindless way and how the soles flapped and the sores on his shins showed. He did not look up. He walked down toward the banks of the river. The girls had stopped singing. His sons did not speak. If the island were not there he would will it into existence. He would rent the skies and call down new creation. He paced more slowly. He turned and brought them along by the shoreline. He let go the reins of the pony and Teige took them. The old man did not look up. He drew in the smell of that river that he knew now better than all the smells of his lifetime. The road beneath his feet turned to mud and sand and at last he stopped. His head was bowed as before God.

'Tell me what you see,' he said.

The heaving of his breath and a little river breeze made uncertain his words.

'Tell me what you can see, boys,' he said again.

They looked. The dog came from the cart and stood at their feet.

'There is an island,' Teige told his father, 'there is a green island.'

12

They sailed to that island the next morning in a narrow canoe-like boat that was made of canvas and coated in pitch. The boatman was a thin fellow with light gait who rode the rise and fall of the waves like a cork and kept his eyes on the horizon as though it were the drawn limit of the world. Blath had to be carried on, and her boarding in the bobbing waters by the little jetty was itself an adventure. The two young girls had never been on the sea. When they understood what was to happen they shook like paper dolls in the breeze and had to be cajoled and lifted by the brothers during which they came more vividly alive and boarded the boat squealing and wriggling and kicking. It was only when they were aboard and the dog jumped to join them that they calmed and looked about and marvelled at the water over the side. Francis Foley had bartered with the boatman and left him the pony and cart until such time as the old man could pay for the ferrying and reclaim what was theirs. The boatman was not much inclined to conversation. He shook his head at things he said only to himself. There were fragments muttered, disagreements, but to those listening there were only bits of language, phrases clipped short and left like the scissored lines of disparate letters.

'Iniscathaig? Scattery?' he had said and nodded. Then, as he stood back and watched them lift Blath aboard, he had added, 'Not that I believe it . . . Oh no. Ha! Blessings and curses says he and that's that . . . Saint Senan himself never and . . .' He stopped abruptly then and said no more and they were no more enlightened as he dipped oars and pushed off.

So, in one canoe then, with Teige looking backward at where the white pony was tethered on the dock, they sailed out into the swift current of the river. What had seemed flat slow murky water from the land soon became a slapping tide where the sea met the Shannon. They tossed upon it like a thing of little substance and the two brothers thought of the last time that they had seen that river with their father. Francis himself was standing in the bow. He knew that he was a man who would not drown. The day was cold and a wind cut across them as they pitched forward. For a time the island seemed to get no closer though the boatman worked hard with his oars and kept his eyes fixed on the destination ahead. Still the island lingered there before them. It appeared for a time as though the current was uncrossable, that though they laboured they would never arrive and were held there in mid-water in a vision at once tantalizing and purgatorial. The canoe lay low in the river. Water splashed and wet the girls and they cried out with glee and Blath held her arms around them. The boatman talked words to the fishes that sped beneath them and rowed on. Beyond the island the coastline of the County Kerry seemed like another country. None of them considered it, so bound were they now on this small green place that Francis Foley had dreamed. Then, as though they had passed through an invisible portal in the tide, suddenly they were near enough to see the gulls walking on the pebbles of the shore.

Francis cried out. He cried out and waved his arms and was in danger of falling overboard. His sons did not know what to do. Tomas shouted to him but the old man kept it up and the girls shouted then too and the gulls rose off the shore and wheeled and screamed and beat their wings in the sky above them. Francis shouted out a long wordless sound of no language that was greeting and announcement and victory. Then to the astonishment of all he stepped out of the boat and made as though he could walk on the surface of the water.

Tomas reached forward to save him, but was too late.

He stepped, but was only up to his waist in the water, for they were in the shallows now. And then Francis walked up ahead of them out of the sea and was in his own mind a fabled discoverer arriving on shores untrammelled by the history of bitterness and betrayal that was his country's. He walked up upon the pebbles and slowly turned around to look at those coming in the boat. He waded out to meet them and carried Blath in his arms. Teige and Tomas took one of the girls each upon their backs and went back again for the small bundles of their things. By the time they had laid the last of them on the coarse sand the boatman had already turned the canoe and was rowing back toward the town.

They stood with slow comprehension. They had at last arrived at the place where they could live in safety and peace, and as this realization dawned Teige looked at Tomas and then smiled and laughed and his brother laughed too, and the young girls ran about and skipped on the sand.

Then the old monk appeared.

He was there before any of them had seen him coming and seemed to have dropped from the sky. He did not look a day older than the last time Francis had seen him. He wore his brown cassock and his hands were concealed where they held each other inside the sleeves. In the moments when Francis first saw him he thought the monk an apparition of his own conjuring. He stared at the monk and said nothing. Then he looked at the others to see that they too saw him. He felt lighthearted with their celebrations. His long body shivered without sensation of cold. The monk's eyes were upon his and seemed of a piercing blue. His bare head was hairless and what grew at the sides of his temples was grey. When he spoke his voice was a warm deep honey.

'Here you are at last,' the monk said.

The sound of his words made him real. Francis's mouth was agape.

'Yes, I can speak to you here. I knew you would come but I did not think it would take so long.' The monk smiled and came forward among them and his hands appeared. 'These are your family,' he said, arriving before the astonished old man and holding out his hand to him in welcome. 'I am very pleased to see you at last.' He stood smaller than all but the girls, and reached and took the hand of the man in his and shook it firmly. 'Welcome,' he said to Francis, 'you are all very welcome.'

The brothers stood with the girls where Blath lay supported against a rock on the shore. They were speechless. The small waves lapped and dragged some pebbles back and forth in watery dance. Gulls arced overhead.

'Come,' the monk said then. 'Let me help you. The place is not very much, but it is dry.'

And he gestured with his hand the way forward and when they did not move he motioned again and led them himself up from the shoreline and along a track in the grass. For a small and older man he was nimble on his feet and sprang forward at times like one hurrying to show a rainbow. And the Foleys followed him, the girls skipping in the windy exposure of the sloping island, Tomas carrying as best he could the woman on his back and Teige and his father loping behind. Happiness lit their faces. They passed up across the island taking the green track and startling hares that darted and zigzagged away. The whole of the island could be seen then and the Shannon waters about it now grey now blue as the sun came and went in high scudding cloud. The way took them through a stile in a stone wall, past tangles of hedgerow and briar and entwined woodbine in early leaf and led them to a tall round tower of stone. Beside it were other small buildings, too.

'There were seven churches here,' the monk said cheerily

over his shoulder as he strode on. 'This is the place of Saint Senan,' he called out, 'it is an ancient site, from before the days of the Vikings,' he added. 'Now, here. In here.'

They entered into the shadows of the stone building of one room where a table and stools stood. In the corner lay a bed of straw.

'It need only be the beginning,' the monk said. The Foleys stood with slow comprehension. They looked at the stools as if to see the figures of themselves sitting there but it lay beyond their imagining. The monk allowed them their bewilderment, but added, 'There are many stones, there can be other houses. And here, come, look.' He stepped outside again and this time Francis was near to him and the monk pulled on the old man's ragged sleeve slightly and led him in through the doorway of the tower as the others crowded behind like visitors to the House of Miracles.

And there in the centre, all gleam and polish and impossible perfection, stood the stolen telescope.

Three

I

And so in the story of our family is explained how the Foleys
came to live on the island called Scattery in the estuary of the
Shannon river. Sometimes the story goes no further. Sometimes
you are left to surmise, to consider how these people became
yours, how your great-grandfather moved out of the stuff of
fable and how the threads of the story unwound and brought
it across the Atlantic Ocean. But if the teller is an old man,
maybe sitting in a diner in Mount Kisco, New York, or speaking
quietly in a corner of a living room when the relations are
gathered after a funeral, the story spins seamlessly on and those
Foleys do not fade into the dark.

Within twelve hours the monk was gone. By some secret
pre-arrangement the boatman came back and the holy man
sailed from the island when all were sleeping in the small light
of the dawn. He left without explanation or farewell. He did
not tell them why he had come there, or why left. He did not
narrate how he had been waiting alone for years on the island
and how he had reasoned it a kind of penance between God
and himself for sins of avarice and covetousness. He did not tell
how his sojourn was a kind of exile from the holy island further
up the river, and that the appearance of Francis Foley there was
a sign from above that he was forgiven and could return home.
All of this the Foleys would only gradually discover in time
from the stories told of the monk in the town of Kilrush.
There, in time, they would learn of his arrival with the telescope
and his taking the confession of the landlord McKean and how

he had bargained with him some portion of salvation for the rights to the island fields that were, after all, Saint Senan's. They would hear of this and other stories and in time all the stories would mingle and join tales of the monk's cures and other miracles and they would come to think of him as a figure fallen from the skies. He would take on the same unreality and magic as had the saint himself and become like the whispering wind in the rushes.

In the dawn when they woke he was gone. Francis stooped out of the low door in the stone house and knew it. He did not need to walk down to the shore. He stood in the light drizzle with the birds of April flitting around him. He shielded his eyes from a brightness that was new to him, for the island had its own light and lay softly sometimes in gleaming opalescence. The stillness was palpable. The simplicity of light and grass and birds and falling drizzle was all there was. And in that landscape the innocence of the world was recaptured for him and was a thing of stone and earth and water. It was the first time in a thousand mornings that Francis Foley did not feel the need to move onward. He stood and did nothing at all. He felt himself an old man and felt the regret and loss that he had caused and endured on his way to that moment wash through him like the tide beyond. He breathed the air of the island as if each breath were parcelled and gifted to him and might not long continue. He stood at the wall and opened his fingers upon it, the stones cold and damp. Briefly he thought to say a prayer but did not. His sons were still sleeping. He watched over the river and the fields for a long time and in that time saw that there was a white swan that seemed to linger there paddling by the foreshore.

Later, when the drizzle had passed and the sky was creased in folds of light from under long sleeves of cloud, Teige and Tomas woke to the sound of metal hitting stone. When they went outside they saw their father digging the monk's little garden. He turned over the ground with such ease it seemed ground of no weight at all. Black furrows were opened in straight lines as though drawn from above. He worked and did not look up. Rooks rose and alighted there and the smaller birds came and went. The dog lay in the freshened earth and watched its new master. Tomas and Teige readied another of the cabins fit for living. They found a low stone cabin where hay and potatoes and cabbages and onions were stored, and another that may have been a stable in ages gone. They made a dry bed there, raised on timbers and facing the door. Outside it, where the wall faced south across the river, Tomas built a seat roughly hewn with the monk's axe, and in the afternoon he carried Blath there wrapped in a blanket and she sat in the thin sunlight and looked out. She was weak and weighed less than a figure of sticks, but she smiled at him and called him her fool. Deirdre and Maeve were all times at her side. They brought her drinks of cool water from the well they had found. They combed her hair with their fingers and smoothed and brushed out her blanket as though it was some fairy raiment. In turn she seemed to have upon them an effect of release, for by the end of that day their tongues were freed and they spoke and then chattered and sang.

So they began. Within two days they had begun to set the patterns of their life on that island. In one of the buildings Tomas had found the monk's fishing pole and line and went up to the southern shore and pulled a silvered salmon from the river. They cooked it over an open fire and the smells of the fish climbed the air. They set seed potatoes, the young girls bending in the furrows and pushing them into the ground and the brothers forking upon them the mulch of seaweed and sand and earth. Daily Teige and Tomas woke in the first thin wafer of light and like the boys of fairy-tales hunted in the dawn fields for hares. They teased and chased and ran and tripped over burrows and tumbled and sighted hares running. At such times the brothers revisited some vanished or unlived part of their lives. The days of May climbed over them. There were high skies of blue with blown cloud. In her seat by the front wall Blath coughed less often and, though her cheeks were strangely flushed with circles of red, in the evenings when Tomas came to her they could hear her laughter for the first time. He made her laugh. It was as though the evidence of his love for her was continually surprising. As she recovered a frail health her language grew more robust. She strung curses and other assorted phrases of colour together for the crows that fringed the garden plot. The two girls delighted in these and giggled and skipped about chanting in sing-song the foul language while the birds lifted in the air. And perhaps it was by this same magic, the effect of words spoken to them like a spell, that soon there came more and more birds, crows, magpies, thrushes, starlings and tits, cormorants, oyster-catchers and such. And these flocked and flew over the island and darted and soared above the opened brown apron of ground and chorused in a nexus of trilling punctuated only by the flat-accented tones of gaily cried Limerick curses.

For his own part, in those early days, Francis Foley lived like a monk, devoted to the making of their home. When the garden was dug, he turned to the building of a cottage. He walked the island and considered all possible sites then settled on a ridge of ground on the northern shore near where the boatman had landed and where they could see the town of Kilrush across the river. One week he made a wooden barrow with rough wheels. The next he was carting stones in it. He did not tell his sons what he was doing, he did not ask for their help. He simply went ahead like one blinded by vision and they watched him and understood and were then there at his side. They made a cottage of dry-stone walls three feet thick. The flesh of their hands dried and hardened in that handling. Their shoulders broadened, their arms hung out further to the side so that even when free of stones the three Foleys seemed to bear burdens. The cottage rose off the ground slowly. Canoes carrying turf sailed past on the way to Limerick. Ferry boats and cargo ships trafficked in the estuary, but to them all Francis turned his back. He did not want to deal with the outside world and for a time was able to ignore it. Then one afternoon when they were setting a flagstone as a lintel above the room door the thin boatman appeared before them.

'Indeed, yes, says he,' he said, and moved from side to side on his narrow legs as though sailing the floor.

'God bless you,' Tomas said to him after waiting for his father to speak.

'Indeed and yes.' He looked at the walls they had made and grinned a slanted grin. He seemed to have nothing more to say.

'What news have you?' Tomas asked him.

The boatman scratched. His head was lumpish like a turnip and grizzled in patches of thin beard like scurf. His eyes rolled about in the motionlessness of the building. 'No, but,' he said. 'Only that, and not that . . . devil a care I give, but . . .'

'Yes?'

'I brought the pony.'

Teige dropped the stone he was holding and was out the doorway then before them. He ran down to the shore to where the horse was tethered to a large lump of wood. She had swum across the river behind the boat on a long line and her mane was matted and her flanks dripping. As Teige ran, the pony sensed that it was he and stirred and hoofed at the sand and turned about. He freed her in a moment and she whinnied and was skittish and puzzled and briefly did not realize that she was no longer tied. He let her have the scent of him and ran his hand firmly along the side of her and then, while the others had come out to see, Teige swung himself on to her back. The motion of it was so fluid and easy it seemed almost as if some inverse gravity was in operation. He held on to her mane and leaned down and seemed to the others to speak soft commands then, for without an apparent action of his heels or thighs, the pony took off. She galloped down the small rim of sand and then up across the bank and on to the uneven green of the low field there, and then pony and rider were gone off away around the grassy domain of the island. The others watched without a word until they were gone. The boatman swayed.

'Teige can ride her, eh?' Tomas said.

His father nodded and stood there and looked at the horizon empty now.

'We need more horses,' he said then.

The boatman did not seem to understand that the words were addressed to him. He was still looking at the place where Teige had ridden away.

'We need other things, too,' Francis said. 'Tools, seeds. We can have cattle here in time.' He turned to face the fellow and the man's eyes rolled and slipped from side to side like glass balls upon a tide. 'We have no money.'

The boatman scratched himself hard.

'Ask if there is one who needs horses broken,' the old man said to him. 'Teige can tame anything and make it run fast as wind. You have seen it. That pony was wild, now she would jump the cliffs for him. He can do it. If there is one who wants a horse for a race tell them Teige Foley is over on the island. Will you do that?'

The man shook himself as though bestirring flies.

'If that, not that...' he muttered with low chin, 'but Clancy, Clancy, Clancy there might says he and...' He stopped, unwound or overwound.

A pause grew.

'And?'

The man trembled as if some charge passed through him, then he said: 'I will.'

Evenings then, when the work was over and their arms ached and their shoulders were stretched and curved and tight with the effort of moving stones, Teige took the pony and rode her off about the island alone. He rode as the light fell into the water and a smudge of smoke hung above the town across the river, crepuscular and dim with the appearance of a thing tarnished. He rode in no particular direction, trotting the pony along the shore or out across the fields they had not named yet. He rode as the stars came out in the heavens above him and glittered and made stars in the water and silvered the grass and made soft silken silhouettes of the rabbits that stood erect in surprise. The pony had become almost too small for him, but she bore him nonetheless with ease and could stride out charging into the half-light, the thrumming of her hoofs the only sound. They travelled back and forth over that small territory. Teige stopped her sometimes on the far shore and watched the hills of Kerry slip into the folds of the dark. Other times he turned her into the shelter of a hedgerow and she stood amidst the sweet breezes of blackberry blossom and lifted her head and her breath hawed and her sides steamed like one becoming vapour. And in that solitude and stillness, Teige studied the sky and thought of all that was and had been. He thought of his brothers gone and wondered in the vastness of space where. He thought of Finbar and his girl from the sea, how he had become almost a gypsy before Teige's eyes. He thought too of Finan, who was more mysterious and dark and whose vanishing seemed a part of his character or a thing foreordained. To each he sent mute wordless missives until the regret tangled in his chest and he had to dismount and squat down in the grass as though about to void himself. He lay then in the May night.

And he thought of his mother.

He had tried to bury her several times now. He had been caught too often by the suddenness of realization that she was gone. It always stole up on him. Time and again he had been on the road or engaged in some work and had stopped briefly to draw breath and then, suddenly, he would think of her and swiftly his spirit would collapse in his chest like a bird made of paper. He would feel the crush of it and gasp. It was as if each time then she died anew, as if by some trick of time and memory she had come alive again and was not with him but only elsewhere and their meeting again was not far distant. She grew near in his mind. The scent of her was in his nostrils. The warmth of her where his head had lain came over him. He heard her tell him stories beneath a darkening summer sky. He asked her always of Virgo, and as she spoke her eyes were proud and deep and lovely. Virgo lies on her back with her feet toward the east, she told him. There are stars scattered over her shoulders like jewels, she said.

At last he had tried to build stone walls of coldness about his heart. He had said to himself out loud 'she's gone, she's dead, you'll not see her again'. He had said it in darkness and light, in wind and rain through all seasons. He had tried to consider it as a fact like winter and so move beyond the continuance of this rhythm of grief. He had chastised himself for a soft fool and cursed like his elder brother and told himself not to think of her again.

But she was still there.

He lay in the cool damp of the night grass and the pony stood attentive beside him. The stars swung westward and were like a map of man's yearning. When at last Teige rose the pony whinnied. She nodded her head thrice. He slipped up on to her and rode slowly back in a wide circle toward the round tower and the stone cabins where the others were sleeping. When he reached them, he dismounted and fetched a bucket of water for the pony and let her into the small paddock where he bid her goodnight. Then, as he turned back to the little cluster of buildings behind him, he saw an eye of light glistening from the doorway of the tower. He stopped and waited. The eye moved and he saw the starlight play off it once again. Then he knew that it was his father, and that while the others were sleeping, through the passing of time and while he should have been resting, Francis Foley was engaged in the one activity that to him made clear sense of the world. He was looking at the stars through the telescope and seeing in the heavens revealed, behind the myriad and seeming chaos of those specks of light, a shape full of meaning.

Teige watched a few minutes as the glass eye moved and reflected the sky. Then he slipped into the cabin and lay to sleep.

Some days later the boatman returned and brought the news that Clancy did indeed have horses for breaking. He took Teige with him and rowed back across the river and Tomas and his father stood upon the top of the wall of the cottage they were building and watched. The narrow black boat slipped away in soft rain and the men fell back to their work wordless and somehow burdened with apprehension. That river had already run so through the family's life that they did not trust Teige's crossing would lead to happiness. Still, Francis had decided he had to go. Gulls flew like ragged pieces of old cloth in the rainy sky. Then it poured down and screened the country from view and was as if some portion of the known world had been erased. The two Foleys stayed working, lifting stones up the narrow ladder while the mud floors of the cottage shell puddled below them.

When he reached Kilrush, Teige too felt the air of apprehension. Whether he had brought it with him or it existed like a thing tangible in the very atmosphere, he could not say. The town was more tired and lifeless than when he was last there. The rain stopped. Those in the streets had a worn and ragged deportment. Wan faces turned to watch him with eyes enlarged and red-rimmed. They were like heads that floated. A beggar boy of no more than ten scurried over to him. He had been the first of a small assemblage to spot Teige and came to him ahead of the others who even then began to drift over.

'A penny, God bless you. A penny.'

The boy's face was browned and stained about the mouth. His nostrils were yellow-crusted.

'I have no money,' Teige said, and tried to walk past him, but the boy, accustomed to first refusals, trotted alongside begging. By now the others, a mixture of young and old in shawls, wraps, tattered once-scarlet petticoats, and apparel that had no name but made its owner resemble a bundle on legs, had come around him. There was a blind woman without legs seated in a small cart, a man wheeling her. A flurry of prayers sounded. The beggars cried out a litany of ailments and Teige felt his jacket tugged.

'I have nothing,' he said more loudly, still trying to move ahead of them. But the beggars were hardened to such and moved as in a promenade performance, their hands wavering and clutching, their brows furrowed and the urgency of their prayers and promises growing with each step. The faces floated there before him until at last Teige tried to shake himself free and in so doing stepped out of his jacket and left them holding it as he hurried up the street.

Clancy, as it transpired, was not the owner of the horses to be broken. They belonged to one of the landlord Vandeleurs. Clancy was a man in their employ, a short round fellow with whiskers and broad curving eyebrows. When Teige met him in the store on Francis Street where the boatman had told him to go, Clancy spat on the ground and asked him if it was true he could make any horse run.

'Every horse can run without my making it,' Teige said.

Clancy nodded and narrowed his eyes in appreciation of the point and spat again.

'Run races,' he said and widened his gait and rocked slightly back on his heels.

'Not all,' Teige told him. 'Some horses are not for races, but I can pick the ones that are.'

'Fair enough answer,' Clancy said. 'Come on so.'

They left there and boarded a wagon that had been laid

with feeding stuffs and sacks of flour and oats and such. Teige had never seen such supplies bought. When he sat up on the seatboard the beggars were clustered about and looked at him like one who had betrayed. The boy was wearing Teige's jacket. The blind woman, small and crooked in her cart, was wearing the sleeves. Clancy whistled and the wagon moved away. They travelled down to the end of the town and out on the road a ways until they came to the gates of the domain and turned in there and journeyed up the avenue past the tall trees where cool green shadows covered the way. So long was the avenue the house was not to be seen. The trees thickened to wood on either side of them. Midges and flies speckled the sky and buzzed and were like patches of imperfect air as they rose from under the branches in the warmth after rain. Clancy whistled a sorrowful tune. The slow notes hung, a melancholy drapery in that verdant hush. They moved on.

'Nearly there,' Clancy said without looking at him and he clicked his tongue and quickened the wagon. The woods were behind them then and the fields that opened on either side were lush and green and fenced with timber posts. They were the smoothest fields that Teige had seen and might have been drawn by a child and imagined into creation. The first of them held no animals at all, just a glossy sward moving in the small breeze. But before they had passed it, Teige could sense the nearness of horses. Then as they wheeled about on a long curve of that road he saw them, thirty or so mares and new foals and two- and three-year-olds, some standing, some grazing, some running to meet the breeze. The wagon slowed. Its horses whinnied and shook their heads in the harness and there was an answering of sorts in the field.

'Well,' Clancy said, 'that's about half of 'em.'

'Half?'

'He's more money than brains,' he said and spat forward and studied the spittle in flight. 'You think you can make something of 'em? It's eight pence a day.'

Teige climbed down. He moved very slowly under Clancy's gaze and went over the fence and entered the field. The horses that were standing there lifted their heads high and raised their tails and then broke into sudden speed like things shocked. They went off away down the field bringing others with them, including a number of the thin-legged foals that kicked two-footed at intervals at the air behind them. Teige watched them all and walked calmly out into the centre of the field. He had about him a kind of ease that was broadcast by some means not known by science to the animals there. It was always so. It was a thing that happened. He came into the company of animals and felt at once a kind of connection. It was something with which he was already familiar, this serene and clear-sighted empathy, and he did not have to try to do anything, only wait for the animals to feel it. He stood and watched the horses that had arrived at the far end of the field as they trotted in the tightened space and turned about and cut backwards across each other, cutting up the grass sod that was softened by rain. They trafficked there for moments, hot and blowing and swinging about, some rearing, some nipping, others, mares, looking for their foals. Then, a black colt with a white blaze on its face spun from the others and led them like a charge back up the field. Teige stood still as they came. He was smiling at them and was for a moment like one within a tide, islanded there by horses of all description, saying the sounds he said in greeting and holding out his hands waist-high as if proffering invisible oats.

Clancy watched him another few moments and then, satisfied that the fellow was indeed what the boatman had described, he clucked his tongue and snapped the reins and took the wagon on up to the stables. Teige stayed in the field with the horses all that morning. Clancy sent a youth with ropes and collars and a long-tailed whip but none of these did Teige want. He walked back and forth among the horses and ponies there. The day moved the rainclouds aside and the sky was then clear and blue overhead. In time the horses grew accustomed to the man in their midst and returned to grazing, standing with long necks craned and swishing their tails at the population of flies. Teige studied each of them. There were many not in good form. He saw the full range of temperament and kind, those already ailing in some manner, those whose hindquarters were stiffened, those in the early stages of colic who turned about and looked at their stomach and made small jabbing kicks at it. There were some with red worm, round worm, whip worm, early forms of spavin and wind galls. Teige did not know the names of all such but recognized in the horses the discomfort of their condition and from this intuited a remedy. By midday the youth who had brought him the ropes returned with warm potatoes in a cloth and a jug of buttermilk. He asked Teige how he was progressing and Teige told him that many of the horses were poor enough and asked how it was that such a wealthy man as Vandeleur had not better stock.

'' Tis Clancy buys 'em,' the fellow said. ' 'Tis he has promised there'll be racers amongst 'em. There's another forty in the fields beyond.'

The youth left then and Teige returned to the slow work of the afternoon. Still he did not take the ropes into the field, but went out through the animals, his fingers greasy from the buttered potatoes. He looked for the black colt and moved in circumambient fashion toward him. The colt's eye caught him at once and flicked his ears back and forth thrice. His jaw stopped. Teige took another few steps. The colt retained the stance he held and was for moments statuesque and posed and serene. The other horses raised their heads and looked and looked down again. Teige moved his buttered fingers together. He was now five paces from the colt. He could see a nerve quiver in its neck and how the sleek black sheen of its flanks showed condition. Slowly he moved his hand out. He let the scent of the butter travel to the horse and watched for the slightest reaction. But there was none. The horse was planted.

Teige took another step and said very softly the Irish word for 'come'.

'Chugainn!'

And within the smallest particle of time, before the words had finished sounding and travelled with the scent of butter across the space between the man and the animal, the colt bolted. He reared and spun and blew and charged and knocked Teige to the ground all in one moment and was gone off down the field, black mane waving and hind hoofs kicking backward in short wild bucks. When Teige began to get up he heard the sound of laughter like tinkling glass. There by the side of the fence were two young women walking the avenue. They looked away from him when he stood up and one of them held her fingers to her mouth while the other nudged her. They did not move on. Their mirth carried and flew about like an exotic bird. They were ladies of the house and wore long dresses, one green, one blue. The girl in the green dress had hair of a light gold that fell about her shoulders. She could not stop herself laughing. Her friend elbowed her time and again but it was as if this action merely released more of the birds of glee and they crossed that field and flickered about Teige as he stood and pressed a hand on the small of his back. The friend took a glance sideways over her shoulder to see him and quickly turned back again and whispered something and then the girl in the green dress turned also and Teige saw her face for the first time. It was less than an instant. Then the friend was pulling on her arm and dragging her around and the two of them were off away in quick steps up the avenue.

The afternoon grew cooler then. Teige worked with the horses with little luck, walking and standing and talking to them. He did not get close to the colt again all that long day. By the time the evening was beginning and there were small bats flying in the air Clancy returned and told him to come with him to the place where he could stay. It was a stone building with a strong roof in a clean courtyard. The coach horses were stabled there and the hunters for the manor house. The youth who was called Pyle came and brought him food and stood by while he ate and then took the bowl away again. Stillness settled over the place then. The May night was calm and mild and held the tangled smells of woodsmoke and horses and the sweetness of the gorse blooming. Teige lay on straw bedding and thought of those on the island. He thought of his father watching the sky as if hunting there traces of the lost portion of his family. He thought of where in the world Finan and Finbar might be and if he would see them again. But from each of these considerations his mind wandered. He stared upward at the blackness that was unstarred. And it was then as if a map had been redrawn and he no longer possessed with surety the coordinates, for he drifted from all things in that sleepless state and time after time returned only to the image of the laughing girl.

The following morning he was up before the cock crew. When Clancy found him he was already in the field with the horses. Teige asked him what the horses were being fed and asked that he be allowed to change their diet. He pointed out some that needed special care and should be withdrawn to other pasture. All of this Clancy agreed to without dispute for he considered himself a judge of men and placed his legs apart and rocked on his heels with his hands on his hips and told Teige that whatever he asked would be done. He left him and Teige returned to the horses. Later Pyle arrived and they separated some and steered the lesser or ailing animals into the further paddock. For the rest of that morning Teige was alone with the remainder. Showers of drizzle came and went. The sky cleared and clouded and cleared again. The birds of that place were many and when the rain passed they chorused and flew and it seemed to Teige that he had never seen such a multitude. From the woods nearby they flickered and darted, thrush and sparrow and tit and robin. They sang full-throated. The song of the corncrake was there, too. And all such harmonies were intermingled in the air like threads of fine colours. Whether it was this or not, Teige progressed slowly with the horses that morning. He seemed to have lost some of his gift and was for the first time uncertain. He walked about the field in circles and held out his hands and spoke quietly but the horses, sensing something in his manner or spirit, shied. He grew impatient then and sometimes jogged futilely toward an animal that soon took off and left him there. He was so engaged when the ladies walked the avenue again. This time he saw them coming, for in truth some part of him had been watching all morning. He stopped his small running and the horses cantered away from him and turned at the far end of the field. The birds were everywhere. He watched the movement of the light-coloured dresses from the corner of his eye. He saw the golden hair. He saw that she was sauntering closer along the fence and felt himself foolish to be standing there in the empty part of the pasture with no horse near him. If he walked down toward the horses now he would be walking away from her. The two desires to stay and go twisted about inside him and he just stood there, the birds flying about him. Then he heard a small tinkle of laughter and there was some jostling and the crunch of the gravel pebbles and then the girl with brown hair called out to him:

'What are you doing there?'

Teige did not move.

'Hello? Oh, hello?'

Again the noise of whispers and urgings and some scuffling of pebbles, and Teige heard the girl say, 'Wait wait, he will.'

He turned around then. They were standing there, the girl with the brown hair looking directly at him, the other turned aside and studying the smallness of her white shoe.

'We were wondering,' the girl said. 'What are you doing?'

He thought to stay where he was and shout across to them. He thought it and decided on it and then was walking closer. There was a drift of perfume there. It hung like a silk. He came within it and stopped and tried to draw deeper than a shallow breath. He was looking past the girl who looked at him. He was looking at the girl now wearing a cream-coloured dress.

'Hello, do you understand? Maybe he can't understand. What . . . are . . . you . . .'

'I am training the horses,' Teige told her.

'You do understand. Well, that's what I said you were doing, but yesterday we saw you get knocked down and Elizabeth said you weren't, you couldn't be, because you're not supposed to get knocked down are you? But I said I do think he is training them, and Elizabeth said that she supposed it could be true and maybe he's just not very good at it.' She arched one eyebrow and her lips curved in a tightened smile.

''Tis true maybe,' Teige told her.

There was a pause of sunlight and birdsong. Then Elizabeth lifted her eyes to him and said, 'I didn't say that.'

'You did.'

'Come on.' Elizabeth pulled at the other's arm. 'Come on, Catherine, I am going back.'

'Wait, maybe he'll show us. Won't you show us? Go on, do some, we'll watch. Train them. You've to choose one for her, you know.'

'I'm going.' Elizabeth took steps away and Teige's eyes followed her and absorbed all that she was.

'Spoilsport,' Catherine said after her and then looked at Teige and laughed and skipped and ran and caught up with her and they were gone.

The rest of that day Teige managed even less with the horses. He moved toward them like one in a dream and they swept past. Sometimes in gathering desperation he ran, sprinting alongside, pumping with his fists and sucking and blowing the air through his teeth. Briefly he was a figure mythic and noble and swift, until the horses opened gait and were gone and he was left panting and slumped in the empty grass. That evening when he lay in the straw bed he watched the image of the woman his eyes had captured. She lingered before him a while as he stretched there with hands behind his head and the hushed darkness filled with the movement of the bats and the noises of the horses sleeping. Then he rose and went outside. The night sky was quickened with cloud. Light from a gibbous moon came and went. He walked barefoot across the courtyard and then out around by the short avenue that he knew led to the big house. When he saw it, all of its windows were dark. Two wolfhounds lay on the top of the steps to the front door. They raised their heads to look at him and Teige shushed at them and they lay down again. He stood there and studied the house and felt the feelings of his father years before standing in front of the house of the lord. He slipped around by the side touching the walls as he went. He arrived at the back of the house where in latter years an addition had been built to the kitchen and this he climbed until he was on the cold slates of its roof. He moved along it low and cat-like until he came to a window. With the tips of his fingers he slid it upward and watched the reflection of his face vanish as a thin curtain of muslin blew softly outward. He moved like a veil and then stepped quietly inside.

4

He was in a corridor. There was timber flooring and it creaked beneath his foot. He heard the noise travel and listened in its aftermath for any response. But there was none. He brought the second foot inside and stood there growing accustomed to the quiet, listening to hear the sounds of sleeping. He moved down the corridor. A pulse in his brain beat and he seemed to hear it along with another in his neck. He paused to still them and failed and moved on. He came to the first of the doors and pressed himself flatly against it, his ear and the palms of his two hands against the timber. Shut-eyed he listened. Then he moved further down the hallway to the next door. With each he did the same, but it was no use. He could not tell. He turned and arched his head back and leaned against the wall and his chest heaved. The moonlight shone on him. He waited. Then suddenly he turned and swivelled the porcelain knob in the door next to him. It made a small click. He held it tight and leaned in and smelled the strong powdered air of the room and saw in the rumpled bedclothes a large woman and a small man. Teige withdrew as silently as he had entered. He moved down the way to the next door. This time he squeezed the lock back and there was no click. The moment the door was only slightly ajar he knew it was hers. He knew, and stepped inside and closed the door behind him.

She was lying on her side. The bedclothes were white. Her right hand lay on the pillow beside her head. Teige stood there. He heard his own breathing and held it and wished it might have stayed so and he only a silent and invisible presence there, timeless, witness to this creature sleeping. The room stilled about him once more. When his pulse had steadied he took a step closer to the bed, and then another. He beheld her. He beheld the way her fair hair fell there and how her eyelashes quivered in sleep, how her lips were pursed. He studied the line of her nape, the delicacy of her ears. Such things. He did not move closer to touch her. He stayed there and the night passed on about him and the sleeping house rumbled sometimes and made airy noises and creaked with the traverse of ghosts and dreams. She moved in dreams of her own, too, and turned away from him and then back again, making small moans in her throat that Teige could not decipher as pleasure or pain. He matched the rhythm of his breathing with hers and when he had achieved this he closed his eyes, and was so, and found a kind of peace in that union.

Time sped on. The moon flew through the sky and dragged her stars and still Teige was there in Elizabeth's bedroom. He could not leave. He stood and was sentry to that beauty and could not have put in words his hopes or desire or told how long he might have stayed. Then she turned in the bed and her hair crossed her mouth and she brushed at it with the back of her hand and opened her eyes and saw him.

She did not cry out.

Teige raised his hands palm outward and made as if placing them gingerly to settle some disturbance in the air. Then he took a step backward, and then another. Without taking his eyes from her he reached behind him and felt for the handle of the door and twisted it and then turned quickly and was gone.

That morning Teige struggled once again with the horses. The day was soft with rain and the ladies did not come on their walk. Time was slow and stretched out and in the absence of the obscured sun seemed not to pass at all. Teige walked about and through the horses and spoke to them and waited, wondering if Elizabeth had told and he was to be summoned at any moment and ordered to leave. In his wet shirt his chest was tight, his eyes were glossed with intensity and glanced sidelong toward the avenue. Where was she? What was she thinking? The sleek flanks of the horses glistened in the rain, their hoofs making short sucking sounds where the ground was churned. The birds stayed occluded in the trees and their song from there seemed to Teige strangely despondent. The long day was like an ache. When the red-headed fellow Pyle came and brought him his food he told Teige that the men said the weather was an ill omen. There was no health in it.

'It is neither true rain nor real sun but lifeless drizzle they say. It is like fine netting, we need a storm to move it off us.'

Teige ate silently and felt the day press more firmly upon him. When the other had gone, he returned to the horses but in a short time realized that it was useless. He had no connection with them and at last hunkered down and sat in the middle of the field in the falling rain. Slowly, in the gradual passing of that afternoon, the horses began to move closer to him and it was as if he were a rock or a bush or a tree or any other part of their domain and they did not shy or move away. Soon they were all about him there and grazing at the grass that was by his side. He sat and a foal approached and then nipped at the shoulder of his shirt. The black colt with the white blaze was less familiar and stood off and sometimes pawed at the ground and blew. But Teige appeared indifferent to all and made no movement toward any of them. At some time he heard noise in the gravelled avenue and lifted his head and saw a coach and horses pass down that way and from the curtained window the face of Elizabeth's friend appeared and disappeared. The coach did not slow or stop and he could not tell how many were inside it. He watched until it was gone.

That night he awaited the darkness. It fell slowly, the light lingering. At last Teige rose and hastened as stealthily as he could past the wolfhounds to the kitchen. He climbed as before, this time slipping twice on the wet slates and pressing himself flat there for moments awaiting alarm. But none came and he made his way to the window and opened it and stepped again into the corridor, darker now without the moonlight. Where he stepped his feet printed wet on the floor. He dripped to her door and held his breath and screwed his eyes tight to squeeze the handle and twist and open it and all the time he was both fearful that she had gone away and expectant of her cry. The scent was the first thing to meet him. It arrived in his nostrils while the door was only slightly ajar and caused a quivering in his spine. The darkness of the room was deeper than the night before and at first he could make out nothing at all. He stood there and heard his breathing and again tried to quieten it and as he did he heard her move.

'Hello.' She spoke across the darkness. She did not seem surprised.

Teige took a step back to the door and they were still as shadows to each other as she spoke again.

'It's all right.'

A pause, in the stillness his breathing.

'I knew you would come again.'

He stood and tried to understand what he should do. Then he heard the match struck and saw it aflame and she was lighting a small waxen candle at her bedside. The amber light glowed and he saw her within it and saw the white linen nightdress she wore and how her hair fell loose on her shoulders to her breasts. She lay back on many pillows then and looked at him with her eyebrows arched.

'Well,' she said.

Teige had lost his tongue.

'You can sit down.' She pointed to a wooden chair near the bed.

But Teige did not stir.

'You can't just stand there,' she said. She moved and released an invigorating scent from the lavender pillow at her side.

'I wanted to see you,' he said at last.

'Yes?'

'Yes.'

She smiled. She smoothed the smooth quilt covering.

'What is your name?'

He didn't want to say. He didn't want to talk to her at all, but only to stand there and look at her and hear her voice and smell that scent.

'I can find out,' she said.

'It's Teige, Teige Foley.'

'Sit down, Teige.'

He did not move.

'You must do what I tell you. Sit down.'

So he sat then and placed his hands on his knees and lowered his eyes briefly from her and felt an obscure shame or guilt as though he was a thing unworthy or had brought her by deceptive means down to this earth.

'Tell me about the horses,' she said. 'Have you found one for me?'

He told her he had not and she told him he must, that she would want to go riding in the summer, that friends would come visiting and he could have horses ready for them, too. She drew her knees up under the quilt. Her face shone in the candlelight. She said she had been to town that day to buy a summer dress. She thought blue suited her but the shops were so dreadfully poor and not at all like the ones in Cork where she mostly lived.

And all that she said Teige listened to, not for its meaning but for the sound of her voice that was like a charm to him.

'You can look at me, you know,' she said. 'You can.'

And he did. He looked boldly at her eyes and her lips and the hollow of her neck and the curving line of her breasts and she turned her head slowly this way and that for his better admiration. And they stayed so for some hours, he seated in the chair and she lain out on the goosefeather pillows telling him things about her taste in flowers and dresses and friends and whatnot. The candle burned low. When at last she tired she told him that he must go now. He stood up.

'You can kiss my hand,' she said, 'before I sleep.'

She offered it in the air.

'My uncle will kill you if he finds you here, you know that,' she said as he approached.

'I know that.'

Teige reached and touched her fingers and balanced them a moment on his and then bent and kissed them.

'Goodnight,' she said, 'go on now. Go.'

She snuffed the candle.

'You can come again,' she said, and in the sudden darkness Teige turned and slipped away.

6

So it was that he visited her there in her bedroom every night after that. All the nights of May and into June he crossed the courtyard in the darkness and climbed on to the kitchen slates and across them to the window. The hounds no longer lifted their heads when he passed. The owls and bats that hooted and flew in the soft crêpe blackness of the night knew his shadow as did the yellow-eyed fox creeping furtively through the dark to sniff at the door of the hen house. To all such he was as familiar as a star and crossed the night with the same mystery and resolve.

By daylight Teige was strangely renewed. Though he had hardly slept at all, he worked among the horses with vigour and energy. Soon he had chosen for Elizabeth a white filly and coaxed her into handling and then lunging on a line. Other horses he managed also, and was to be seen riding some or walking them as Elizabeth and Catherine, who was her cousin, came for their daily exercise along the fence. They came now even in the drizzle that spoiled the weather all that early summer. They carried light parasols and twirled them on occasion in a manner that suggested mirth. At no time did Elizabeth show him any recognition. Sometimes she stopped and the ladies stood and studied and appraised his progress. Sometimes Catherine called out to Teige and waved for him to approach and the high clinking of her laughter carried out across the pasture, but he did not respond. He stayed closely engaged with the horses and whistled and whispered and gestured to the animals in ways he knew they understood, and then he drew one to him and caressed its flank and stroked and pulled its ears while all the time the ladies watched. Within a few weeks many of the horses were under his dominion. All those in his care improved steadily in form. The ones whose diet he oversaw lost the bulge of belly or beginnings of laminitis, colic and other ailments. Clancy came and stood by the fence a long time and scrutinized Teige working. Then he turned on his heel and went off and said nothing.

But Teige did not care. He had lost all care for the world as long as he knew that he could each night escape into the bedroom above the kitchen. When he opened her door it was like lifting some pressure from his heart. He sighed in relief. Sometimes she had the candle lit and was waiting. She was sitting upright and her hair was loose and her eyes fixed on the door as he entered. He came in and stood and she told him to sit down and he did. Every night it was the same. He did not presume and this she enjoyed, delaying sometimes her invitation and stroking some imaginary flaw in the quilt while he stood. He did not touch her. He sat on the wooden chair by her bedside.

'You think I am beautiful?' she asked him.

'Yes.'

'More beautiful than Catherine?'

'Yes.'

She smiled and made a small laugh and looked at him. She leaned a little closer and then wrinkled her small nose.

'You smell like horses,' she said.

And to that he answered nothing, and flushed and sat there entangled in the same feelings of shame and guilt and unworthiness whose source he did not understand.

And she was contrite then to see him so and looked across the candlelight at him and was moved.

'Promise me you won't do anything,' she said. 'Promise.'

He did, and she fixed her eyes on his and slowly drew down

the quilt over her knees until her feet were bare. Then she raised herself up and stood on the bed and her hair fell down and her scent assailed him, and slowly, looking at him all the time, she reached and found the buttons of the nightdress and one by one opened them. Then when the garment was fallen open she stood there on the bedclothes and raised her two hands and drew it back away from her on either side and it fell without noise to her feet. She stood. The candlelight made her skin lustrous, her eyes were glazed. She took her hands and placed them on her breasts and then moved them down along her body swaying them outward like wings.

'Well?' she said.

Teige looked at her.

'See, I'm not so terrible.'

She turned on the bed as on a podium and she let him study her from the back and take his time and absorb into imagination and memory the detail of that beauty.

'Now,' she said, 'am I terrible? Am I, Teige Foley?'

'No.'

'Is that all you can say?' She turned disappointed and lay down on her back on the bedclothes. Teige did not speak. His throat was too tight for words. If he freed his fingers from their grasp on his knees they would shake and waver. He sat. She lay there naked before him and spoke calmly of the flaws she found in her body. She said her legs were too short. She said she did not like her toes and held one foot in the air for his inspection. After a time they heard footsteps in the corridor outside and they hushed and listened and the room was tight with the beating of their hearts. When the footsteps had passed she told him he had better kiss her goodnight and she held out her hand. He stood then beside where she lay on the bed and he was twisted in torment and his lips trembled and dried.

'Goodnight, Teige,' she said.

And he kissed her hand and was gone.

The following night when he came to her she was already undressed. She was standing in the far corner of the room and held open over her breasts a fan of peacock feathers. The candle was placed on the ground.

'Who can this be?' she said and lowered her face in a pretence of shame. She moved across the room then and fluttered the fan and Teige caught anew the scent of her. 'Do you know how to dance, Teige Foley?' she asked him.

'No,' he said.

She stood right in front of him. 'You never say my name. You can, you know.'

He said nothing.

'Go on.'

'Elizabeth.' It was a whisper. Her face was next to his.

Then she stepped past him. 'That's a pity you don't dance. I was watching you at the horses and thinking what a fine dancer you might be.'

'I'm sorry.'

'Don't be silly.' She walked back down the room again and his eyes followed her. 'You're in love with me, aren't you?' For a moment he did not want to say. 'Well?' she asked him.

'Yes.'

And that seemed to please her and she smiled and raised her head at an angle and then moving the fan swayed with grace as if music played.

'You could never marry me, you know. You know that, Teige Foley?' She swayed still to that unheard music and her eyes looked directly at him. 'You're a stable boy.'

'I know what I am,' he told her. He did not move.

'I could not be in love with you.'

He did not answer her and she swayed about him and danced and he watched the movement of her neck and her breasts in the candlelight and how her hair fell and he thought he had never seen anything so beautiful.

'Do you love me more than your horses?' she said and she

lay on the bed and moved her legs and held the fan so it covered her face.

'Yes.'

'Well, then. You can touch me if you want.'

And for an instant Teige was not sure. It was as if the moment his hand reached her some tender and perfect thing might perish and tragedy and grief begin their long fall downward to him through the stars. It was as if with that first touch the entire and myriad constellation of all his future would be mapped and foretold and fated and he a mere and powerless nothing lost to the inevitability of that suffering.

Then he touched her. He touched the calf of her leg and it quivered. Elizabeth kept the fan covering her face and her leg moved under the firmness of his fingers. He knelt beside the bed and caressed her. His hands moved palely across the flesh of her stomach and circled and traced patterns intricate and ephemeral. He watched his own fingers in their tender exploration, he watched where they travelled to her breasts and how she arched and moved on the bedclothes then. The room grew close and crowded with an infinity of desire. She rolled to the side and still held the fan to her and rolled again and lay luxuriant and sighed and was to him a goddess from the fabled stellar world and he a mortal transgressing or elected by the mystery of fate.

'My name,' he said in whisper. 'Say my name.'

But she did not. She said nothing at all. She turned on the bed beneath his touch and his own eyes he squeezed tightly shut with bliss and his face he lifted back where the thin moon and starlight glanced upon it and made of his features a mask of anguish and pleasure and desire.

7

The following morning when Teige was working with the horses Clancy came to see him. He came fast on the cart down the avenue and reined the horse roughly and jumped down and came out into the field with a purposeful stride. He moved too quickly for his girth and sighed and blew with agitation. His cap he drew back by its peak right-handedly and with his left he forked up the hair that was flattened. His cheeks were red. When Teige had reached him Clancy did not speak at first but seemed to be weighing words like lead measures in the near distance just left of Teige's head. They stood so and the horses in the field turned to look at them. The sky soured.

'There's been a death,' Clancy said at last. 'You're to go.'

'What?'

For a moment Teige imagined it to be Elizabeth. His face whitened and Clancy saw this and reached and held on to his shoulder stiffly at a distance.

'There's one dead. The word has come. On the island. You're to go.'

'Is . . . Who is it? Who is dead?'

''Tisn't said. The boatman came with it. He's waiting to take you back. Here,' Clancy said and from the sidepocket of his jacket drew out some wages. 'Get in the cart.'

They rattled down the long avenue, Clancy leaning forward and making whipping sounds at the horse with his tongue, Teige sitting upright mute and blind and impassive as a figure cut in stone. When they arrived in the town the haste of the cart turned the heads of those standing in the street. Some looked and kept looking, following the two men with their eyes and enjoying in some way the sense of calamity and grief that was evident. Teige and Clancy paid them no heed. The horse raced on down the streets of the town and the island appeared green and low and tranquil in the grey waters of the river. They came to the jetty where the boatman was waiting. He looked at Teige and then looked sharply away over his shoulder as if at a perching blackbird.

Clancy offered his hand.

'Sympathies,' he said.

'Who is dead?' Teige asked the boatman. But on the mention of the word the boatman shuddered and threw his shoulders and glanced quickly from side to side as if dodging the same dark bird as it sought to land upon him.

'Who is . . .' Teige tried again, but the boatman had stepped down into his boat and lifted his oar. He splashed at the water with it and then sunk it into the top surface, shuddering and throwing his shoulders, saying sounds of words that were lost to Teige as the boat slipped out into the estuary.

The dip and slap of the oars; the glitter of the water as it fell from the raised blades; the weak sunlight of that morning; grey clouds coming up the river like ghost galleons; the fish that moved beneath them; all such entered Teige and became part of memory. He stared across the river for signs and saw none. Where the river met the sea the boat lifted and fell and achieved a kind of jaunty precariousness, and the boatman stopped rowing altogether. He swayed there and felt the motion in his body and waited and then dipped the oars and rowed once more. Seagulls flocked and beat hurriedly across the air. Then the rain came. It fell heavily almost at once and dimmed the light of day and made the waters murky. The boatman jabbered some curse and shook his head and let the drops scatter, then he curved his back and pulled harder to draw them to the island. Up from the shore Teige saw the cottage they had been building was now as high as the roof timbers though these were not yet thatched and looked dark and skeletal in the rain. There was no sign of life. The boat reached the shallow waters and the boatman single-oared it about and waited and Teige stepped out and walked up on to the island. He went up along the beaten track that was shouldered with the yellow furze, heavy with the rain. The day seemed pressed down upon the land. He walked and felt the air of death and still did not know who had died. And while he walked the images of his father and brother were before him and he feared for both of them and tried to banish the fears and not bring himself to have to choose between them. And tangled in his mind too was the sense of an obscure guilt, a vine like a complex algebra that wove and entwined and at last related the X of illicit love and the Y of death, binding cause and effect and turning improbabilities into fact.

He reached the doorway of the cabin and stood and looked into the dark. The dog came out to meet him. He could see a figure lying on a table but he could not distinguish who it was. Then his father said his name.

'Teige come in. It is Blath.'

She had died of typhoid fever which was already in the close damp air of that place. Francis Foley sat by her and the girls, Maeve and Deirdre, looked up at Teige but did not speak. They looked away again. They had been returned to familiar Death like ones recaptured after brief freedom. Their faces were pale.

'Where is Tomas?'

'He's gone off,' Francis said. 'He was pitiful with her. He did all a man could do. He made her drinks and remedies and things he had heard of and she could keep none of it in her. And we sent word for a doctor to come, and we waited and he did not come and she losing strength all the time so that she could not take even a drink of water. Tomas would go up and stand on the hill and watch for the doctor and still no sign of him.' The old man's eyes watered in the shadows. He paused and held the anger in his chest. 'Why would the doctor not come? What is the matter with us, are we beasts in the field?'

'He did not come at all?'

'He did not. She died in the afternoon. Tomas went out and I found him beating his two fists on the stones of the house over. He bloodied himself red-handed and when I came to him he threw up his fists at me and spun around and went off and would not be spoken to since.'

Teige stood there in the gloom of the cabin and he looked at the dead woman and saw the blue and purple shadows about her mouth and eyes.

'We must bury her,' he said.

'There is a place here on the island. Gort na marbh,' his father said. 'It is where they bury some from over the water. They bring them here because of the old churches.'

Teige went out then to find Tomas. He went and whistled the white pony and she came to him and he let her smell the other horses on him and he nuzzled and stroked her and then rode off down the shore in the falling rain. He rode fast. He galloped her because of the urgency and because he found relief in the speed, racing away from many things. He rode and stopped and scanned about for his brother. Then he saw the boat coming across the water with the black figure of the priest sitting erect in the bow. He hurried back and told his father.

Francis Foley came out of the cabin into the spoiled daylight.

'Now he comes,' he said and scowled and took from the doorside his stick and walked brusquely ahead of Teige toward the shore.

The rain muddied the way. Francis tramped along it and swung and beat at the furze randomly, scattering petals of yellow. At the place where the shore shelved off and there was a small drop to the sand he stopped and watched the boat coming. The priest could be seen clearly now. He was a thin figure with a wide-brimmed black hat. His nose was sharp and this combined with the prominent narrow edge of his chin to lend his face the appearance of having been pressed in from either side. Clutched at his chest was the Bible. Beside him in the boat sat another, a younger man also in black whose head was hatless and whose cheeks were polished a purplish hue by the rain. The boat bobbed in the shallow water. Then this boatman whom the Foleys had not seen before stepped out in the small waves and offered his back and the angular priest stood and climbed on to it and was carried so on to the sand. The younger priest did not wait for this transport but paddled across and kicked water from his shoes. They stood and the Foleys walked down to meet them.

'I am Father Singleton,' said the priest, 'show me to the deceased.'

He raised the Bible slightly at his chest and made as if to hasten on with his business. But Francis stood.

'Come on,' said the priest. 'What is the matter? Do you understand me? The deceased. The dead.'

His tone was exasperated and sharp and in his eyes was a silvery scorn.

'What is the matter with this man,' he said and looked to Teige. 'You. Do you understand? Lead us. We must hurry before the tide turns. We have other matters. Father Boland, can you?'

The younger priest looked at them and his lips quivered as if uncertain whether to smile. When he spoke his voice was soft as a girl's.

'We are here for the burial. There is a woman who died.'

The old man stood and he was appalled at them and felt a riot gather in his blood. The rain dripped off the priest's hat. He sniffled.

'Are you Christians?' he snapped then. 'Do you know this is a holy island?'

'We do,' Francis said at last and stepped forward and was

now not a yard from the priest and could smell his dinner off him.

'Do you know it is the island of Saint Senan, and that he decreed that no woman was to set foot on it? Do you know that?' He paused and looked and Francis did not move an inch and the priest's ire raised a purplish vein in his forehead. 'And what kind of woman was she? Will you answer that?' he said. 'Because I know. I know what she was. You see. Nothing is hidden, remember that, if you are Christians. Have you other women here?' The priest's sharp features were raised and he let his righteousness and judgement be seen and felt by them and was awaiting some demeanour of reverence and contrition when Francis stepped quickly forward and pushed him back in the chest.

'Go away!'

'What? Stop!'

He was pushed again and he staggered back two steps and a fringe of raindrops scattered from his hat.

'Are you defying the word of God?' he shouted. 'What are you that you can face damnation?'

'Go away! Get back in the boat! We don't want you!' Francis swung the stick now and came forward with it and the priests retreated, the younger one hurrying back into the water and his superior raising up the Bible like a weapon or a shield.

'Have you other women here?' he cried out.

Then a stone flew through the air and splashed in the water beside him. Then another, and another. They hailed from the higher ground where Tomas was standing now, bending and lifting and firing. The priest retreated. The boatman was in his boat. The waves lapped at the priest's shoes and he lifted his feet and put them back down again in the water vainly trying to outstep the tide. The stones whizzed and plopped and the priest raised and brandished the Bible and his hat spun off and he reached for it and lost his nerve as the stones flew through the rain.

'You'll be cursed,' he said. 'You'll all be cursed here. This is a holy island!' A stone clipped at his shoulder and he yelled out and waded quickly backwards and climbed into the boat. The hat turned and tumbled in the waves. The boatman rowed them away.

Teige turned to look up at Tomas. He was standing behind them on the small bluff, his arms out by his sides. His face ran with the rain, his shirt was marked with mud and blood and he looked risen from some nether region where he had been wrestling with furies.

'Tomas,' Teige called to him, but the brother did not respond or look at him and went off running through the bushes.

'Come on. We must bury her now,' the father said.

The two of them returned up the island. The sky darkened further, the spillage of rain from the heavens a portent now hiding the mainland. They seemed sealed there and moved as if imprisoned in a dream of desperate business. They came to the cabin and took shovel and iron bar and then crossed over by the wiry craze of the blackthorn ditch and in to the Field of the Dead. There were tombstones at every tilt and slant and others fallen and embedded now in grass the hares dunged and burrowed and made their own. There were sea captains and boat pilots and fishers and their wives, some from centuries since forgotten whose names if once carved were now erased by the sea wind. There were many children, doomed weak things who perished from every ailment and disease. All lay silent now in the falling rain as Francis and Teige uncovered a place in the brown earth for Blath. They worked without words. They did not try to blunt the sorrow with any meaning or purpose or to reconcile inequities. They dug the hole. Then they went back and Francis told the girls to step outside and wait, and he took two of the cloths they had and with Teige's help wound them about the body. These he tied then with cords of hay rope. They had no timber for a coffin.

'I will go and tell Tomas,' Teige said.

'He knows. Leave him,' his father told him.

So the two of them came out then and ungainly bore the corpse to the graveside. The two girls followed with arms crossed and eyes faraway, and behind them the dog. The rain fell. They trod anew the ancient path in the grass and made mud along it. The brown hole in the ground appeared shockingly, and was like a rent in a green garment otherwise perfect. When they were beside it, Francis took the body in his arms alone and bent down and knelt with her and then climbed down the side and was then in the hole itself where he lowered her gently to the clay. He stood so a moment and looked upon her there. Then he climbed out and scanned about for sign of Tomas, but could find none. He waited. The girls shook but made no sound.

'God bless her,' Teige said.

But his father said nothing, and after a moment bent and picked up the shovel and pitched the earth in upon her, and shovelled at the small mound faster and faster until the hole was made up to the level of the grass once more. Then he raised the shovel above his head and beat and beat on the grave with it, and tramped on the fresh earth and beat some more, and was still doing so when the others left him and walked away in the rain.

8

In the days following the Foleys did not see Tomas at all. He did not visit the cabin or the grave. The weather was still broken and the island hung in mist and drizzle and the light was veiled. The girls Deirdre and Maeve, mute and hollow-faced, went off about the fields and gathered flowering boughs and branches and wildflowers and brought these to the bare grave each day. There they sat in the dampness, their coughing soft and continual. Teige rode the white pony and looked for his brother, but often imagined that, seeing him approach, Tomas had hidden or run off and did not want to be seen again. And after a time Teige stopped and let the pony graze and let his own mind leave the island and travel across the river and up over the slates of the roof to find his way to the bedroom of Elizabeth. He sought for her image amidst the desolation and grief and loneliness that weighed there and wondered how long he must wait before he could return. For no reason he could name he avoided his father then. And the old man seemed to do likewise. They were separate as stars, and as silent. The house that was almost built lay untouched down near the shore.

Then one night when Francis had disappeared to the tower and his telescope, Tomas came into the cabin. The girls were sleeping a jagged sleep of sharp coughs. Teige was sitting in the corner mending the fishing line. He started when he saw his older brother, for Tomas was returned to the figure they had met on the road. The ghost of dead love harboured in his eyes.

A ragged beard climbed his cheeks. Teige stood and held out his hand to him but Tomas was looking at the empty place where last he had seen his wife.

'Tomas, sit down, you are wet through. Here, take my shirt.'

Tomas stepped softly past him and bent down and laid his hand on the shoulder of first one and then the other of the sleeping girls.

'They were good to her,' he said. He stayed bent low there and phantoms sojourned the while and he seemed to see them and watch the brief invisible happiness of his life take ephemeral form and then vanish anew.

He stood and looked at his brother.

'Maybe it's true,' he said. 'Maybe we are all cursed.'

'You know it's not. Here, my shirt. I have another one.'

The shirt was pressed in Tomas's fingers and he held it and sadly smiled.

'Teige,' he said. 'Teige.' He said the name with slow weight, as though the sound of it was somehow entering him, as if he was aware there was some conjuring in names themselves. It was as if he knew that by saying it so he could both take the spirit of his brother inside him and at the same time express outwardly some of the love that lay all steeped and banked and inarticulate within him. He lifted his hand and held Teige by the shoulder. He gripped him like that and did not move and did not speak, and in both of them the moment sunk deep like some aureate treasure, to be found and fingered years later.

Abruptly, Tomas turned then and went out the door and Teige came out after him and called out to him to stay. They were in the muddied grass yard. Tomas was striding away. His brother called out to him for Teige felt the purposefulness of Tomas's stride and knew there was finality about it.

'Tomas, where are you going? Stop.'

The elder brother was already out by the track that led down toward the unfinished house and the shore. Teige ran behind him in the night.

'Where are you going?'

A voice flew back out of the dark.

'Leave me, Teige. Go back.'

'No.'

'Leave me!'

'I won't.'

'Tomas? Tomas?' The father's voice boomed then from the tower. Then Francis had come out into the night and as he approached Teige had reached and grabbed the arm of his brother who shook him roughly off and then ran off.

'Teige, Tomas?' The old man saw the back of his eldest son as he flew into the dark. He blew and sucked at the air. 'Where is he going? What did he say?'

'I don't know. He's going somewhere . . . he's . . .'

'Tomas?' the old man shouted. 'Tomas!' He shouted the name again and then took off and ran after it and Teige after him. The father ran with ungainly stride. He bumped and swayed. He ran past the furze bushes that were speckled with gleam in the nothing of light. He ran and found uneven footing and plunged into briars and waved his arms at them and flayed the skin and felt blood rise and sting. He cursed the world and the darkness and the bushes. Then he called his son's name again and got up and ran on and Teige beside him. They ran down the dark path and heard the sea grow louder and heard the noise of its breaking on the small stones. Teige shouted the name of his brother too. They stood there on the night shore and swung about and looked like ones who had lost their shadows. They glanced sharply right and left along the sand and the stones. They hurried a few paces along and arrested and came back again, and cried his name that the soft night swallowed and took within its deeps like the sea.

'What did he say? What did he say to you?'

Teige saw his father's eyes wide and near and felt the sour desperation of his breath.

'He said nothing. He came and looked at the girls sleeping,' he said. 'He said nothing else. Then he just turned and went off.'

The old man bowed his head, then he looked out at the water, and he and Teige stood there a long time seeing nothing but the passing motion of the tide darkly hooded with unstarred sky.

They did not see Tomas again after that. Teige rode all corners of the island in the light of the next day, but could find no trace of him. He rode and searched, although in some part of him he already knew that his brother was no longer there. His searching grew aimless and petered off in fields where the hares stood and watched him and then ran into cover where none appeared possible. It rained a soft rain that was neither one weather nor the other, but a malady of season that lingered without remedy. It did not seem summertime but for the long pale light of evening.

A boat came to the island one afternoon and a river pilot stepped out and brought news of Tomas. He said he had come because he had given his word he would. He said it was the queerest thing. He said he had been sailing down to Limerick in the dawn light leading in one of the cargo boats and hadn't he seen the man swimming. He had thought him a seal at first. He thought to bat him with the oar, he said. But he pulled him on board and the man told him his name was Tomas Foley and would he take him to Limerick because he was on his way to America. The river pilot said he took him to be one evicted or otherwise fugitive, but the man was not inclined to talk, he said, and they sailed on down to Limerick and arrived there as the morning came up. This Tomas got out, the pilot told them, and his clothes still wet and cold, and a second shirt tied skirt-like about his waist.

'He thanked me right well enough and asked me if I was passing back down the river to give ye word that he was not drowned. He made me promise it. And that's why I came.'

The pilot stopped and Teige and his father and the two girls were about him like stones standing in a field.

'America?' Teige said.

'That's what he said. America,' the pilot replied.

'We can go and get him back,' Teige said at last.

'We cannot,' his father said. His voice was old and tired; his head was anchored on his palm. 'He is gone.'

The girls turned mutely and went to the straw bed they shared. The rash that was on their bodies for weeks climbed that night to their cheeks. They cried and fretted and moaned in the dark and Teige and Francis came to them and cooled their fevers with what means they had. And the girls called them mother and other soft names out of long ago and looked at them as though they were from another world. Both girls were like one then and the fever rose in their bodies and they seemed to be burning up from within until all the tragedy and loss and regret of their lives perished in conflagration and they arrived in a place elsewhere and their eyes softened and they died.

9

This time the priest did not come at all. They buried the girls alongside Blath and left the shovels there and walked away while blackbirds flew and landed. They set ablaze all clothes and bedding. The dog barked at the sparks spinning in the air where disease smoked and fumed and was vanquished. Francis folded into himself. He thought all endeavours now were futile. For Death came for everything.

'Somewhere your mother is buried,' he told Teige. 'I am sure of it.' And seeing him deep in such grief and resignation Teige did not dispute it, and in his own heart partly believed it, too.

The spoiled summer passed on.

The boatman came and told them the potatoes had failed. The stalks had withered and the leaves blackened and the potatoes crumbled in the hand. There were thousands unable to pay rent. By the shore, when he was leaving, Teige asked him if there were still visitors at the Vandeleur estate and the boatman shook his head and said they were all gone, there were none at the house and it was closed up now. Only Clancy and some of the workers were there. Teige asked the boatman to come again and to the man's bashful mutter and sway he gave an armful of their own potatoes that were undamaged. These the boatman placed tenderly in the boat as if they were infants. Then he rowed out into the Shannon and was gone.

Teige and his father tended the potato field carefully. They watched for signs of failure and rot. Francis stooped and crawled between the furrows and turned each leaf and rubbed softly with thumb and forefinger. Once Teige thought he heard him say prayers while he lay in the dirt. But he could not be sure, and his relation with his father now did not seem to allow much dialogue. They lived on like ghosts in the ruins of the old man's dream. Francis's eyes became dull and his skin began to turn a papery white. He came and went from the tower at nights and seemed to age there faster than before. After long sessions in the stars he would re-emerge into the thin light of morning like one dazed or newly arrived on the earth, fistfuls of his hair gone and his limbs weak and frail as a centenarian's. He seemed to have passed beyond language and little by little it began to fade from him. He nodded and made small sounds when leaving the table and the food that Teige made for him, but he did not say his son's name. The old dream of finding a home for his family mocked him now, for there was only Teige left and the island was suddenly large and empty and bare and the cries of the seabirds above it harsh and forlorn and beyond consolation.

All the rest of that summer they did not move to finish the house. Teige fished in the river and watched the pilots and fishermen and sea captains and turfmen as they sailed past. Sometimes they passed close enough for him to call out to them but he did not do so, as though such communication would be a betrayal of some kind and his father would disapprove. He sat there and watched and they watched him, the boy from the cursed family on the island of Saint Senan.

But later in the dark Teige sailed free of that place in his mind and found and reassembled his family. He lay and imagined them and they appeared before him. Beginning always with his mother he made of them a story no different from all the others he had learned and told. To himself he spoke of them as if they were stars. In stories extravagant and magical he imagined his mother still living. He followed her through various narrow escapes, moments of outrageous hardship and fortuitous chance, always allowing her the slimmest hope so that she could survive and travel on down the winds and bends of the long road that was leading to him. He saw his brother Tomas slip through the city of Limerick and walk out on the road to Cork where there were crowds of pale and skeletal people moving. He imagined them, those gaunt figures with ghosthood already immanent, their long thin arms holding cradled the bundle of their world, their hunger and frailty, the mewling of their children, the ragged faded worn quality of their spirits as they journeyed homeless toward the impossible idea of home. Teige imagined them and cold sweats surfaced on his body and he feared for Tomas then and wished the story would turn him around and bring him back to the island. But the story continued, nights and weeks and months after that, and was horrific and relentless. Tomas saw men and women and children fall by the roadside. He saw Death move across the fields like a summer shadow and bodies falling beneath it like ribs of hay to a scythe. He saw the wagons of corn escorted out of the country of the starving, and the same wagons attacked by some without weapons, whose shrill shrieks and yellowed eyes made of them fierce and pathetic clowns, waving their arms for food while they were shot to the ground. He saw mothers without milk press their babies to their breasts and wail then to the heavens and suck on plants and flowers and grasses and anything they could find in the futile hope of lactation. He saw children die and their fathers and mothers sit by them waiting to join them while coaches passed.

On the road to Cork Tomas witnessed it all, and in each story grew thinner and thinner himself, and was more indifferent to his own survival. He tramped forward each night in Teige's mind because he could not stop and because in some way the restless journeying toward some impossible end was part of that family's inheritance and would not and could not finish this side of death. And in truth this was what he was going to meet, for he could not knowingly bring it upon himself or sit still and wait for it to come. At a place above Mallow, he came upon a hellish scene reeking and smoking where wild-looking bloodied men scrambled about with knives hacking and carving at the warm carcasses of three horses. These had been slain to stop them from bringing away the corn. The horses' heads were cast in forlorn twisted postures in the dirt. Their flanks were opened inexpertly in haste and their insides spilled out and trod over as the men butchered and swayed in the foul air and sought to bring away steaks. Flies buzzed there. A hundred crows cawed and darkly opened their wings in the field nearby and were so many that they seemed like missals or Bibles unused and thrown from the sky. Tomas came upon the scene and voided the nothings in his stomach. Two of the men paused and glanced at him and held their knives and were momentarily frozen with shame, stunned like some caught in God's eye. Then the moment passed, they lowered their eyes from Tomas's and bent and hacked at the horses once more.

In Teige's story Tomas saw the dead horses and thought of his youngest brother. In Teige's story, Tomas's heart wept then as he remembered the innocent times when he and his brothers had ridden horses and ponies in fields daisied and green. Tomas remembered all their days and nights and weakened there on the roadside and did not think he could continue, until some time later a family came passing and the emaciated father asked him if he would carry one of their boys.

Tomas carried two. Without discourse, without nicety of introduction or comment of any kind, they left that scene where the horses were denuded of even their tails and the crows pecked the glassy eyes with impunity. They travelled silent and with graven inconsolable expression among many others of that kind into the city of Cork.

There Tomas walked along the dockside in scenes teeming with all humankind. The air was sharpened with men's cries and commands as families stood and jostled and bargained and bought passage across the ocean. Women wore grim stoic expressions. Their mouths were small and thin-lipped as though food were a fading memory, and their children sat and lay curled on the ground and made a low wailing that issued without effort. In the story that Teige told himself in the long nights on the island Tomas found work there on the docks loading chests and supplies on board tall ships that creaked on the changing tide. He worked and was paid pennies and stayed in a cramped and crowded boarding house with others waiting to escape. And in four weeks he bought passage for himself on a ship called *Liberty*. He stepped below decks for the first time in his life and as he went deeper down into the ship found the daylight fractured and then gone altogether. He stumbled and reached for his way while the bo'sun's whistle sounded and men ran to and fro and commands were called out on the decks above him. He heard them hurrying about over his head. At last Tomas arrived in the quarters of the poor and sat amidst the huddled hundreds who stared through the gloom and said nothing but coughed in the queer damp air of that place that was to be their home below the surface of the sea.

Of the twins, Teige's stories were less sure. He imagined Finbar in extravagant worlds of myriad and mortal dangers. He dreamed pirates, raging armies, weird weathers of hurricane and typhoon, thick suffocating snows of white goose-feathers, huge floods red as roses, tigers sabre-toothed and snarling, snakes, elephants, a whole terrain crawling with spiders, strange exotic natives with pierced tongues who ate the skins of others. Mammoths, dragons, flocks of blood-sucking bats, mutilators, murderers, thieves and bounty hunters with skulls dangling and knocking like coconuts by the sides of their saddles. All of these and more populated Teige's stories of Finbar and the gypsies. Of Finan the stories were less clear. He had killed a man and was gone off for contrition. He had become a healer, a layer-on of hands, or had joined up with a troupe of actors and performed in Shakespearean tragedies and made all weep with the deep and potent veracity of his grief. He wore greasepaint and his eyes were darkened hollows and nightly he was struck down and died and from such was his own soul briefly healed. Sometimes, when Teige could not bear the tale or the vision he saw of his brothers' afflictions, he summoned a land of lovely women. He closed his eyes on the night and smelled the remembered scent of the room of Elizabeth and saw her multiplied a hundred times and standing naked and tender and beautiful like flowers in a field. And for the remainder of that night then he did not leave that imagined place, but stayed with her and forgot the world of pain and allowed his brothers rest and peace.

And all this while, across the way, his father sat in Saint Senan's tower and bowed his head and stared endlessly through the telescope at the sky. He placed his eye to the glass and for hours did not move it away, and this though the clouds did not pass and there were no stars to be seen.

In truth, by that time Finbar Foley had led the gypsies on the long walk south out of the snowy mountains and bartered with what things they had and those they found for the timber to make new caravans. It took some time before they were again ready and equipped to travel, but the pause was welcome to all.

During those weeks they did not move on. Now their leader, Finbar, imagined he must announce to them a destination, but he himself had no clear idea of one. Not being of gypsy blood, he did not understand that such was not required of him; the gypsies never journeyed toward an end, for motion was an end in itself. Nonetheless, wrongly believing that this was needed to validate his leadership, it was what Finbar Foley sought to give them. So, one dawn, he rose from beneath the blanket where Cait the mer-girl was grown large with his twin daughters and he walked out where the embers of the fire smoked and called the gypsies to rise and move on. They did so, coming to life in the grey light and tackling up new horses for the way ahead. When they were ready, Finbar looked along the line of them and felt a surge of pride as if he were some valiant captain trooping into battle. He sat beside Cait in the front caravan and snapped the reins and drove the line of caravans down across that country that lay to the south of the Maritime Alps. Nor by then was Cait the only pregnant woman among them, for in the weeks that followed one by one all of those within the perimeters of child-bearing years announced themselves to be expecting, as well as two prune-faced women who boasted they were a youthful sixty. Finbar did not announce then that he would bring them to Bohemia, or make speeches on the notion of a homeland, though these loomed in his mind. Indeed, he did not know where Bohemia was, but had like others before him fallen upon the idea of it being a spiritual home for gypsies and did not for one moment imagine that he could be wrong. Still, he kept the destination secret. He told the gypsies only that he would bring them to a place where they belonged, and where the weathers would be clement and the people welcome them like lost cousins.

That this was a fantasy of his own making, and born out of the need to believe such a place would exist for his own children, did not stop him from believing in it. Nor did he realize how his hopes fell into the selfsame shapes as those once dreamed by his father.

So, travelling with care for the pregnant, and with such slow indolence that measurement of progress was impossible, the gypsies moved through Liguria like an oil of olives. They arrived at the banks of the River Po and followed along them and bargained and traded with villagers there and heard tales of wars and battles and the affairs of a world in which they were no more than shadows. One of the older women who was expecting her fourteenth child had a vision of yellow birds flying in her stomach. A night later three more of the women had the same dream and two nights later six more. They were uncertain of its provenance, but to set their wives at ease and to make real the thing imagined their husbands went and returned with a dozen canaries in wicker cages. The visions vanished then and the canaries hung outside the front hoop of the caravans and rocked there on perches and sang sometimes to the swaying of those roads. It was discovered the birds' humour foretold the weather; how they sang or perched or flew predicted the rains or wind to come, and the men, learning of this, were pleased to pretend they had known all along and not bargained for the birds merely to placate their women.

Before they reached the sea the gypsies left the Po and turned northward around the Gulf of Venice. It was the summer. The canaries sang sweetest and the sun shone and the swollen women took to lying in the grass and lifting their shirts and smocks and exposing to the warmth the pale orbs of their future progeny. They said the sun would give them sons. Leaving them so, Finbar sailed to the fabled city that was a thousand islands, and there in the shop of old Fabrizio Benardi saw his first map of the known world. He could not believe it. He unfurled it across four tabletops and moved his palms outward upon it like two flat-bottomed boats travelling in opposite directions and revealing places of which he had never heard. Old Benardi, who himself had never left Venice, had purchased the map from a navigator who had arrived from the Indies. He had been assured the map was an authentic and accurate rendering even to the point of those islets previously considered too minor to merit inclusion. On the map, Finbar studied the place where they were and where he imagined Bohemia to be. It was not so very far away. His sons could be born there, he thought at once, and the sons and daughters of all those in the caravans. It would be a glorious new beginning. He lifted his hands and the world rolled closed. He spun around in the dust that flew upward off all the handmade papers and scrolls of that shop and brought his face close to Benardi's. Finbar Foley was still an impressive figure: the breadth of his chest, the thickness of his eyebrows, his firm chin and fiery stare all lent him the air of one not to be denied. He told the Venetian he had to have the world, and he offered him gold coins he did not possess for it. The old man agreed the sale, and that afternoon Finbar Foley stole the coins at knifepoint from a Jew he followed from the Rialto. He returned to Benardi's in haste and later took the map back to the gypsies, along with several bottles of ink, some sheets of yellowish paper, and a half-dozen masks that Fabrizio Benardi thrust toward him when he caught the scent of violent desperation. That evening the gypsy men gathered to look at the map, but to Finbar's surprise were only briefly interested in it. They could not match the shape of the lines drawn on the paper with the endless terrain they had traversed back and forth in their lifetimes. It was no more like the world than the sketch of a man was like a man. Though Finbar could not see it, it made less of the gypsies' one great wealth: their intimate and unrivalled knowledge of all the richly varied landscapes that existed. For they alone knew the world.

Despite their indifference, later that night Finbar showed the map to Cait with all the excitement of a New World discoverer. He fingered their route through the mountains, and pointed the way ahead, and was too rapt in his own fervour to notice her brown eyes turning longingly back to fix on that western island where they had begun.

When they left there the caravans and wagons creaked under the weight of the pregnancies. They passed northward through lands governed by Habsburgs and met old peasants on the roadside who asked them what the world was like to the south. There were some among them who remembered the armies of Napoleon and when those same places they stood in had been renamed the Illyrian provinces. And they told of how the maps of that country had been drawn and redrawn many times and the people lived on hungry among the linden trees no matter who their sovereign. And the gypsies agreed and understood this and took their time there and shared what they had and sang songs in the night ancient and sorrowful.

At last the caravans moved on and the summer passed into a mild and tender autumn. Misreading the map, Finbar took them east across the great Hungarian plain when they should have gone north. He allowed the road to take them and they journeyed ever more slowly as the women's pregnancies neared their time. In the vast wilderness of steppe they saw none but foxes and trundling boars and herds of deer standing or moving like dancers to some music in the wind. It was a place great

and empty and crossing it the gypsies felt the smallness of themselves and their caravan, as though all others in the world had
perished. Even the canaries hushed. Finally they came to the
shores of the huge Lake Balaton. And, as though there were
some ancient folkloric mechanism that operated there, once
they saw and heard the lapping of the waves the women's waters
broke in unison. Their cries rang out from each of the caravans
and at once the canaries burst into song. The gypsies made
quick camp and the men lit fires and stood about them and
were silent while the few women who were not with child
hurried back and forth with bloodied cloths and sleeves rolled.
The night fell like a velvet curtain and while the women cried
and the men waited stars were spun upon it out of the dark.

All this time Finbar had feared in secret for Cait's pregnancy.
He had suffered dreams where he saw her sex bleed a river. The
blood was thick and gushed alarmingly and flowed across the
floor and out the door to the sea, and all the time Cait was lain
on her back and the gypsies were gathered about her awaiting
the birth. Then in the dream the child was born and its birth
was a kind of fluidity or issuance without effort and the gypsies
were amazed and applauded. Then they began to laugh. And
the laughter took the shape of white gannets and these then
were beating in the air above where Cait lay. And when Finbar
looked down to see his child the birds were swooping to attack
it, and he had to wave his arms about and it was still moments
before he looked down and saw the infant had been born with
the lower body of a fish.

He woke then, lathered in a white film with his eyes wide.
But the dream recurred on many nights through the pregnancy,
and sometimes in the dark he had woken to find the air beneath
the hoop of canvas heavy and putrid with the smell of fish and
silvery scales upon his tongue.

So, on the night of labours, Finbar Foley passed into a kind
of torment that, though not equal to that of his wife, wrung
him like a cloth. The first of the children was born just after

midnight to the sexagenarian mother who made no cry at all but claimed the birth felt like a hairball dropping softly out of her insides. Her son, Primo, was borne out on the night by his ancient father, and the others who were still attendant on the arrival of their own offspring greeted it with half-glad nods and thin smiles. The child did indeed resemble a ball. Its head was very large and covered with a downy fur, and although the other fathers-to-be did not say anything there passed through each of them the same painful vision, imagining how such a huge ball could pass out through the smallness of a woman's sex. The births came on in waves then. The cries and excitements of the midwives passed along the caravans and flamed torches were held aloft and there were embraces among those who were uncles and cousins and bottles of a clear fiery liquid flashed in the starlight. It was a wonder, the synchronicity of those births like some vast clock set in the heavens and chiming the beginning of a new gypsy age. Or so the fathers said. Hot-faced and exulting in their achievement that was nothing at all, they proclaimed, they made announcements, they sawed the air with their hands and predicted marvels. Moving from one to the other, and taking the congratulations he was given for bringing them there, Finbar secretly studied each child for oddities. Secundo was a big boy also, born without defect. As were all the others that were pressed into his arms as if for benediction during that long night. Finbar took them and held them an instant and tried to look pleased, but the truth was that with each perfect one his soul was tormented further by the certainty that his own child would emerge a monster.

But as the night drew on and it became clear that Cait was to suffer the longest labour and her screams came piercingly out of the caravan where three women attended her, the fear grew to certainty. He went up to the caravan and dared to lift the flap of the canvas to look in and see the river of blood. But one of the women spun around at once and cursed at him and shook her whiskered chin and pulled the canvas closed again.

233

He stood there and heard his wife cry and briefly he thought of his own mother and whatever world she had gone to. He threw back his head then and shouted out a sound, and the gypsies about him did not understand it for it was in a language not theirs. And he shouted it again and added before it the name of his family, and shouted it out to the swirling stars of that night by the great lake in the country that was like none any Foley had ever seen before. He shouted the words and boars in the woods stopped, foxes froze. He shouted the words and in so doing echoed his own father years before when teaching the boys, in games of hurling, the cry of defiance that led to victory.

'*Abu! O Fhogli abu!*'

Finbar shouted it out and then raised his fists and shook them in the air as if at the face of some celestial beast.

The other gypsies who were about him were startled but saw the urgency of his cry and were moved to join him. They all raised their fists and shook them and were a chorus that would not be denied.

And like all swift and traceless epiphanies it came to Finbar then that he must catch a fish. He looked out across the dark mutable waters of the lake. He heard the laps and slaps of soft collapse as the waves sighed, and then he was running out to the water's edge, followed by the loud surge of the newly made fathers. None had any idea at first what he was about, but each had drunk the burning juniper-flavoured whiskey that was of that place. They splashed into the chill waves and yelled as the cold bit at their calves. But Finbar was further out still and was waist deep and then dived out of sight. The gypsies stopped and were like puppets suspended, not knowing if he was to come back again. They knew the tales of whole lands hidden beneath the surfaces of lakes, they knew the lore of demons and watersprites and other fairy enchantments and of the many who had disappeared without trace. There was a long moment in the stillness and silvered dark of the lake. Then Finbar broke the surface again. He stood and shook a wide corona of lake water from his long hair and then dived again. This time the meaning of his actions translated itself to the fathers, and in a great rush they too dived down into the lake. The scene if not beheld was one such as beggared imagination. Like strange nocturnal seabirds the gypsies plunged in the cold waters, some rising as some were vanishing. Bodiless heads appeared and bobbed and then flapped out wing-like arms while next to these were the disappearing legs and lower bodies of others. The lake was alive with them, diving and surfacing again, breaking the glittered reflection of sky and its scintillas of stars. They were like some that had drunk a potion or been charmed under a spell. As though their lives depended upon it, the gypsies dived for fishes. These, coming through the lake in vast schools of gentle fluttered motion, can only have been amazed as the men's bodies crashed down and appeared bubbling before them, the faces wide-eyed and blind in the night water. The men's hands reached and grasped, they made slow broad arcs of attack causing wild underwater currents and whirling eddies so that the fish themselves were spun about and swam flatly and sideways like ones demented. Still, the gypsies caught some of them. They made nets of their shirts, some of their trousers. Others managed the impossible and bare-handed the fishes into the air. They broke up through the surface with a cry and held aloft in the small light the flashing trophies. The gypsies bobbed there on the cold water and did not know what to do until Finbar himself appeared with a great thrashing fish and shouted the same cry as before and stepped forward and waded out of the lake with the capture in his arms. The others followed then. They walked up the banks in the night with the fishes in their arms, and were like an image out of some perished mythology, fathers cradling with bewilderment the changed forms of their sons. They came to the caravan where Cait was silent now and they stood around in a throng, the men with fishes and the others who held torches. Then Finbar knelt down and placed the one he had caught on the ground before the caravan. All of the gypsies followed suit until there was a small hill of fishes flapping and thrashing out of their element.

'Cait!'

Finbar called out her name as though he were summoning her from a far shore.

'Cait!'

He made the short name long and filled inside it the volume of his own longing and love for her and the gypsies remained quiet and lowered their heads and once more the lapping of the lake water could be heard.

Then the whiskered woman drew aside the flap of the caravan.

'She is all right,' she said. 'She's come back.'

'How is my son?' Finbar called up to her.

'Oh,' said the whiskered one, 'your son has no penis.' She watched as all the fathers' heads came up and their eyes opened and their mouths dropped and there was a kind of moan that passed among them like a wind.

'No penis! But two heads!' she shouted, and brought her hands up to the sunken sides of her leathery face and leaned back and hooted a kind of hoo-hoo of owl-like laughter to the astonishment of all.

Then from inside the caravan came the other two midwives and wrapped in both of their arms were newborns. Their heads did not appear from within their swaddling.

'You have daughters!' one of them said and smiled. 'You have two daughters! Twins!'

'Hoo hoo, no penis!' hooted the whiskered one. And the breath of relief of all the gypsy men could be felt as Finbar stood up and moved toward the infants. And as he was doing so some of them came and shook him by the shoulders and he stopped as if just then grasping some urgent matter and told them quickly to return the fishes to the lake. They did. Finbar took his children in his arms and went inside to Cait.

'Our sons are not born fishes but daughters,' he told her and smiled. And he lay down the two infants on her breasts and lay himself next to them and he kissed the side of her face where her tears were slowly running and tasting like the sea.

11

They were both beautiful. They had their mother's skin and their father's eyes. They slept and suckled and seemed children of such serenity that the turbulent passions of their futures could not even be imagined. Cait recovered from the ardour of her labour quickly, but retained a kind of sensual fondness for her bed and lay there pillowed and luxuriant and told her husband she did not want to move. This mood was soon discovered general throughout the caravans. The mothers were abed. They did not want to travel on. The entire camp smelled then of warm breast milk and cotton and made the autumnal air by the lakeside heavy and drowsy. The gypsy men, suffering a deep nostalgia for their own infancy, were soon of a like mind and happy to stay the winter there. For in the aftermath of the momentous night of births all were ineluctably altered and it was as though in the days following minor roots had sprung from them and were twisting down into the ground. They watched with drooped lower lips of envy while their sons and daughters sucked away at these milky matrons that were their wives. Even the sexagenarian, whose breasts were bluish and flat, with nipples that were wide brown knobs like the plugs of copper baths, and who had to have her son carried by his aged father to the next caravan for a further sup, was strangely glowing. Her eyes shone with contentment and her silver hair was very fine.

The mothers stayed in their beds for a month. Then they stayed for another one. The men and the older children cooked and burnt the food and bore it on tin plates into the caravans where the mothers lay back listening to the songs of the canaries. That the bond between the women and their new children was overly strong, or that this might cause difficulty in time, did not yet occur to Finbar. He accepted the somnolent mood of the camp and watched as, for the first time in many years, the gypsy men came to understand what it was to stay still. The winter was slow in coming. The horses were left to graze the long grasses that feathered the lakeside, and sometimes were taken and ridden bareback into the woods in grey dawn deer hunts. And it was a good time. They lived on there in the strange desolate beauty of that place. And some of the men who had felled trees worked at these with long jagged tooth saws and cut out shafts of wood and placed these at angles off the sides of their caravans and bound the rough hewn planks together with hay rope. There were three of these shelters made before Finbar realized it. He did not know whether to knock them down or offer his help, and in the end did neither, retreating into himself and secretly studying the map of the world while all about him the gypsies built their winter houses. By the time the first snows came his was the only caravan without extension. He lay on the bed at night beside Cait and played his face like the moon coming and going before his daughters.

'We'll stay here now until the spring,' he said. It was more of a question than he pretended, for he was testing her wishes. 'Then we'll go north. Do you want to see on the map?'

'I do not,' Cait said, and she held the child they had called Rose in the air above her. 'I want to stay here, or I want to go home.'

'Home?' He could not believe she had said it, and he furrowed his brow as if it were something beyond his comprehension.

'Yes.'

'Home?'

'Your hearing is working then.'

'Where is home?'

'You know where it is.'

'I do not. This is home,' he said. 'This caravan, this is all the home I have. All the home we have. Cait. Cait?'

Cait did not answer him. She brought the child down to her and held her close and said no more.

The snows were thin until Christmas. They fell into the lake and lingered only on the margins of the road. The gypsies lit fires and traded with those who passed that way. They told fortunes to some that came out of the snowy roads with thick capes and thin horses. The gypsies played them music on wooden pipes and sang the songs they knew. The strangers told them sorrowful tidings of the greater world, and it seemed to the gypsies it was always so. They built high their fires and kept warm their children. An air of contentment had settled over the gypsies and they did not hanker after open roads. Even their features softened. When the snows grew worse, Finbar expected they would come to him and look to move on. But this did not happen. Instead they barricaded their caravans more thoroughly and cut wood for fires.

Gradually, very gradually, the line of caravans grew to resemble a street.

Storms of wind and hail and sleet came and went and still the gypsies did not look to move on. Finbar talked no more with Cait of bringing the gypsies to Bohemia, and did not unfurl Benardi's map except when she was sleeping. She loved him for that, and some nights lifted Rose and Roisin to the other side of the blankets, and rolled her bed-warm and sensual amplitude to him and let his face be lost in the roundness of her breasts. Then, when the spring arrived, she, like almost all of the gypsy women, announced that she was pregnant once more.

So they stayed on again there. Finbar came out to the campfire and gathered all of them around him and announced what he knew they were already wishing. Finbar's broad arms were crossed on his chest, his long hank of fair hair hung down his back and he stood before them like a god.

'It will be good,' he said, 'for another year. Then our children will be strong.'

'Yes,' the men mumbled. They nodded and shrugged their shoulders in acquiescence and raised the palms of their hands slightly outward as if showing stigmata. 'Our children. Yes. For our children we must.'

Finbar left them and went away down the lake and felt ashamed and dishonest.

Rains fell. One night, when all were sleeping, a gypsy by the name of Nimez hitched his caravan and dismantled its extension and moved down to the beginning of the line of caravans and made camp on the opposite side. When the others woke up he was already established in a superior trading position and had set out a stall of tin pots, ladles, bent spoons, two-pronged meat forks, keys without locks, spikes, hooks, tin Vs of no particular use and other such oddments. He had put on a purple shirt and was standing before his caravan looking down the road. Some of the gypsies were disgruntled but could not say so, for it would reduce them to no more than petty merchants. But the following night, several of the caravans were hitched and moved about in a dark ballet until the dawn arrived and found them settled in two lines either side of the muddied road. No one said a thing.

'Have you seen what has happened?' Finbar said to Cait as the girls rolled in her lap. 'They have made a street.'

'What is so bad about that?' she asked him. 'Don't be afraid of the new thing. It might be wonderful.'

And he did not believe her but neither did he know how or if he could stop it.

The place changed before his eyes. As the warm days of May came with hordes of flies, the pregnant women grew irritated under the canvas. They told their husbands they were useless.

They heard that the wife of Nimez had cool silken sheets and Moroccan perfume. When their husbands lurched over in the bed to kiss them the women shooed them away and said how could there be love in a place that smelled like horse manure. They asked why was it that their men were so slow to see the future. Did they want it to bite them in the arse? The women said the future had arrived. For, since the gypsies were no longer going to sell and barter and tell fortunes and stories and beg their living travelling miles along the roads, they must now make it from all that passed there along the road between the caravans. It was that simple.

In the morning the gypsies moved the horses further toward the woods. By that afternoon any traveller coming down the road took two hours to pass the various booths and stalls and pitches and hagglers that were in his way. Some did not pass at all. So it was that there was soon a dealer in mirrors, a brewer of medicines, a maker of elaborate mechanical contraptions, a scarred man who offered body piercing, a trader in boar hide, a sharpener of knives, a woman who needled tattoos, and others various and sundry of that kind.

From these who were delayed along the way, the gypsies heard tales of the greater world. The travellers and traders spoke in all languages and their meanings were not always clear. Nonetheless soon the gypsies understood that there was calamity everywhere, and they were better off staying there by the lake. The summer drew on. The street lengthened and the flies buzzed over it. Without anyone noticing it, the caravans themselves began to lose their origins. Nimez worked in the dark to build a kind of foundation beneath his, and was one day able to sell the wheels to a passing Macedonian who bore them off tied either side of two oxen. Other wheels were soon removed, too. Then, when a bearded Magyar stopped around the fireside one night and told them that in the empire of the Ottomans gypsies could still be bought and sold as slaves, the following day the horses were sold and the gypsies cut short their hair.

In all this trading Finbar Foley took no part, and although still their leader he was soon the poorest among them. He kept his horse and did not remove the wheels from the caravan. In the mornings when he woke he caught in his nostrils the bitter smells of the street that were the smells of envy and avarice, and he was disgusted at what he had allowed to happen. He rose and took his daughters in his arms and took them off away around the lake to where the birds flocked and plashed in the waters and where things were simpler. He caught fish for their dinner, and they ate it every day though Cait wondered why he did not barter some of it for the vegetables of Kaleth the grower.

'I will not,' he told her, 'and I don't want you to ask me again.'

'This time maybe your son will be born a fish,' she shouted back at him.

When the time for birth came it was not like the year before. This time there were many along the street who were able as midwives, and they visited in and out of the wheel-less caravans without betraying excitement or tension, either deeply weary of this action of life or fearing displays of emotion would soil the decorum of that neighbourhood. Nor did the gypsy fathers come out and gather, but there was a muted and melancholic dullness to the street, and the births took place one by one without announcement or celebration. For his part, Finbar again went out to the great lake in the darkness and wished that his son would be born well. He dived into the waters and made a net of his shirt and swam there until he had a trout thrashing in the raised bag of it. He came up to the caravan where Cait had finished her labour.

'Is he born a fish?' he asked.

And the whiskered midwife again came out and said:

'He is not. But he has no penis.' She smiled the whiskered smile. 'He has two heads.'

The second pair of twins was identical to the first. When he saw them for the first time Finbar threw back his head and exploded with laughter. He laughed and Cait laughed and the first twins Rose and Roisin made a noise like laughter, too. He laughed until the tears ran from his eyes and he looked down at the two newborns and saw their red and tiny faces and said:

'Two more roses.'

And he kissed his two forefingers and flew them down on to the infants' heads.

'Roseleen and Rosario.'

'Is there nothing else that springs from your penis but roses?' Cait asked him, and she smiled and his heart grew large inside him and might have taken the form of white birds with wide wings for he felt then so light and full of hope.

The days thereafter were soft and warm. The street became a small village. But, without the constant journeying of the past, the gypsies grew restless easily in the mild late summer nights and took to sudden knife-fights for little reason. They visited the giant-bosomed whore Cassandra in the small hut she had erected at the end of the street, whose loose planks creaked and sometimes fell outwards as her customers' heads banged against them. Not to be off-put, in mid coitus she called out to those who were queued outside to repair the damage unless they wanted their wives to see. While some ecstatic customer bobbed up and down on her chest she made above his head the gestures of hammering to the gaping others and told them to hurry up in case she caught a cold and closed. After such loving, the gypsies came out into the night with an empty dissatisfaction they could not explain and took to flashing their knives without provocation and spilling the innards of each other in the street. They did not fight to the death, but slashed at chests and midriffs and took a kind of perverse glee in how the blood slowly emerged like dye on the fine white shirts their opponents wore to visit Cassandra. To arrive in that street in the summer nights of that year it might have seemed the gypsies were rivals for the love of a fabulous beauty, and were engaged in a fight for her honour. But it was in fact not hers but their own honour that they sought to recapture. They knifed each other to be men, and whether you were the gypsy wounded or wounding did not really matter. In the daylight the scars were bandaged and masked and the little village seemed as normal. The bloodstains in the street vanished under the traffic and trade.

Now all of this Finbar Foley knew, yet could do nothing to stop it. He grew more and more isolated from those he was supposed to lead, and when the gypsies saw him in the street it seemed to him they lowered their eyes and busied themselves with merchandise. He said nothing to any of them now. In the evenings he did not unfurl the map of Benardi nor mention again the notion of Bohemia. Secretly he allowed the first seeds of returning to his home country to settle in his mind, but he did not tell this to Cait for he could not face the idea of such defeat. Then, one morning in the month of October, there arrived in the village a ghost whose name was Malone. He was a figure ancient and thin unto transparency, with baleful blue eyes and the bones of his cheeks like stumps polished and poking outward through the flimsiness of his flesh. His head was bruised and scabbed. As he walked down the street he blinked incessantly and when the gypsy traders called to him of their wares he babbled words they did not understand and stepped on in his shoeless way. They cursed after him then and disregarded him further though he stopped in the middle of the street and said something back to them which was again indecipherable and easily mistaken for ravings. Then he drifted on slow and ghost-like and without baggage and in the dim brown light of that season seemed little different from the dead.

Then Finbar saw him. And in a moment recognized some trait of physiognomy or bearing and knew he was from that old country where he himself had been born. The ghost-man stopped and looked at him and said:

'*Ta an domhain ag dul ar siar.*'

And although Finbar had not heard that language spoken in a long time he recognized what it was and knew that the man had told him the world was nearly over.

Finbar brought him inside and sat him by the low oak table in their caravan. He brought the man cold smoked fish and water and he and Cait sat there and watched while this same fellow took the food and drink in slow small mouthfuls as if these were painful to him. The man's jaws moved in a crosswise crooked motion. He was without teeth and crushed the food on his palate with his tongue. He was bent over and rocked softly all the time. Then Finbar asked him in Irish where he was from and the ghost-man stopped and turned his ruined face to them and said his name was Malone and he was from the place that was the County Galway.

'Was?' Finbar asked.

Malone nodded. He said none were alive there now. He said a plague had come in that country and killed the people that had once lived there. He wet the lipless gap of his mouth with a little water and then he told them. He told how the potatoes had rotted in the ground and the people been unable to pay their rent and how they were driven to the roads. He told of some gone insane and others who leapt from cliffs into the sea. He told of those who ate the grass and the nettles and the green leaves of the hedgerows and how their bodies twisted in the ditches six days and more before they died. He told of bailiffs come to tear houses down lest the families think to lodge there without rent. He said how he saw a mother of ten children offer to tear her own house down for two pennies, and how she did, with terrible tears and lamentations until there was nothing left but rocks in the road.

The night fell while he talked on. For once he began the stories flowed from him like a river of grief and Cait nursed the new twins and rocked them in her arms with her eyes weeping and Finbar said nothing at all. The old man had lost his daughters first. These were twelve and fourteen years old. They had sickened on the road to Waterford and fallen into a fever with frightful visions and eyes white with terror. When they died he had not a spade to bury them, and dug the ground with his hands and made a cross of ash and tied it with the cord of his trousers. His wife would not leave the spot, and though he begged her and tried to drag her along the road she would not go, and he was forced to let her stay where she sang sad songs all day long to their daughters. They watched the thousands coming and going there, those doomed and futureless and travelling to nowhere. His wife died of hunger by her daughters and he buried her alongside them in the same grave where their bodies were not yet rotted. Then he himself walked on. For he could not bear to stay there and thought Death would find him quicker if he went to meet Him.

Malone paused and looked and saw that Cait was bedding the children, and then he whispered other terrors to Finbar that he did not wish her to hear. He told of death in all its forms, of some shot, some throat-slit, others hanged and swinging in the trees of the fields of north Munster with crows eating their eyes. He told of a man in delirium who cut off his arm and cooked it in a fire to feed to his son. He told of roads where the smells of putrefaction rose and how he walked on through them to meet Death and could not find him. Only ghosts. For that country had become peopled by these. They rose from where they lay unburied in weeds and thronged the roadways. He saw them himself. They wandered listless and wan and without purpose. There were families entire. There were small infants with encircled eyes. There were gaunt great-grandfathers, all ghosted and silent and grave and journeying as things without a home. Malone had walked to Waterford and still not met Death, and then taken a boat thinking he was to drown. He had arrived in France one day without knowing the name of the country he stepped out on. Then he walked southward and eastward. He had heard then that those who had survived the first year of the famine were killed the second, and any last remaining starved in the third, until there was none left in that country now but a multitude of phantoms.

He finished and lowered his eyes and looked at the timber flooring of the caravan. Finbar and Cait were seated about him. They did not speak. A long time passed and all three sat in still and mute contemplation of the horror that had been told. The candle burned out and they were shadowless shades there until at last in the small hours of the morning Malone spoke and asked them if in fact he was dead.

12

On the ocean, the eldest of the Foley brothers sailed for seventy-one days. The journey was to have been forty, but the captain of that ship, Abraham Huxton, chose a course more northerly than usual and brought them into seas as tall as trees. Almost all of those who sat in the gloom below decks had never been to sea before. The distance of the journey was unimaginable to them, and in the times they were allowed to climb the stairs and take air and see the ocean they thought it endless. Within ten days there were many who chose to stay below rather than feel the fall of their hearts as they gazed out on the churning grey emptiness. They lived then in the small cramped quarters where the air was soon fouled and where cholera and typhus and dysentery were in their first stages. Many were ill with seasickness and lay groaning day and night as the ship swayed to and fro. The drinking water was too quickly drunk and was then rationed to two cups a day, and then one. The flour was infested. Children bawled and were hushed or beaten quiet and lay then on the damp timber floor with defeated brooding faces and horror at how the green world of fields had vanished. There were mothers and grandmothers who brought with them small trinkets or minor belongings that recalled the homes they had left. These they fingered, a brass ring, enamel spoon, braid of doll's hair, small carved cross, such things, turning them over for hours on end long after any talk had fallen silent. They sailed on. Sometimes they kept the small candle of their hope burning by asking each other about where they would go in the

New World. They did not speak of the farms and villages they had left behind, but tried to be forward looking whenever the terrors they had seen ghosted before them and made their throats rise. So, they spoke of places their imaginations could not yet begin to shape, of New York and Philadelphia and Boston. And these appeared in their minds like shining citadels in the Bible wherein all their travails would be ended and their families live in peace and plenitude. But then the sea grew rough and the filled chamber pots that lay in their laps spilled about the floor and the children cried again.

Huxton sailed them into storm after storm. He was a broad-chested man who walked the decks with his clean-shaven jaw thrust forward and his hands holding each other behind his back. Even as the seas rose and threw the ship sideways he tried to keep his hands behind him. He stood in the gales and sweeps of rain that whipped across the decks and he kept his legs planted as though defying Neptune to throw a storm that would unbalance him. And so they came. The wind cracked in the sails and the decks were awash as waves broke in froth and spume and painted the boards in thin white foam that came and disappeared down through the deck into the quarters below. The ship was like a toy and within it the families of O'Connors, Barretts, Keoghs, Considines, Kirwins, Mulcahys, Moriartys, Doohans, and others were thrown from their seats and tumbled in the dripping darkness with white eyes and screams. The barrels of drinking water came loose from their bindings and crashed. They clung to each other and awaited their death. But for most of them it did not come and at times the storms began to ease. A junior accommodation officer appeared at the trap above and looked down at the bowed heads and counted them and went off to make his report of losses and sometimes to arrange for bodies to be buried at sea. Within days there was another storm. And then another. Huxton kept his balance. In time the passengers grew to read the wind in the creaking of the hull and know the signs of tempest before it arrived. They learned how to sit in braced positions and secure such things as would roll and cause breakage and injury. They drank empty the cloth-stoppered bottles of poitín they had brought with them.

They endured.

Then, when the shores of America should have been near, they sailed into deep fog. The ship slowed and then seemed to stop altogether. The passengers came up excitedly expecting to see land and stood silent craning forward and narrowing their eyes into the soft grey blanket that surrounded them. The foghorn sounded. The day passed. The passengers grew accustomed to that sound. Some said it would summon whales and that these were gigantic and would stove in the ship and sink her. Others said the shore of New York was less than a few miles and the fog would rise in the morning and like a cloth lifted they would see the great buildings. Neither proved true. The fog hung on. Huxton stood on the poop with his hands behind his back. There was an eerie silence there. In the absence of storm the water made small sounds now and the sailors did not speak. The food supplies dwindled. The fog remained. The air was cold and windless and no seabirds flew.

The fog lasted another week. It seemed to the families gathered below that they had been chosen for a special purgatory. It was as though they had entered some location whose coordinates were unknown and that after the long history of tragedy they had survived they were now to be kept there enshrouded and apart from human contact where the memory of their hardships would perish with them. They sat and waited. Days passed.

Then the ship swayed.

It swung into a breeze and the sails flapped with a kind of urgency and even there in their quarters below the emigrants knew they had come through. They shouted out. Tomas climbed the stairs and looked out through the air slots of the trap, for it was not their hour to come on deck.

'I can see the sky,' he called. 'I can see a clear sky!'

Two days later they reached land. Huxton stood and watched them enter America.

It was not marvellous or beautiful. They did not feel the sense of welcome they had dreamed of or the richness of opportunity they had been told was there. Instead there were small offices and papers and questions and waiting rooms and certification and cramped huddled crowds moving from one place to the next without yet entering the country proper. They were in quarantine. There were medical examinations and bewildered faces and naked bodies standing in the cold. In all of this Tomas Foley moved indignant and restless. He felt like a trapped animal. He was reminded of his days in the gaol in Limerick and suffered sharp memories of the tenderness of Blath. Once when an officer gazed in his opened mouth at his teeth he thought to lean forward and snap off the man's nose. But he resisted and only blew his breath out and ended the examination.

It occurred to Tomas that he had not fully expected to survive and arrive in America at all. He was to have died already, and had no plans for any future there. On the long voyage he had heard the dreams and hopes of the others and wanted the ship to reach the far shores for their sake only. For himself there was nothing.

But then he arrived in those cold examination halls and suffered the indignities of inspection and somewhere within him an anger fired. He stood in the long queues and saw about him the forlorn figures of the dispossessed and the whole history of his country seemed etched in their faces. They shambled forward and gave their names, and these were Seamus and Sean and Aodhain and Brigid and Maire, and were given with quiet humility and sometimes had to be spelled out slowly for they belonged to another world. And in those moments perhaps Tomas Foley resolved not to be defeated. He tensed like a coil. He stepped forward and had already resolved to make good there, to show all such inspectors and officials and others that he was a Foley. Determination burned in his eyes. His mouth took the firm straight line it was to wear for the rest of his days and his shoulders curved as though he lifted a burden.

He would make good there. He would work at whatever work there was and then send the money for Teige to join him. For the image of his youngest brother left on the island remained with him and he knew he should not have abandoned him so. Guilt muddied all his thoughts. Of Teige's shirt there remained only a rag, but this Tomas kept rolled as a keepsake in the small bundle of his things.

At last he was free and walked into America. He moved out in the uncertain and innocent cluster of his fellow passengers, who looked about them with wide dream-filled eyes and the fear of being out of place. They shambled into the streets with their few belongings. They stayed within ten feet of each other for a brief time, like a herd, and then the crowds of Polish and Germans and others intermingled among them and they were lost to each other and slipped away into the great teeming life of that city.

Tomas had no money. He had arrived in New York, and the air was beginning to turn cold. He followed his oldest instinct and made his way through dusty streets down to a river whose name he did not know was Hudson and then lay down there as the stars appeared. But he could not sleep. He kept seeing figures moving about, shadows, the nameless multitude of the city's doomed. They were like so many leaves, blown, and then blown away. When the dawn arrived he saw for the first time the silhouette of that city, and walked to a street corner where men gathered and stood and waited as at a hiring fair. He was taken then in a wagon and worked on the docks carrying crates of tea and other dry foodstuffs that had come from England and sailed around the shores of the country of famine. Those about him were from a dozen countries. Among them he found the faces of Mayo and Galway and Roscommon and acknowledged them with a small lift of his head but no more, working on until the darkness carrying boxes on his back.

He found a place to live in a tall building that was little better than a workhouse. There were twenty-four iron frames for beds and upon these each night the exhausted fell for sleep. In the dawn Tomas Foley was back on the street corner. Soon those hiring grew accustomed to looking for his face. They chose him quickly and he sat in the wagon while others looked up and tried to broaden their shoulders and contain the coughs that jumped in their chests. The winter came. It stole in along the docks in chill winds and frozen fogs, and then made the streets bitter tunnels of gelid air where people hurried with heads low. Tomas had never felt anything like it. The skin of his face cracked. He had grown a beard by then and it froze hard upon him like an iron mask. Huge snowflakes fell. The city whitened in an hour and within two slowed to a standstill. Horses slid and neighed in alarm, hoofs clopping and breath misting in dragon-like plumes. And the snow kept on falling. It fell at first like blossoms in Maytime but then thickened until the streets were blinded. It fell on the shoulders of the men as they worked and made them briefly blanched like incipient angels. But it did not stop them working. For a week the snow continued. The city stopped and became a frozen image of itself, beautiful but for the dirtied smudge of tramped foot-prints. In the boarding house, men held up their feet and peeled bandages and bloodied bindings from them and made hushed inner groans at frostbite and sores. They were unable to pay and so were told to leave and come back when they could. The place emptied by half. Down at the docks Tomas was kept on. His value as a labourer was already known and he was employed by the firm of Joshua MacMaster, Shipping Merchant, for all that winter. When the snow stopped the ice sealed it hard, and the city of New York remained a dirtied white, stained with grit and grime, and was the image of innocence tarnished.

On his first payday, it had been Tomas's intention to take

half of his money and put it aside for Teige. He planned to do this every week and put the notes under the heel of his boot until there were too many to allow him to walk. Then he would send them back to the island. But in the first weeks of the frozen winter he had come to know an old man in the bed next to him. His name was Patrick O'Loughlin. He was a small wiry figure without hair on his head and quick flickering grey eyes. He had come from the County Galway years before and travelled up and down the eastern coast there in various jobs of uncertain honesty until rheumatism had made claws of his hands and curved his spine like a bow. That winter his money ran out and he could not find work. The day he was told to leave the boarding house he spoke to Tomas, who took off his boot and gave him the money he was to save for Teige. He did not think of it beforehand. He did not consider that it would only last a time and that O'Loughlin would be again on the streets. He gave the money and waved away his hand at the thanks that began on the other man's lips. That evening Tomas sipped from O'Loughlin's whiskey bottle and felt the warmth of goodness flood up through him. It was the first decent thing he had done in America, he thought. It was his way of giving thanks for the good fortune that was now his at MacMaster's. There would be more money for Teige.

Ten days later, after ten nights of sharing the bottles of O'Loughlin, the man told him he was out of money once more. Tomas took off the boot he wore even in bed and gave him another handful of notes.

'You're a great man,' O'Loughlin said. 'If we'd had more of your kind of man we'd never have lost our country.' He paused, and watched the other's face from the side. 'I'll surely have work when the ice is melted,' he said.

And so, somehow, as simple as that and without exactly meaning it to happen, Tomas found himself in the position of sharing all his wages with Patrick O'Loughlin. He worked for two men. He grew stronger. His legs were thickly muscled, his shoulders huge, but the wad of notes in his boot stayed thin. Through the months of January and February the city remained frozen. There were spells of further snow. Tomas wore a heavy greatcoat that he found in the storeroom of one of the ships. It had belonged to a Russian general and still had the epaulettes before he tore them off. He worked on. He heard from some new arrivals mention of the continued famine in his country, and felt rage and impotency both, and that evening told O'Loughlin to get him a bottle of his own. He drank himself unconscious, but managed still to wake in the morning and trudge to the docks.

The spring arrived. It arrived without any of the signals of the springs he had known. He did not see it in buds and birds and grass. On the long avenues and streets it arrived in the air itself and was there almost before he knew it. He left the coat open, then off, then worked in rolled shirtsleeves. It lifted his heart. He imagined seed settings in the island and the terrible year of famine put behind. He worked with the crates that seemed natural now to his hands and shoulders, but his mind was away in the other country.

With the spring came blooms of violence. In the warm evenings hot-headed gangs marched with bats and clashed in street battles over territories unmapped. There were feuds and enmities that the spring fuelled, and men appeared on corners and in alleyways like soldiers without armies but bound to continue in long nameless wars that pre-dated their grand-fathers. They rampaged some nights and battered each other and cried old slogans from campaigns long passed. There were Italians and Slavs and Irish and others and all that spring they clashed by night and released the restless turbulence of their disappointment in that new country by renewing hostilities of old. For his physique, Tomas was soon petitioned to join. O'Loughlin asked him one night as Tomas lay in his cot bed. He told Tomas they had to hang on to whatever they could or they would be run out of that country the same as they had been their own. The Irish had to stick up for themselves. He dressed it greenly so and watched across the semi-darkness of the April night to gauge Tomas's response.

'I told Burke Tomas Foley would be like ten men,' he said.

Tomas lay with his great arms crossed behind his head. The small night noises of the street sounded.

O'Loughlin leaned over. His voice was a whispered laugh.

'You can bate the heads off 'em and the police won't even come near. They're afraid. They're off in the next street and they don't come over. One night Burke's going to go over after them. Bate 'em, too.'

Three nights later Tomas went with O'Loughlin. He met Burke who was a big thick-bodied man with a top lip that sneered permanently upward as though balancing there some droplet of righteousness. He nodded at Tomas. His eyes were hooded. He had large pink hands that were like the skinned flesh of fatted fowl. He said something to one next to him and Tomas recognized the voice of Mayo. Then they were a crowd moving forward. There were cries and shouts and the men beat their sticks and bats into their hands and flowed down the street as one, though flagless and without even the knowledge of the face of their enemy. They erupted into a charge. Some shouted 'Up Ireland' and others cried out the place names of their origins, towns and villages and townlands that they would never see again. These, though cries of war, revealed a sorry truth, for they betrayed the deep-down angers of men landless and adrift in the anonymous vastness of that continent. They were cries of belonging, and as the gangs crashed there on the streets they might have been engaged in some terrible act of reinvention whereby the blood spilled could make good the loss of home.

Or it might have been nothing but the running amok of hot bloody-minded thugs. Tomas watched it happen. The ones they charged against were Italians. He did not know what feud they were engaged in or on which side lay right. He stood back, and though O'Loughlin urged at his elbow and pointed out fellows he should charge and throw into the river, he did not move. Burke was at the rear of the scene. He studied Tomas with tight-lipped expression and turned away when O'Loughlin failed to get him engaged.

'You could kill a dozen of 'em,' O'Loughlin said. 'You could take any of 'em you wanted.' His eyes were crazed and shallow, and Tomas turned from him and walked away up the street with men shouting and beating at each other at his back.

He did not go out again on the night streets for all the rest of that month. He worked overtime for free. He volunteered to stand await for ships in the night. He tried to exhaust his body and then shut down his mind with the whiskey O'Loughlin got for him. Still, sometimes the image of open fields came before him and he felt the closure of his life and its constraints and he wanted to strike out against these. He ran the crates then up and down the gangways, he worked the great mitts of his hands and the deep muscles of his shoulders until the sweat ran glistening off him and his eyes attained the faraway look of one beaten and whipped a long time.

Then one summer evening when he was still at the docks Burke came to see him. Two others who stood back attended him. Burke gestured Tomas to him with a fat pink finger. He told Tomas that famine had struck again in their country. He made a sneer of his lip and told him they were dying again in the fields and roadways and that this would only worsen as the harvest time drew on. He said they could all be dead soon. He asked Tomas what he was going to do to help, and did not wait for an answer. He said he was sure Tomas would do what every good man of their country would do.

Tomas said nothing. He looked out at the Hudson river sleek and black and he thought of it flowing all the way across the world and into the mouth of the Shannon.

Burke put a hand on his shoulder.

'You have family there. We all have family there,' he said.

'We have to help them. We need a rebellion, and for that we need funds.'

By the time Burke left there Tomas Foley's wages were to be halved. The money was to be his contribution towards helping overthrow the enemies of his country. He could think of it as money for Teige. It was what had to be done.

That summer the city boiled. Waves of heat floated and bent the streets and burnt off the shoulders and arms and faces of those unused to it. There was no air. Some, freckle-faced men of pale skin, fell at their work in spells and faints or drank the river water and felt their brains swell and bulge in the baked shells of their skulls. It was hotter than they had ever known. It seemed they breathed in the oven breath of a giant beast that towered over the city. Workers who had come from other countries were less afflicted, and could be seen then in a kind of swaggering ease, their tanned bodies slick with oil and their smiles white.

Through it Tomas Foley laboured on. He became nothing, another in the myriad of emigrant workers in that city who lived without hope a thing too empty to call a life. He worked, he drank, he gave over his money to O'Loughlin and Burke.

He burned in summer, he froze in winter. It was only during the short springs or in early autumn that he felt any ease, and in these he was tormented with memories of the country left behind.

And years slipped by.

He learned that the famine had struck again. And then again. He saw the ships of the wretched come and knew well the wan and hollowed look of those families who had survived starvation and sickness and the sea. They seemed to him to look in more desperation than those of the year before, and were like casualties in some long horrific war. He could not bear to look in their faces. They were grey figures, sunken-cheeked, with ruined teeth and bloodied gums, collarbones poking outward, flesh dried and dead and flaking. There were forlorn grandmothers and mothers and children thin as sticks. A hard wind might have snapped them. One day he saw four boys of eight and ten in dirtied shirts and the expressions of old men with coughs making their eyes water. Their father had been buried on the sea. Tomas's throat rose at the sight of them. He held his teeth tightly together to stop his jaw from shaking. He looked about at the sorry assembly arrived there and thought: these must be the last left living in my country. And now they are here. He did not ask them. He did not go forward and tell them that he had been one of them too. Instead he kept his head down and worked on and banged the crates and spat angrily into the river whenever the vision of suffering assailed him. That night he came back to the boarding house soured and bitter and told O'Loughlin to get him two bottles of whiskey. When the little man returned Tomas told him he would give no more money to Burke. He told him it was useless, what had they done? O'Loughlin tried to say great progress had been made, plans were afoot, but Tomas turned and grabbed him by the throat and held and shook him like that and then threw him back on the bed with a curse. The small man said nothing more then.

In deep sleep that night Tomas dreamed his country was a woman who ran a knife across the surface of her womb. Her blood ran out like a stream and he watched it, that awful emptying that flowed over the ground. And it took the form of ghost-like faces. Tomas saw his father and his brother among them. He woke. There was a cold sweat over him.

My father and Teige are dead, he thought.

He blinked his eyes at the darkness of the long room. He lay there like that a time to steady himself. Then he leaned over and reached in the canvas bag of his things that he kept beneath the bed and he took out the tattered rolled rag of his brother's shirt. He held it in his hands and sat so, and it was some time before he noticed that Patrick O'Loughlin was gone, along with both of his boots and all the money he had in the world.

13

He could not stay there after that. When he gathered his senses Tomas Foley walked out of that place barefoot into the streets and never returned to the dockside warehouse of Joshua MacMaster, Shipping Merchant. He just walked away. He walked westward, trying to increase with each footstep the distance between himself and his country.

He is lost then from any history. He disappears from the story, vanished into the crowds of those nameless and without domain until one winter's night some years later in a small town not far from the city of Cincinnati.

It was snowing. The flakes whirled out of the dark. Tom Foley, for so he was now, walked out of a bar and a man came after him and hit him across the back with a swung rifle. He fell face-forward into the slush of the street. The man said nothing. He raised the rifle by its barrel a second time. He wore a coat of furs and a hat of beaver skin. His face was blotched from raw whiskey and he blinked his eyes as he swung again. The rifle arced through the snow air and on the ground Tom Foley rolled to avoid it. He kicked out with his right leg and the fur man toppled and soon both were tumbling over in the mud of the street. Men came and stood to watch in the yellow lamplight. The fur man was large and grunted and tried to make fist blows from the side. But Tom paid them no heed. He rolled the man easily and then struck him hard in the midriff. Then he stood up.

He stepped two paces away in his Russian greatcoat and

brushed at it with his hands. And in so doing he did not hear the man cock the rifle at his back. There was a moment upon which his life balanced. The snow, the mud, the yellow light, the smoke that hung there, the horses and the smells of sweat and dirt and whiskey, all were part of it. Somewhere in him he sensed his own death. It was as if Death himself suddenly appeared there as a grey phantasm in the street and in that same instant Tom Foley knew that He had come for him. For then the rifle fired. He saw his own blood spurt out through him and briefly rouge the snowy air. It shot out in fierce and sudden leakage and his brain fuddled with incomprehension as to whence it came. He looked down. The coat was holed clean through below his ribs. He fingered it and like a child then pressed the finger further until it was inside the hole in himself. The bleeding ceased and he fell on his knees. He was there in the street unhanded by any and studied by a few as the snow fell upon him. The fur man staggered to his feet. He swayed with the rifle that smoked thinly still. Some element of conscience fought within him for he turned to those watching and showed an expression of both strange pride and bafflement that he had shot a man in the back.

Tom felt Death lay hands upon him. The snow touched his face but he could not feel it. He wanted to close his eyes. His hand upon his side was soaked in blood and it squelched when he lifted and replaced it. He was cold. He knelt there and did not fall over, like one faulty in the performance of dying. The fur man behind him held the rifle another minute. None stepped out from the sidewalk. They shuffled there and murmured and held their glasses and waited. The rifle passed along the line of them as the fur man turned and gazed upon them as on a jury. Then he threw the rifle on the ground and hurried away through the falling snow.

A man walked forward then and touched Tom Foley on the side of his neck and then called to others and these came and carried the wounded man from the street.

Three days later Tom Foley learned that the bullet had passed through him. The doctor that attended him was Philip James Brown. He was a strongly built man of about sixty years with a round head and thin reddish hair. His eyes were kind and his manner assured. He had had Tom brought to a room at the side of his own house where men of various kinds had lain to recover. There he had dressed and wrapped the wound and doctored it. He had said little at first, the gravity of the situation denying it, then as Tom Foley sat propped on the bed Philip Brown asked him where he was from. To the response he did not say anything at first. He nodded his head and offered Tom a drink. He watched him while he took it. He asked him what his plans were.

'I have given up making plans.'

'That a fact?'

'I plan to live until I die.'

'Glad to hear it. Hate to hear a man wanted to die after I stopped him bleeding all over my floor.'

'I'm grateful for what you did. I will repay you.'

'I didn't do it for the money.'

'Why did you?' Tom Foley asked him.

'I'm a doctor,' Brown said, and he sat there in a chair by the bed and held his drink and the two of them dwelled in the amber hush of twilight and said no more as the noises in the street came and went.

Less than a week later Tom was able to walk. The first thing he did was go outside of the house and around to the back where he managed one-handed to swing an axe and split the many logs that were assembled there. When the doctor returned he looked at the timber and thought to admonish the patient but simply thanked him instead.

'I will be gone tomorrow,' Tom said.

'Gone where?' Brown said.

'On.'

'I see. Plans?'

'No.'

The doctor said no more then. He waited until the evening had drawn in and the street darkened and he and Tom Foley sat one last time on the porch seats where the doctor liked to smoke in the chill winter air.

'How're you going to repay me?' Brown said. He was looking away over the small fence that separated them from the street.

'You didn't want me to.'

'Not money, I said.' The doctor kept his eyes far away. He seemed to be engaged in some study of the air in the middle distance.

Tom Foley looked at him.

'What?'

'Well, let's see here,' Brown said. 'I saved your life, that's for sure, right?'

'Yes.'

'Well, then, there has to be some payment, otherwise every fool in the street'll be shooting down some other fella saying Doc Brown will patch him up no charge. You see my point? Where would that leave me? No there has to be something,' he said and drew on his cigarette and waited. A moon was rising through clouds and suddenly the snowed street turned a dirty yellow.

'What?' Tom Foley asked him again.

'I have a lifelong interest in this country,' the doctor said then. 'Had it since I was a small boy and my mamma told me she had come here on a ship from Scotland and that this country had been her saviour. That's what she called it. Her saviour. And I often got to thinking about that. How can a country be your saviour? And I didn't know then about all she had suffered and her sea voyage and all that. I didn't know her father had been hunted down and hanged and that she had seen him swinging from a tree. She told me that only when she was lying in a bed dying and raving with fever.'

He paused and pushed his lower lip out and back a little, then he took his right hand and rubbed at his chin stubble and waited a time.

'So, she had a good life after that beginning. That's what struck me. That's what it is about this country. You can begin here. It can be your saviour. Long as you don't get shot down in the street,' he added and made a small smile in the corners of his lips.

'There's a man going to make this country better,' Brown said. His voice was soft but firm. 'He's going to find a way to bring the railroad all the way to California.' He paused again and let the smoke drift on the cold and seem a measure of the vastness of that distance in geography.

'I want you to go with him, Tom,' he said at last.

The night was still. The chairs creaked on the old porch.

'I want you to keep an eye on him. He's been shot two times already.' The doctor rocked in his chair and the clouds came and passed across the face of the moon.

'Who is he?' Tom Foley asked then.

The doctor did not turn to him, his features obscured in the poverty of clouded moonlight.

'He's my son,' he said.

14

Tom Foley left the doctor's house two days later and rode westward on a chestnut gelding that once belonged to a man who had been gut shot in the street and cut and patched and sewn up by Brown. That man was General Isaac Stephens, under whose command a unit of the Corps of Topographical Engineers of the US Army was engaged in surveying the land west of the Mississippi river for a rail route that would join the two sides of the continent. In that unit was one Lieutenant Philip J. Brown, engineer, draughtsman and map-reader.

'When Stephens sees his horse, he'll know I sent you,' the doctor had said. 'He owes me. You'll ride with them. Give him this.' He handed over a letter. 'Say nothing to Phil, mind. But send me a letter sometimes. You know, to say how he is.'

Tom Foley had sat the horse and nodded at the old man. He did not say he had never written a letter in his life. The doctor blinked his eyes and then raised a hand in sudden salute and went off inside.

15

General Stephens was at that time in a fort near Quincy on the Mississippi river. It was further than Tom Foley had ever travelled over land. He had been shown where it was on the doctor's map, but only knew it as a point directly westward. Still, he would find it. It was not yet spring and the wind blew cold and bitter as he rode. He wore the collars of his greatcoat up and his hat low. The land spread out before him. He galloped the horse through terrain green and rolling and fringed with mountains. He travelled on. He did not stop for he feared the army unit would be gone and the lieutenant with them. He came out into bright hard days and followed for a time the stagecoach road to St Louis. Then he left this and cut northward as was his understanding of the map. He crossed a hundred small rivers and sometimes stopped and watered the horse and crouched down to taste the current before continuing. He rode with a sense of mission. He heard the hoofs of his horse beat over the ground and took from that some kind of ease and satisfaction. He was happiest in motion. Sometimes he saw a coach or wagon or a lone rider or more, but all he left alone and did not seek any company. The vastness of the land made his spirit tranquil, for the more he journeyed on in the same relentless way, day after day, the more the griefs of his past became numbed and then slipped away. He was a figure in the landscape, nothing more. He was a momentary speck on the huge open space he crossed and he took from this some portion of peace.

At last he arrived at the Mississippi river. He was south of the fort and travelled along the muddied banks where rains made swift the flow. When he came into the fort he asked to see the general and was told by a soldier in blue uniform that this was not possible and was asked what was his business. Tom told him he had a personal message for the general and it was to be delivered by hand. Ten minutes later he was standing at a table in the log-built quarters of Stephens. He was a stocky man with heavy sideburns of brown hair. He wore his hat. He looked above the pages of the letter at Tom.

'You ride?' he said.

Tom Foley said he did.

'You can shoot a rifle?'

Tom Foley lied that he did.

Three days later, he left the fort with Unit 49 of the Corps of the so-called 'Topogs' division of the United States Army. Lieutenant Philip J. Brown was the commanding officer of their number of eight men. Stephens himself had decided not to ride. He had already been on various expeditions through Minnesota and North Dakota and Montana, and this time he left Brown the job of reconnoitring the lands through Nebraska and beyond the Wyoming Territory.

The general had told them that Tom Foley was scout, cook, rifleman, water-diviner, and horse doctor. They led pack mules with supplies for six months and rode out of the fort with the pale March sun at their backs. They had all manner of maps, accurate to a degree, some sketched by trackers, crusty pioneers and Indian hunters. Of the eight men, seven of them knew intimately the paper geography of the country ahead. They had studied it at length, could name gullies and canyons and mountain passes that were eighteen hundred miles further than they themselves had ever been. They rode that morning with the confidence of such knowledge and were tall in their saddles. Some of the men were younger than Tom. They had been at schools in the east and joined the army not to fight but to be part of that other enterprise of the advancement westward of law and justice and civilization. They were to be part of Manifest Destiny. When they had first heard heady talk of the railroad that would shrink the continent, a railroad that when completed would make possible the circumnavigation of the globe in ninety-three days, their heads caught fire. It was a fire that was easily fed, for it burned on the stuff of young men's dreams, of voyaging into the unknown and leaving there a mark inviolable and absolute. They saw the railroad in their sleep. They saw the iron tracks running on and on across untrammelled terrain of prairie and desert and were drawn to the dream of tracing a line on that vast emptiness. In rooms in cool evenings by the fireside they fingered ways across the Rocky Mountains, the Sierra Nevada, deserts west of Missouri.

And now there they were. They rode out those fine spring mornings with the air soft and the world like a thing newborn. The broad sky was before them. They rode in single file without discourse and assumed the manner of such men who knew that the way was to be long and tongues would tire before horses. They rode from the Mississippi westward and crossed the Missouri river above St Joseph and were as yet on lands already well surveyed for rails. They crossed then into Nebraska and soon their progress slowed as the engineers stopped and studied and charted the land. They opened maps and knelt on them in swift, capricious winds. They marked coördinates and spoke among themselves and did not say more than two words to Tom Foley but to ask him to fetch something or ride out and see what danger lay beyond the next canyon. He did so without pause. It was bigger country than he had ever dreamed and when riding alone across the prairies and open spaces he felt himself vanished from the world of men and achieved a kind of serenity there. Still, his rifle was at his side. He had seen Indians at the fort and and he had thought them peaceable and proud. But he had not as yet encountered what the engineers referred to as hostiles.

Brown he found to be energetic and earnest. He was blue-eyed, had a peak of thinning blond hair and a way of addressing the others that made his statements seem urgent. When he spoke at the fireside about the railroad his eyes glittered. He gestured with his hand and waved it like a wing. He told them to think how it would be if they were the ones to find the true route. He told them that the way they would chart the rails would endure for all time afterwards.

'It will be like this,' he said, and reached and marked with the blade of his knife a straight line in the sand. 'That. Done. See. Marked out on the ground. Once. And never changed.' He looked across the fire and they looked at the line in the sand. For some time the men retained their gaze there and mutely considered it, and as the firesmoke wavered to and fro it was as if they could then imagine the great iron engine moving along ever closer until it was beating down through the very darkness behind them. As if, while the men each day moved on, behind them sprang up stations and telegraph offices and saloons and smithies and all manner of lean-to clapboard premises to fulfil the needs of man and become the cities of tomorrow.

Then Brown scuffed at the line with his heel and made it vanish. But his eyes glittered yet. The night passed.

They rode on. They crossed lands that had once been covered by glaciers and later by beasts unnumbered whose names were unknown and, later still, which were part of Indian country. And all that vast and empty landscape seemed to Tom Foley to echo still with a chimerical after-presence. They passed over a plain where a great herd of bison moved before them like a brown tide. As the animals ran their dust hung in the breezeless air and was a cloud low and sad and slow-fading. None of the men had ever seen such a herd and they stood upright in their saddles and pushed back their hats. Then one of them who was young and whose name was Cartwright let out a cry and spurred his horse and galloped in pursuit. He pulled a rifle as he rode and the others sat and watched as he tore into the dust and let off a shot at the blue sky. The bison charged. Their noise travelled over the plain and was the noise of hoof and bellow and fear. Cartwright raced on. The rifle he raised to his shoulder but the motion of the horse and his own lack of expertise at such caused the weapon to waver right to left like the upturned rod of some demented diviner. He fired. The report of the bullet was a sharp and hard crack. The shot would have missed all but the widest target, and as the herd thundered on a beast lay fallen in the dust. Cartwright rode past it. He fired again at the air and then again before he reined the horse and turned about a small circle in the passing cloud. The bison passed on. Slowly as the dust settled there resumed the air of tranquillity over the plain, but it was like a thing fractured and repaired and ever fragile now. The troop rode on to where the animal lay and Cartwright next to it still astride his horse.

'This is the US Army, Cartwright, do you hear me?' Brown asked.

'Yes, sir.'

'This is not some band of renegades, or wild men or hunters.'

'No, sir.'

'We have orders.'

'Yes, sir.'

Brown studied the distance.

'If I want you to shoot an animal I will say so.'

'Yes, sir.'

A pair of birds, dark shapes high in the blue, glided toward them.

'Very well,' Brown said, 'you shot it, you skin and carve it. We'll be at camp down there.'

He squeezed his thighs and they moved off then and left the soldier there and Tom Foley stayed with him to help. Later, when he and Cartwright's arms were stained to the elbow with blood and they looked like perpetrators of some foul savagery, they sat exhausted on the plain. The sun beat down. Scavenger birds cut arcs in the blue. After a time the soldier thanked the other for his help.

'Do you know writing?' Tom asked him.

'What kind of writing?'

'Letters. I'm long out of practice.'

'I suppose I do.'

That night Cartwright wrote a short letter for Tom Foley. Because Tom did not want the soldier to know his business, he asked him the words in jumbled order and later copied these in his own hand. When it was done his letter read:

Dear Doctor,

He is out in country big and grand. He is right well. He is finding a route. I am watching out for him.

Yours,

Tom Foley.

They journeyed on. They did not see the Indians that saw them. They camped by the many lakes in the sand hills there and ate pheasant and quail and waterfowl. Summer thunderstorms crashed over them. Coyotes and foxes and badgers ran across the evening light. The men passed up over the grasslands and sheltered betimes in forests of oak and hickory and cottonwood where the shade was welcome but harboured thin clouds of insects that ate at their faces. These trees would be felled, Brown told them.

'These are our sleepers,' he said.

They traversed the North Platte river into Wyoming Territory and came to Fort Laramie and refreshed supplies. Tom left his letter there and after four days they travelled on again. They rode north to the pale red horizon of mountains. They came to desolate lands where alkali dust was deep to the knee and the water had to be rationed to drops and the horses and mules lifted up their lips to suck in vain for moisture in the air. The men's faces burned and tanned like leather hides. They followed the routes of fur traders and gold seekers and those who had sought to make homes in the far land of Oregon. The days stayed dry. A high wind blew without cease and moved the sagebrush and buffalo grass. Whitened skulls and brittle ribcages of beasts long slain lay in disassembled poses like things struck and shattered by time. Sunlight dazzled there. The small troop passed along the boundaries of forests of pine and spruce and fir and sometimes saw moose step quickly away. They rode all the time with the knowledge of the great barrier that lay before them, for in the high-ceilinged rooms where men had dreamed of the railroad the Rocky Mountains always lay, like God's defiance, in the way. To bring the rails through the mountains would be a kind of ultimate proclamation, a statement sent heavenward of all that man could attempt and master.

This all the engineer soldiers knew. They rode with their gaze fixed on the peaks ahead. Slowly then they ascended through narrow passes and dry gullies. They wound their way upward beneath the blue sky and found themselves in the stillness and silence that seemed of another world. The sun burned its relentless fire. The men dismounted and led their animals and were a thin ragged line of blue coats and might have been the last remnants of a vanquished and forgotten tribe, wandering there until they fell thinly and the sun blanched their bones. The harsh majesty of that place assailed them. They progressed almost not at all, yet all day moved about trying to find routes that were not impossible. Sometimes they tethered the horses and then Tom and Cartwright and Brown made their way up through the mountains on foot, scrabbling over the warm rocks, to find viewpoints for surveillance.

One time on such an occasion they scrambled up the mountain only to meet a bear. The bear saw them before they saw it. It had smelled them coming and laboured a time between curiosity and fear. Then when the men's heads appeared the bear froze. It watched them like creatures landed from the moon. Briefly it crouched and in those moments seemed to belie its own reputation for ferocity. Brown's head came up above the rock to the ledge. He saw the bear and let out a curse and whether it was the noise or the wide whites of his eyes or the sharp tang of fear that burned on the air then, the bear rose. Brown called back to the others behind him. He tried to get them to retreat but already the bear was coming forward. It was less than an instant, then the noise of the bear and the size of the bear both achieved that aim and the men turned about and sought places below them to jump. But there were none. The bear roared. It stood and made as yet no other action as if such were not required but that the evidence of its own magnificence was sufficient to make all enemies surrender. The men pushed backward and were close together and reached for weapons. The bear opened its jaws and roared again and slavered a whitish loop. It moved forward in a massive lunge at the blond head of Lieutenant Brown. Then Tom Foley shot it. The bullet hit the bear in the forehead. Its head twitched backward as if tugged by wire to something greater than itself. The men saw the puzzlement register in its eyes and then the bear dismissed it and came forward again, and Tom Foley shot it once more and Cartwright shot it too. The bear howled out and shuddered and twisted and its right leg gave beneath it and it fell.

The silence regathered in the mountains.

'You saved our lives,' Brown said. Then they moved away from there and left the great corpse of the bear on the ledge.

They went on. All through the rest of that summer and into the autumn that unit of the Topographical Engineers of the US Army travelled up and down the various ranges of the Rocky Mountains. They drew maps and charts and sent these sometimes by rider back to Fort Laramie. But they did not find a way to bring the railroad through the mountains. The air turned cold in the beginning of October. The rider brought back two mules laden with heavy blankets and other supplies for the winter. The first snows fell. Mountain lions came down and prowled and Tom and Cartwright sat watch and fired rifle shots. At the campfire Brown told the others they could go back. He said the winter would be harsh and long. He said he himself was going to stay on, that he could not give up now, but that for any that wanted he could issue orders to return to the fort.

None of the men left him. They watched the way his eyes burned when he spoke of what they could achieve and the candles lit in their own eyes, too.

The winds became knives. The skin of their faces peeled off, then the new skin dried hard and cracked and in wrinkled lines turned scarlet as though branded by the burning feet of crows. Their lips blistered and opened at the corners and the burst skin puffed with pus. Their legs froze on the flanks of their horses. In their long boots their toes turned numb and they had to jump down and fall over and pull off the boots to try and beat the blood back into their feet with their hands. Two of the horses died overnight. They froze like things iced in a fairy-tale. From then on the men tethered the horses together and blanketed them and made their own rests beneath their legs so the meagre heat of their bodies might rise to the animals. They came on snows thick to the waist. They dug out small tunnels and made tiny progress and one time encountered the upright body of a frozen man with bluish face and finger pointing as if at the way to eternity. The fierce season made even emptier that empty place. They seemed the only ones then, as if the rest of the world had perished or been taken in judgement and they alone were overseen and endured in that white and pure domain.

In those days, in that place where time seemed ceased and the very change of which they were to be the agent was nowhere evident, Tom Foley's mind wandered into the past. He thought often of his youngest brother. He lay beneath the wide magnificence of the night skies there and tried to recall the stories of the stars Teige had told when they were younger. He looked for the Great Bear and Cassiopeia and Cepheus and he remembered stories of winged horses and charioteers and deeds heroic and fantastical. In his mind he heard Teige tell them the way he had learned them from their mother. For days then Tomas's mind drifted. He rode with visions. He passed a white day moving through the mountains but was in all but body thousands of miles away in the green fields of the island of the saint. He was there with Teige and his father. And his mother Emer was there, too. And the twins. And all were as they had once been and were not aged or changed and his mother's hair blew on the soft breeze in that place she had never seen. They were walking over the way toward the tower. He saw the blossoms on the berry bushes. He smelled the furze and the blooms of May and let his hand touch against them as he went. And all of that verdant loveliness that had entered him once now rose and screened the other world. He sat on his horse and let the reins hang limp and walked it forward behind the others, rocking softly in the saddle and drifting back to that place where he last felt a sense of home. Snow flurried and crowned his hat. The muffled clop of hooves made a rhythm slow and hypnotic and Tom Foley's eyes dulled into that look that in his country was called 'away with the fairies'. It endured for a certain time. But it stopped abruptly when he saw the face of his wife, Blath. Then the grief rose through him. He saw the ghostly faces of those multitudes dying on the roadways and their shrunken bodies and pulled himself upright on his horse and lifted his face into the wind that it might sear him.

They are dead now, he thought. All of them are dead now.

16

They did not find the route for the railroad that winter. Nor at any time in the year that followed. They sent plans and drawings and their suggestions east, but heard nothing in reply. They imagined themselves forgotten. Brown used this as his principal motivation. He told them the politicians were arguing among themselves. He said there was probably no one who thought it could be done and that the finances of the country were being spent elsewhere. He said he believed the gold in California had finished and so greed no longer fuelled the enterprise. He told the men this and they sat hunched and worn and aged about a fire. And then he raised his voice and said that he was still going on. Who would continue with him? After a time it became needless to ask. They rode on. They passed across the mountains and down into Fort Bridger but were met there with looks curious and askance, full beards and tattered uniforms lending them the air of renegades. None felt welcomed. For they were not engaged in the business of that army proper, and might have been like some figments or ghosts travailing in a shadow-world. They left and rode back to the mountains and felt they were men grown intolerant of all but each other's company.

They travelled northward up into the lands of Montana. The seasons slipped past them. They crossed over the Rockies and down past the Big Horn. They rode wide of the villages of the Indians. And not Crow nor Blackfoot nor Cheyenne nor Arapaho did they kill in all that time.

But by then time itself was vanished for them. They existed outside of any history and knew only their horses and the land. They did not know of wars and treaties and treaties broken. They did not know how the maps of that country were being redrawn even as they rode over the land. They did not know that in Fort Laramie they themselves were reported murdered by Indians, that their relatives had been informed, and that another troop had set off likewise to find the best rail route west. Brown's men rode on. No maps and charts and graphs were drawn any more. The relentless immensity of the land itself made weary the vision of the railroad and at times they forgot what it was they were seeking. Days and weeks could pass without mention of it. In three years Tom Foley had written three letters to Doctor Brown about his son. But only the first of these had reached other hands. The other two Tom had given to traders and these had never been seen again.

So it was. They rode in the mountains.

Then one day, in the April of the year, they came down to a clear running stream and dismounted and ducked their faces and shook the great hanks of their knife-cut beards and were in general ease when arrows landed in the chests of three of them. They fell forward on their faces. The arrows had made such small noise that at first the others did not understand. They looked along the stream at the fallen soldiers. Then arrows landed in the throats of two more of them and pierced them through. There were Indians on horseback in the stream. The water plashed and made broad translucent arcs either side of the horses as they came and such things seemed to be in slow motion or exist in fragments and shards where the mind's perception shattered with shock and fear. Another arrow flew, the sound a whirr. Then Cartwright fell as he ran to his horse and rifle. Then the Indians were upon them. There were five or seven or maybe nine. Tom Foley could not be sure. He saw the one coming on a white pony with toma-hawk waving and saw the triple scars across his chest. He saw the feathers in his hair. Then he jumped up at him and there was a moment and he was airborne and grappling the Indian about the midriff and the tomahawk was being raised to sink in his skull. Then the two of them were crashed in the stream and went below the surface of the water, and Tom's hands found the neck of the other and closed upon it and drowned him there. Beneath the water he heard the sound of gunfire. When he stood again Brown was aiming his pistol and pulling the trigger time and again without a bullet firing. There was a long arrow in his thigh. Two of the Indians lay in the water. Another was running at him with knife drawn. Tom shouted out. He saw the Indian sink the knife in Philip Brown and was then upon him. He pulled him down as Brown fell back, and they tumbled on to the wet gravel of the riverbed and wrestled there. The Indian was younger and smaller than him and twisted and rolled like one demented. He broke free and stood and pranced on the ground, as might a dancer. He had no weapon. Tom Foley stood up and looked at him and they were so some little time, the Indian jostling in the space and ready to leap and the other still and braced and looking him in the eye. The moment held. There was the small noise of the stream and the groans of a man. The water ran red past them.

Then, the moment snapped, the Indian turned and ran and jumped on to the back of his pony and was gone.

Tom Foley stood there.

He watched where the other rode away. Then he walked past the fallen to Brown and knelt down and put his hand before that man's mouth and then placed his ear on his chest. He was living still. Tom reached down then and took the shaft of the arrow low as he could and snapped it. Brown did not open his eyes. The blood from the knife wound pumped freely.

'Oh God,' Tom said. 'Oh God in heaven.'

He went and took the shirt of one of the men and tore it lengthways and came back and applied pressure to the wound with both his hands until the blood stopped coming between his fingers. Then he bound the wound as best he could, and crossed down to his horse and brought up the canteen and poured the water over the lieutenant's face.

Brown opened his eyes.

'You can't die,' Tom Foley told him. 'I promised your father.'

It took Tom Foley thirty-two days to get Lieutenant Philip James Brown back to fort Laramie. And another five months before the son was fit enough to take the stagecoach back east to meet his father.

When it was done, Tom decided to ride back up into the mountains. But before he did there came into the fort a wagon train, and among the homesteaders was a family whose name was Considine. He saw their freckled faces and he stood and asked them how long it was they were in that country. They spoke with the accent of the County Clare and told him they had come over only six months ago.

'Are they not all dead there?' Tom asked.

'No, indeed. No,' said Mary Considine, who was the man's sister, struck by the sadness of the question.

That night, with her help, Tom Foley sat and wrote a letter to his brother Teige.

Dear Brother,

I do not know if you are living or dead. I do not know if our father is living or dead.

I am in America. I came here to make the railroad. I am in first rate health. My mind wanders some times to the days long ago. I had your shirt a long time Teigey and I intended to send you money to come. Then I thought all were dead there on account of the famine was in the potatoes.

This is a big country. I have been in the mountains. And sometimes there I thought I saw the ghost of you passing.

I miss those times we had. I have lost all feeling of people here. I'd like to see you coming over a green field on the white pony.

    I remain,

        Your devoted brother

          Tom Foley

Four

I

The story leaves him and returns to the island. Always the story returns there. The teller changes the lens and the green slope of the island reappears in focus. And it is as if the teller understands that the island is an image for all Foleys thereafter, that there was something passionate and impetuous in the character of the family that made each of its men islands in turn, and that this was a trait deeply fated and irreversible. It was their nature.

On the island of Francis Foley in time the telescope aged. The hundred seasons of the rain, of drizzle and mist, shower, sleet, spells sudden and violent of cloudburst and downpour, worked their way into its timbers. The wet winds that braced the river came inside the tower of the saint where all that time the telescope lay propped at an angle to see the stars. Its timbers shrank. Fissures worm-like climbed with slow persistence toward the brass rims. The beeswax that had once been worked into its surface by the monks was long since desiccated and returned to the air. Now it grew more and more to resemble the man who, grave and silent, visited it each night like an eremite. The golden curls that had once been his were white now. The strength of his body that had one time been a vision of potency and inviolable faith in his place in the world was now vanished. As if wires had been cut the musculature was slackened, and his was a figure wasted with the angles of his elbows and other joints in odd protuberance like fallen tenting. His past was longer than his future now and haunted his eyes and gave to them an expression at one time vacant and deep as if seeing but not what lay before him. By that time Francis Foley's manner was quieter than a whisper. In the daylight he slept in the corner of the stone cashel where he and Teige had survived the famine on fish and berries and the rabbits that lived there. When he woke Teige fed him. They sat either side of the low fire and the smoke travelled about them.

Language had slipped away from them. It passed in the first season after the disappearance of Tomas and did not fully return. It was as if the winds that blew were a keening or requiem and father and son said nothing but sat and listened, until in time they found they had passed beyond dialogue and were in a place now where such was impossible. In the place of words were sometimes small gestures, the least lift of eyebrow, wrinkle of lip or nod of head. But even these were barely required. In the afternoons the old man went out around the island. He walked in a slow ramble and kept in his hand a hazel rod, always going around by the shoreline and doing so in all weathers as if it were a station of penance and while he trod there he revisited sins of his past. Then, when the night fell, swift in winter, slow in summer, he returned and went to the tower. One night the noises of his efforts as he moved the telescope into place alarmed his son. The father's chest made a soft soughing as if sycamores in full leaf rustled there. And Teige came to him and appeared in the doorway of the tower and then came inside and helped him get the telescope into position. His father made the half-smile of gratitude that always verged on weeping. Then Teige left him and crossed back beneath the stars and wondered for the millionth time at how nothing else in the visible world now seemed to matter for the old man. All nights after that Teige came and prepared the telescope. It made no difference if the night sky was occluded or rain fell. Francis Foley would still take his place there, lying down on a bed of hay and opening and closing his mouth as he brought his face to the eyepiece and fitted it there. He lay there until the dawn gathered in the stars. He lay in what private perusal Teige could not for a long time imagine. For it seemed a practice cold and aloof and without purpose other than a fascination the father should have outgrown. Still it endured. And it was not until one night in the October of the year after Tomas had left that it finally fell to Teige to discover what the old man was doing.

It was a night brilliant with constellations. And all the stars from Pisces to Pegasus to Hercules and on above to the Canes Venatici glittered. Teige could not sleep. He lay in the stone building where the air was cold and damp with the coming of winter. The mud floor, as if it received the season ahead of time, as if winter and summer and spring rose from below and did not fall from above, exhaled a chill dark breath. It travelled inside the clothes on Teige's back and made him shiver so that he rose and beat his hands against his arms. The plume of his effort came and went visible on the pale starlit air. The dog raised its head and lowered it again. Teige looked to the bed of hay where his father never slept in the night, then he stepped outside beneath the sky and stood and watched all that was still and yet slowly moving there. The river was quiet. Across on the farther shore the town of Kilrush slept in an unlit huddle. Teige walked out and went, to where the pony was standing. He stroked her neck and her flanks and lay his head against her. Then he went back across the wet grass to the wall where he saw the glass of the telescope glinting. He crossed to the tower, but not in such a way that his father would see him. When he reached the wall he pressed in against it and came around the curve so, until he was next to the doorway where the eye of the telescope peered out. Teige squatted down then, and from that position aligned his naked eye to the view of the stars his father beheld. He found Cassiopeia and Ursa Major and Minor and the myriad of others that gradually revealed themselves the longer he stared. The night slipped on, the stars wheeled another fraction in their endless turning. The cold made Teige embrace himself and he crouched there small and shivering and attendant to that ancient pattern wherein his father's mind roamed.

Then he heard the whisper.

At first he was not sure if it was his own dream speaking, or if at such a time in the night sprites or other such came and whispered for mischief and devilment. He pressed his ear closer to the doorway. Then he heard his father say words in a tone barely audible. He could not know what they were. His father was lying on his back with the telescope to his eye and the sounds travelled upward in the high acoustic of the tower and were all but lost to him. Teige heard them like the smallest noise; the footstep of fox or badger coming from some covert might have been louder. He leaned more forward still and turned his mouth back that his breath might not give him away. Then he heard them again. The old man was speaking. The words slipped off his lips and rose and faded and still Teige could not make them out. Then he took a greater chance and leaned in below the angle of the telescope and was in the same space where he could see his father's prone body and hear now what he was saying.

'. . . what sorrow is mine is mine. I am not asking for less,' he said. 'Do you hear me?' he whispered. 'Listen.' He paused. His breath was a sigh. Teige heard his heart thumping.

'I am asking for her. And for my sons.'

His voice then was thinner still. It seemed to Teige that he said some words that did not escape his mouth, that these were formed in the air like silent promises or prayers and ascended into the ether of space as so many credos must have in the centuries since that tower was constructed. Teige moved back and sat once more outside against the wall. He pressed back his head and felt his body shake. He looked up at the stars and blinked, for they swam in water like swans.

Every night after that Teige came and listened outside the tower where his father watched the sky. He understood then that the constellations had become for the old man the face of God and that while gazing upon it Francis Foley confessed sins of pride and others that he hoped might redeem the souls of his wife and sons. To the pitch of his whispers Teige grew accustomed and soon could hear almost all his father said. There, he heard the old man tell God the name Teige. He heard him ask of Tomas and Finan and Finbar. Some nights he heard him say the name of Emer only, and whisper this over and over as if reminding the ear of a forgetful deity. Other times the whispers spoke of that country and the blight of the potatoes and the stories the boatman had brought of those thousands dying. Francis made appeals. He asked if all were suffering some sin that was beyond atonement and if He above might not consider the punishment only of some. He offered bargains of damnation eternal. He promised his soul. Then again on other winter nights he asked God for signs. He asked Him to show Francis in the heavens some small glimmering that he might know he was being heard. He turned the telescope slowly across the skies and seemed to Teige to aim it northerly at the Coma Berenices. These, that were the constellation named for the beautiful amber-coloured stresses of the Queen Berenice, obscured a thousand galaxies too distant to be seen, and were the first astral story that Emer had told Francis.

Whether there was a sign in the sky or not Teige could not

know. Through all that autumn and winter, he came each night and listened to his father talk to God through the telescope and always the same topics rose in whispers off his lips. And from this Teige was strangely comforted.

One day in the second year after Tomas left and when the blight was again in the potatoes, the boatman came. He came up from the shore and stood at a tilt before Teige. He was thin and grey about the cheek and swayed in the small wind-rain. He said nothing. He passed a hand up over the crown of his head where the hair was vanished and an oily dirt streaked. Then he muttered something that Teige did not catch and made a sudden shrugging which led to coughing. His body racked. He stopped and looked at the ground, then back over his shoulder where his boat lay near the shore. Teige looked beyond him and there saw sitting in the hull the sorry assemblage of rag and bone that comprised the boatman's family. There were twelve in all, his nine children, his wife, her sister, and his own mother. The children sat to the front, aged from four to fourteen, and were a mass of faces wan and doomed and obscurely contrite. Behind them huddled the three women. They had lost their house, the boatman mumbled to Teige. They had been evicted the night before. He turned about as he said it, as if something sharp and coiled twisted within him. He did not want them to take to the roads, he said, and then said no more, because Teige told him not to.

'You can stay on the island,' he said, and when the man said nothing, Teige touched him briefly on the shoulder and walked down before him to where the boat lay on the water.

Their name was MacMahon, but had through use and familiarity become Mac, and then, to distinguish them from multitudes thereabouts with that appellation, the BoatMacs. They were a mute congregation of souls and seemed sundered from the world, with only the strange music of their name to recall their origin. Nanna BoatMac, Livy BoatMac, Tibby, Tabby, Oonee, Aggee, Gra, Bu, Prun, and the others that their father, BoatMac himself, had christened. Now they looked at Teige with that same expression of mistrust and guilt and shame that had become habitual in that time. They did not speak out. They slumped and endeavoured to make themselves seem a burden smaller than they were. One of the children shivered. They were cold and wet and the cold wetness of them translated itself into the morning and lent them the air of travellers from the Country of the Drowned. Their hair was matted, their eyes stinging. Sores had opened at the corner of two of the girls' lips and these they had torn with their nails until they looked like some caricature of down-mouthed desolation. Teige stood before them and did not know what to say. He reached out his hand to one of the small girls and she pulled back. Gulls that had followed the boat screamed in the air. The dog that stood on the bluff waited. Slow rain began.

Teige turned to BoatMac.

'You are all welcome,' he said. 'Tell them to come.'

The man nodded and shook in himself and swayed. Then he stepped down into the water and took the first of his daughters in his arms and bore her over and placed her like a proven treasure on the sand. While he did this with each of the girls, his sons tumbled out. Slim splashers, freckle-faced, weedy-armed fellows in torn shirts and rags of trouser, they came on to the island and variously spat and kicked at the sand and looked as if considering its worth. When they were all ashore – the grandmother borne on the boatman's back in a vision that crumpled Teige's heart like paper – they stood about in a little cluster and did not move as the rain mizzled upon them. They were like climbers arrived on the thin ledge of hope and dared not budge. The boatman coughed. Gulls rose and fell again. Waves broke. At last Teige told them to come with him and see the places where they could stay. He walked off a few paces but the BoatMacs remained behind.

'Hereabouts,' the father called, 'hereabouts is fine.'

'What do you mean?'

The man twisted. His shoulders turned like a sail.

'Hereabouts,' he said.

'There are ruins up here, there is the house we were making. It is not finished but . . .'

'Hereabouts,' was all BoatMac said. Then he made a sudden nodding and raised the palm of his hand and turned and told some of the boys to go off and find timber and they ran like hares and were gone. By night there was a mound of materials gathered on the shore. When the darkness fell the girls and the two sisters and the grandmother got back aboard the boat. While the boys and their father slept on the shore the women slept on the water, believing the island still held a curse for any woman that spent the night there. The following morning the boatman and his sons set about building a long platform along the shore. It was a crude raft-like structure loosely moored with rope lashings. But it sufficed. The sisters and the tiny grandmother and the daughters all came on to the island by day. The little old woman set herself on the rocks and stitched at a shirt. The boatman's short sturdy wife helped like a man, while her sister sat disconsolate with empty eyes and hands limp in her lap. The younger girls recovered their energies quickly. They ran about and went searching for mussels and periwinkles beneath the swooping and crying of the seabirds. They gathered mounds of seaweed. When boats passed up the Shannon river the two youngest of them yahooed and waved their arms like the happily shipwrecked, heedless of loss and tragedy. By the second evening the women and the girls slept on the platform. By the third it had already begun to resemble a home. Teige worked with the boatman to make three-legged stools, and a hunk of driftwood became their salty table. The women thanked him graciously. The grandmother, shrunken and curved like one rescued from depths, worked without end at her stitching. She rocked as she did so and did not stop even when she told Teige he was their saviour. Her eyes followed him a long moment, but she said no more.

In the week that followed the house-raft was roofed with stitchings of canvas and other cloths the BoatMacs had with them. The seaweed the girls gathered was mounded at a place nearby where they would dig a garden. Soon the home was done and was a weird raggle-taggle assemblage of blankets and sacking and twisted sticks of blackthorn and sally bush and rods of hazel and bags of goose and gannet and other feathers, and all adorned with thrown clusters of wildflowers the girls gathered. It made an image at once homely and desperate, and could seem a place inventive and bohemian, or what it was, the frail, decrepit and tumbledown remnant of a family ruined.

Francis Foley did not come down to meet the MacMahons. On the first evening Teige told him they had arrived. The old man paused briefly and studied the steam that rose off his broth. Swirls of vapour ascended and vanished. Then he made an all but imperceptible nod, and ate on.

The season turned. Rains fell all day and night and made swollen the tide. The Shannon waters ran more swiftly and in the starless moonless dark the home of the BoatMacs creaked and moaned and threatened to break loose. But it did not. The father and his sons would not let it, plunging in the river, hanging on to the raft-house, making new lashings with knotted ropes while on the platform the girls huddled against their mother and grandmother, and attended their doom like those fabled in the antique times of the Flood. Still they survived. Then in the winter of that year gales came down from Iceland and carried within their force fierce flint-like showers of hail. These streaked out of white-grey skies, and were multitudinous as arrows. They pierced the flesh with ice. No man could raise his face. Borne on the power of the frozen winds they seemed to foretell the end of all seasons and be the precursors of some new age, boreal and quiescent. In such weathers the raft-house of the BoatMacs was daily destroyed and rebuilt. The rough tenting of their shelter took off and flew across the water. Stones were brought from further down the shoreline and built like walls along the wooden flooring. The family sat and hung on to what they possessed, and still would not move up to the safety of the island buildings. The gales continued. Teige came and went and offered what help he could, and through the continued inclemency of weather all that winter, the boatman's family became his. For though the gales and hails and sleets and storms remained brutal through February and on into the month of March, the BoatMacs did not despair. They did not curse their misfortune nor decide to return to the mainland. Even the sister of the boatman's wife, who had buried her husband and her children, remained stoic and crouched in the bitter season as if in quiet assent, as if such were a kind of purgation.

And so they endured.

A spring arrived. Birds, starlings, sparrows, golden orioles, thrushes, chats, swallows, corncrakes and cuckoos flew and sang. The skies were a light blue and the breeze a mild and soft gentling. On those days the boatman took by turn one of his sons and went off and ferried passengers from the town of Kilrush down the river, or acted as pilot for the bigger boats that sought to navigate the waters called the Scattery Roads on their way to dock at Limerick. He returned in the evenings and brought a basket of fish, some of which were always carried to the table of Teige and his father. So the BoatMacs lived on there, and their moored raft-house became more secure still, and in the daytimes any number of the children could be seen going about the island, chasing birds and hares, skipping in dance-step, hunting fairies, and gathering the assorted sundries that are the treasures of childhood.

In May Mr Clancy appeared. He was rowed across in a long skiff and stood up in the bow when the children of the BoatMacs gathered on the sand to greet him. He came on to the island and asked one of them to get Teige Foley. While the boy ran off, Clancy did not proceed further. Instead he stood with legs planted and examined without comment the extraordinary sight of the ramshackle home at anchorage some few yards distant. He held his hands behind his back. He moved his lips in a tight line from side to side, as though struggling to contain exclamations. The children of the Boat-Macs clustered before him and stared. They looked at his green jacket and his long boots. When Teige at last appeared coming down the rutted roadway to the shore Clancy strode swiftly up to meet him. He said some words the others could not hear. He gestured with his right hand a kind of onward motion. Then Teige left him and went back up the roadway and the other man returned to his place on the shore and stood there and waited. The children looked at him. Under their scrutiny he tapped his pockets and found coins and drew some out and proffered these to the smallest of the girls standing near him. In his palm they sat like brown buttons. The girls did not move. Their eyes studied his face and he moved his hand further out to them. Then the girls turned to see their mother who stood up with arms on her hips from the clothes she was scrubbing.

'We have no need. Say "thank you", girls,' she said.

'Thank you,' they said.

And Clancy pocketed the coins with a mixture of rue and shame and like a darkness passing felt what sufferings this family had survived. He stood and waited. One of the girls brought him an earthen jar of spring water. She watched him while he drank it back. Then Teige came and went to the BoatMac's wife and told her he must go and would be gone some days and he asked her if they would give care to his father until he returned. She told him he did not need to ask, and then Teige said goodbye to them and the children came to him and he embraced many of them and lifted high two of the girls and kissed their heads. Clancy stood nearby. Then he turned on his heel and led the way down to the boat where the oarsman was waiting. Teige followed him and climbed in and then left that island for the first time in a long time. The boat pulled out into the river and Teige looked back and saw the congregation of the BoatMacs standing there, and the sky high and blue, the fields greening with the renewed hope of the turning world, and there, in the distance, the lone long finger of the saint's tower.

3

On that crossing neither man spoke. They arrived in the town of Kilrush where at the dockside were the usual congress of petitioners, mendicants, ragged ones of mock-genteel bearing, and others – hags, crones, aged-looking urchins, men toothless and head-bandaged in cloth filthy and frayed. Clancy waved all aside and Teige walked behind him and they reached a place where a boy minded the horse and cart. Clancy threw him a coin. Then they climbed up and passed on out through the streets of the town where some paused and stared at them, gaping with a kind of naked inquisitiveness at the one who had come from the island. They reached the estate and passed in through the stone pillars and along the tree-lined avenue where the new leaves rustled in tender breeze. Teige's throat tightened. He thought of the girl Elizabeth and felt the weight and loss of time and was like one given a glimpse of his younger self. They travelled on. They came to the big field where Teige had worked the horses and there were many there again that day, and some stopped grazing and raised their long necks and stood statuesque and beautiful, and others equally so started and ran and traced a long arc through the fresh grass. Clancy slowed as they passed them. He let Teige watch and for the first time made comment to say some that Teige had broken were fine horses now.

But it was not for these that he had been brought, and soon they were turning the wide bend and proceeding on up to the yard and the stables. The closer they got the more Teige suffered a deep longing which took the form of visions almost palpable and of such a verisimilitude that he risked reaching out like the mad to touch them. He saw the figure of the girl standing and undressed. He saw how her hair fell. He saw her walk across a floor and keep her eyes fixed on his as he watched her. He saw the purse of her lips. Then Clancy was calling to him to get down and they were stopped in the yard before the stables.

Teige got down and felt the solidity of the cobbled ground restore him. He filled his lungs and drew in the smells of that place that were of horses and blacksmithing and woodsmoke and honeysuckle and ivy.

'She's in here,' Clancy said.

Teige went to the stable half-door. When he got near enough to see only the shadows the mare inside turned and swung around away from him and snorted with her face to the wall. Teige placed his hands on the top of the door. He leaned there and looked in at her. She was a five-year-old, high and fine and white.

'She's ready for him,' Clancy said. 'But you bring her near and she won't take him. We've brought her three times last year. He's Bonaparte Lad. You've heard of him?' he asked and at once knew it was foolish. 'Well, he's over east Clare. He's the one himself wants for her.'

Teige opened the door and was inside the stable before Clancy could tell him not to. He was whispering the sounds he whispered in that language that was not language in any sense other than as it existed between him and horses. He stood still and whispered and raised his hands very slowly until they were flat-palmed up to the air as though holding a most delicate and invisible wall. He breathed outward and let the presence of him establish and mix and become inextricable from the sunlit motes of straw dust and the fumes and odours of dung and urine and sweat that hung and made thick the air there. The mare whinnied. She did not turn back her head. Thrice she stamped her hind leg on the off-side of him. The damp straw of the bedding was moved aside by that action and the hoof hit the stones of the floor under and made a sharp and angry retort.

'She knows her mind,' Clancy said.

Teige turned and looked at him and Clancy understood and said he would leave him to it and they would take her to the stallion in the morning.

For the rest of that day, Teige and the mare became familiar each with each. Pyle, the youth that had before brought him his food, was now a redheaded fellow, muscled but callow, who came and stood with a bowl of potatoes and a sullen expression. Teige thanked him for the food, but the fellow said nothing, only stood and cracked each of his knuckles and then went off. The day was fine and warm. Flies travelled the sunbeams. They buzzed about the horse and felt her heat and she whisked her tail to little avail. The signs of thirst were on her but she would not take water and was restless and nervy and seemed ill at ease in her own horseflesh. After a time Teige put on her a halter and brought her out and led her clopping across the yard and out down the avenue. He walked her with short lead firmly and said things and kept his head close to hers and allowed the softness of the day to ease her and let her feel her liberty from the stall. He took her on down the way, but then turned at the fork and crossed to follow the main avenue so as not to bring her past the grazing horses. He was some way along this when he saw the carriage coming.

The mare flicked her ears then locked and planted her feet and stood like the semblance of a horse cast in iron or bronze. The noise of the wheels and the beat of hooves and the sleek dark black colour of the rushing carriage all quickened the air there. Teige tried to coax the mare to the side out of the way, but she would not budge. And the carriage bore on toward them. Its dust rose in a cloud and hung pale and luminescent like the fore- or after-presence of a deity. Teige could see the coachman in livery and see the fellow wave his free hand to clear the avenue, but the mare snorted and snuffled and shook her head and turned about on the short lead and did not step out of the road. She sniffed the excitement out of the air and though Teige *shush-shushed* her and reached his hand to pat the side of her neck still she frisked and turned and tried to step about in a small circle. The coach was all but on them. In moments the coachman cried out and stood upright and reined hard back to his chest and at last the mare moved off the avenue on to the verge of grass. The coach stopped and the mare grew more anxious still. Teige released its lead to the full and let the animal sense it had its freedom. When she moved back so did he. He was in a small, scuffling, pulling, dragging scene then, with the mare moving this way and that and he following with the line fully extended, when the woman in the carriage looked out of the window, and he saw in side view in the briefest instant that it was Elizabeth.

He saw her. Then he saw the other figure, a man in a black suit of clothes sitting close by her side.

4

The coach passed on. Teige tugged sharply on the mare's lead and brought her closer to him and they stood then in the wake of dust and fading noise and the slow reassembling of the world. He could not breathe. He stood a time looking at only the soft curved line of the mare's back and the fields beyond it and all was tranquil and still like the changeless and unreal country of dreams. He did not look after the coach. Then the mare pulled up her head twice and he snap-tugged at the lead and admonished and turned her about and brought her back up that avenue to the stable where that time she drank water. He left her there and went across the yard and worked the pump hard and fast until it gurgled and a frayed water came. He stooped and doused his head and the water was first slightly sun-warmed and then cold and then colder still. He shook off the drops and then cupped his hands and drank some and looked across his dripping fingers to see the youth watching him. Teige walked over. Pyle's eyes lowered and were gone then beneath a fringe of lank red hair. Teige stood next to him.

'Busy at the house, are they?' he said.

'I suppose they are.' The fellow cracked his knuckles.

'Visitors?'

'Feck all I care,' Pyle said, surly and short, his gaze fixed on the ground at his feet. 'More logs, more water, more logs, feck,' he said.

The afternoon sunlight beheld them. Flies and honeybees

flew. The snout of the pump dripped a slow heavy drip of aftermath.

'Feck,' said Pyle again, daring beneath the blind cover of his hair. 'What fires do you need and it fine as any summer's day? But fires in every room it's to be. More logs. And more. For the married ones. Feck.'

Teige did not speak. The blue sky seemed to pulse. He turned about and found it best to squat down against the wall a moment, as if to study the cobbles of the yard. Then the other fellow got up and went off and Teige stayed there and held his face up to the sun blaze.

For the rest of that afternoon he did not take the mare out. He sat outside and watched across the yard where the maids and butlers came and went briskly. From time to time he got up and went inside the stable and spoke to the horse and stroked her, but she was restless in the heat and the flies. The time passed slowly. He turned in his head the news that Elizabeth was married. He turned it this way and that as if trying to find comfort while a stake was in his heart. He told himself it was to be expected. He told himself he must have known all along, that she was certain to be married as soon as she left there and went back to Cork. She would hardly even remember you, he said. You were nothing to her. You were how she tolerated the boredom of being here, nothing more. She probably told her friend and they laughed at you and how you came across the roof in the night to sit and see her naked. He told himself such things, as if bitterest medicine worked strongest. He derided all notions of love and made of them pathetic constructs of artifice and lies for innocents and fools. Anger roiled in him and came and subsided and came again. He saw his life like a story and one without great event or passion, but instead a long dwindling of days islanded with his father. He took from this the solace that such was meant to be, but soon this too was found frail and its comforts thin and chimerical. In the labyrinths of such considerations the after-

302

noon passed. The lustre of the sun was slowly diminished and the walls of the yard transformed from yellow to gold to an umbered brown. Red-combed hens walked about and pecked the straw stuff, scrabbled three-toed, stood one-footed, dunged a blanched dung, and made sharp head turns, quizzical and affrighted. To these Teige tossed powder of crushed oats that lay in the deeps of his pocket. The hens flurried and ran in startled swoop-like movement. They pecked fast and frantic and in the still emptiness the tiny tapping of their beaks on the cobbles sounded. When the ground was cleaned they stood attendant and Teige got up then and flapped his arms and they scattered in all directions with noise and feather and were in riot so when Elizabeth came into the yard.

He saw her. She wore a dress of pale blue that touched the ground. She carried above her head a parasol and crossed slowly to the stables. There she stopped not ten feet from him and made to look in on one of the other horses stabled there.

'Are you going to say hello to me?' she said at last. She had not turned. She was hidden beneath the parasol and studying the gelding that had come forward for her touch.

Teige stood. He looked across the yard, but there were only the hens in retreat. He turned back to the door of the mare's stable and stood and looked within.

'You heard I am married now?' she asked him, still not showing her face.

'I did,' he said. His voice was low, his breath seemed to move through ashes.

She reached out her right hand and touched the long face of the gelding.

'And what do you think?' she said.

'I have to tend to the mare, that's what I think,' he said, and opened the door and stepped into the darkness.

'Teige?'

He heard her say his name but he did not answer. He took brushes from where they lay in the straw and with swift arcing motion set about grooming the horse. When he paused later he listened and then came up to the door and looked outside and she was gone.

That night he lay in the straw and could not sleep. He watched the moon cross the partly clouded sky. He heard owls and bats and others nocturnal traverse the dark. The mare shuddered in dream and lifted her hind hoof sometimes and stamped. Then she stilled again and her breathing resumed its slow and steady heave, filling and venting the vastness of her chest in hypnotic rhythm. Mice myriad and minute scuttered over the stones, vanished into the walls and under the doors. Teige rose and walked out. The vaulted hood of stars glittered in revealed fragments as the clouds passed. Cassiopeia shone her tale of tragedy to all who might read it there, but Teige did not delay. He crossed the yard and by instinct and memory moved to the shadows beneath the wall. He pressed himself close to these and followed their line around by the house. He did not see the red-haired fellow that saw him. He came around by the kitchen and found then the holds between the stones for his fingers and climbed up on to that first low roof. He crouched low and was a shadow and again did not see the shadow of the youth below in his wake. He came to the window and found the sash partly raised. He lifted it with two hands and waited to still his breath before he stepped inside on to the floorboards of the hallway.

All was an umbrageous hush. Ghosts and their shades ambled and paused momentarily, quizzical to see one living among them. Then in the grave and somnolent manner of their kind they passed onward and were as shadows as they went about their ceaseless business in the halls of that old house. Teige stood and listened, the dreaming and the dead alike making the softest sounds. Then he stepped forward barefoot and with hands out as if to fend off attack or to balance on a rope. He came to the door of the room where she had slept before and he pressed his ear against it and could not hear the breath of any. Slowly he squeezed the handle around and opened it inches and then he leaned in and saw that the bed was empty. He blew a long thin breath and tried again to still himself, and while he did he passed through brief sharp agonies of indecision familiar to all such lovers, and then he went down the hall to the next door. He listened. She was not there. He went on, around the turn of the corridor, emboldened now and grown more reckless as he proceeded. The floorboards creaked, ghosts and dust and dreams astir. He came to a door then and stopped and knew that she was within. He tried to still himself. Then he reached and opened the door.

There were shadows on the bed. The darkness was jumbled with shapes and shades, tones grey and pewter. Teige stood, strange like a creature incorporeal. He waited, attendant on some discovery and incipient disaster, and with the passing of each moment could not quite believe that none came. Slowly the shadows assembled and were the shapes of a man and woman sleeping. He moved a step closer and could see her then where she lay with the man's arm outstretched across her, a pale raised line like the weal of a scar. Teige moved again, and this time knelt down on one knee and was close enough now to be enveloped in the smells of her. Her face in sleep was calm and very beautiful and Teige studied it without haste or anxiety, as if the progress of all time had since ceased and such perusal was his eternal business. Then she moved and the man's arm moved and she pressed her head back and angled in the pillow and showed the line of her neck that was fine and white like a fabulous bird's and Teige reached and touched it.

Elizabeth opened her eyes. She opened them quickly and wide as if seeing a vision though yet she did not seem to be seeing at all. There was a brief hiatus, a frozen instant. Teige's fingers touched her lips and her eyes turned to look at him. The man beside her sighed like a sea cavern. None moved. Then very slowly Teige got up and her eyes followed him and he stepped a step back from her and another and all the time she watched him. He came to the room door and reached and opened it and already she was easing herself from the body that lay by her. Teige stepped outside into the corridor and turned and pressed himself flat against the wall and tried to draw his breath.

'You're mad.'

She closed the door. Her voice was a whisper and when he heard it he wanted to hear more.

'You will be killed. You know that?'

He said nothing. His eyes studied her.

'They will take you out in the fields somewhere and . . .' She stopped. Something in her wavered as though in a sudden warp of heat.

Teige reached and kissed her mouth and lay his palm against the side of her neck. They stopped and she looked at him and then kissed again and were one twisting shape among the shadows and the soft ghosts and silent dust that assembled there.

5

In the dawn when Clancy came to him Teige was lying awake in the straw of the stable. Neither man spoke, but went at once as if by mute accord and brought out the horse and stood her briefly in the yard. The day was thickly clouded as if there were no heavens. The air smelled cool and damp and flies were not yet abuzz. The horse's eyes studied with long slow circumspection the horsecart in which she was to be loaded. She had never yet travelled so, but it was the squire's belief and shared with others of his kind that the exertion of the ride over to the east to the stallion would weaken the possibility of a strong issue. So Clancy said. She must be loaded and brought. In the thin light Teige and Clancy set about it. A line was run from the horse's halter on up the gangway and into the cart with high creels. Clancy took this and led it through the top bar and waited for Teige to begin to coax her on. But the moment the horse felt the tension on the line she pulled back with her head and took two steps backward and Clancy tugged at the rope harder and called out a curse. The cobbles of the yard rang out with the sharp clopping of hooves. The fellow Pyle appeared with tousled hair and looked at Teige with a crooked grin. Clancy shouted to him to get behind her and urge her forward, which business he set about in a manner wild and mad. But Teige already knew that it was hopeless. As if it travelled along the very rope, fear reached every sinew of the horse. She backed and shook and twisted her head about, thrashing the rope-line sideways, for all the world as if she was some fabulous marine creature hooked on a fishing line descended from above in the realm of the gods.

'Stop, leave off,' Teige said. And the tension on the rope slackened and he undid it and let it fall to the ground. 'Get off, go away from there,' he told Pyle, and the youth scowled and scratched at his freckles and did not move back.

'Do it!' Clancy shouted.

'But I'm coming to . . .'

'Go away!' Clancy roared.

Pyle stepped back then and his eyes narrowed and were lost beneath the falling fringe of his hair.

Teige turned the horse about so she was headed in the direction opposite to the gangway. He stroked her neck and spoke to her and felt the heat in her body. Then he ran his hand firmly down the length of her long face and stopped, and with one hand held there across her nose and the other flat against her flank he coaxed her backward. She stepped a step and then another. When her hoof reached the wooden planks she hesitated only for a moment then clattered up backwards with Teige holding her so. She was loaded. Clancy came about and swung up and closed the cart. He did not say anything to Teige.

'Am I not coming?' Pyle asked.

'You are not,' Clancy told him. 'Do you think I want her maddened? You will clean out the stalls.' The fellow's face crumpled into a sour twist.

Clancy climbed up and sat beside Teige and they drove the cart away down the avenue.

In slow rocking motion, the cart pulled by two black horses and labouring on all hills almost to the pace of walking, they passed out through the town of Kilrush and eastward along the road to Ennis. They travelled past wild brown boglands and small roadside cottages with doors open and dark dim interiors whence the face of a man or woman peered like a frightened animal. Long tracts of the road were empty of all living. There were many cottages ruined, thatch torn down or tumbled inward and standing now with roofs gaping, strange and sad in the aftermath of famine. At a place where green fields opened to the south, Clancy passed Teige the reins and rummaged in a bag and brought out hunks of bread and a stoppered jug of milk. They did not stop as they ate. The morning came up over them, the sky grey and sunless. At the town of Ennis a shower of rain fell and stopped and then came again and continued falling. They passed on, as if veiled within it. The backs of the horses shone. The road, softening beneath them, tuned the pitch of their clopping a semitone lower.

At that town they drew the attention of many. Some who were stopped in doorways studied them like a show. Small children, boys and girls alike, ran along in the rain and shouted and tried to hit with sticks the sides of the creels. Clancy swung a short whip back-handed toward them in warning and Teige stood up and turned back and tried to soothe the horse. But soon the children slowed of their own accord and stood in the rain and faded off, mucked and white-faced and melancholic as some dwindling image whose meaning was potent but hard to fathom. The road east took them out of the town and soon they were again without company on the long brown ribbon bordered by green. The land was still and the cattle within it stood in the falling rain. Berry bushes dripped in the hedgerows. The flowers of the fuchsia hung and fell red and purple on the roadside.

They passed on. In the pallid light of that afternoon they came to the place where the stallion was at stud. When they passed through the gateway the mare lifted her head and neighed and moved about in the narrow confines of the cart.

'Stop here,' Teige said. It was the first words he had spoken in some hours. Clancy did as he was told. The cart stopped and Teige got down and walked along by the side of it and spoke up to the mare. Then he went on ahead into the yard and across to the stable where already the stallion was turning and making long ratcheted sounds to be released. There was a man there with eyes he opened wide every second, as if a reverse of blinking. Teige looked in at the stallion.

'You'll take him out? And be able to hold him?' he asked the man.

The fellow widened his eyes. 'I will.'

'Wait until I say. I'll close the gate.'

Teige went and brought out the mare on a line and told Clancy to shut the gate between her and the stallion. And when this was done he called up to the other and told him to bring out the stallion, and soon both horses were frisking on lines either side of the shut gate. He backed the mare to the gate and held her there and let the stallion approach and take the smell of her and raise his head as if savouring it and twist it about thrice in the heavy rain air. He came to her and his nostrils widened and his sex rose and he pressed and angered at the gate impatiently and still the man held him. The mare did not kick back as was her wont.

'Let her through to him now!' the man called. 'I won't be able to hold him.'

'No, hold him, wait. Wait.'

Teige took the mare then and turned her away and walked her in a small muddy circle there where she could see the stallion. He held her back when she would have stepped forward. The rain ran on his face.

'Now, now open the gate,' he called and Clancy stepped across and did so and the stallion came forward pulling the man with the wide eyes like some minor nuisance. Then the two horses passed alongside each other and the mare tried to bite and her teeth showed in the air and each neighed aloud and Teige called out for the ropes to be loosened. Then, with the men standing muted about them in the pouring rain and holding the long lines limp, the stallion mounted the mare and became briefly a thing colossal, high and muscled and shuddering as if with the charged currency of the earth itself.

In moments it was over. The men came to and sharply reined the horses apart and with swift economy of movement brought each back to the places of their confinement. The mare was backed up the platform and it was raised with a clatter and shut. The stallion, subdued and dull-eyed, was led inside the stable and the door bolted. Clancy went off to the house with the other man and performed what matters of business were required. Teige waited. He looked at the mare, tranquil now, her coat damply matted, and the coupling already passed like some figment into the deeps of her memory. If there was such, Teige thought. If it's not just then, done, and then gone. He waited. No sound came from either horse.

When at last Clancy came out he had the flushed cheeks of strong whiskey and his eyes were brightened like polished glass. He climbed up on the cart and told Teige he was good, by God he was good, and they would stop and get a drink to celebrate. They would, so they would. He clucked at the horses and they wheeled about and out of there. A short time later they came to the town of Killaloe on the banks of the river. The rain stopped then and the place hung in sorry wet aftermath like a child half-drowned. Clancy looked along the street for a place suitable to their needs. No sooner had he found one than there appeared a small boy ready to hold the horses and keep all safe while the men went inside. Teige and Clancy got down and Clancy gave the boy something. Already there was a little cluster of some too proud to be called beggars who assembled to beg there. They stood in the men's way with no menace, but urgent persistence. Their begrimed hands opened palm upwards like rough petals. Their clothes steamed a strong sour odour that was the perfume of rain and sweat and poverty. They offered prayers and blessings and intercession with saints of all name and manner and appeals to the Virgin herself for the cause of the good travellers. As if wading in murk, Clancy raised his arms above them and tried to move forward. He saw the doorway where he was headed and pushed towards it parting the beggars and telling them he had nothing for them. He did not look back at Teige behind him. He did not see how they gathered about the younger man, and how Teige stopped there.

Teige stopped and his mouth opened and he felt himself weaken as though a surfeit of air had arrived in his lungs or he was suddenly out of his element. His outstretched hand was taken by one of the hands offered to him. Others joined this and took him gently. He near staggered but did not and yet seemed almost asway as he came forward. His expression was of one caught and transported in revelation even there on the grey wet street of that town. The look of his eyes must have bespoke something for the little crowd followed the gaze and turned and saw at whom he was staring.

It was a woman, one amongst them, who hung back and waited on the side of the street. She was wrapped in a shawl, and stood with patience and a faraway look. She did not turn her face to see Teige coming to her. She did not lift her eyes from the scene infinite in distance upon which her mind gazed. He came to her and the little crowd came with him. Some held his sleeve, others the hem of his jacket, but none said anything now. Dream-like, as if the moment did not exist but must be lived anyway, Teige reached the woman and stood before her and a cry escaped from deep in his throat and seemed to buckle him. For he fell down on to his knees and then reached up and touched the face of the blind woman who was his mother.

6

And sometime in the darkness of the night many miles away
Finbar Foley woke and felt the left side of his body was dead.
Beneath the covers he reached across himself and with his right
arm made short tapping motions as if to gently awaken the part
that was numb. When this failed his actions grew more urgent
and Cait woke in the bed beside him to find him beating at his
left breast with his fist.

'God almighty, what are you doing?' she said.

'Half of me is dead,' Finbar told her, and no sooner had he
uttered the words than their reality struck him and he let out a
sharp cry and stopped still.

'What is it? Tell me, what?'

'It is Finan,' Finbar said. 'My twin, he is dead.'

When the light dawned over the lake that morning, he went
down the ramshackle street to the house of the fortune-teller.
By then the feeling in his left side had returned but an ache
persisted as if he had been lanced and he walked crookedly, his
right hand clutching at his left side. He did not wish to be
noticed on such consultation and wore a green felt hat pulled
low on his forehead. When the fortune-teller saw him at her
door she nodded sagely, as though his future was already with
her or she was already many pages ahead of him in the tale
of his own life. She waved a pendulous arm and he entered.
With his hat on he sat in a room that no longer resembled
the caravan it once was. There were silks and other thin cloths
draped and curtains of purple beads that swung and clacked

minutely in the afterwards of his arrival. Candles burned and made the air dense as a soup of flowers. The fortune-teller sat on a kind of cushioned throne and raised her bejewelled fingers and made of these a gesture as if playing an invisible concertina. She remained so, feeling whatever vibrated there in the space between them, for some time. A large woman, she had passed her seventieth year but scorned all such measurement of time and was on that her fifth lifetime lipsticked and thickly painted and bewigged in a tousle of flame-red hair. She watched Finbar with steady gaze while fingering the air. When at last she stopped she asked him if he wished the cards as well.

'Do you need the cards before you can tell me?' he said.

'I do not. I can read the future like script on paper. It is there,' she said, and waved a heavy hand toward his face and stirred the soup so its scents swirled.

'Well?'

'Men come for only two reasons. Love or death.' She paused. She watched him move as if in some discomfort in the seat. 'You are not a man in love.'

'Is it true then?' he asked her.

'Yes,' she said.

'He is dead?'

'He is.'

For a moment Finbar did not react. He was like one transfixed before an altar. His face betrayed no expression. His eyes did not move from the eyes of the fortune-teller. And he stayed so.

'Tell me,' he said.

Then as the air of that room grew steadily warmer, the fortune-teller told him the story of Finan, his twin. She told him Finan had sailed from his own country and gone south and arrived in a port in the country of France. His heart was heavy and his soul could find no ease in the world, she said. He met a priest there and confessed his sins and though the priest did not understand his language he absolved these, but told him he was one called by God. He kept Finan with him in a monastery for five years, and then one day told Finan he must sail to the continent of Africa and do God's work there.

'More?' said the fortune-teller.

'More.'

He boarded a ship then and was on the sea for many weeks, she said. He arrived in the port of Sierra Leone in the blaze of summertime. His head burned, his ears crisped. He moved among slavers and callous men and others who had come there to live outside the law and the rules of human decency. He wore the black clothes of a priest and in these suffered the heat like a further penance. He preached in vain, for none there would listen to him. He grabbed a man by the arm to stop him beating a slave and was himself knocked down and beaten in the dirt.

The fortune-teller paused. She asked Finbar again if he wished her to continue for she knew the story that lay ahead.

'Tell me,' he said again.

'He did not know what good he could do there,' she said. 'He asked God and got no answer and went from there eastward.'

He crossed scorched places in the dry interior of that country where there was no one, or where passed figures silent and nomadic. The first signs of malaria were already in his eyes. He walked toward the foothills of the Wologisi Mountains. There was a tribe there that scattered when he came. He travelled in open country past herds of elephants, and came to swamps of stewed heat where herds of pigmy hippopotamus lay. At a place where caves opened in the ground he came upon a wretched tribe withered with the scabs of leprosy.

'Here he stayed a while. He tended to them for they were frightened and dying and had been long outcast and lost the trust of human contact.'

In the night he told them the word for God, she said, and he pointed at the heavens and they mistook God for the stars. But when God could not cure them, his faith weakened. He asked God many times to come and show a sign. But there was none. Then when his own sickness was worsening he left there and walked on.

'I see a forest of trees dripping. There are trees of fig and palm and rubber.'

'And he is there?' Finbar asked.

'Yes.'

He was in that forest where monkeys screeched and crashed above and where the bright wings of birds fluttered and vanished in the high branches. He was unable to walk now and sat down and tried to pray but no prayers could form in his mind and he suffered delusions and saw in mirage the face of God. But it was the face of his father. His mind buckled then and he was not sure if there was a God or if he had had a vocation and if his devotion was not simply the expression of lost love. There was only the long figure of the father who had not seen Finan as a child in his own right and who had vanished in the river before the boy had become a man. There was only the boy's longing for his father to acknowledge and know and love him, and that this impossibility had become his yearning for God.

'And with that revelation he cried out there in the forest,' the fortune-teller said. 'He cried out your name.'

She stopped and waited a moment and the heat in the room was such now that it was difficult for Finbar to breathe.

'He cried it out loud and then the other names of his brothers and then cried for his mother. He cried out and saw one coming to save him. He saw it as clear as if it were real and that was the one he had prayed to and was his own father who in his vision then lifted him like a child in his arms and bore him away in a place distant and lovely as the stars.'

She stopped. Finbar held his face in his hands. Sweat glistened in the creases of his brow.

'He died alone there?' he asked her.

She nodded. 'Yesterday,' she said.

Africa lingered in that room for a spell. Time passed, or did not. The heat of the room rose and rose then to such a degree that at last there appeared in translucent mirage the wavering sunburned figure of the lost twin Finan Foley. He stood there before them, his face placid and his arms by his sides. Then Finbar could bear it no longer and let out a cry and reached his left hand to his brother and at once the image like a fever broke and was gone.

'Now,' said the fortune-teller as the room cooled, 'what will you do?'

Finbar touched his side where the ache had passed.

'I will go home,' he said.

He got up then and paid the woman and went back down the street to Cait and his six children. He told her to get ready, they were going on the road.

Her hands flew to her mouth, as if she had to hold her hope a moment.

'Where?' she asked him.

'To dip our daughters in the sea where I found you,' he said.

Then he went outside with a shovel and dug at the grass that had covered the wheels of the caravan. He dug for two hours and some of the gypsies came outside to see what he was doing and some were glad and others vaguely ashamed. He told them he was going on the road and any were welcome. He was not going to seek their ancient home, he said, for a Magyar traveller had told him that it was not Romania but a place in the north of the country India from which they had long ago been banished and come across Asia Minor and Byzantium like seeds in the wind. He was going west and north, he said, to see the sea again. For those that were gathered in curiosity he unrolled the map of Benardi, and upon it he traced a route, like one showing the way to the lost.

Then he went and bought two horses and hitched these and after some efforts moved the caravan for the first time from the deep ruts in which it was foundered. And with the first great sway of motion in their cages the canaries sang. Two other families of the gypsies joined them. Their caravans were beyond recovery and they came instead on foot with bundles tied. Then, without further announcement, in the warmth of the afternoon, they left there, Finbar Foley and Cait and, with the two youngest, the now half-dozen Roses. The caravan creaked out on the road past the lake, some following behind in slow file and the children of others skipping and hopping alongside for part of the way as if witnesses to some strange and fabulous carnival.

7

If the story of Emer Foley could be told the telling would take the days and nights of the rest of her lifetime. The sorrow of the words themselves would weigh so upon her that her heart would crack, making the skies weep and blacking the stars. Such was Teige's understanding the moment he knelt before her in the town of Killaloe, for so it seemed written in the lineaments of her face. He did not ask her where she had been. He touched her face and told her he was Teige. Those assembled murmured and pressed forward the better to witness the scene of annunciation and to them Teige raised his right hand and said nothing and did not take his eyes from his mother. The beggars stopped. They clustered there as if at the edge of some invisible arc drawn about the man and woman, as if these were upon a stage and they the chorus. The mother's face crinkled in a puzzle.

'Teige,' she said, 'is it Teige?'

Her voice was cracked and whispery and frail and seemed like a thing left long in harsh weather.

'Mother.'

She reached out both her hands and they hung in the air slightly aflutter until her son leaned forward and put his face between them. She drew him to her then and they seemed to melt upon each other, and not the horses or the carts or the people that moved in the street mattered for them at all. Understanding this, the crowd of onlookers slowly stepped back and then dispersed down the street to speak of what they had seen and to console themselves of their own losses and the many of theirs that were missing or gone.

Teige and his mother embraced there in the thin wet afternoon light. They wept. They held to each other like ones rescued in a drowning. They said nothing at all. After a time Clancy came out to see where Teige had got to and he came upon the scene and in his mood made buoyant by whiskey he called out loudly and clapped Teige on his back. Teige stood up then and told him this was mother who had been long lost. And Clancy offered her his hand that she could not see and he said well well well, and Emer stood up from the street and was now a woman small and light and crooked though she held her chin high.

'You'll be coming back with us then?' Clancy said. And when neither of them responded he nodded forcefully and answered himself. 'Yes, indeed. Indeed you will.' He waited a moment, his legs planted, as if unsure whether he could suggest to the others to come into the public house for a final drink before the journey. Then some torch of self-consciousness shone upon him and one-handed he smoothed down the tuft of his hair and said: 'Well, we'll go now then.'

They left there in the late part of the afternoon with the light poor and the mare hungry in the cart. Those who had been her company stood by the wayside and though she was blind raised their hands in farewell. They watched her go and stood out in the street after she had passed, taking solace from that reunion and studying the horizon upon which the travellers diminished. On the seatboard softly the mother rocked. Her head she kept at a slight angle away from Clancy and toward her son, and sometimes she freed her two hands from where they held each other and opened them in the air and Teige placed his right hand between them and they closed about it. Now in the easy drifts of his intoxication Clancy said nothing. He was comfortable in himself and was as one who has suddenly discovered his spirit larger than he imagined. They moved on.

The countryside passed in its ceaseless green unrolling. Carts and coaches and men on horseback journeyed across the dying of the light. Farmers and sons drove two or three cows with sticks and these dunged the road and the last flies found them. As the day fell into twilight those coming and going on that road took on the unreal form of things without substance. Riders appeared and faded in the gloaming. Soon they were travelling in the first darkness of night and it came to Teige that this was the world his mother saw and he reached his arm about her and held her against him. On the outskirts of the town of Ennis Clancy stopped the cart and palmed flat his hair and looked at the darkness and then reined the horses to the left and brought them to a large farmhouse. There he climbed down and went inside and came out to the Foleys some time after and told them they would stay there the night. Teige brought his mother down from the cart then, leading her upon his arm to where Clancy's sister was standing at the open door. The woman welcomed them and brought them inside where she said food would be ready for them shortly. Teige went outside and untied the mare and took her to a stable and fed and watered her and crossing back he moved beneath the stars which were clear now and arrested him a moment. He looked at Orion and Pegasus. He thought of his father that night studying those same constellations, and knew that he must tell his mother about him and about his brothers. And he thought too of Elizabeth and lingered there in the stillness of the yard and looked across at the yellow lampglow of the house and stood and felt the existence of such a thing as grace.

Later that night, in a small room that was off the hearth, mother and son lay sleepless in a cover, their separate histories vast and unspoken in the dark above them. Slender stellar light fell. The sill of the small window shone and showed in the corner lace-like tracery of spiders. Mice worked. At last, though he did not know if she was awake or sleeping, Teige said: 'Mother?'

It seemed strange to be sounded aloud. It seemed a word he had never heard himself say.

'Mother?'

'Yes, Teige.'

'They are all gone,' he said, 'Finbar, Finan, and Tomas, too. I am the only one left.'

She did not say anything at once. He wondered in her dark world if shades or shadows fell. He wondered if there was blackness and then utter blackness. He reached his hand towards the shape of her and his fingers arrived at the softness of her face that was like a fallen fruit wet in the grass.

'I thought I had cried my last,' she said.

He told her quickly then that none of them may be dead. He told her of the river crossing with the telescope and the chase from Limerick and the gypsies and the races on the sands. He told her of Tomas and his love. He told her of the twins vanishing and how they had never returned. He paused and did not tell her then of his own searching or the years of solitude tramping the roads. He heard her sighs. He heard the new sorrows make room in the confines of her spirit. The night moved on a time. Clouds came from the west and darkened the window. Then rain began.

'I found him,' Teige said then. 'Father, I found him on the road. He was looking for us. He was looking for you. He knew of an island.' He stopped himself a moment and did not know if she wanted to be told. But he felt compelled and said: 'He is there now. He is sorry. He looks for you in the stars.'

There escaped from her the smallest cry, as if some great weight had been pressed against her chest and she could utter nothing more. Teige did not continue. Then out of the darkness his mother's hand reached for him and touched his face and then her other joined it and she held his head between her fingers and kissed his forehead.

'I came back,' she said. 'The day after. I came back.'

She paused and her breaths came in sharp gasps.

'We had a fight. He wanted to go, I wanted to stay. I went out the door. I only meant to be gone a day until he could see how he needed me. God forgive me. I came back the next morning the house was on fire. They were hunting him. I thought you were burned. Oh God.' She cried out and she moaned as if torn and Teige drew her closer and they held to each other, weeping in the darkness of the night. He stroked her silvered hair, he touched her blind eyes, and murmured to her *shush-shush* sounds while all about them in the fields of that countryside a bitter rain fell.

8

In the dawn the skies cleared. A buffeting wind like a busy housekeeper moved about and took down the first leaves of autumn. Sycamore trees around the farmhouse made whispers and shivers, sea-sounds. Birds were sent about and arced and whirled on air that gleamed. Teige rose and went to see to the mare and then led his mother to the table which Clancy's sister had laid. Clancy himself did not appear at first, and his sister knocked and called to him several times before his head came around the door. He would take no food. He would be ready shortly, he told them. They ate, and rose and thanked the woman. Then Teige backed the mare once more on to its transport and they left there.

The road west was already busy that morning with market-goers. Drovers had been out moving with cattle since before light. Now their customers followed in their wake. There was a stream of buyers, hawkers, gawkers, and others on foot and cart, travelling into Ennis. Wisps of straw and hay blew down the wind, the pungency of a congregation of men and beasts leavened in that blustering weather. All studied the mare as she passed, but Clancy, who had returned to his taciturn manner, did not give them so much as the corner of his eye. He clucked at the horses and brought them through the town and out the further side on the road to Kilrush. They travelled on, the blind woman seated between the two men and her son sometimes saying to her brief descriptions of what country they passed. She wore a shawl against the breeze. What visions of those she loved unrolled as the landscape passed could not be said. She sat and was like a revenant from other worlds burdened by what she had witnessed and what could never be told. The horses clopped and beat down the road. Gusts of wind rose across the hedgerows and leaves and smaller birds briefly dallied in the polished light. At cottages along the way some had bedding and blankets out and beat at these and made thin clouds of dust in which hens scattered and flew. At others faces of men and women watched from just within and gave scrutiny to all without show of emotion as if they were themselves no more than milestones and merely measured all that passed in the long continuum of human sorrow.

They went on. When they neared the town of Kilrush, and the grey estuary waters could be seen, Clancy looked to Teige and gestured with a motion of his head in the direction of the island. Teige nodded in response and Clancy turned again to face the road with the woman between them none the wiser of their discourse. They came in about the town and there in its windy streets were those familiars who had seen them go and saw them return now and saw the strange woman on the seatboard. They studied her as the cart passed and asked aloud of one another who she might be and what trouble might be abrewing. Some moved along the street then after the cart as if hooked.

Down at the water's edge by the small pier, Clancy left the Foleys. He told Teige to come back to them when he could, that there would be more work for him, and he bowed his head to the blind woman and seemed about to say something when the words escaped him. So he turned away suddenly and climbed up and clicked with his tongue and was gone. Mother and son stood there in the wind. The water slapped. Some of those who had followed down through the town stayed a short distance away and watched surreptitiously.

'We are going to the island,' Teige told his mother, 'we are going to father.' He hesitated a moment then said, 'Some say there is a curse against women there. They say . . .'

'We will go,' she said, and held up her head and was briefly the proud and headstrong image of her former self. She raised her hand for him to take it and he did. And she said nothing more. Clouds fast-moving swept above them. The light there came and went. Gulls and other seabirds hovered and plunged and rose again briefly dripping. The noon and afternoon passed as they waited for a ferryman to take them across. The fishing boats were long gone and had not yet returned. Only small skiffs and other canoe-like boats of canvas moved on the water. One of these, piloted by a man of ragged beard and neck boils, at length arrived at the pier and Teige asked him for their passage. The fellow shrugged, as if such was not his business but rather some purgatorial labour, as if he was bound to ferry all until he died. He sat there and held the moor rope and waited while Teige tried to help his mother to board. The boat bobbed alongside them. Timbers creaked. The light was swiftly dying. The little crowd of onlookers came down along the pier.

'Where are you taking her?' one of them called. 'Are you taking her out there?'

But Teige did not reply. He stood in the boat himself at last and reached his arms and told his mother to step to him. And she lifted a small blind foot and it wavered an instant before she stepped forward on to the air. Though the boat rocked it did not capsize. The ferryman dipped his oars. Teige and his mother sat. He hooped his arm about her. The wind that was moving fast now fluttered her shawl, and soon they had left that shore she would not walk upon again and they were out in the twisting currents of the waters where the river met the sea.

9

The children saw them first. They came from the rafthouse and ran on the shore and peered in the grey light and waved to Teige and he called back. Before the boat had reached the shallow waters the young girls were standing in the waves. When they saw the figure of the blind woman they hushed with the mystery and stood with their arms hanging. The pilot brought them to where Teige stepped into the water. Then Teige reached and lifted his mother and walked in with her in his arms until he was on the pebbles of the shore. The children came about him, for it seemed a thing of marvel. When he told them this was his mother who had long been lost the marvel seemed doubled, and some of the children laughed and spun instant cartwheels as though giddy with the turning of the world. The old woman smiled. She said she was sorry she could not see them for they seemed so lovely, and some of them stood next to her so her hand could alight upon their heads. Their own mother came out then and greeted the Foleys and asked if they were not hungry and would they come and eat.

They went on board that creaking home of salty logs and rope lashings and sat at a table and ate the fish and potatoes and buttermilk as if in any inn. They took no notice of the breeze thrashing at the canvas and sacking coverings. The children stood along the table. Mary BoatMac came and went about them with quiet solicitude. Her husband, she said to the old woman, was gone up the river to Limerick and would be sorry to have missed her arrival. 'But we'll welcome you here any time, any time at all,' she said, and looked and her eyes watered. 'Your son Teige,' she added, 'he is, he is . . .' She seemed to lose language adequate to her needs. 'He is so good,' she said shortly, and then said no more for a flush of sentiment ran through her and she turned about and went out to her sister.

They ate. The children teased and pushed and made jokes. Outside the evening fell and at last Teige looked across at his mother and knew that they could delay no more.

'We must go,' he said.

'Yes.'

Then he took her hand and placed it on his arm and led her away out into the darkness and up from the shore along the stony pathway toward the tower. The wind was blowing. Clouds raced before the coming stars. Late hares fleeted and vanished. Thorn bushes in their twists of growth whistled and did not move. Out in the waters nothing trafficked and the long black line of the river was slick and cold and fast-moving. Teige drew his mother closer to him. The way was uneven and she stumbled. He steadied her and was moved again by the slightness of her and how the woman he had looked to as a boy was now this frailty on his arm.

'It is not much further,' he said. 'I will carry you.'

'No. You will not. I will walk to him.'

And she raised her chin and her blind eyes looked away at an angle and held so as if seeing what he could not. She stood. He took her arm. They moved on. When they came close enough Teige could see the glass of the telescope and he told her: 'He is there. He is watching the sky.'

'Lead me right to him.'

'I should tell him.'

'No.' She clutched at his arm with her fingers. 'No, Teige. Stay here.' She stepped away from him then and was a shape in the dark against the darkness, holding her hands out and moving forward in the night wind like a thing of flimsy sail.

She walked toward the tower and Teige watched her and then when she thought she was close she called out.

'Francis! Francis!'

And he must have heard her and not believed her voice part of the corporeal world for he did not move and she called again and still he stayed there lain on his back with his eye against the eyepiece. The wind took her words the third time she called. It played them across the night and swept them into the tower. And Francis Foley heard his name said in her voice and thought it a sweetness long gone out of the world and imagined he was near the precipice of this life and she calling him to cross a bourn into the next. He took his eye from the stars. He looked at the stone walls as if in puzzlement that he was still not transported. He touched the straw on the ground and then lifted his head to look outside and he saw her there. She stood some feet away and behind her stood Teige and all about them the blowing darkness. He looked from one to the other and back again and seemed to reach understanding slowly, or was slow to overcome his fear that the moment was mere vision. Then he said her name. He said it and stood and she opened her arms and something in him seemed to buckle and it seemed he would fall down. But he did not. And he came forward and said her name again and reached out his hands to her face and knew that she was blind and then he raised his head to the dark and swirling heavens and let out a cry long and hard and pitiful and cried it again and voiced there the grief and regret and loss of all his days. Then he held that woman to him and kissed her head and her face and did not let her go.

10

Later, when his father sat beside the bed where his mother was sleeping, Teige left the stone cabin and went down to the shore. The night was wild now. The wind thrashed at hedge and tree and made moans in the gaps of the stones. The river and the sea surged. Waves broke on the shore and dragged the pebbles in an urgent music. Tethered on its moorings the rafthouse sang, but the BoatMacs were soundly sleeping. Teige paused a moment to be sure, then he went on down to the boat and pushed it out into the water and climbed in. He rowed out into the cross-current but was inexpert and was soon marking a course westerly on the outgoing tide. He pulled on the oars. He tried to steer across the darkness for the few lights of the town. The wind threw rain slantwise down the night. The waves were capped with white and slapped and churned and his progress was slow. But he was not to be stopped, and he made his way into the centre of the river and across and arrived at the shore some ways from the pier. He drew the boat up there and turned her over upon the oars, and he left then and walked along the grassy shore to the town. All was dark and empty. Rain lashed and stopped and fell again. Buildings grey and cold and grim of disparate size with roofs tiled and mismatched and at levels up and down stood and took the weather and seemed things of some inhuman order that had no fear of time. As if such were the faces of that town and would stand there forbidding and severe for ever. The wind howled. Teige walked up the street with head low. Rain stains saddled his shoulders. Cats in an alley mewed. A dog, lone and wolf-like with coat forked with dirt and gutter water, passed down the centre of the town and gave no heed to any. It appeared to have journeyed a long distance, and returned there perhaps in such metamorphosis from another life, so grave and decided was its manner. It padded down the darkness and was gone. Teige walked on. He went out the end of the town and was soon in the blackness of the country road to the estate. The night starless, he saw not four feet in front of him. He shut his eyes and stood some moments blind. He heard his own blood racing in his ears. Then he opened his eyes and was accustomed and saw the way in the dimmest light that fell from sources obscured and years on. He went on. Cold was inside his clothes now. He hurried on, running into the darkness as the storm that was not a storm yet gathered overhead. Trees on the roadside whooshed and let down their leaves. Teige knew his way in the darkness. He came to the gateway of the estate and went up the gravel. He passed the fields where the horses had grazed and where he had first seen Elizabeth. He took note of the fields and the fence and the places he had seen her as if such were talismans and assured him of love. He came to the stable yard and saw that the horses were fastened in and the doors bolted. Still some neighed and whinnied when he came there and he went to one and through the door said words though these were gone in the wind.

The night whirled. As he crossed the yard Teige turned and looked into the heavens as if some rent might appear there, and he thought of his mother sleeping on the island and the lore of the curse, and had he the time to make a prayer he would have done so. He went, as he had before, around by the back kitchen. There he scrabbled at the wall for finger and toeholds and finding these between the stones he began to climb. The slates of the roof where he arrived were wet and the soles of his feet slid upon them. He crouched and moved on all fours and found his way to the window. It was shut tight. The latch was turned over. He pulled at it as hard as he could but could not open it. On the wind another shower of rain fell. Teige cursed it softly and looked along the dark of the house but all windows were likewise latched against the storm and there was no way he could get in unless he broke the glass. He squatted there and the rain blew on him. What desire fired in his body flamed then. He would break the window. They might not hear. They might be so soundly asleep. They might think it the crash of thunder. There on the roof before the window he took off his shirt and wrapped it around his fist. He looked at the glass. He knew the ruin that might await. He knew his life might all have come to this one moment, and that for ever all happiness or sorrow might be traced back to this. And he did not care. He drew back his hand to break the glass and he saw her there framed in the window. He stopped. She was there in her nightgown. She had heard the noises at the window. She had been waiting.

There was a time that froze and was held. There was a stilled moment that entered each of them, a moment in which Elizabeth did not open the window and Teige did not move. A time in which the meaning of that moment was only then becoming apparent. And then Elizabeth unlatched the window and the curtains blew inward and Teige climbed inside the house.

He was wet and cold and half naked. But she shut down the window and then turned and kissed him there in the corridor. They kissed as if hungry. They seemed like creatures whose condition was to be joined at the mouth. Then they stood and she touched his face and he tried to kiss the hand and she drew him along the corridor to a room that was her dressing room. He closed the door behind them and came to her and kissed her nape and she moaned out and pulled at his hair and then he bit into the shoulder of her nightgown. He lifted it high to reveal her. He stood and looked at her and she trembled and she said in a whisper his name. Then he lay her down on dresses of green and yellow brocade and silks of scarlet and black, and she said to him to take off his clothes and she watched him as he did so. And then there in that room while the storm thrashed the world outside and her husband slept not fifteen feet away in the next room Teige Foley loved Elizabeth Price and changed his life for ever.

11

When they came outside the night was in hurly-burly. Teige carried her small case. They came out the kitchen door and at once the wind whipped it from Elizabeth's hand and banged it hard. They ran then. Leaves flew in circles in the yard as they crossed it. They went to the stables and Teige opened the door on a chestnut gelding that neighed and stamped in alarm and turned about in its narrow confines as if visited by nightmare. Teige approached it palms extended and spoke to it in what seemed tones of urgent beseeching. Then he laid his hands along the horse and moved beside it and so was able to fasten a bridle. He led the horse out into the storm. He took Elizabeth's hand and brought her closer and then cupped his fingers for her foot and helped her mount the horse which side-stepped and made shivers of nervy reaction until he soothed it once more beneath his command. They set off then out of the yard and down the avenue, Elizabeth bareback on the horse and Teige carrying her bag and leading it at a quick trot alongside. The wind sang demented in the trees. The starless moonless dark seemed itself a creature poor tormented by some flagellant merciless and huge. Noises crashed about. Branches snapped. Boughs moaned in long ache, and still the wind blew. Rain lanced sidelong and vanished and came again. Down the end of the avenue they went, the horse wild-eyed and on the point of frenzy and Teige mastering and coaxing it and taking rearward glances to see if their pursuit had begun.

They reached the gates. He looked to Elizabeth. There was

an instant at that threshold in which they might have turned back. She had already discarded her bonnet. It hung in the branches of an oak where it would be found in the morning. Her face was wet and her hair was blown free of pins and came across her mouth and she moved it aside as he looked at her. Then he climbed up on that horse and she held to him, and they rode off down the road toward the town of Kilrush.

They arrived there in darkness still hours before dawn. They came down the centre of the streets between those buildings where all lay in grim repose, clutched in fearful sleeps while the wind took the slates off the houses. Nothing moved. The air smelled of salt and squalor. Gutters and sewers ran sleek and black like festered wounds opened. The night howled. At the end of the town they came to the shoreline and rode along it to the grassy place where Teige had left the boat. There they got down and stood before the river that now was like the sea. Teige turned the horse about and waved his arms and slapped its back and it went off and was lost into the rent and velvet dark. There, he told Elizabeth, was where the island was. It was not far, he said, when she looked and could make out nothing. She stood there while he overturned the boat and laid it on the water. She seemed in all manner one unsuited to such adventure. She seemed too fine and delicate in appearance, too long used to the broad high-ceilinged drawing rooms and dining rooms of elegant china. She seemed of a different world and stood there on the brink of this in the thrashing of the storm like one not quite awake but lingering in the vestiges of a dream. Her toed shoes were muddied. Spatters, muck-splashes, painted her legs.

'Come.'

She stepped into the boat. It dipped and righted itself and dipped again and then Teige had pushed it off and they were fast in the current. The river took them. The tide that had been unruly before was wild and swollen now. The boat crashed against waves and was taken without course. Elizabeth cried out and clung to the sides. She called Teige's name. She cursed. They spun off into the dark and were like the smallest toy of the sea. Teige pulled and angled the oars and tried to steer about in that blackness, and the town came before them and then the mouth of the river and then the island and all seemed as if in some dark dioramic scene played for those watching from above. Teige rowed. He pulled and shouted at the storm as if it were a thing animate. He let out long wordless cries and these were lost in the wind. Elizabeth's face was white. She called to him that they must go back. Water slapped in the boat at her feet. She called to him again, and he shouted back to her that they could not. They were in the current fast and strong. Above and about them the storm thundered. It let down its rain in cold sheets and darkened the dawn.

But at last, whether by chance or design, the small boat crossed the mid-point of those waters and Teige was able to row it to shore at the eastern end of the island. They came up on the stones and Elizabeth stood and retched and Teige held her about the waist. Then she took three steps and had to sit in a weakness and he let her back into his arms and held her there on the open ground where the rain fell upon them still.

After some time slender light opened to the east as at the rim of the world. Clouds heavy and regally purpled were revealed sailing across the sky. The field the lovers lay in was littered with small leaves and twigs and feathers and other debris. Pieces of sacking, cord, cloth, such things. The wind like a ghost departing moved about the place a final time. And then it was gone. The fields of the island settled in the dawn light and in that serene and unreal aftermath Elizabeth clung to Teige. They were soaked to their skins. Their faces were cold when they kissed. They stayed there a time still and gazed out and watched the morning come across the fields. It was as if they could not move yet into the new world they had brought about. As if the full realization of what was now their life was only just arriving and they were as yet only beginning to comprehend it. So they held to each other and said nothing and when she felt the fright of what lay ahead of them Elizabeth kissed him hard. Small birds ventured across the air. Hares that came, it seemed, from shadows darted out and down the fields and painted tracks of dark in the silvered grass. At last Teige stood up and offered her his hand and they walked off down the island toward the tower.

He brought Elizabeth to the cabin where he slept and he set a fire there and blew the flames alight. Then he left her briefly as if she required privacy to undress and he went to where his mother had slept with his father and was afraid he would find her dead. He stood in the doorway and saw there an image that he would carry with him for the rest of his days. His mother lay small in the arms of his father. Both of them were sleeping. Their breaths came and went in slow easeful rhythm. Upon their faces was the same expression that was an expression he would return to and see in the air of nights far distant from there and would tell himself was the look of peace and forgiveness. He watched them a while. He watched them and did not want to step away and did not want the world to spin onward and the rough consequence of all our actions to follow. Then he went out the door and down to the rafthouse where already BoatMac was standing on the shore looking for his boat. Teige told him he had taken it and that it lay now on the far side of the island. The boatman looked at the stones.

'It was a fierce storm,' he said.

'It was.'

'Bad night to go out in a boat.'

'It was. I am sorry,' Teige said, and did not know if he would tell more. Then the man's wife appeared and was standing there and saw him in his drenched clothes and must have read in his comportment some affliction or beneficence for she asked him:

'Are all well?'

Teige looked at her. Her face was kind. Her eyes seemed to contain deeps he had not noticed.

'She is very wet,' he said.

'Your mother?' said the boatman.

'No,' said his wife.

A moment held. The water sighed.

'Gather her wet things,' she said then. 'I will have food for you both soon.' And she turned and went back to the house and left her husband standing there and studying the ground as if for pieces of the missing story.

Some time later she crossed up the pathway to the cabin and called in and Teige came to the doorway and welcomed her. She stood inside and saw Elizabeth and saw the beauty of her and seemed to understand at once that she was some man's wife, for she looked at Teige and took the wet clothes and asked him if he thought they would be going soon.

His judgement was impaired and he told her no.

'Eat and then sleep so,' she said, and took the clothes and went off back down the path.

And they did. They slept before the fire in that small stone cabin while the morning after the storm lightened outside. They slept in fits of dreams and shuddered sometimes like things fearful. Their legs lay entwined.

They woke with the sounds of the children playing. Elizabeth turned in Teige's arms and she studied his face. She put her fingers in his dark hair and traced his brows and closed his eyes.

'He will come after me,' she whispered.

'He'll never know where to find you.'

'He will,' she said.

They lay there. The yelps and cries of the children rang out. Smoke in slow ascension twirled inside the chimney. Neither of them moved. They lay still and were as creatures white and bare and beautiful fallen from another dimension.

In the noon they rose and Elizabeth came out by Teige's side and saw that ancient site of church and tower. She saw the town across the water which seemed nearer than she had hoped and nearer than their night-sailing had suggested. And she said to Teige: 'He could almost see us.'

'He will not look. He will think you are gone to Cork or Dublin or finer places than this,' and he smiled and put his arm about her.

Outside the tower on a stone trestle sat Teige's father and his mother. Francis Foley had awoken ten years younger than he slept. His face had dropped from it weariness and doom and his eyes were lit. He stood up when he saw the lady.

'This is Elizabeth,' Teige said.

'Elizabeth.' His father held out his hand.

'She is to be my wife.'

His mother took Elizabeth's hand and then to her son opened her arms and he leaned over and she embraced him. 'She is very beautiful,' she whispered, 'I know.'

'We'll start on the cottage for you tomorrow,' the old man said and smiled. Then he sat down again by his wife's side and took her hand as if as guarantee against the world sundering again.

It was the first day of the new. Storm-cleansed, green and tranquil, the island lay in the waters as an idyll or the vivid dream of Francis Foley years before. Boats sailed again along the Shannon. The traffic of white sails or men-at-oars proved the world moving but to the two Foleys, father and son, it seemed to be moving only out there, away from the island. They were each likewise gifted a pure innocence that morning and were like men under some enchantment in which time did not pass and loveliness endured. Teige walked with Elizabeth about the island and the children of the BoatMac came along and they gathered the red and orange wild flowers of montbretia and the feathered plumes of late purple loosestrife. They sang singsong chants. They chased and ran away and

Teige and Elizabeth sat down on the grass and kissed and then lay back and watched the vaulted blue sky.

They were lying so when the children came running again. 'Come come! Mammy says come! There is a boat coming.'

Teige took Elizabeth by the hand and they ran then across the fields down to the rafthouse by the shore. Mary BoatMac was standing there with her husband. Approaching steadily across the estuary was a long boat and in it sitting grim and purposeful were the sheriff and three constables, the wronged husband in a plum suit, and the red-haired youth Pyle.

There was a moment in which they all stood and watched, in which the slow and steady action of the oarsmen seemed in some world not this wherein the laws of force and motion did not apply and the boat did not come closer. It was like a picture or a scene posed, the little crowd on the headland and beneath the blue sky with white clouds the figures of law approaching.

'Quickly, you must go quickly.' It was Mary who spoke. She turned to Teige and shook him by the arm until he looked at her and broke from his disbelief that they could have found Elizabeth so soon. 'You have to go,' she said. 'They'll be here. Take them,' she told her husband, 'Mac, take them across the island to the boat. Go up to the tower with them and tell Mr Foley. Go! Go on, go quick,' she said, and as they turned to go, added, 'God bless ye.'

They ran up the beaten path that was soft and muddy after the rain. Teige took Elizabeth by the hand and with the shambling stride of one unused to dry ground BoatMac hurried behind. They went up past the long grass and the jumbled bushes of blackberry and the brambles wild and scented. Birds flew up. As if the world was freshened in the aftermath of the storm, all the natural wonder of the island seemed like a thing charged, alive, emanating from some source secret and holy. There was a tang in the breeze. Late blossoms of that season that had survived yet held the last bees and these hummed the air. The beauty of that landscape in all its detail, what sights and sounds and smells, all of these registered with Teige Foley as he ran and were to be there still in some part of him years later.

Francis Foley stood from the stone bench when he saw them coming.

'What is it?' he asked. 'Teige, what is the matter?'

'There are constables coming. They will say I stole a horse. There will be a man who is Elizabeth's husband.' He stopped and drew his breath.

'Teige.' His mother held out her hands to him. He came to her and she embraced him. She held him a long time. 'Go,' she said. 'Go and be happy.'

He stood and she gestured for Elizabeth and she held her, too. 'Do you love my son?' she asked her in a whisper, and what answer she received was not heard, but she embraced the young woman hard and then released her.

Teige faced his father. 'I sent the horse back last night. They will find it. It's . . .'

'Teige.' His father stopped him. 'Teige,' he said again, and said it slowly and burdened the sound with such tenderness that no single vocable seemed capable of carrying such or no word as dear to him then as the sound of his son's name. 'I will beat the heads of any of them that walk up here,' he said. 'I will let none stop you. Go.' He reached his hand and laid it on Teige's shoulder.

And then they were gone running. They ran across the island with BoatMac coming behind them. They ran to the place where the boat lay upturned on the far shore and this they righted and slid it down the weeds and mud into the water. And then BoatMac held the boat while they climbed inside it and he pushed it further into the water and then climbed in himself and took the oars and pulled away. And they did not see Francis Foley stride down the path to the other shore and meet there the little party of the wronged and the righteous. They did not hear his booming voice as he called out damnations against those who trespassed there or accused his son. They did not know that the sheriff would say the youth Pyle had given them reason to suspect Teige and that Pyle would grin and the plum fellow alongside would scowl with pale effete manner and show his distaste at this discourse with rabble such as these. Nor would they know that Francis Foley's ire would burn then and he would say he had answered all queries and that even had his son taken the horse and the woman it was no more than God's own will for any could see the kind of man this was. And the sheriff would perhaps in secret agree and stand back and instruct the constables back into the boat and say they would return if the horse was not found. And the plum fellow would cry out that the island must be searched for his wife, and his voice would be high and thin in a timbre that would be mocked in games by the children later. His cries would go unanswered and at last he too would get on board and all would sail away, in gloom and dismay as they had come, the youth Pyle with crooked grin looking back all the way.

None of this did Teige and Elizabeth know. Their boat carried them safely to the town of Limerick. There BoatMac left them with subdued farewell after Teige had thanked him and offered in vain to pay from the money Elizabeth carried in her bag. They took a ship that same afternoon and sailed from Limerick up to the town of Galway and spent that night there where they purchased passage in the morning on the *Mary Ann*, bound for the coast of Nova Scotia.

12

In the week after Teige was gone the BoatMacs moved from the rafthouse into the unfinished cottage by the shore. Francis Foley insisted on it. He came down with his wife on his arm and asked them please to move there and said that he would help finish the building and they would be the first true settlers on the island. It was what Teige would have wished, he said, and was the least they were owed. He told them to take a field and grow what they wanted, and take another for sheep or cattle. By the beginning of the following spring there were lambs born there. The cottage was thatched. Another was built next to it by the boatman and his sons, but when they came to offer it to the old man Francis said they would prefer to stay where they were and that soon enough there would be takers for it, indicating the oldest of the daughters.

The season was mild and easy that year. The waters of the river ran smooth and blue-grey. Swans that had not been seen in some time sailed off the shore. Michael, which was discovered to be the name of BoatMac, came up to the tower one morning and told Francis Foley he had been asked to enquire if other pilots could settle with their families on the island. The old man studied the blue sky where high gannets flew. His wife sat by his side. His gorge rose and fell with some emotion unsaid and he waited a time for it to pass.

'They want to live here?'

'They do.'

The old man nodded. 'A village should be made down by the shore,' he said.

And by the early summer there were seven more cottages underway. Seagoing men with short legs and stout chests and with sons thin and wiry scattered over the stones hauling and tapping and knocking edges. Walls rose. Thatch was mounded on the sand. Buckets of mud and lime and water were borne along the shore and soon such traffic made there a printed trail that the tide took in the evenings. By night the pilots sailed away and the assemblage of their unfinished cottages appeared like ruins of some earlier time. Doorways and windows looked like eyes upon the starry river. In the silence soft and crepuscular hares, badgers and foxes visited and moved as shades stealthy and inquisitive. Francis Foley came down then, too and walked along the way that would become the street. The dog followed him. He stood in each of the roofless houses where none were there to see him and he touched sometimes details of masonry or joinery and let his fingers rest there. He stood so for long moments, his hand upon a wall, as if such were a connection of profound necessity and it restored him to do so. It did not escape him that these were to have been the homes for his sons and he thought of them in the world and looked upon the night sky and went up then along the path to hold his wife in her bed.

In the dawns the black currachs of the pilots returned weighted in the water with supplies. The boats were drawn up and turned over on the shore and lay long and dark like strange insects warming in the sun. The cottages rose as in a race, their walls three feet thick with broad sills and deep lintels of hewn oak. With lighter timbers the lattice of roofs were made and seemed in broad day the bleached ribs of once great sea-creatures. When they came to the thatching the pilots were less expert and brought from the town some tawny fellows with dark hair and long needles and hooks and other tools secured in their belts. Bare-chested, these thatchers ran up and down light ladders and worked and sewed above and sometime whistled and were like brown birds nestled there. They ate and drank in those lofty perches and looked betimes out to the sea as if gauging what weathers their work would have to withstand. When they were done and gone again, the pilots brought their families across. A flotilla of figures wrapped and shawled and bearing bundles, they came from the district of Kilbaha to that island with a quiet and humble gratitude. They moved up about the small village and saw for the first time their homes. Children ran along and whooped and went in and out behind the houses. At once the women went about making their homes. They untied bundles of blankets and put clay pots, earthenware and tin canisters on sills. They hung crosses and some had other images of their religion and they placed these like shields in corners or over doorways. The pilots meantime stood outside in a small gathering and watched the Shannon. One made small comments on the tide or weather and others concurred in soft mutterings. Their eyes were narrowed and their faces crinkled, grown accustomed to long scrutiny of the horizon. In the evening one among them played a concertina and they gathered outside the houses and smoked pipes and some sisters danced together. Others of the women joined. The men bashful and slow sat or leaned against walls and watched. Only later were some cajoled to step out there, but when these did, their movements light with the drink they had taken, the whole swayed and spilled over and broke with laughter. One sang a song then shut-eyed and sad. He sang for the drowned and those gone and these sounds travelled out across the mild night plaintive and grave. Then a hush fell and spread and all said their goodnights and went to sleep there for the first time.

And so another summer drew on. In the first light of each day and in all weathers the pilots launched their currachs into the water and sailed out in a race against each other and were like so many waterborne beetles as they travelled out to meet ships bound for Limerick. Whosoever reached the ship first drew the entitlement of piloting it in through the dangerous currents and past the sandbanks. Others bobbed in the heavy waters and scanned the horizon and waited. They watched the sky for seabirds to tell them if ships were coming. They lived all day on the water and in the falling dark returned and stepped with jaunty gait up the street where children and dogs came to meet them.

These men had little contact with the Foleys. Their wives sometimes went with potato breads and griddlecakes and such up to the house by the tower and they were welcomed and thanked by the old man. But he rarely came down among them. Michael and Mary visited. They sent meals with the children, and came themselves on many evenings and told them about the antics of the Brennans or Behans or McNamaras or Scanlans or any of the families that lived there. They told of sea escapades and boats overturned and news brought on the ships from the world outside. And these things the old man and his wife listened to politely and nodded and made little comment, for it seemed news of a place fictive and unreal.

The seasons turned. Cousins of those living there came and built houses, too. A girl of the Griffins married and for her a house was made in the half-acre behind her father's cottage. Winter and spring and summer and autumn chased each other across the sky and the constellations wheeled and the moon rose and fell like hope and still none of the sons of Francis Foley returned there. One night as they sat outside in that silent and peaceful way that had become their custom before sleep, Emer asked Francis to tell her what the stars were like now. She sat there in her darkness absolute and turned her face upward. She knew he had not gone to the telescope once since she had been returned to him and knew him well enough to know that such may have been a pact promised to be kept if indeed she came back.

'Tell me,' she said.

He did not think he should at first. At first he thought it

346

risked her in some obscure way. He thought fortune and misfortune so close to each other that there was the thinnest sliver between them and the slightest error could bring the latter.

'It's all right,' she said, 'I would like to hear you tell me about them. I will place them around my dark.'

And so he did. He looked up high into the sky at Cassiopeia and told her its form, and then took her down through the sky to the Bears Minor and Major and over to Castor and Pollux, too. These he named and with that she sat attentive and did not tilt her head but seemed to be gazing nonetheless upon a panorama of inner stars.

'You love them so, don't you?' she said one night when already such mapping of the dark had become their custom.

'I do. They are so pure,' he said to her. 'They are like something perfect. From the time of Adam. And I cannot look at them without thinking of you. Thinking of the days we met and the nights we went out roaming and you told me stories of them.'

She did not say any more. She held his arm. They sat there.

'I will think of them now as the boys,' she said.

The night was still. A moon gibbous and bare hung overhead.

Francis's voice answered softly: 'Yes.'

Five days later Michael McMahon came up to the tower and brought with him a letter that had been left in the town of Kilrush, he said, for he didn't know how long. It had lain in dirt in a corner for none had wanted to bring it over. It was the letter from Tom Foley to Teige. The old man read it aloud. He finished by saying the name Tom. Then he said it again. Tom. Then he started the letter from the beginning and read it over once more.

'We must send a letter to him,' Emer said. 'And when Teige writes to us we will tell him where he is. And when the twins come back we will tell them, too.'

That night, when they sat for their stellar vigil, the air had turned cold, and Emer Foley asked him then to take her to the telescope. He led her there and lay her down alongside him and he blew on the eyepiece and cleared webwork and dust. She placed her head upon his chest over his heart.

'Now,' she said, 'I will tell you about my stars.'

13

And Teige and Elizabeth arrived off the coast of Canada just before ice forced the closure of the ports along the St Lawrence River. They arrived after a long journey in which Elizabeth had suffered sickness and woke from fitful sleeps crying out in fright. Her face grew paler and her cheekbones more prominent. Teige served her food and drink and brought to her what comforts he could find. He urged her to come on deck and take exercise, but she had a horror of her fellow passengers. They were walking dirt and disease, she told him, and she would not move from the narrow bed. When he came to her and tried again to have her walk with him, when briefly the ship found calm blue waters, she shouted at him.

'I don't need exercise! I'm not one of your horses!'

For the remainder of that grey voyage she lay below deck. She turned her face in her pillow and was like a rag twisted. Her eyes took a haunted look. The further the distance travelled the deeper she fell into despair. She berated Teige for clumsiness and smacked away the plate when she saw his thumb above it against the pork. She despised how he befriended others of the passengers and found in his very appearance faults she had not noticed before. Sometime after she had screamed at him she calmed and sobbed and opened her arms to him and asked for forgiveness and said it was the wretched sea. It was the wretched boat, it wasn't her at all. He was not to mind.

And for the most part, he tried not to. He tried to imagine the life ahead of them. When he walked on the windy deck or held to the rails in the sheets of rain he looked at the blank horizon and tried to be emptied of his fears. He lifted his face to the weather. He sought in his mind the image of the island and his father and his mother there. Long hours while Elizabeth lay below he thought of them and thought of his brothers gone and wondered where in the vastness of the world was Tomas. He stood and held on in that swaying ocean that was like a watery bridge between the old life and the new. He stood until his loneliness weakened him. Then he came down the steps and along the passage to where Elizabeth lay and he took off his coat and knelt beside her and caressed the top of her head. He lowered his forehead to her until it rested against her shoulder and he could stay so a long time and she would not move and no word would pass between them.

For reasons not explained to its passengers the Mary Anne did not arrive in Halifax but came about Cape Sable and docked at Saint John, New Brunswick. When Teige and Elizabeth disembarked they gave their names as Foley and were man and wife. Elizabeth told the officer they met that their luggage had been sent ahead of them. They walked off down the gangway in the chill air of late autumn in a place where the air was pungent with fish and gulls made raucous sounds overhead. Fishermen, bearded high on their cheeks, worked with crates and barrels wherein the silvered catch slapped in spasm. Some spoke but not in words that Teige understood. Elizabeth lay her hand upon his arm.

'This way,' she said, indicating that they should not follow the clump of their fellow passengers, those freckle-faced Galwegians who moved like some slow lumpish porridge all together up the street.

There were men in peaked caps and others in suits of black that studied the arrivals there. There were some that called out offers of lodging and food and more still that cried out sailings on ships bound for Boston and points south. Past these Elizabeth guided Teige and past those too who stared wide-eyed upon her beauty and followed her with their heads. They went along a street of mud upon a walk of loose boards. The heel of Elizabeth's shoe caught and she slipped and cursed and stamped at the plank.

'We're getting out of here tomorrow,' she said.

They took a room in a boarding house run by a woman red-faced and large. She was Mrs Flump. She wore an apron tied about her from neck to knee and within such lost all shape but was a great mound smelling variously of flour and carbolic. Her eyes were bright blue like things lit. She asked where they were bound.

'We are not sure,' Teige said.

'Boston,' Elizabeth replied. 'Our trunks are sent ahead.'

'I see,' said Mrs Flump.

Their room was small but tidy. Elizabeth sniffed at the sheets and found them clean and then lay upon them in her dress. Teige undid her boots.

'This is Hell,' she said. 'We are fallen into Hell.' Her eyes stared at the ceiling boards where a web had recently been woven.

'I will take you to a better place,' Teige said. 'This is only tonight. We have just arrived. There is a huge country here. We will be happy.'

'Oh God, Teige.' She held out her arms to him and he came to her and they held each other and kissed and waited for the fall of night while keeping mute their separate fears.

In the morning Mrs Flump gave them a breakfast of eggs, but these Elizabeth could not stomach and she retreated to her room at once.

'Is she expecting?' Mrs Flump asked Teige. 'I often find those expecting can't eat the eggs.'

Teige's face was blank, and Mrs Flump saw his surprise and quickly added, 'No, I suspect probably not. It's probably just the long journey.'

Still the thought remained with Teige, and when they left

there and Mrs Flump stood in her doorway and gave them a carbolic-scented napkin of her scones he thought her eye studied Elizabeth for some further sign.

'Good luck to ye,' she said. 'I hope ye'll be happy.'

They returned to the dockside. Men watched them. Some with knives bent over fish barrels stopped and looked at the woman in the green dress. A wind blew her hair. She stood alone a time and waited while Teige made enquiries. Then he returned to her with another man who was thickly whiskered and stood very close to her while he told her of the schooner that would take them to Boston. They sailed from there at noon. Some passengers of various origins stood on the deck in frayed and sea-soiled finery and watched the coast pass. Trees dense and evergreen lay along the shore. Impenetrable forest seemed the landscape and to the eyes of those just come from the distant continent the whole seemed wild with as yet little mark of civilization. They imagined therein were the Indians they had heard of and that these were even then watching the ship with arrows in bows aimed as she moved down the coastline. The voyage was without incident. Cold wind made the waters choppy and slowed the progress of the schooner, but when she arrived in Boston none of the passengers cared. For they were cheered by the elegance of the buildings and the sight of the streets. Elizabeth too smiled and stood on the deck as the ship came in. She squeezed Teige's arm, her face flushed and her eyes travelling over the thoroughfares. When they disembarked a man stepped over to them and speaking to both but looking at Elizabeth said he could tell they would be seeking fine accommodations and would they allow him to guide them to the best? He carried Elizabeth's one bag. They went to a hotel finer than any Teige had ever seen. The man tipped his hat and stood and waited and Elizabeth gave him some money in their own currency and he thanked her and was gone. They took a room with flowered paper on the wall. Above the posts

of the bed was a canopy of cream-coloured linen. Their breakfast was brought on a tray of silver.

They stayed there. In the daytimes Elizabeth went out and
bought new clothes and returned with these and tried them on
before a standing mirror. Teige told her she was beautiful. He
searched for signs that she might be pregnant but did not know
what these were and if he found them or not.

'We should think of moving on from here,' he said to her
one evening after they had dined in the grand room where the
chandeliers that had come from Milan glittered above them and
let fall brilliant splinters of broken light.

'Why should we?'

'I have no work. We cannot stay here. We must be near the
end of your money.'

Her expression turned cold.

'Money is vulgar, Teige. Please don't speak of it.'

'But . . .'

'Please Teige.'

He looked at his plate.

'Thank you,' she said, 'you are so sweet. Always so sweet.'

The following morning she went and bought him a white
shirt and black suit. He tried them on in the room. When he
stood before her she considered him a time and then told him
to go to the barber's and to buy new shoes. Then he would be
perfect, she said. He did. In that same afternoon returning
he crossed the lobby of the hotel and caught in a gilt-framed
mirror the image of himself and felt almost another. He went
around and came back to pass the mirror again. He looked then
like none in his family ever had and was the copy of others who
sat with newspapers in the leather chairs there. That evening
Elizabeth was in light humour and sang as she dressed for
dinner. Her hair was pinned above and about her neck she wore
pearls he had never seen.

'How long do you think we will stay here?' Teige asked her.

'Until we find a house.'

He said nothing. His heart sank. She came to him and touched his shoulder.

'You can get a job soon. I asked today for you at the bank.'

'I can't work at the bank.'

She turned her cheek as if it had been struck.

'We'll be late for dinner,' she said after a time.

They went down the carpeted stairs and entered the dining room, she upon his arm with her head erect and her pearls shining like defiance. They ate roast beef and potatoes with gravy and were served a bottle of wine courtesy of a man at another table. They said almost nothing. As if they had come into a country of extreme civility wherein all discourse was predicated upon polite formulae, Elizabeth addressed him in dulcet tone over such matters as the passing of the salt and the pouring of the wine. But nothing more. She sat and was the loveliest woman in the room. When the meal was ended the man who had gifted the wine came to their table and asked them if they were coming in to hear the piano played. He was French with a name Teige did not catch.

'Oh yes,' Elizabeth said, 'thank you. We would love to.'

They sat with the man whose hair was black and sleek and cuffs linked with studs bejewelled. He asked what plans they had and Elizabeth told him they were as yet undecided but that Teige would probably take a job he had been offered at the bank. The Frenchman looked at Teige and smiled. He said it was a good job. Men get rich in banks, he said. He bought them champagne to drink a toast to their beginning. When Teige asked him what business he was in he said he was in the business of seeing opportunity. He accented the last word so, such that Teige was unsure at first of his meaning. There is much opportunity in this country, he said. More than in France. France is old and tired now. Elizabeth agreed.

'Very old and tired,' she said, and giggled and touched her fingers to her mouth where the champagne had left a fizz.

354

The Frenchman smiled.

'We should go to our room,' Teige said.

'It is early,' said the Frenchman.

'Yes it is early,' Elizabeth scolded.

They stayed on. The piano music was played and ended and the umber light of that room dimmed further until all were but shadows slumped here and there. At a moment without warning Elizabeth's head suddenly rolled and she swayed sideways and the Frenchman caught and held her. He sat her upright once more and removed his arm. Teige lifted her to her feet and she staggered and said small nonsense and the Frenchman offered to help but was declined. He stood to wish them good-night. They went then, tilting, wavering, going over and back in staggered progress and were like a thing of sails traversing into dangerous waters.

14

The Frenchman's card arrived with their breakfast. Elizabeth could not eat. She moaned and put her head beneath the pillows. The tray was placed outside the door. Teige rose and went out about the city in the black suit. He went to the bank she had mentioned and entered and stood beneath the high domed roof and watched for some moments the business transacted there. His chest pounded. He watched those men, bald, bespectacled, as they bent over papers, collars pinched beneath their chins. Light suffused through high windows and lit dust motes as they swirled and fell. The air was arid. Across the marbled floor a guard came and asked him if he needed assistance. He turned and went outside and stood on the steps and tried to catch his breath. He had felt as if his life had been taken away, as if it were a document of sorts he guarded in his chest and the instant he walked inside the bank it had been withdrawn to be kept by another. He stood and watched the sky where clouds moved brisk in the wind. There were signs of the coming winter. He stood and did nothing and considered and then he crossed down the street to the railroad station and bought two tickets for the afternoon train. Then he went back to the hotel and asked at the desk for their bill. When it came he saw the figure and did not know how they could pay it. He went upstairs and woke Elizabeth.

'Come on, you have to wake now. We have to go.'

She shook her head with its tousled hair. It was as if she was being asked for a dance.

'Yes,' he said. 'Elizabeth, how much money have you got?'

She opened her eyes to look at him.

'What?'

'How much money have you got? We have to pay, or give them something if we can't. We have to take a train this afternoon.'

The urgency of his tone roused her.

'What are you saying?'

'We can't stay here.'

'Yes, we can.'

'No. We have to go.' He began to gather her things that were too many now for her bag.

'Stop it. Leave my things.' She sprang from the bed and was beside him pulling back her dress. 'How dare you,' she said. She struck at him with her hand. It landed on his cheek and he stepped back and raised his two hands as if to still the angry air.

'I cannot work at the bank, Elizabeth. I have to go into the country. I have to work on land with horses. This is what I can do, you know that. We can have a good house, for our child.' He gestured right-handed to her midriff.

'What?'

'Are you . . .'

She shouted, 'No! No no, stop!' She turned back to the bed and threw herself upon it and wept.

Teige stood and felt the life go out of him. He put down the bag. He took off his jacket and he sat beside her on the bed and he stroked her hair. When at last she turned her wet face to him she said: 'Can we stay?'

And he answered her, 'All right.'

15

So they did not take the train that afternoon, and Teige went
down and told them at the desk of the hotel that there had
been a mistake and the man there smiled and was most gracious
and said how delighted they all were. The first snow flurries
blew. The fire in the lobby was loaded high with logs and the
scent of woodsmoke hung thickly. Elizabeth bought a coat of
fur. It was made she told Teige from wild bears that ran about
in the rest of that country. Imagine. She told him to get one
for himself, but he declined. He sat in the hotel room and
despaired. He went out to the outskirts of the city where the
land opened and the treed skyline told of the wilderness beyond.
He found a blacksmith's yard and stables and passed some time
of the day examining the horses there. He surprised the smith
with knowledge of hooves and offered to help, and showed such
skill as belied his fine clothes. He went there several times
thereafter. When he returned to the hotel he was again in his
black jacket but his skin smelled of horses.

On many evenings the Frenchman joined them for dinner.
Such was his frequency that Elizabeth and Teige were custom-
arily seated at a table for three and sat in attendance until he
arrived. Evenings when he did not come they sat muted over
the noise of their knife and fork. When he did he came with
many apologies and kissed Elizabeth's hand and ordered champagne. He made jokes about extravagant heiresses with triple
chins. He told stories of the glamour of New York and the fine
houses he had stayed in and told too of his favoured place in

that country that was called New Orleans where the ladies wore jewelled garters sent from Paris.

When they came upstairs after one such night, Elizabeth told Teige he should ask the Frenchman for a job.

'You cannot sit around for ever.'

He came to her and held her about the shoulders. 'Elizabeth,' he said, 'I want us to leave. You know that. I want us to go west. There is . . .'

'No.'

She spun away. She went to the dressing room. He came there and opened the door where she was taking down her dress. When she saw him there she stopped.

'Once you wanted me to see you,' he said.

She held her hands across herself.

'Please, Teige,' she said. 'Go to sleep.'

She closed over the door.

The day following he rose before her and went out across the frozen morning to visit the smith and the horses. One that had recovered from lameness he took for a ride and went out at a gallop across thinly crisp and whitened grass. The plumes of his breath and the horse's breath were like signals of some release. The land they crossed was fresh and unspoiled and open and the sky above clear and bluer than any he had seen. He took the horse down the steep of a valley and journeyed along this until he came to a stream. He paused there and dismounted and let the horse drink and he squatted and scooped palmfuls of icy water for himself. He doused his head. He shook the wide ring of drops and then shouted out. He shouted again and the horse startled and went a few paces in the stream but intuited there was no call for fear and stood then looking sidelong. Teige stood and opened his arms and shouted again, and the shout travelled up that valley and was heard by what birds and beasts dwelled there and perhaps by these alone was comprehended.

Teige whistled and the horse came to him. He stroked its flank. He lay his forehead upon its shoulder. In fields at the north of the valley some cattle stood. A hawk high in the blue travelled a wide arc. Teige climbed on the horse and rode on. He rode all that day and afternoon. He rode along the edge of woods and stopped to smell the trees and to recall that smell from a time long ago when he and the twins waited for Tomas with a swan. He rode across the fast fading light of that winter's day and stopped sometimes to let the horse graze and rest and to consider the world in which he found himself. Then he went on. He went in an arc no different from the hawk's, as if upon a long invisible tethering, and by the coming of the darkness he was back at the smith's. He returned the horse. The smith worked at a fire hammering. He told Teige he could have the horse for little money for the work he had done. Teige said he had worked for the horses and not for payment and the man said he understood this and this was why he offered.

Teige told the smith he was unsure if he could take the horse but would return. He went back to the city on foot and his suit was soiled and worn-looking and about him was the smell of the land. He came in the doorway of the hotel and from what signals he could not say knew at once that something was awry. It was as though all was canted slightly, or a glass opaque had been placed between him and what he saw. He went past the desk where the clerk at that moment spun to study the keys. He went up the stairs and into the room and saw at once that she was gone. Her clothes, her bag, his eyes looked for these though he did not move. There was only her scent. Upon the bed he saw the note she had written him.

Dear Teige,

I am gone. Please do not try and find me.

It will only embarrass both of us. We are finished. It was my fault.

I have paid the hotel bill.

I wish you every happiness,

Elizabeth

16

He stood and held the note and looked it over again. Then he crumpled it and threw it across the room. He went to the chest of drawers where his old clothes lay and he stripped off the black suit and put them on. With the suit bundled under his arm he left that room and went down the stairs quickly and caught the eye of the desk clerk who looked askance at him in that old apparel. He crossed the marbled lobby beneath the chandeliers and went out to the street. There was snow trafficking in the air. Those moving in that thoroughfare were thickly coated in furs and other heavy materials and at once Teige had a glimpse of what the winter would be like there. He went out the way he had come. The snow fell but did not seem to land. It crossed the air and vanished when it touched the ground. Yet still more fell, spiralling in windless descent out of the evening dark. Teige turned his face to it. The stars were gone. His breath rose briefly and then passed into nothing. He went on. He walked out the end of the streets into the utter dark. The road was softened beneath him. The snow falling was visible only barely when it passed his eyes. He tramped into the night and went on out to the blacksmith's. He found that man's low house by the roadside and went and knocked on the door.

The smith came out in a vest and trousers.

'I need the horse,' Teige said. 'I could work for you for a week.'

The smith blinked as if there was something he was just seeing. 'Have you nothing you can trade?' he asked.

'Only these.' Teige held out the black suit.

The smith took the suit that was too small for him and turned it over in the half-light.

'For funerals,' he said and smiled and Teige smiled, too.

'You have already done the work. The horse is yours,' said the smith. He told Teige to wait a moment and went back inside where the figure of a woman moved and then he came out with a lantern. They crossed the yard where the snow fell across the amber light and the smith held the lantern aloft while Teige unbolted the door. The horse neighed and Teige went and calmed her.

'You have no saddle,' said the smith.

'No.'

'Take the bridle.'

The smith watched while Teige brought her outside and he held the lantern and considered what tale untold underlay this scene and of it he did not ask. Teige turned and offered him his hand.

'It is a cold night,' the smith said. 'You should wait.' He indicated with his left hand the stables.

'I cannot,' Teige said. They shook hands. 'Thank you.'

Then he slipped up on to the horse's back that was already starred with scintillas of melting snowflakes. He said some words to the animal and then he turned her out of there and they went out of the lantern light and down the dark.

Teige rode out on the road in a direction south of the city. Of the geography of that country he had only the vaguest knowledge and even prior to that moment had not exactly considered where it was he was to start his life with Elizabeth. He had heard men speak of the west as if it were more than a compass point, as if captured in that appellation was a territory majestic and free and without parallel. But he did not know where it was nor did he comprehend the vastness of that continent. That night as he rode he rode for distance only, to be further away than it was possible to be. The road wound away from the coast. He went down through woodlands where the snow stopped and a small chill wind tunnelled. He passed on and met none coming or going and found in his very bones the sad familiarity of such lone travel, as if re-encountering there a truth about his own condition. In the hours yet before dawn he slowed the horse and walked her and then drew her to the side of tall trees where he bowed his head and for some short time slept.

He woke with birdsong. Light was breaking and the country thereabouts was revealed in verdant and purple colour. He rode on. South of there he came upon two boys and a man hunting cattle in the dawn. The gate to a field was open but the cattle in their own peculiarity broke and ran past it and the boys ran after them with the man shouting. Teige turned the horse and headed the cattle off and turned them back. The drover boys joined him and they returned the cattle to the field proper. Then the man indicated the farmhouse not distant and said breakfast would be readying now.

Teige stayed there a week. The boys called him Ty. The woman of the house caught the melancholy of his demeanour and fed him double portions of eggs and meat as remedy for such sadness. He helped with the cattle and winter fencing. The days were cold and bright and the sky like a sheet of blue pulled taut over the world. When the man tried to pay him for his work Teige would take none. The man offered him an old saddle then and said he would not be refused.

He went off south and west again and crossed the valley of a great river whose name he did not know. He saw mountains ahead and kept these to his right shoulder. He stopped occasionally at places and worked a few days and was sometimes paid and sometimes given food. He stayed always briefly and made attachments to none. What history was his and how he had come to be there he kept like a parchment folded inside him. As he rode the horse his mind was sometimes erased of all and he achieved in the rhythmic motion a state akin to innocence absolute. But in the evenings when he had to rest the horse and sat on a stone in the grass he was often assailed by the memory of what he had left behind. He saw the woman's face as he had first seen it. He returned to the old country and saw himself there in scenes as if from the life of another. He thought of his father and mother on the island and he looked at the big sky there and considered what stars he could see. He knew he should attempt a letter, but in the ruins of his dreams felt a vague uncertain shame and could not begin.

All that winter he rode south. Then when the spring came and the waters ran in clear streams everywhere he turned the horse west and headed up through a pass in the Appalachian Mountains. By the summer of that year he had reached the Ohio river. He had thought when he reached it he must be nearly most ways across the country. The heat of the day scorched his forehead and he began wearing a hat. The horse took lame and he had to rest her a while on the outskirts of a town where in that season all was dust. He went and found a smith's there and from short exchanges learned of those multitudes who considered that merely the starting point for their own sojourns west. The country was vast beyond imagining, he understood then. And from that knowledge he took solace, for destination was not what he sought and there was in endlessness a certain comfort born of the recognition that there would be no turning back.

He went due west then, and came upon many wagons and riders and walkers, too, all as if under some heliocentric influence following the falling trajectory of the sun. Such were the numbers moving on the roads that it appeared as though the earth herself were flat and had been tipped on the side and all manner of men and women were then propelled to travel westward. Teige rode at times among them. Each had their own tale and without exception had left their lives behind on the basis of stories they had heard of the land that lay ahead. They were a long loose caravan of faith. Their countries were many.

By the time he had crossed the Mississippi river Teige had heard described the gold of California that some believed was plentiful yet. He had heard of similar riches at the end of the Oregon Trail and of untouched land there said to be only waiting for farming. But to none such was he drawn. He could not envision himself a farmer, could not now imagine being in a house fixed and still. He went south. His skin crisped in the sun. His forearms blistered in a line of watery moons. His horse suffered and whole days he spent then only seeking water. He had come into Nebraska. On prairies there he saw herds of bison for the first time and paused his horse upon a crest and sat and watched over them a long time. He slept on a bedroll beneath the huge sky. In dreams he saw the face of his brother Tomas and saw him on the night he had last seen his face as he left the island and woke and wondered if he were living or dead.

For days he went nowhere at all. He rested the horse and spoke to her and brought her to water. If she died, he thought, I would, too. For such was the empty vista he beheld that travellers there seemed less than sporadic and his bones would have whitened before he was found. Nonetheless this same emptiness soothed him, too, and there was in his silent and solitary state a kind of peace. He stayed in that country a while. He watched the birds of prey high against the heavens like smallest flaws in the blue. He heard the prairie dogs in the night. When the ashes of love gathered in his mouth he stood and went off across the dark sending badgers and foxes and coyotes alike in scattered retreat. He walked and sometimes howled out and sometimes stopped and bent over and wept. He felt like a disease in the blood the shame of failed love and could not explain to himself how it had happened. After a time he returned to his horse and his bedroll and lay until the dawn.

One noon clouds heavy and black rose up in the western sky. They came quickly and gathered as they did so, crossing the land like a grim assemblage. Teige watched the shadow coming. Then he brought his horse to shelter in some rocks and waited. Thunder crashed. The horse's ears went flat and then she let out a cry of alarm and stamped backward and he spoke to her and held up his palm and lay it on her nose. The thunder banged again and the rain fell. Lightning forked. It flew from the sky so close that Teige turned about and at once the horse ran. She raced off out of the rocks and down into the prairie below. He saw her go and he called after her but then she was gone. The rain came on. It fell in torrents. Again and again the thunder rolled grave and declamatory. The air flashed electric. Teige turned his face to the sky and let it fall upon him. He wanted it to be the rain of home. But it fell too hard and was dark and stiff and urgent and seemed, with its thunder crashing, the ancient locution of some primitive god. It rained on. It made floods in the darkened ground. Night was made of the daytime as the clouds crossed. Still Teige stood. He thought for moments of the lightning falling through the sky and striking him. And if such had happened he would not have regretted it, he told himself.

But it did not. The clouds rode on. The storm had made clear the air that in that aftermath was briefly cooled like a drink. Teige took his bedroll and walked on down into the prairie after his horse. He whistled for her and called out. He crossed the dampened ground where the dust clung to his boots and made upon them a reddish coat. The land all about was empty of man or beast or bird. The herds that had grazed there were all elsewhere and the scene entire was tranquil and vacant. He might have been the sole creation left extant.

Time passed. He walked on and the white eye of the sun reappeared overhead and the air wavered with heat once more. He crossed land where the hoof prints of the bison had left a trail wide and broken and there lay bones of some fallen long ago. He called for the horse. He stopped and considered the endlessness of the terrain and the futility of his attempting to walk out of it. He sat down then. He had some few supplies, enough for maybe two days. He had a canteen of water. He had a pistol. The night fell. He was aware of Indians and knew of tribes such as Sioux and Cheyenne but he did not fear these for he held his life lightly. A moon climbed above him. Her stars arrived. In the stillness of the dark of that prairie Teige Foley lay down and after a time as though to the company of his brothers began to tell the stories of the constellations above. He spoke aloud. His voice carried a little in the windless night. And in such dark and beneath the canopy there he told of Pegasus the winged horse and Equuleus the foal and he traced with his eyes the pattern of stars his father saw. He spoke until his lips dried and his voice became a whisper. The enormity of that landscape was spread out about him in the night and upon it he less than a speck of light or dust and with as little consequence it seemed to any in heaven. The moon slid down the dark.

17

Upon the island winters wet and cold came and were followed by wet and cold springs. Like time the river ran. Smoke climbed from the cottages of the little village and in the damp seasons did not ascend but hung in the air like a presence or a spirit without form. Uncertain summers followed. A drift of light rain came up the estuary and drizzled in the windless air and this remained and the autumn was winter once more. All moved in a slow yet ceaseless falling. Upon a ledge in the stone building, Francis Foley kept the letter of Tomas. He awaited news of Teige, but none came. The letter like a thing returning to some former state had grown thinner, its single page read so often it was light as a wing. When Francis took it from the ledge and lifted it in the candlelight he saw the ink that was faded from black to grey and he did not tell his wife the words were vanishing. In the season that followed when the rain swept down and the dampness of the climate threatened to turn all rheumatic the letter soaked up the watery air and in the brief warmth afterwards the ink evaporated altogether. This did not stop him from reading it to his wife. While he read it he watched her face and saw there how her blind eyes settled on some vista of her son and how imagination in some way redeemed the absence and loss.

They endured. The years passed over them. Then in the April of a year there came across the river a flotilla of boats and upon them a colourful crew of figures. The men were dressed in shirts of red and yellow and such and the women were long-haired and wore bracelets and golden hoops from their ears. They came ashore where the village women and children had gathered to meet them. The men stood with legs akimbo and hands on their waists. The women studied with brazen looks the clothes and manner of the females there. The island children held to their mothers' skirts and stared. One among the arrivals, a man with hair to his shoulder and a white shirt, stepped forward. Behind him was a beautiful woman with about her an array of a half-dozen figures in steady progression from girl to woman, each the twin of another and each more lovely than any there had seen before. The man spoke in an accent that made the words seem made of wood.

'We have come from the town of Kilkee yesterday,' he said. 'They told us there that there was a man here with an eye on the heavens.' He paused and looked over them. Mild wind blew. None moved or showed recognition.

'A glass,' he said, and made with his hands the shape of a great telescope and aimed it at the sky. 'A man who looks at the stars.'

'He is here.' It was a young boy of the BoatMacs'. 'He is here,' he said, 'in the tower.'

They went then like a wave and passed all together up the path and past the hedgerows of thorn and bramble. The children ran ahead and made noise of high-hearted cries and excitement and in the fields thereabouts rabbits paused in alarm and then darted away. They came within sight of the tower. The man in the white shirt strode to the front. His face was browned from climates not theirs and his dark eyes contained deeps from scenes none there could imagine. Yet all could tell he was upon one of the moments of his life.

The crowd reached the tower and the clamour deflated and they stood thereabouts in a roughly drawn arc. Then Francis Foley came out into the daylight and Finbar his son saw him for the first time since he had thought his father drowned in the river.

There was a moment in which they looked at each other like ones newly re-encountered in the mists of the hereafter.

'Finbar?' The old man said then. 'Finbar?' He raised his hand to pause the air and seemed as if he would fall down. Then he went back to the doorway of the tower where Emer stood and he led her out into the light and told her this was her son Finbar come back again.

She came to his arms and at once the gypsies cheered. They cheered and clapped and some laughed and pushed each other about. Children embraced in giddy mock performance and ran off then with shrieks and wild yahoos. Finbar brought forward his wife Cait and the half-dozen Roses.

'My lovely daughters,' he said, and then laughed himself with head back at the blue and white sky.

As if this then were a latch released the gypsies turned and went down the village and began the business of celebration proper. Some of them were those originals who had left the lake with Finbar years before, who had wintered by the great forest and crossed the mountains into France in the spring. Others were some they had met along the way, ashen figures wandering lone in the aftermath of wars, vagabonds, pedlars, loose strings of families dispossessed and tramping the roads without direction. There were men and women of various nations, their look and language each their own. All for reasons unsaid had taken up with those gypsies and journeyed westward toward the ocean. Their progress had been stopped often. Sometimes in the softness of the season when crossing a river such as the Saône they had found themselves turned south and slowing to a languorous motion while the sun shone. They had drowsed and drunk the wines there and seemed in a place Elysian. The perfumes of that landscape wafted and wound about them. Their journey westward then had been stalled. Their horses grew fat on summer grass. Then, a morning of changed wind, and without announcement or discussion Finbar yoked his caravan and the others did likewise. Leaving the flattened imprint of their stay upon the grass and the blackened eyes of their fires, all had turned about and headed north and west once more. They had little sense of time, only season. They followed roads that led to others. They crossed up through France. They met a troupe of actors who performed in frayed and gaudy costumes the plays of Molière. They came upon some that were soldiers deserted from a war of which none had heard. At last they reached the sea at Cherbourg and sailed from there to Plymouth. In England they did not stay long. Rain made grey that country and they crossed up through it in the last days of winter and so wended onward toward the place Finbar imagined home. In the town of Kilkee they had found none of Cait's family living. Nor was there sign of the Foley brothers. Upon this discovery Finbar had led his wife down to the white strand with their daughters, and while the other gypsies camped on the high field that overlooked the sea, he had walked with his family along the sand there and said little and watched the waves breaking. 'Here I saw your mother the first time,' he told the girls after a while, and they smiled widely and their eyes shone, for this was a story they had often heard, of the mer-girl and the seaweed, and they giggled at this sudden proof of the actual. The Roses ran off then into the tide, the younger ones only to their ankles and kicking high cold splashes that glittered. Their mother and father watched them and were in some fashion restored by this.

Two evenings following Finbar heard of the man on the island with the glass.

Now to each gypsy of those originals the long journey there seemed as nothing. Though none were cousin or kin to any, the instant the mother had embraced her son there had passed through them like a charge the sense of something right in the world. They did not explain it to each other. But there the travail and effort, the long uncertainty of their shapeless lives, all fell away. They clapped backs. They hung arms over shoulders. They went down to the village again and from there to their boats wherein were stored all manner of items none there had seen before. The gypsies carried up on to the sand chests with iron padlocks. While children ran about they opened these and brought out strange wood and paper goods. Others set up a yellow tent on the sand. A gypsy with open shirt held his hands wide and then clapped and clapped again a beat and then to this rhythm sang in what the islanders did not know was Italian. A fire was lit there and flames crackled and twisted this way and that in the small breeze. The gypsy women showed jewels and hoops and bangles. They proffered in their palms blue stones mined from countries in Asia and ran between their fingers Indian silks they had gathered on their wanderings. None of these they tried to sell, but showed them like gathered evidence of the wonders of the world and their part within it. By the fall of darkness the pilots had returned. They came ashore with some amazement and passed up through the fires and singing and roasting meat like ones somnambulant in vivid dream. They went to their cottages as if to confirm the island was the same they had left in the dawn and then came down sheepish and circumspect and stood on the edge of the firelight where their children were dancing.

When the dark was deepest blue a small assembly of the gypsies carried in bundles sticks with wads of cloth wound about them. One other bore a firebrand. They went to the shore and the crowd murmured and the singer stopped as did the one playing the blue guitar. Then a touch-paper was lit. Into the sky streaked a trail of light. It blazed upward and turned the heads of all below and upon a moment then exploded with a bang. Splintered light fell. Those watching ducked down their heads at first and held them fearful so until the same fragments faded like things erased into the dark. Other fireworks were shot into the night. All manner of trajectory was briefly there illumined and in all colours of the spectrum. Wheels of fire spun above them. Blue balls of flame whirled. Now the gypsies did not await the decline of one to send another but flashed some that fizzed fast and others that flew and climbed the dark in slow ascent and met there the falling tendrils of scintillas yellow and gold. The night sky flared and was shred in ribbons. In the crowd below some held their arms up as if to reach the sky-blooms and cried out and shouted. More rockets were fired. Each rose in swift short bursts of fury and released itself high and bright above like things in glorious failure unable to reach some higher plane. Then the music began again. The strings of the guitar were plucked in dance-time and the island women linked arms with each other while their men watched. The gypsy men were less bashful. They clapped wide claps and threw back their heads and made swaying body movements as if in time to some inner rhythm of the universe deep and secret and ancient.

That night they slept where they fell down. By the next the islanders were less unsure of their visitors. In the day they shared food with them and their children played together and went off hunting about the island. When night fell the festivities resumed. The Roses came and danced there. Some fellows from the town of Kilrush rowed the night-river and came up on the shore and saw those sisters and weakened to their knees at their loveliness. These same were then told by the pilots to be gone, and they returned to their boat and rowed a small way and then sat in the tide and looked back upon the scene with yearning. The Roses danced. Their mother and father came down from the tower and watched them.

'There will be boys to beat away every night now,' Finbar said.

'I hope so,' Cait replied.

The month of April passed. A warm and easy summer began. At times the pilots took with them some of the gypsies when they rowed out to meet the ships. These delighted in the race and took off their shirts sometimes and held them flapping in the wind like flags or banners. They saluted the victor with broad operatic gestures that threatened to capsize them and then called out to each other gambles on who would win the next. In the night, when the men returned, they took to predicting the races of tomorrow. The gypsies turned over cards and made inexpert prophecies and pretended for a time that they had seen the unknown. But in truth what future was yet before them none there knew. They did not ask Finbar how long they would stay and neither did he mention to any of them his intentions. The days rolled on. Bees and birds of summer flew. The buttery almond scent of gorse was spread over the air and then sweetened further by honeysuckle and fuchsia. Sun dallied the day long. The river ran blue as a southern sea. And in that season the island seemed a place from which none would ever leave. Clamour and battle and bitterness were history and seemed to exist in an elsewhere. The summer hung there, its weather like a gift.

Then, in the end of August, the old restlessness returned in the blood of Finbar. He woke and imagined he was moving. He went out into the day and stood a while and watched the water and the sky.

'We have to go,' he said to Cait, when he came back.

'I know,' she surprised him by saying. 'I have been waiting. There's no home for the likes of us.'

'We will come back every year.'

'You need not worry. Your daughters will see to that,' she said.

Finbar went then and walked up to the tower to tell his father and his mother.

'We will go north to Ballinasloe to the horse fair in October,' he said. 'We will go on but promise to come back.'

His father nodded and held Emer's hand in his lap.

'Every man must live his own life,' he said. 'You will come back?'

'Every year in the summertime.'

'God bless you, Finbar,' said the blind mother and she raised her hands to feel his face.

The following morning, the gypsies sailed from the island. Before they went Finbar brought to his father the map of Benardi. 'Look at this and you will think of us,' he said. 'We will be back when the blossoms are on the trees.'

They left and the island women and children watched them go, and some youths swam alongside the boats a ways and then stopped and gathered breath, their heads like dark blooms on the water. They swam back and came ashore and the boats receded further and bore off with them the imaginings of many. For the islanders had grown used to the gypsies and now in their absence felt the silence fall like a heavy curtain. In the night there were no festivities or gatherings. Mists grey and wet enshrouded the island and the season turned. It was a place again hushed and alone and when the rain fell it seemed to make dreary and dull the world and many there dreamed in secret of what adventures had befallen those gypsies now.

The islanders looked for them in the summer. And when they came, good as their word, they came with the same flourish of colour and revelry, of song and music and dancing and fireworks. They came this time with canaries. They brought them in many cages and hung these in the twisted trees where the canaries sang to other birds there. They brought kites of stick and paper too, and flew them on long lines from the shore. Such flying was good for the spirit, one said, who did nothing else all day but tugged softly on the unwound spool and gazed up at the distant fluttering as if at some furthermost extension of himself wild in the breeze. Their gifts were many and varied and became like tokens of goodwill exchanged between those who arrived and those who welcomed them. They were the beginning of what would become a custom. The things they brought carried within them stories of the greater world and whether the islanders laughed or raised their eyebrows at such as winding music boxes or hot peppers or slippers of silver with curved toes, they enjoyed all and were grateful. In the beginning of autumn they left again and promised to return and did so. There were no more than the half-dozen Roses but these with each visit became more beautiful still. And in time the gypsies' caravan itself would come to seem like a touring carousel crossing the earth back and forth, bound by some antique covenant, and sheltering within it those beauties. They were like Grecian figures reincarnate and had dark eyes and pale skin that maddened many. No sooner would they land on the island than the river would fill with night-boys crossing in boats for glimpses of them and the pilots would run down and pitch stones and yell and wave their arms as if able to shoo away fate. Finbar himself did not join the pilots. He knew his daughters' beauty bore with it some seeded destiny and knew that one day too he would have to meet it. He grew older and strangely wiser. He came to his father and brought him always a chart of some kind. He brought maps and drawings of islands newly named. He brought the latest cartography of their own country and scrolls and parchments inked with mountains and rivers and shorelines. The old man took these with grace and thanked him each time. He told Finbar he studied them when he was gone away and placed them to one side. To his mother Finbar gave scented oils and powders and such. He gave her candles though he knew she could not see their light, for he said they could be lit for remembrance. Then he sat with them in that old place of stone and none of them spoke, and the summer breeze blew and each of them thought of the brothers gone.

Then one year the gypsies did not return in the summer.

The islanders watched for them. They invented reasons: how the gypsies may be delayed in mountains, or on sea-crossings, or in any manner of trouble that may be abroad. Into August they waited for them to come before they began to accept the chill of autumn was arriving. The gypsies never came, only the winter with sleet and ice.

Then, a day in the following June, a boy ran through the village calling, 'They are here! They are here!'

The boats they came in were laden low. They had been in countries in the east and brought all manner of strange and exotic goods, some of whose uses were unknown to themselves. They brought there also a form of early bicycle, an angular contraption of iron rims and timber handles that looked in some ways like an assemblage of garden tools on large wheels. This one of the gypsies demonstrated, wobbling out down a sloping field of grass, cheered and chased by the children until like a proof of some law of science he slowed to standstill, balanced an instant, and finally toppled. There were other such near-inventions, three-handed clocks with cuckoos that sang, sheets of carbon upon which faces could leave their imprint, socks that were soled like shoes, thick glassed spectacles that made all look far away, a pendulum that if hung over the expectant foretold the sex of the unborn.

While all these were uncased and held out and shown to the islanders, Finbar went up the pathway to the tower. Even as he approached it he felt some change had happened. It was as if there was a warp in the air, a rumple in the fabric of things that was all but imperceptible. As he came past the last of the stone walls to the little opening there his father and mother were not sitting outside. A shiver passed up through him. His breath was caught. When he came to the doorway of the tower itself he stopped and called out to them. Birds were singing. Sunlight made light and grey the stones. That moment he noticed such details and they entered him and adjoined his memories.

'Finbar?'

The voice of his father was softened. Finbar stepped inside the shadows and saw the two of them lying in each other's arms beside the telescope.

'Is it you?' his father said, and his hand rose white and slim and wavering until Finbar knelt and took it.

'She is gone,' the old man said. 'I am waiting to go with her.' And his hand returned to stroke the grey hair of Emer and then came to rest upon her once more. Finbar said nothing. He bowed his head and held his hands together and from him like a river invisible ran his grief.

'You must let me take her,' Finbar said.

'No.'

'I must bury her.'

'Bury the two of us. She is waiting for me. I will be with her tomorrow.'

'Father.'

'No.' The old man's eyes flashed again as they had often done before and he fixed them upon his son only a moment yet sufficient to still all argument. 'No, Finbar, please. Tomorrow.'

Finbar walked outside into the sunlight. He lifted his face to the warmth and the brightness of that June day and he heard the birds singing anew and the sounds from the village travelling upward to where he stood. He watched the cloudless sky a long time. The dog came and lay at his feet. Then he went back inside and told his father he would be back to him in a short time. He ran down the pathway he had come along and said to Cait and the Roses and the gypsies and the islanders that his mother was dead and his father dying. Mary BoatMac put her hands to her face and wept.

'I am going to stay with him tonight,' Finbar told them. 'Light no fireworks for this evening. I will see you all in the morning.' He embraced his wife and children then and took some bread and smoked fish and from one of the canvas bags the latest charts he had brought for his father.

He went back along the way to the tower. His father was as he had left him.

'I need no food, Finbar,' the old man said.

'Drink this.' From a bucket in the corner his son scooped water and brought it to his father's lips and held it there while it spilled and was some part taken.

Finbar sat then beside them both. The sunlight that fell did not reach inside the tower but lay only at its doorway like a golden cloth that was slowly withdrawn throughout that quiet afternoon. The father and son said almost nothing. In the stillness that assembled Finbar listened for his father's breaths and heard each one as if each were a thing singularly gifted and counted and measured out in some accountancy finite and exact. At times Finbar thought the breath that came was final and he would not get to give his father the last charts. There seemed stalled moments in which the continuation of life paused and held and was uncertain, then Francis Foley sucked in again. As the long daylight diminished and began to fade into night, Finbar told his father he had another chart to show him. The old man opened his mouth but did not say more than a thin sound. Then Finbar brought it out for him and unfurled a scroll that was long and yellowed and marked in ink of black. The writings upon it were in a fine hand. But it was not upon these that the eyes of the old man fixed. For it was a map not of countries known but of the heavens above. Therein were scored all the constellations and the planets on what were called the First Plane, and then below these was another diagram, called the Deeper Heavens where stars were given that Francis Foley had never seen.

'Here,' Finbar said, 'is explained how to see the future.'

The old man's eyes read what they could for the writing was in several languages: Latin and Greek and some English and other scripts from lands in Arabia. He studied for a time the planetary cycles shown there, the cycles of Pluto, of Neptune and Uranus. There were further cycles shown, too, of Saturn and Jupiter, and lastly of Venus, Mercury, and the Moon. There was more there that Finbar did not understand, the symbols of the Zodiac, the patterns and repetitions of history that were constant, the planetary clusters in Aries, Taurus and Gemini. There were details of all manner of calculation and methods of interpretation, birth signs, astro-morphology, the Thebaic calendar, and a brief account of various cosmogonies.

Finbar held the scroll open and his father looked at it a long time. He did not speak. When Finbar asked him if it wasn't a marvellous thing the old man did not reply to him but smiled a weak smile and gestured to his son to bring the telescope to him. He laid the chart aside. The darkness had fallen. Finbar turned the great instrument and brought the eyepiece close to his father, and when it was in position the old man brought his face to it.

Finbar sat there in the darkness. He listened to his father breathing. He mourned in silence for his mother.

The night was mild and the sky cloudless and the stars therein shone. Francis Foley made only the slightest sound as he surveyed all above and studied there what galaxies were unveiled. He did not cry out or exclaim or make otherwise known what he saw but while the hours passed one upon the next and the stars turned he seemed to slip through some portal in his understanding of the universe and enter a dimension of revelation. In that sky then he saw Finan dead in Africa. He saw, too, his son Tomas, and saw him in a homestead in a territory of tall grass and trees. He saw him with a wife called Mary Considine who was kind and gentle and a mother to their three children. He saw the farming they did there and the seasons harsh of snows and heat.

Teige, too, was in that sky revealed to him. Francis Foley paused when he saw him and lifted away his eye from the telescope and blinked it twice and Finbar brought him something moist to his lips. The old man swallowed and it seemed a labour. He made a moaning sound in his throat, as if he would speak but knew he must not. Then he resumed his gaze and saw Teige with the strange clarity of how one sees the unreal figures in a story. He saw him alone in the dark in a desert place. He saw the dust there blow across the night and sands gather around the boy's boots and cover them over while he hunkered there and waited for the dawn. He was without his horse. In the breaking light he rose and walked and was a speck in the landscape of desolation. Teige went on. He crossed that empty terrain that seemed endless and about him skirted small animals that ran and scavenged there. He walked through the blaze of sun. A hoop of red was burned about his neck, as if he had been in hot irons or once held by thongs. His eyelids were caked. His brows wore the dust of that place in deep wrinkles. When he had no water he stopped walking. He squatted down and broad-winged birds encircled black against the sky. For two days he lay so. The birds came and landed nearby and stepped and pecked at nothings and looked sidelong and waited. The night came on. Teige imagined he would die then. He said some words to his father and his mother and shut his eyes.

In the morning he was found by two riders heading south ahead of a herd of horses that were bound for the army in the war that was threatened against the rebels. They came upon him and sat him upright and gave him water. They asked him his name. One of the men was by the name of MacNamara. He took Teige on the back of his horse and they brought him out of there. He joined with those herdsmen and rode south with the herd. He showed in time what knowledge he had of horses and moved through that land that was wide and majestic and various. He rode through canyons and through the passes of mountains and by forests vast and serene. All that land he passed along and sat by night at campfires where flames twisted and died. He grew accustomed to the life and its rhythms. They delivered the horses and went north for more. Sometimes they encountered Indians that were hostile and there were rifle and pistol battles and some fell and died. Other times the natives they came upon merely watched them from bluffs and grassy crests and kept them in long and grave scrutiny but took no action, watching the herds of wild horses pass in clouds as if seeing the spirit of the land itself traversing there. In such a life years passed. And these were already in the future as Francis Foley saw them. And in that future he saw the day when Teige Foley would stop with a lame horse at a homestead in the Wyoming Territory, and the woman who came out on the porch would silently remark on the familiarity of his face and ask him his name. And then she would send her son running and Tom Foley would hurry back from the fields and brush the dirt from his hands on his pants and come into the yard and see his brother Teige for the first time in many years.

And perhaps it was so.

And perhaps all was so revealed that night to Francis Foley as he lay with his wife silently gazing beneath the stars. And in that fall of light from heaven to earth perhaps all our stories were told, all actions of the living and dead explained, and all time past present and future there revealed. In such eternal patterns perhaps the old man gleaned secrets and mysteries hitherto undisclosed and saw there in the stars the future generations of his family, saw the children and grandchildren and their grandchildren and theirs. Perhaps he saw in the sidereal light all the times to come. He saw those like me, the great great grandson of Teige Foley, who years hence would return to that island seeking his spirit, who would walk over the windy fields and watch the river and think of the long story and that it should be written down. Perhaps he saw the others who would leave there for America. How in time the last family would go from that island and it would return to a place empty and green once more. Perhaps that last night Francis Foley saw there the whole history of endeavour and understood as none can its meaning. And perhaps in so doing he found peace.

By the dawn he lay back on the straw bed. He placed his hand upon his wife's back and breathed his last.

The sun rose palely and made vanish the stars. Birds of morning sang.

NIALL WILLIAMS

As It Is in Heaven

PICADOR

Love is not easy, especially if you find the woman of your dreams and then lose her – as Philip Griffin and his son Stephen each discover in turn.

Stephen is just a boy when his mother and sister are killed in a car crash, and his father never recovers from the accident; he wasn't involved but is subsequently consumed by grief, his only desire to be reunited with his wife. Before that happens, though, Philip wants to ensure the happiness of his son, Stephen – now a grown man.

'*As It Is in Heaven*, Niall Williams's tale of love and tragedy, will leave you in tears'
Tatler

'The novel is all delicious coincidence and tragedy, as these extraordinary lives begin to unravel and intertwine'
Guardian

'A tender and sober novel with a faith in romance that is absolute'
Daily Express

NIALL WILLIAMS

Only Say the Word

PICADOR

In a cottage in County Clare, Jim Foley sits before a white screen and begins a love letter to his wife, hoping the words he writes will bring her closer to him. In the upstairs rooms of the cottage, his children, Jack and Hannah, are asleep.

Retracing the journey of Jim's life, from childhood in County Clare to early adulthood in America, and eventually back to Clare again, this is a story of desire, of stolen books, missed moments and contemporary fatherhood.

'A wonderful book, uplifting and hopeful. Give it to
everyone you know'
Sunday Tribune

'A conscientious, assiduously crafted novel where what
strikes you about the writing is how deftly Williams's prose
mingles sensitivity to nuance with a more remarkable muscularity.
With its powerful sweeps and blending of imagery, this is
a compelling, serious and deeply persuasive novel'
Joseph O'Connor, *Guardian*

'For Jim, words are a kind of redemption – and nobody reading
this subtle, meditative and beautifully written book will be
inclined to disagree'
Peter Parker, *Sunday Times*

AVAILABLE FROM PAN MACMILLAN

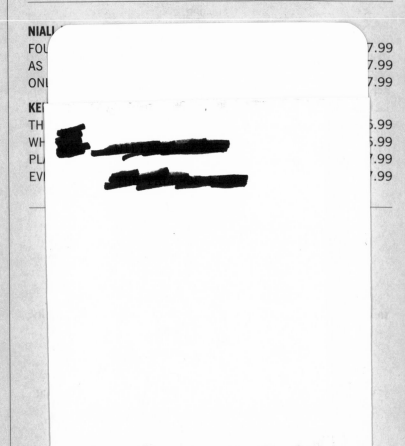

which may differ from those previously advertised in the text
or elsewhere.